MW00814255

HARRY SEVEN

by

d.a.hill

Copyright © 2017 D.A.Hill
All Rights Reserved

This is a work of fiction.
With the exception of known historical figures,
any resemblance to actual persons,
living or dead, is purely coincidental.

Also by D.A.Hill

Cerelia's Choice

The Emulation Trilogy
Newton's Ark
Fuller's Mine
Book 3, coming 2018

A note on spelling: the chapters narrated by
Harrison Seely, an American, use American English,
while the chapters narrated by Alicia Rowntree, an
Englishwoman, use British English.

Contents

For Paula
who always reminded
us what lucky ducks we are.

PROLOGUE

2015
Thursday, August 27
Princeton, New Jersey

My front door hangs open, as strikingly large and incongruously blue as ever. Outside, the now familiar sight of wartime London calls. July 1945. The past, but my inescapable future.

I must go. Despite the best of intentions, all I've done is change the course of history for the worse. The Russian got the better of me. I'll warn Harrison about him and the other lessons I've learned. Prepare him better than *my* Grandpa Harry prepared me. I can't let him fail again. Correction. *I* can't fail again.

How many times have I had this same thought?

I've done what I can to wrap up my affairs. The strangers who consider themselves my parents can take care of the rest, the things that can only be done once I'm officially declared missing.

I grab one last glance at my house. My grandfather's house. It's both disconcerting and comforting to know I will see this place again, even though I won't be coming back.

I tense my muscles then spring into action, charging forward like a rampaging bull, committed now to this course of action. *Seventh time lucky* I tell myself as I rush through the open door…

ONE

2015
Tuesday, June 30
Princeton, New Jersey

The weight of the ridiculously large sapphire blue door impedes my efforts to close it behind me. I pull harder, banging it shut, then reach into a pocket for my key chain. Once it's free, finding the right key is easy. Old-fashioned, with a long cylindrical shaft and two large, square teeth, it looks every bit as ancient as the lock.

A dull tingling in my fingers persists an hour after I stopped the car, the lingering effect of driving five hours straight without even a bathroom break. Pushing so hard wasn't necessary — classes don't start for several weeks yet — but the house beckoned. A thick layer of dust covered everything inside, but I was relieved to discover the place in good condition after being unoccupied for so many years.

I wiggle the key back and forth before finding the spot where it slides home. The key resists my effort to turn it. I push harder.

Damn. The shaft may break off in the lock if I twist too hard. Perhaps I should just leave the place unlocked in the hope someone will save me the trouble and cost of dumping Grandpa Harry's appliances. How did anyone ever think a refrigerator or range hood looked good in mustard yellow?

I'm half-serious, but no one would take them, and I can't risk the furniture. It's even more dated — from the fifties maybe — but quality workmanship in a classic style. I like it, and not only for its sentimental value. One more try of the lock.

This time the key turns.

I slip the keys into my pocket then tug at the door. It should hold. I'll replace the lock with something modern, something secure, before I fill the place with white goods and electronics actually worth stealing.

As I turn to leave for my hotel, I dream of a long-awaited dinner — room service, but better than nothing — followed by a steaming hot shower and a comfortable bed.

WHAT THE F —

There isn't time to finish my question in the

instant between missing a step and kissing the pavement. And far too little time, or information, to answer it.

I lie there long enough to recover from the shock before sitting up with a loud groan. My right shoulder seems to have taken most of the impact. I rotate my arm in a slow, lazy circle. Just a little mild discomfort.

My neck hurts too, and now a dull, burning pain in my hands reaches my consciousness. I turn them over. Gravel rash on my palms. I drag my hands along my thighs, removing as much as possible of the dirt and fine pieces of concrete embedded in my skin.

Otherwise I seem OK. Wouldn't I hurt a whole lot more if I broke or dislocated something?

Even my glasses are undamaged despite my inelegant face-down landing. It's my pride that's injured, far worse than my body. *How stupid.* I haven't even moved in, and I've fallen down the front steps. *The neighbors will think I'm a drunk.*

When I look behind me, shock replaces anger at my own carelessness. At the top of the steps, four more than should be there, stands the door I just closed...

Attached to the wrong house.

Wrong because a few minutes ago this door was attached to *my* home. Although I must admit that architecturally speaking it fits this house much better. This grand Georgian structure is worthy of a door ten feet tall and five feet wide. Even the color that was so out of place in the Princeton house fits the style of this building. It is as if someone designed this door for this specific home.

Nevertheless, it doesn't belong here. It belongs to my grandparents' house, my house now, where it has stood for as long as I can remember.

I climb to my feet.

What is that smell? My nose twitches. Something burning. I take another breath, drawing the curious scent deep into my lungs. A hint of... sulfur. Gunpowder?

My God, did someone shoot me? Is that why I fell? Both hands pat furiously at my chest and stomach but find no blood or bullet wounds.

Slowly spinning around, sniffing as I go, I search for the source of the odor.

While subtle, it seems to be coming from every direction. Burning coal? Nobody burns coal anymore, other than in giant power stations, and even that's on the way out.

Left, right, left I swivel my head. Buildings three

or four stories tall fill the street from end to end. There's no sign of the detached suburban homes that should be here. And where are the majestic oaks lining my street? Or my car? I left it parked right out front.

The other side of the street is the same, townhouses abutting each other from one end to the other. Except for the house directly opposite. What's left of it. Only a few walls and part of the second floor still stand. The rest spills onto the sidewalk and into the street, a pile of rubble mixed with the sad flotsam of a family's life — splintered furniture, the shredded remains of bed linens and clothing, a headless doll. It reminds me of the bombed-out houses I've seen in dozens of old black and white photos of wartime London.

Don't be ridiculous. That would be impossible.

But it sure isn't Princeton. Everything here is out of place. And dark, so dark, though it's only a little after 5:30 pm in the middle of summer. Sundown isn't for three or four hours yet. Even at night it should never be this black. Not a single streetlight pierces the darkness, there's no traffic, and not even a scrap of light escapes a window anywhere.

What is going... My vision blurs. *Now I understand. I have a concussion. I'm hallucinating.*

I sway, in small circles at first but they grow larger with each rotation. I can't stand for another minute. My knees hit the ground then I tilt forward at the waist. Using my already injured hands to break my fall, I slump to the ground, once more face down on the pavement.

Everything rolls ninety degrees to the left. My cheek presses against the cold, hard concrete, and then this strange place disappears behind closed eyes. *Everything will be fine when I wake up...*

TWO

1943
Thursday, July 1
Kensington, London

The staccato rhythm of my high heels striking the pavement echoes down the empty street. So eager am I for the familiar comfort of my London home I rush along despite the deep gloom of the blackout. Three nights in my own bed will be a welcome and much anticipated respite from the dull room in a drab house where I have spent far too many evenings since this horrible war started.

I pull up sharply at the foot of my front steps.

In my imprudent haste I almost tripped over a human lump lying at my feet.

What is he doing there? Passed out in a drunken stupor is the most plausible explanation. I kneel and smell his breath. To my great surprise there is no hint of intoxicating liquor. If falling down drunk is not the explanation, what is? At this closer range I can see a graze and the beginnings of a lump on his forehead, entirely consistent with a fall, or a fight. But robbery is an implausible motive given the sleek gold watch still attached to his right wrist. Left-handed. *Interesting… but not germane.*

Yet an explanation there must be; a man should never find himself lying unconscious on the foot-path without good cause.

Though he is under-dressed — no waistcoat, no jacket or overcoat, no tie or cravat, and no hat — his trousers have the sheen of silk, his cotton shirt is finely woven, and his shoes have the shine of the best patent leather. Expensive garments and an elegant watch suggest a gentleman, or at least a person of means. And well-dressed, well-groomed, and bespectacled does not describe a man accustomed to casual violence.

The most plausible hypothesis is therefore that he was the victim of an assault, a troubling enough thought to compel me to involve the police. I move towards the stairs, then stop and turn back. In good conscience I cannot leave an injured man alone in the murky darkness whilst I go inside to telephone.

I kneel beside him once again. "Hello there." He does not respond. I shake him by the shoulder. "I say, can you hear me?"

He moans as he turns onto his back and opens his eyes. They trace out a strange elliptical path as they roll around in their sockets. His eyes widen then narrow then widen again as he struggles to focus his vision on me. "What happen…"

"It appears you struck your head."

The man pushes himself up with one hand. The other lightly touches his temple, the fingertips exploring the injury.

"Oww," he says with a wince. "Where…" He shakes his head, his breath coming in ragged, panicked bursts. "Where am…"

"Please, you must rest easy. There will be time for questions once we get you inside. Can you stand?"

A hand reaches out. I take it and place my other hand beneath his elbow. He begins to rise but then releases my hand and drops forward onto his knees.

His palms rest on his thighs, his chin on his chest. "Sorry, but not under my own steam."

An American accent, only hinted at in his earlier, monosyllabic utterances, is unmistakable now. What is his business in London? The obvious answer, that he is an American serviceman, does not fit his appearance. First, he has a beard. Though cropped short and neatly trimmed, it is not the mark of a soldier.

But the Royal Navy, unlike the other services, allows beards. Does the US Navy?

I do not know, but even if they do, it would not explain his civilian attire. Or his hair. It reaches in unruly, dark-brown waves to his shoulders, a style that does not belong on the head of any man, no matter what his profession or nationality. Certainly not a military man.

For now the mystery of his identity and his purpose here shall have to wait.

But can I carry him inside? Perhaps I should summon Father to help move him. Or he could telephone while I stay with the man…

Is Father even here? He may still be at the War Office. Mr. Churchill often keeps senior officers until the small hours of the morning. He may not even be in London. I did not check before I came down.

Mrs. Collins, on the other hand, is always present. But she would object vociferously to bringing a stranger inside. I would never hear the end of it. There must be a more palatable alternative.

I assess my subject again. While tall, he is quite thin. Lanky is the word to describe him. How much can he weigh? I am an independent woman. I will deal with this situation myself.

I squat, keeping my knees together as a lady should, even at night with no one around to see, and slip my shoulder under his arm.

"One, two, three," I say then lift with my legs.

A long, deep, unladylike groan escapes my lips. *More than it appears*, is the answer to my query about his weight. Unsteady on his feet, the mysterious American cannot support himself without my help. I half-lift, half-push him up the stairs.

By the time we reach the landing my back aches, my heart thumps, and my chest heaves as I struggle to regain my breath.

With my key already in hand, I unlock and thrust open the door before I guide him inside and lower him to the floor, involuntarily letting him land with a thud.

THREE

Wide, narrow windows set high in the wall remind me of the tiny basement flat I rented in Chelsea.

So I'm in a basement? London townhouses all have basements. Back when they were built, these grand houses had armies of domestic helpers. 'Downstairs' was their domain.

Is this the basement of the townhouse that for some inexplicable reason has a door identical to mine? Wherever this is, it now appears to be some kind of informal sitting room, every inch decorated in the style of 1940s England.

I look around the room, my gaze settling first on a painting on the wall, then on a piece of furniture, then on some small trinket sitting on a shelf. The authenticity is staggering. Though military rather than social history is my primary field of interest, WWII is my specialty, and the fashions of the 1940s are familiar to me. Yet I can't fault a single thing, not even small details.

A teacup and saucer sit on the table in front of me, the delicate bone china decorated with an antique pale blue floral pattern.

Yes, there's tea in the cup. I lift the saucer, then raise the cup to my lips, closing my eyes as I take a long, slow sip.

Ahhh.

It took the Brits some time to convert me, but they're right—a 'nice cup of tea' is the universal tonic. If you know how to make it properly. Which most of my countrymen don't. *Boil the damn water, people.*

The cup warms my hands as I hold it, staring into the milky liquid and hoping for answers. *Where am I and how did I get here?* I remember a fall. Then blackness until I'm sitting in this armchair.

My head aches. I examine my palms. Someone has cleaned the skin and applied what looks like iodine solution. A little old-fashioned, but effective. Grandpa Harry swore by the stuff.

Is this an elaborate prank perpetrated by my new colleagues, some kind of initiation ritual, my fellow history geeks' idea of a joke gone wrong? But they would have needed to drug me or something to bring me here, wherever here is. That isn't the sort of thing the faculty at a prestigious university like Princeton would do. Perhaps they took me for welcoming drinks and I consumed a few too many. I can recall nothing of the evening, not even before

I started drinking, but what other rational explanation could there be?

A door opens and a woman I've never seen before enters the room. Is she one of them? I don't remember her from the faculty directory.

I stand. Feeling lightheaded, I have to steady myself on the arm of the sofa.

My effort at politeness is ruined by my staring, but I can't help it. She is slim and willowy without being bony and androgynous like those hideously skinny runway models. With a classic English complexion — pale freckles dance across her alabaster skin beneath strawberry-blond hair — she seems to draw all the light in the room to her, reflecting it back in an angelic glow.

But it isn't her radiant beauty that stuns me. Rather it's the forties hairstyle and her clothing — a perfect replica of a woman's Victory Suit — which fit the purported time and place every bit as well as this room's decor.

Lively green eyes gaze back intently at me. "You have quite a bump on your head," she says.

Her upper-class accent is every bit as faithful as the rest of this elaborate deception. I could easily imagine this woman invited to tea with the Queen. Someone went to a lot of trouble. But who?

She raises her hand with three fingers extended. "How many do you see?"

"Three."

"Splendid. And do you recall your name?"

As I transfer my tea to my left hand, the cup wobbles on the saucer. Steadying my arm before I spill any, I extend my right hand. "Harrison Seely."

Her hand, soft and delicate, rests in mine for a brief second as she says, "Lady Alicia Rowntree."

In a man such a handshake would be considered a sign of weakness. In her case it seems elegant and refined, and somehow an unspoken assertion of social superiority.

"It is a pleasure to meet you, Mr. Seely."

She motions for me to sit as she lowers herself into the seat opposite, her back ramrod straight, and her knees pressed together and tilted to one side. From the ease with which she assumes the pose, the movement appears well practiced.

"Perhaps pleasure is not the best word given the circumstances," she says. "How are you feeling? Quite a deal better I hope."

I groan theatrically. "I think I'll survive."

"Do you know where you are?"

There it is. Should I call her bluff or play along? Which choice is more likely to lead to answers?

Play along. For now. "London. Though I can't tell you the address. Or how I got here."

"32 Hartness Street, Kensington. I found you outside in quite a sorry state and brought you in."

"You're in the habit of collecting strays?"

"Certainly not."

"Well thank you for making an exception, for sheltering me in your home. It is your home…"

"Title resides with my father and will pass to my brother, but yes, it is my home. In a manner of speaking."

"In a manner of speaking?"

She waves the question away. "As to the broader question, perhaps if we knew what brought you to London, we might determine how you managed to end up lying unconscious on the footpath outside my front door. Are you part of the United States military? I ask because there are so many American soldiers on our shores now, but you are not wearing a uniform."

"Only indirectly." I touch the side of my nose with my forefinger. "I'm not at liberty to say more, you understand."

Her eyes widen. *Aha.* Whoever is behind this ruse didn't prepare her for this particular answer. But before I can think of a follow-up, her face stiffens and her shoulders relax, indicating she has regained control.

"Absolutely," she says. "Loose lips sink ships and all that."

"Exactly." For a moment I thought I was on the front foot. If only I could think of something to put her off balance again.

"And you remember nothing of the events preceding your unfortunate mishap this evening?"

"Nada. Zip."

Her brow furrows.

"I remember nothing. Nothing at all."

"Do you at least know where you reside?"

I place my cup and saucer on the side table then stand. "I do."

It's not a good idea to engage an unknown enemy under the best of circumstances. But with my brain as foggy as it is, continuing this battle of wits would really be asking for trouble.

"And on that note," I say as I move toward the door, "I really should thank you for your kindness and be on my way."

"We should telephone for someone to fetch you."

She slides to her left, just enough to obstruct my path unless I push rudely past her. "You did lose consciousness. Notwithstanding your remarkable ability to count fingers, I fear you may have suffered a nasty concussion."

Whoever this woman is, she is a talented actress. Her concern, an obvious ploy to get me to stay, seems so genuine. All the more reason I should leave. Immediately.

"That won't be necessary. If you would direct me to the nearest tube station, I can take it from there."

"It is after midnight, Mr. Seely. Underground services will have stopped by now."

"Then I'll find a taxi," I say as I step around her. "Or walk," I add as I rush for the stairs.

— o —

The woman playing the part of Lady Alicia Rowntree closes the door until only her head is visible through the six-inch gap between door and frame. "A very good evening to you, Mr. Seely."

"And to you, Ma'am."

Her lips move as if to speak, but she stops and shakes her head instead. "Good evening," she says again, before closing the door.

At the top of the steps I pause, gazing out into a

dark and unfamiliar street. What's my next move? If this is London, I can find my way to a hotel; it's just over five years since I lived here. If not, I'll find out soon enough and take it from there.

Behind me I hear the sound of the key doing its work.

The key.

I spin around. All I can see is dark outlines. I reach out in the darkness, groping for the door.

My smartphone beeps. I pull it from my pocket. A reminder to call Mom. As I swipe to dismiss the notification, illumination from the screen, though faint, spurs a mental connection. Flashlight app!

Two quick taps and I have useful light.

Now I can see the lock. It looks identical to mine, except the brass on this one is shiny, like it's been freshly polished. I remove my keys. Will mine fit?

I turn the phone off and slip it back into my pocket. After waiting a few minutes in the dark, I press my ear to the door. No sound. I guess she's in bed by now, somewhere on one of the upper floors.

I hold my breath as I feel for the lock. *There.* I place a finger beside the keyhole, rest the key against it, then guide it in. Unlike the lock on my grandfather's house—my house—the key slips smoothly into this one. Too easily. No jiggling required. It can't be the same lock. Of course it isn't. But I rotate my wrist to the left anyway, even though I expect the key not to budge.

It gives way without resistance, the bolt retracting with a smooth click.

Damn, what do I do now? I have a key, but the law is clear. This is still breaking and entering. I can just imagine the headline in *The Daily Princetonian*: **NEW ASSISTANT PROFESSOR ARRESTED**. Mine will be the shortest appointment in the history of the university, fired before I teach a single class.

But I have to find out what the hell is going on. I have no idea where I am, who this house belongs to, or how I got here. Somehow the key to the front door of my house in Princeton fits the lock to this door, the entrance to a house that looks for all the world like it belongs in wartime London, not modern day New Jersey.

I lay a palm against the door then push it open inch by inch, biting my lip when the hinges squeak.

I don't know what I expect to find. But it isn't this. The inside of my own house.

—o—

I charge into the living room and press my face against a large picture window facing the road. Oak trees, single-family homes, my almost new Subaru Outback still covered in the grime and splattered insects of a cross-country road trip, all illuminated by the long, soft rays of the afternoon sun sitting low above the western horizon.

The sight of a normal suburban street has never been so welcome or appeared so welcoming. Relief at being back in Princeton crashes into me like a wave, one of those big ones that comes out of nowhere and dumps you head first into the sand.

I drop to the floor and sit with my head in my hands, overwhelmed by this strange ordeal.

Am I going mad?

About an hour passes before I summon the will to stand. Maybe in the morning I will find the answers, but for now all I want is to return to my hotel. Dinner and a shower can wait. I need to crawl into bed, pull the comforter over my head, and wake up tomorrow to a normal, boring, time-travel-free day.

I open the door to leave.

Not again!

Outside is the gloomy streetscape I thought I'd escaped. I rush back to the living room window.

Princeton.

Then the front door.

Kensington.

Back and forth I shuttle, running in circles like a cat chasing its tail.

Princeton-Kensington-Princeton-Kensington.

Stepping outside, the soft afternoon light spills from my door into an otherwise all-encompassing darkness. I turn, tilt my head back, and look up. The upper floors of the townhouse loom over me in the night, like an evil giant. Yet through the open doorway I can see the inside of my house. *How is any of this possible?*

—o—

I pull the door closed behind me and look up and down the street once again. I'm more convinced than ever. This *is* wartime London.

The implications of my discovery are astounding. Shouldn't I tell someone?

An image appears in my mind, influenced by too many movies I'm sure: men riding in black

SUVs screeching to a halt in front of my house, helicopters hovering overhead, scientists from some unknown three letter government agency clad in HAZMAT suits commandeering my home to study this wormhole or whatever it is.

No, this is my find, my secret. If I can move at will between the past and the present — or seen from here, the present and the future — the possibilities for my research are endless. I could gather data for a dozen groundbreaking papers, any one of which would launch me on the fast-track to tenure.

But how to be sure?

A newspaper. I need to see a newspaper.

In the inky gloom of the blackout I must walk at a painfully slow pace to avoid tripping. But it's still less than fifteen minutes before I come to a sign pointing to the Underground.

Finding my way becomes progressively easier as my eyes adjust to the dark, and five minutes later I stand across the road from the entrance to Gloucester Road Station.

The station is closed. I duck into a nearby alleyway, disappearing into the shadows. In a country embroiled in total war, paranoia is epidemic. At all costs I must avoid looking suspicious. That's not easy though—lurking in a dark alley is exactly the sort of thing a German spy would do.

I'm forced to wait more than two hours. It's deathly quiet at first, but around 4:30 am the city begins to stir. Every passing vehicle and person strengthens my conviction I have traveled to London in the 1940s.

By the time the newsboys arrive, between 5:00 and 5:15 am according to the large clock mounted above the station's entrance, I know what I'll see. But it's important for my research to establish the exact point during the war this day falls.

Leaving the security of my hiding place, I take one step into the road before jumping back. *Shit, I looked the wrong way.* Fortunately, there's no traffic, but it was still a stupid rookie mistake. I should know better; I almost got wiped out that way when I first moved to London.

I step off the curb again, this time checking to my right first, forcing myself to do the exact opposite of what Mrs. Walton taught us in the first grade. The road is clear, so I dash across, stopping on the other side a few feet in front of a boy waving a paper above his head.

RAF PUMMELS RUHR AGAIN! the headline shouts triumphantly.

The bombing campaign against German industrial facilities in the Ruhr Valley occurred in the first half of 1943, only stopping when Bomber Command's Lancasters and the Flying Fortresses of the US Eighth Air Force switched to the pointless and inhumane firebombing of Hamburg. But I have no idea when this particular raid occurred.

I move closer, stretching my neck as I try to read the date on the masthead.

"It ain't no library, Guv."

"Huh?"

"You want to read it," the kid says, "you pay your money."

I hide my face as I slink away. I would have bought the paper if I could have, not just to satisfy my curiosity, but for the paperboy's sake. He can't be any more than eleven or twelve. His sallow face and skinny arms and legs suggest he can only dream of three square meals a day. In my time, kids his age don't get out of bed this early, they don't work, and obesity is a far bigger problem than hunger. This is definitely not 2015.

If I'm going to come back — of course I am — I'll need to do something about money. That might not be so easy, getting hold of British notes issued before 1943.

But for now I've got what I want. The date.

July 1.

I stare up at the awning overhead as I recall the events of July 1943. From the corner of my eye I catch the sideways looks I'm getting from passing commuters. I must look like a madman.

Before leaving I glance up at the station clock. 5:25. My watch, still on Princeton time, shows 11:25 pm. The time difference between the east coast and the UK should be five hours… but the UK was on Double Summer Time during the war.

The time difference is right. Apart from the seventy-two years, to the minute, I've traveled into the past.

FOUR

I pause in front of the mirror for a final wardrobe check. A wide smile beams back at me from underneath a charcoal-gray fedora. With my hair tucked into my hat, I could have stepped straight out of 1943 London. My new look is the result of a week of meticulous preparation. Every moment not devoted to moving in, I've spent scouring online markets for period clothing and shoes, an antique watch, and other vintage items.

But I'm sticking with modern eyewear. My prescription would require super-thick lenses with 1940s technology, glass rather than plastic. I don't want to look like Mr. Magoo. Fortunately, the style, small, round lenses in a tortoiseshell frame, should fit right in. They'll only be a problem if someone examines the lenses closely, not easy to do if I keep them on my face. As for seventy-year-old under-wear—*used* underwear—I'm not going there. Not that anyone should see my boxers.

Though pleased with my disguise, I'm less happy about the effect on my finances. 1940s chic doesn't come cheap, and junior academics are

notoriously underpaid. My new position pays better — once I start. And I'll save on rent living in this
house. Cash flow is my problem. My credit cards
are almost maxed out. If I keep spending this way,
I'll drain my meager savings before the paychecks
from my new job start arriving.

I'll have to think about that one. Time travelers
solve the problem in the movies by giving their
future selves stock tips or, *hello Biff Tannen*, by bet-
ting on sporting events. Of course, Hollywood isn't
real life. Neither is time travel, or so I believed until
recently.

I touch my pockets, feeling for the pouches of
tobacco. *Check.* I don't smoke, but cigarettes were in
high demand in wartime England. U-Boats sent so
much of Britain's vital imports to the bottom of the
Atlantic, dedicated smokers turned to the black
market. Such is the addictive nature of nicotine,
they would pay astronomical prices.

In contrast, a pound of loose tobacco cost me
just fifty bucks. Though I did feel vaguely dirty going into a tobacconist. These days, to be a smoker is
to be an object of pity.

My original plan was to put the tobacco in vintage tins, but I need them to appear new. The ones
I found online were scratched and dented, the paint

dull and faded after seventy years. So I've wrapped my wares in brown paper pouches tied with string instead.

I also bought all the pre-1943 British currency I could find for sale. At a hundred dollars for a 'tenner' it wasn't bad value. Ten pounds was a lot of money back then—what a skilled worker might earn in a week or two. But the £143 in old, worn notes tucked into an antique billfold in my pocket still won't last forever. Selling tobacco should be a more sustainable strategy for acquiring local cash.

I check the time on my phone and make a quick calculation. The time in London should be 4:30 am. Sunrise will be a little after 6 am. The idea is to arrive while it's still dark. That way I shouldn't run into Alicia Rowntree while using her door, but not be there so early I'll have to wait for hours to get on with business.

I put the phone away. From the drawer of a small table standing in the entrance I grab the old key, now detached from the keyring.

Making a point of leaving the lights on, I open the door and step outside.

— o —

I sit hunched over a table in the back corner of a pub called *The Hand and Flower*. A thin, smoky haze fills the room, giving it a warm, intimate, and mysterious air, like a key scene from an old movie, one where you know critical events are about to unfold.

The smoke drove me mad at first, irritating my eyes and nose. But I've been here long enough now for that to stop, or at least to learn how to ignore it. And to be most of the way through my third drink.

Or is it my fourth?

I'm making notes on wartime London in a pocket-sized spiral notebook. Things like street curbs painted with white stripes, to help drivers see them when there's no street lighting and car headlights are masked so all that emerges is a narrow, inadequate strip of light.

I want to record everything I've seen. But I'll have to stop writing soon because my pencil needs sharpening. I Googled the history of ballpoint pens to discover the RAF is about to order tens of thousands for their bomber navigators, to replace fountain pens which tend to leak at altitude. But they're a novelty in 1943. *It's the little details which trip a time traveler up…*

As interesting as my observations are, it's not the kind of hard-hitting historical research I hoped to do today. I didn't have time. For fifteen hours I wandered the streets of London searching for an outlet for my contraband tobacco, and still I sold nothing. The locals don't want to risk doing shady business with the stranger they pick me for the second I open my mouth. As soon as I even hint that I'm moving illicit goods, everyone I approach suddenly remembers they need to be somewhere else. *Should have expected that.*

The whole day has been a total disaster. My feet are sore. I have blisters on my heels, probably the size of quarters but I'm too afraid to look. And the vintage watch I paid a small fortune for doesn't seem to keep time properly. So much for Swiss craftsmanship. Somewhere along the line it lost a few hours.

The building rattles again as a train rolls by on the line running behind the pub, mere feet from the rear wall by the sound of it.

I lift my glass and drain the last of its contents. The beer, a hearty dark ale served at cellar temperature the way it's meant to be, is excellent. Unlike the food. The dishes I've seen them serve other customers look unappealing. More than half the items on the menu are based on canned meat. *Spam.* There's a reason we've named unwanted email after such an unappetizing substance.

But despite my best attempts to fill the emptiness in my belly with beer, I'm so hungry after eating nothing all day I'd happily swallow any of it. If I had that choice. For all my detailed planning, it didn't occur to me I'd need ration coupons, not cash, if I wanted food.

It's not quite dark outside yet. At least an hour before I dare head to the townhouse and back to Princeton for a decent meal. Perhaps I'll try that Indian place I drove past yesterday. They'll take cash, American dollars I can get from any ATM. Or any of the seven or eight credit cards in the wallet I left at home. And they sure as hell won't serve fried spam. *Is it possible to overdose on curry?*

I slip the pencil and notepad into one pocket and pull a handful of change from another, spilling the coins onto the table. As I try to determine an appropriate tip, I stumble over the relative values — what's the equivalent of two dollars in 1943 England? — and the complexities of a system where twelve pennies make a shilling and twenty shillings comprise a pound. The Brits still use pounds, but they converted to a decimal system before I lived here—a simple one hundred pence to the pound. And with no weird denominations like halfpennies, crowns, or guineas.

A stocky, well-worn man slips into the chair opposite while I'm still battling the unfamiliar cash. "Buy you annuver?" he says in a thick accent, rough and unrefined, definitely working class. Cockney I'd say, but with a touch of... Irish? It's only a guess. I'm not Henry Higgins.

I narrow my eyes and inspect him warily. Has he noticed something about me that's out of place, a neglected detail that doesn't fit? Why else would he want to talk to me? "Thank you, but I think I've had enough."

He throws himself back in his chair. "Lord luv a duck, a Yank." The man smiles, a crooked, gap-filled grin that reminds me just how far dental treatment has come in the past seventy-two years. "I should 'ave known."

I don't smile back.

He leans forward. "Perhaps ya sellin' then."

"What makes you say that?"

"Maybe I'm a genius. Nuff said, yeah?" The man chuckles and points at my coat. "Or maybe 'cause you look like a barrage balloon with yer bulgin' pockets."

I didn't realize it was so obvious. Better be more careful next time. But what's done is done. "Then it depends if you're buying."

"Might be your lucky day."

I slip a hand into my jacket to retrieve a sample.

The man plants a hand on my arm, stopping me. "Not 'ere. Outside. If I decide I want what you got, I'll tell you where."

"Tobacco," I say quietly. "A pound. But I can get more. And papers. You know, to roll your own."

"Ten quid for the lot of it."

Is that a good price? I looked for academic research on black market prices in wartime England. Unsuccessfully. Google turned up several oral histories, but they contained no usable data. All the old-timers admitted knowing about the black market, but none of them ever did business there. So they swear. History is so often like that; selectively edited to make the storyteller look good.

There's a research paper for me right there, and I have my first data point. A tenner for a pound of tobacco.

Unless he's picked me for a newbie and offered way under market price. I have no way to know, but turning $50 into ten pounds is twice as good as the rate on eBay. I can bring more tobacco next time. If I repeat this trade regularly, I won't run out of cash.

"You have a deal."

"Rightio." The man stands. "Wait five minutes, yeah. Left out the front door, then take the first right until you come to an alley on the right."

My heart pounds in my chest as I watch the man leave. Is this a setup? Will the man be lying in wait with his gang—he looks the type to have a band of toughs at his command—ready to take what I have and leave me for dead?

No. There was money to be made on the black market, good money. If you could provide a reliable supply. As long as the man sees this as an ongoing arrangement, which I already hinted at, I should be safe. And I won't have to waste my time looking for a buyer every time I visit.

—o—

My partner in crime is waiting where he said he'd be, leaning against a grimy brick wall. His tweed cap is angled low over his face and a smoldering cigarette hangs from the corner of his mouth.

I approach slowly, glancing around in every direction, but trying hard not to seem nervous. He appears to be alone. Not that I can tell, the way he's hidden in the shadows. But who am I to criticize? I've been doing plenty of skulking myself lately.

The man tips his cap back and winks. "I'm not plannin' to roll you, Guv, if that's what's got you worried."

"No, of course not. Just making sure there aren't any coppers about."

He laughs. "Look at you, a septic tank, usin' the local lingo." His expression turns serious. "The constabulary won't be a problem. I give 'em, shall we say, regular encouragement to be wherever I'm not."

I nod, acknowledging the man's assurances, then remove the tobacco pouches from my coat pockets — inside right, inside left, outside right, outside left — and hand them over in a single bundle I grasp awkwardly in both hands.

My buyer stashes the makeshift packages into a canvas bag — all but one, which he unties. He pulls out a small sample of the product, rubs it between his thumb and forefingers, then sniffs it.

My pulse quickens as I wait for the man's verdict. Is there something wrong, something not authentic? Tobacco is tobacco isn't it? Or has it somehow changed in the last seventy years?

The man smiles. "Top notch." He places the final pouch of tobacco in the bag.

His hand emerges holding a roll of notes. "Five, ten," he says as he pulls two five pound bills from the roll, so crisp they could have come straight from the Bank of England.

"Here's to doin' business with ya, China," he adds as he delivers the agreed payment into my outstretched palm.

I slip the cash into an inside pocket and turn to go.

The man grabs my arm for the second time tonight. "You 'ave anythin' else in'erestin'?"

"Such as?"

"Razor blades. Alarm clocks. Pots 'n pans. Sugar?"

"Not with me."

"Don't be daft, man. Of course yar don't. But can you get it?"

Modern alarm clocks and cookware won't pass muster, but sugar is sugar. Though bulky. But razor blades would be easy to carry. "I can get blades."

They still make the old-fashioned ones, don't they? I'm pretty sure he doesn't mean the modern shaving miracles with three, or four, or even five blades. "Maybe. But how will I find you?"

"Just tell the lass behind the bar you've got a package for Riley."

The man stares at me, waiting for something. "Now I've told you me name, the polite thing would be for you to tell me yours..."

I don't know if Riley is the man's real name, or his first or his last, but I'm not going to give him mine. Instead I say, "Jackson Browne," because I like his music and it's the first name that comes to mind. "Browne with an 'E'," I add.

"You do right by me, Mr. Browne, and I'll do right by you," Riley says before he disappears, swallowed by the dark, narrow alley.

FIVE

I look up and down the street to be sure nobody is watching, then bound up the stairs, key in hand. Today ended much better than it promised only an hour or two ago. I'll be able to do a quick deal with this man Riley next time, then spend most of my day on research.

Getting ahead of myself, I fumble as I pull my keys from my pocket. They slip from my hand and fall to the ground.

The sky is clear and the moon almost full tonight, but it is hidden behind the buildings and deep shadows obscure the door and landing. My keys may be only inches away, but I can't see them.

As I stumble around blindly, my toe kicks something. Metal clatters against stone, falling. They could be anywhere now. On hands and knees I work down the stairs, my outstretched hands dancing frantically from side to side like a demented pianist's.

Minutes pass. I inch my way back up the steps, going over ground I've already searched, but I'll never get home if I don't find them.

Relax. Worst case, wait until the sun begins to rise. Five or six hours… If only my phone…

I reach into my pants pocket. I shouldn't have brought that along, but it's lucky I did. A tap opens the flashlight app. I hold the phone out at arm's length, sweeping it around in a wide arc.

There they are, in the middle of the third step. How did I miss them? I grab the keys and rush to the door, hurriedly pushing my key into the lock and twisting it.

As the tips of my fingers touch the handle, it turns. I pull my hand away with a jerk, taking a step back as the door swings away from me.

"Kill that light!" whispers a dark outline.

Oops. The blackout. "Sorry." I lock the screen and slip the phone back into my pocket.

"You had best come inside," says the familiar voice.

The door clicks into place behind me as soon as I step through and the room fills with a dull light. A large, crystal chandelier hanging overhead ought to bathe the room with dazzling illumination, but only one of its many sockets is in use.

I turn to find Alicia Rowntree standing behind me, her back to the door. She's wearing a thick dressing gown that comes to mid-calf, below which protrude the last few inches of a silk nightgown reaching her ankles.

She grasps a cricket bat in both her hands, the wide, flat blade raised above her shoulder. "Explain yourself, Mr. Seely. At once."

I close my left hand over the key before raising my hands above my shoulders, retreating until the wall presses against my back.

"Begin with how you opened my door. I distinctly remember locking it." She shakes her head. "First show me what you have in your hand."

Should I turn and flee while I still can, before she calls the police? If I stay I'll be lucky to get away with being thrown in prison. The prospect of incarceration in a foreign land, in an even more foreign time, is horrifying. Yet that isn't the most frightening potential outcome. Since I'd be unable to explain who I am or where I came from, an encounter with the authorities could end with me standing blindfolded in front of men pointing guns.

Though she's a full six inches shorter than me and fifty or sixty pounds lighter, the bat is a great equalizer. Even if I avoid a beating and get away, what then?

I need to figure out what went wrong, how to get home. This is the center of it all, the place to get answers. But for that, I need her on my side. I have to tell her the truth, as incredible as it will sound. I need to tell someone. It's killing me, keeping a secret this big. She's already involved. Who better to share it with than her?

I lower my hands to my waist, then open my fist to display my key.

"What? How did you obtain my key?"

I remove my hat and run my fingers through hair damp with nervous sweat.

"I'd love to explain. But it will take some time." I tilt my head toward the cricket bat. "You'll tire yourself out before I'm done, Ma'am, holding that up there."

She lowers her improvised weapon. "The term you are searching for is My Lady."

"Pardon me?"

"You Americans believe you are being polite with your Ma'am this and Ma'am that, Mr. Seely. But do I appear old enough to be Madam?"

"No, M—Miss?"

"An improvement, but the correct form of address is My Lady or Lady Alicia. I will, however, accept *Miss Rowntree*... given that you are foreign."

"I'm afraid I'm something more complicated than that, Miss Rowntree. Far more complicated."

— o —

Here we are again, sitting across from each other in the basement. At least I descended under my own power this time. I'm still not sure how she hauled me down here before when I was semi-conscious. If that, because I don't remember coming down those stairs.

Alicia Rowntree studies the two keys resting alongside each other on her palm. They are identical, though hers is a bright brassy yellow while mine is brown and dulled with scratches.

She looks up and fixes me in her gaze. "You say you inherited this key. From your grandfather?"

"Along with the lock and the door."

"That is impossible."

"What is the date?"

"Mr. Seely, I do not see how — "

"Please, Miss Rowntree, indulge me."

"Very well. Today is the 17th of July." She glances up at a clock hanging on the wall. "For another fifty-seven minutes."

"But what year?"

"What do you mean, *what year*?" she says in a tone that questions my sanity. "It is 1943. As it has been every day for the past six months."

I can't help grinning at her, knowing I'm about to deliver the punch line to the joke. Only it's no joke. I suck my cheeks in and take a deep breath. "My grandfather installed your door in his house in Princeton, New Jersey, sometime in 1947."

She jumps to her feet. "Preposterous."

"And he left his house, including your door, to me when he died at the ripe old age of ninety-one, in the year 2004. For me, that was eleven years ago."

Rather than the shock or confusion I expect to see written on her face, what I see is seething anger.

"I may be a woman, Mr. Seely, but I am no fool."

"I never said you were."

"I read both Pure *and* Applied Mathematics at Cambridge, I will have you know. My doctoral dissertation was almost complete when this terrible war started."

It's obvious her intellect is a matter of great pride. As someone also devoted to the pursuit of knowledge, I understand. *Appeal to the mind she is so proud of.*

"Then you must possess the capacity to evaluate my claims rationally, logically," I say. "To weigh the evidence scientifically."

She puts her hands on her hips and glares at me. "I would, were you to present any proof, something you have utterly failed to do. I suggest you leave."

I do not move. "You're a math wizz, right?"

"A wizz?"

"Like a boffin."

"The term 'boffin' is a touch condescending in the minds of most who use it, but I will wear the title proudly."

"As you should."

My compliment draws a tight-lipped smile and a nod for me to continue.

"By 1943," I say, "all the top British mathematicians are at Bletchley Park, breaking the German Enigma codes. You must know some of them since many came from the math department at Cambridge. Alan Turing perhaps?"

Her throat tightens in panic, but she does not speak.

"So you do know about Bletchley," I say.

She avoids my eyes.

"No. It's more than that, isn't it? You work there." *What hut is she in?* "Do you know about the Bombes? Or the new machine? Colossus."

Miss Rowntree stares straight ahead, her expression a determined, but not entirely successful, attempt at neutral. She wants me to believe she's ignorant of the work in the other buildings.

Or perhaps she doesn't know. Code-breaking operations were tightly compartmentalized.

I pull my phone from my pocket.

She recoils with a panicked gasp.

"It's OK," I say. *Does she think it's a gun? That I'm here to… arrest her? Or kill her?* I place the phone on the table between us. "This is just a far more advanced version of your code-breaking machines."

She resumes her seat, leaning forward to examine the phone. Her eyes narrow, the terror draining from her face as she studies it.

"History is more up my alley than math," I say. "But I'm guessing that finding the square root of a large number is hard?"

"It depends what you mean by *large*, Mr. Seely."

"Say you have half an hour. How big a number could you find the square root of?"

"Seven or eight digits. Excluding perfect squares of course. Those are trivial."

I look at her questioningly.

"An integer whose square root is an integer." I must still look confused because she continues with, "Like twenty-five. The square root is five."

"Got it." I can't help sounding a little peeved. I'm not great at math, but not so bad I can't work out the square root of twenty-five.

I press the power button and unlock the screen, then tap the calculator app.

She stares at the phone, looking confused, then the light of recognition ignites in her eyes. She looks at me, half in wonder, half in disbelief.

"Just press the buttons. Like this." I touch 6, then 5. I point at the screen. "See how it displays the numbers I enter right here?" I place the phone on the coffee table in front of her. "Now press the rest of the digits you want."

She extends her hand toward the screen, but doesn't touch it.

"Don't worry, you won't break it."

The phone vibrates as she presses 4, making an 'errrr' sound as it crawls across the table. "Oooh," she squeals as she pulls her hand away.

"I should have warned you. That's normal." I grab the phone, turn off the vibration, then place it back down in front of her.

Her hand returns to the phone, tapping 6 – 3 – 2 – 9 in quick succession. The calculator now displays 6546329.

Her forefinger hovers over the square root symbol.

I nod. "You're a fast learner."

She smiles then taps the surface once more.

The calculator flashes up a new string reading 2558.579488700713.

"There's your answer," I say.

Her lips move ever so slightly as she reads the digits. "That looks about right," she says in a disbelieving tone.

She stands and rushes over to a desk in the corner, rolls it open, grabs pencil and paper, and takes a seat.

I watch her for almost twenty minutes before she throws her pencil down and turns to me.

"How can you be so unmoved by the miracle performed by your marvelous device?" she says, shaking her head.

—o—

"How does it work?" Miss Rowntree says.

I point at the phone. "This?"

"Oh, I have many questions about that device, but for now I wish to understand time travel."

"You and me both. I have no idea how it works." The matter-of-fact way she says 'time travel' suggests she accepts my claim to be from her future. Which is more than I can say for myself. The little voice in my head is still telling me this is all some kind of delusion, a dream or hallucination. "Time travel is supposed to be impossible."

"Yet here you are."

"Yet here I am." *I think.* "All I know is I pass through my front door in Princeton and I land outside your door. Simple as that. Don't ask me how."

"But how do you return home? To New Jersey. To your time."

"I pass back through the door. That's what I was doing when you threatened me with your cricket bat."

"My brother Jonathan's bat. And I did not threaten you. Well, perhaps I did. But I am well within my rights to defend myself in my own home."

"Point taken. I didn't mean to scare you."

Her jaw stiffens. "You did not frighten me, Mr. Seely," she says. "But why are you still here?"

I stand, though I don't know where I'll go. I know an invitation to get the hell out when I see one. Her anger is justified, her desire for me to leave understandable.

If I use the door again will it take me home? I can only hope. But for the moment it's time to beat a tactical retreat. "I apologize for the intrusion."

"What are you doing, Mr. Seely?"

"Leaving…"

"Nonsense. We have not yet finished our conversation."

"You asked me to go."

"I most certainly did not." She pauses, then her eyes light up. "You misinterpreted my statement. Why are you still *here*? If my door takes you home, why are you here, in my home, in my time?"

I drop back into my seat. "Oh shit."

"*Mr. Seely, please!* Have you no shame? I am a modern woman. To my mother's despair I even prefer slacks to skirts when the occasion permits. But I would like to think I remain a lady."

"Sorry. No offense intended, but standards are different where and when I come from, Miss Rowntree. I'll try to remember that, if you would too."

She stares at me, her lips pressed together, unmoved by my suggestion. But then her face softens. "That does seem a reasonable request. Very well, I shall make the effort if you do too. Now back to the matter at hand. On previous attempts, you have returned to your own time through my door?"

"Twice."

"And yet on an equal number of occasions you crossed the same threshold and remained here in 1943. Tonight, and several days ago when I found you in the street. It cannot be an alternating pattern, so there must be some other variable. What is it? What was different?"

A long silence passes between us.

"My presence!" she announces. "Each time you entered this residence I was at the door with you. The other two times you were alone, correct?"

"I was."

She stands and leaves the room without explanation, reappearing in the doorway a few minutes later dressed in the same Victory Suit she wore when I first met her. Maroon gloves and a matching felt hat tilted to one side provide a dash of color and, to the extent I'm a judge of such things, an element of style.

She gestures toward the stairs. "Are you coming, Mr. Seely?"

"Where are we going?"

Though she doesn't answer, I follow her from the basement to the ground floor and then outside.

She closes the door behind us, then says with an uncertain smile, "Testing your theory," before pushing it open again.

Beyond the door it's dark. "Not my house."

"How can you be sure?" she says.

"Because I left the lights on."

She closes the door. "Perhaps if we are touching." She locks her elbow in mine and opens the door again.

Still dark.

"Allow me." I reach for the handle and push. The door swings in, drenching the landing and steps in a mix of artificial and natural light.

She releases her grip on my arm and leaps forward to pull the door closed. "We do not want to attract the ARP Warden's attention."

"That was definitely my house. Interesting. It seems to be who holds the door which determines where it leads."

"A plausible conclusion. But we should try again, to confirm."

"What about the light?" I say.

"We step inside and close the door behind us as quickly as we can."

I push the door open and rush inside, then turn to close it. The landing outside the townhouse is still visible, but Alicia Rowntree is gone.

SIX

I follow Mr. Seely as he advances through the door. The light flickers once before darkness engulfs me.

After exposure to such intense light, it takes my eyes a minute to adjust enough to detect the outlines of my own entrance. But I already know where I am, or am not, before I turn on the light.

Did I truly expect an ordinary wooden door to transport me to the future?

Of course not, but there is still a twinge of disappointment. What a marvellous adventure that would have been! Yet I beheld it — the inside of another house. Was it simply an illusion?

I turn and leave once more, now ignoring the blackout. From the landing, I see my own home through the open doorway.

Is this a form of hysteria? Has the work at Bletchley proved too much for me, a woman, as some of my colleagues and superiors have often insinuated it would?

There is another brief flicker, and then a painfully intense light from which Mr. Seely emerges as if it were a wall, only those parts of him outside the plane of the doorway visible while the rest of him remains hidden.

He pushes through until he stands beside me, fully formed. "Are you coming or not?"

"I followed you through." The door is still wide open and flooding the street with light. I'm too pre-occupied with this astonishing new development to care. "But it took me back into my own home."

He wrinkles his brow and rubs his chin. "I have an idea."

I let him take my hand and pull me through the shimmering wall, into an entrance which is not mine. As he reaches past me to push the door clo-sed, I turn and look over my shoulder in time to see Hartness Street wiped from view.

"Welcome to Princeton, Miss Rowntree," he says. "And to the future."

— o —

Though delicious, the biscuits differ from proper Scottish shortbread, presumably because they come from Denmark. I lift one and inspect it before taking a bite. I find it hard to conceive of Danish imports when in my mind that unfortunate land still languishes under Nazi occupation.

I sit in Mr. Seely's living room, our roles now reversed as he serves me tea — if one stretches the meaning of 'serve' to include placing a teapot and a tin of biscuits before a guest and then waiting for her to help herself.

There isn't a piece of decent porcelain or silverware in sight, only rough pottery — I suppose one could call it rustic, if one wished to be generous — that is every bit as casual as his manner.

My mouth moves, ready to object to his poor manners and lack of effort.

I press my lips together. Am I looking for impoliteness and disrespect where none is to be found?

He already reminded me that standards have softened with the passing of three or four generations. My great-grandparents would not regard my daily habits favourably either. And the Americans have always been much less proper than we English, at least since their revolution, almost taking pride in their casual ways as a marker of their independence.

The choices are either he seeks to offend, or his behaviour is acceptable in this time and place. In the absence of evidence to the contrary, it would be logical, prudent, and charitable to assume the

latter. Instead of stewing on an imagined slight,
I return to drinking tea and quietly examining my
surroundings.

The living room furniture is quite formal, not
what I would imagine of this era, had I ever stopped to consider interior design in the twenty-first
century. Even in 1943 it would be considered dated,
at least within fashionable circles. It reminds me of
Father's library or his London club, all dark leather
and dark wood.

But there is still a great deal in the home's
contents to surprise me. His house appears humble,
a simple two-storey dwelling perhaps half the size
of Hartness Street. But those parts of it I have
seen—this room, the entry, and a glimpse of the
kitchen through an open door—contain numerous
wonders.

Even the device he calls a 'smartphone' is far
more miraculous than I initially thought. It can do
so many astounding things; as if performing complex mathematical calculations in the blink of an
eye were not miracle enough.

But am I imagining it? Is any of this real?

Some of these marvels, like the 'calculator app,'
appear to be an electronic version of mechanical
devices familiar to me. Even his television is based

on a concept extant in my time. It is still astounding. Only two inches thick, fifty inches wide, the quality of the sound and picture are breathtaking, and in the most vivid colour! There is a personal cinema in his sitting room and he thinks nothing of it.

But other technologies, like the Global Positioning System he tells me about, are stunning in their originality, each appearing to be *sui generis.* Could my own mind manufacture even the idea of such creations? Perhaps, but unlikely.

When I question Mr. Seely he provides answers filled with extensive scientific detail. Though he claims it is the sort of general knowledge most educated people possess, it exceeds anything I could conjure from my own body of knowledge. And I believe he is being entirely too modest. Most of the professors I know can barely operate a wireless, let alone explain the principles by which it works.

Other times he points me to something called 'Wikipedia,' accessed with his smartphone. For example, when I ask how this 'GPS' works, he retrieves an article of several thousand words, written by volunteers in every corner of the world he informs me.

Almost every paragraph is filled with new and ground-breaking concepts: 'multi-stage' rockets, 'satellites,' 'geosynchronous orbit,' and on and on, each of them explained in another detailed article available at the 'click' of a 'link.'

An hour and a half goes by in a blur while I 'surf,' as he calls the process of jumping from one article to a related one, and then another, and another, until I cannot quite remember how I arrived at the current topic, like Alice pursuing the White Rabbit down his burrow to Wonderland.

I would need to be the greatest mind since Da Vinci to have conceived all these marvels, smarter than all the true geniuses working at Bletchley combined. The only alternative explanation is that what I see here is real. It must be. *Lex parsimoniae* — Occam's Razor — says so.

Though relieved to find my sanity intact, the logical implication is that I must therefore believe the unbelievable — this truly is the future, in all its dazzling and awe inspiring glory. This truly is Wonderland.

I have a million questions. About everything. And if this is how a junior don lives, what unimaginable miracles do the wealthy and powerful command?

But as much as I thirst for answers to those questions, a different matter presses at me.

"What happens now, Mr. Seely?" I say, hoping to discover the answer to my most urgent question: *what is his agenda?*

SEVEN

What happens now? That depends on you, Miss Rowntree. "Obviously I'd do everything possible to minimize any inconvenience to you…"

"Do go on."

I had a reason for bringing her here, for sharing this secret, so there's no point dodging and weaving. "I wish to continue traveling to 1943."

"To what end?"

There is nothing shameful about my goals, no reason not to tell her. And it will be easier in the long run if she understands what I'm trying to achieve. "To continue my research. Britain during the war is of great historical interest to me."

"Yes, I do recall you mentioning an interest in history, though I struggle to think of 1943 as the past."

"It's slightly more than just an interest. More of a calling, I'd say."

"A calling?"

"And a profession. I am Assistant Professor of Modern History at Princeton University. Well I will be, starting the fall semester."

"You should have mentioned that."

"Why?"

"So that I might address you properly."

"Properly?"

"Yes, *Professor*. Properly. By your correct title."

"It's not that big a deal."

"I beg to differ."

"Well, not to me. What I care about is my work. That's why I need your help. Or your cooperation at least."

"And what is it you hope to do in 1943, Professor?"

"Observe events first hand. Not just the big events, the ones documented in the history books, but the small ones too. Life in London during the war.

"I took my doctorate from Kings College London you know, just so I'd feel closer to the place and the people I was studying. But that's a poor substitute for being there while it's all happening. This is the most incredible opportunity any historian has ever had."

"You wish to study us in our darkest hour? To watch us like you would watch wild animals fighting to the death in a cage?"

"That's not what I —"

"This war is not history. Not for me. It is the present, my reality. And the reality for millions of brave men risking their lives. How many more must be sacrificed to the wrath of Mars before it is over?"

More than ten million is the answer.

The coming years will be far deadlier than most people in 1943 imagine, though the dead will be overwhelmingly Russian, German, and Japanese. For her country and mine it's less horrifying, though another million and a half combat fatalities before it ends is tragic enough.

I don't know whether her loved ones are in danger or what their fate might be, but in the midst of total war there must be someone she cares about at the sharp end. A brother, a cousin, a boyfriend or fiance. So I simply say, "Too many. But what would you have me do?"

She takes a deep breath, puts down her mug, and straightens her back. "The decent thing. The proper thing. Use your knowledge to end the war."

I sigh in exasperation. "It isn't as simple as that."

"But you have already asked yourself the question," she says.

"Yes."

"Because you know it is the only decent course of action."

"Because I wouldn't be human if I hadn't." I shrug my shoulders. "Whether it's the right thing to do is much less obvious."

"How can you say such a thing? Surely the moral choice is clear cut."

"Not really. History is contingent. Will your future be better or worse than the future I know if the war were to end in 1943?"

"Of course it would, Professor."

"Next year, for sure. But long term? There are far too many possibilities for anyone to predict. Anyway, it's too late for anything I do to make a difference. The war will be over by the end of 1945."

"Another two and a half years of this... it is an eternity."

"It may seem so to you, Miss Rowntree, but there's a lead time to anything large enough and decisive enough to deliver victory. Allied forces will land on the beaches of France in May 1944. Planning began in earnest almost as soon as we — the United States that is — entered the war. Training and mobilization of the necessary men and machines is already underway. There's nothing I can tell the Allied commanders to stop the Wehrmacht d.a.hill

pushing them back into the sea. Other than *don't go*. But that won't win the war, will it?"

"You must at least try. Share your knowledge and allow the authorities to decide if they can use your information."

"And how do you propose I do that? Knock on the door of the Cabinet War Rooms and ask to speak to Mr. Churchill?"

"We shall begin by consulting my father."

"Your father?"

"Yes, my father. Once you have established your *bona fides*, Father can secure you an audience with his commander, General Brooke, and ultimately with the Prime Minister."

— o —

It is hard to believe Miss Rowntree would speak so nonchalantly about direct access to senior officers of the Imperial General Staff. Perhaps even to the British Prime Minister, the legendary man himself, Sir Winston Churchill.

I've read all the official documents of the period. The Cabinet Papers, correspondence between Churchill and Roosevelt, military plans and after-action reports, and tens of thousands of pages of personnel and supply records. There is much to be learned from the latter; logistics so often determine the outcome of battles.

Not to forget the memoirs, the reflections after the fact of those prominent enough to have their version of history published. And in an unending search for the complete story, I've also read masses of unofficial documents — diaries and journals and occasionally mere scribblings on scraps of paper — written by ordinary men and women who couldn't predict how long they would endure, or if they would survive at all.

Their writings were sometimes despairing, often filled with anxiety, and at other times humorous and irreverent. They wrote not to establish their place in history but for their own sanity, to make sense of their own personal nightmare, and for the comfort of their loved ones if they didn't make it home. Theirs was a narrower view of events, but typically painted a far more honest picture.

But to see the strategic decision-making process first hand, to have a window into what the leaders were thinking at the time? Was Brooke's relationship with Churchill as fractious as he portrayed it in his *War Diaries*? Did Roosevelt really not understand what Stalin intended for Europe after the war, did he not care, or was he simply too ill to respond effectively? So many unanswered questions.

For such unprecedented access I'll play along with her plan. Hell, I'd run naked down Fifth Avenue in the middle of a winter storm if she asked.

This opportunity is too good to be true. If it's real. "Major-General Sir Geoffrey Rowntree is your father?"

She reels in surprise. "What do you know of him? Father insists his post at the War Office is quite obscure."

"Not to a student of the period. He's an earl or something, if I remember correctly."

"The 7th Earl of Hamley."

"Just tell me when and where to meet him."

"If you truly know the future, then you know much that you should not. Official secrets." She glances around the room. "And, as they say, the walls have ears. Therefore, it must be somewhere private and secluded. With appropriate precautions we could meet at Hartness Street, but my father's movements are unpredictable."

"Makes sense."

She pauses, biting her lip. "Elverstone Hall would be just the ticket."

I can't help chuckling.

"What do you find so amusing, Mr. Seely?"

The English have this quaint habit of identifying even the most humble and obscure building by the name alone, without an address. It would be like me saying 'Grandpa Harry's House' instead of '21876 Washington Avenue' and expecting strangers to know where it is.

"Nothing," I say, I hope with a straight face. "Elverstone?" I pronounce it _Elv-stun_ as she did.

"Our estate in Warwickshire. Father will be there the night of the twenty-seventh."

"We can't do it any sooner?"

"There are a great many demands on my father, as you can imagine. Rarely does he know where he will be on any given day. Fortunately for us this is an exception, the 27th of August being my parents' wedding anniversary. In addition, I must be back at Bletchley tomorrow, and I am rostered until noon on the twenty-fifth."

"The twenty-seventh it is then."

"We shall take the train up together," she says. "Let us meet me at Hartness Street at 8 am."

"Yes, but there's one other problem."

"What is it?"

"The passage of time doesn't seem to be the same here and there. It was at first, but not now."

I hold up my smartphone. The display shows the current date as July 9. "You said today is the seventeenth, didn't you?"

"I did." She has me explain exactly what time I left Princeton, and what time I arrived in London.

"And it was almost midnight when we left Kensington…"

She looks up, staring at the ceiling, then a minute later says, "It appears time is passing in 1943 at twice the rate it is here."

There is another brief silence while she stares vacantly into the distance, before her gaze returns to me. "You should leave here around 11 pm on the evening of the 13th of July."

EIGHT

Bright sunshine hits me as soon as I step through the door. Something is wrong. I planned to arrive several hours early, before dawn, having filled my pockets with contraband to sell to Riley first.

I shield my eyes with my forearm as I turn my face to the sky. The sun is already high overhead, so I'm five, six, maybe even seven hours late. *Damn, how did I mess up?*

I spin around and pound the brass knocker against the door. Will Miss Rowntree forgive me? She must.

The door opens half way.

A small, plump woman with short, silver hair tied up in a severe bun greets me with an unfriendly stare. "May I help you?" she says, her impatient tone suggesting she wants to do anything but help me.

"Hello. I'm Professor Seely. Miss Rowntree is expecting me. Was expecting me. I was supposed to be here earlier today. Is she still —"

"You must be mistaken, Sir. *Lady Alicia* spoke of no appointment with an American."

She starts to close the door but I press my hand against it, stopping her. "Wait, please."

"Lady Alicia is not here."

"Do you know where she is?"

"It is not my place to share such information, especially with a stranger."

"Can you call her and tell her I'm here? Professor Seely. Please. It's extremely important."

She shoots me a skeptical look. "Wait here," she says before closing the door in my face.

A few minutes later the door opens again, wide this time. "Lady Alicia invites you to wait inside, Professor." She steps back and waves me in.

I follow her into the entry.

She glances disapprovingly at the small suitcase I'm carrying, then raises narrowed eyes to meet mine.

I can guess what she's thinking. A young man packed for traveling, meeting with a young woman who is neither his sister nor his wife — in 1943 that spells scandal.

"Please remain here, Sir," she says. "I will return when Lady Alicia calls back." She darts off as fast as her short, thick legs will carry her.

Standing there alone, time passes slowly. After

a wait that seems interminable, but is only fifteen minutes, the telephone rings.

The plump woman rushes in from another room and then down the hallway to answer it. After a brief conversation she calls me over. "Lady Alicia wishes to speak with you, Professor," she says coldly as she hands me the receiver.

"Miss Rowntree?"

"Hello, Professor. I apologize for the delay in calling back. You caught me on the hop. I needed to find my supervisor and ask to be excused from my duties."

"I'm the one who should apologize, for being so tardy. I don't know how it happened. I followed your instructions to the letter."

"Clearly we do not possess all the facts," she says. "Therefore, this is not the time to concern ourselves about it."

I've just upended her day. She sounds stressed, but not angry or annoyed. More perplexed, or intrigued, by our unsolved mystery. Nevertheless, I feel guilty for the disruption I've caused.

I'm also confused. Why is she back at Bletchley? If she wasn't going to wait for me here, surely she would have gone on ahead to her family estate.

"What do we do now?" I say.

"We are in luck. My father will be at Elverstone the next two evenings, and I have managed to swap shifts with another girl. Can you meet me here?"

"At Bletchley?"

"Preferably at the station."

Bletchley Park is an important historical site, of interest to a war historian, so I've been there. Even in my time, the railway is the best way to get there. "The train still goes from Euston?"

"It does. See if you can make the quarter past two. That should get you here by three-thirty. I will meet you in the waiting room. If your plans change, here is the number to call. Do you have a pencil?"

— o —

A red double decker carries me from Kensington to Euston Station. I stand on the rear platform. Hanging off the back, I savor the wind in my hair, reveling in a level of personal freedom that isn't allowed anymore — *for health and safety reasons* — not even on the modern version of the iconic London bus.

While waiting on the platform for my train, my mind fills with romantic images of wartime railway travel: pretty young girls saying fond farewells to brave soldiers carrying duffel bags slung over their shoulders, many of them still more boy than man; riding in richly paneled compartments with men and women dressed in fine clothing who conduct intelligent, sophisticated conversations; chugging our way through idyllic rural landscapes behind sleek black steam engines.

The locomotive finally arrives forty minutes late, looking like something left over from the previous century. The carriages appear just as old and worn and grimy. My journey to Bletchley will be far from romantic, or comfortable.

I wait for the worst of the human crush to disperse before boarding. The interior is as much in need of cleaning and maintenance as the outside. I find an empty seat, stow my small suitcase in the overhead rack and sit down, but not before another two passengers push their way into the compartment, filling it beyond its intended capacity.

There is a grayness to my fellow sardines that darkens my mood even further. Perhaps they are weary of a war they never expected to last so long and which asks so much of them. Though forced to sit pressed up against each other, for the next hour and a half the occupants of my section avoid eye contact and speak not a word to each other — apart from the woman sitting opposite who scolds her child repeatedly. "Sit still and be quiet, Jimmy," she says so many times that it grows almost as annoying as the boy's constant squirming.

Dragging out the pain, our train stops at every siding, allowing trains carrying troops and war materiel to roll past, doing what they were meant to do — move — while we impersonate a rock, motionless and impotent.

I try to lighten my mood by focusing on the scenery outside. The English countryside is every bit as lush and green as I remember. The small towns and villages we pass look so peaceful — deceptively so when so many of the residents or their loved ones are involved in the greatest military struggle in history.

By the time I alight, all I can think about is having room to move and breathe, and the fact I'm running half an hour late. I pay no attention to the one other passenger who gets off, a man who exits from the door at the other end of the same carriage.

I go straight to the waiting room. Miss Rowntree isn't there. No reason to panic. She said she might be late. I can always call her if she doesn't arrive soon. Anyway, it's exciting, a rendezvous with a woman doing secret war work. I smile in amusement. *Like something out of a spy novel.*

I take a seat and settle in to wait.

The smell of food coming from a tiny shop tucked into the rear of the building reminds me I haven't eaten since dinner last night. But I won't be buying anything to eat this time either. After going hungry on my last visit, I decided to print my own ration coupons. I attacked the problem with enthusiasm. Having dealt with many historical documents, I assumed it would be, if not easy, at least straightforward.

Even the *free* computer graphics tools are amazing, so producing a good facsimile of the design was simply a matter of investing enough time in learning to use one of them. But the quality of the physical output was far too high to pass as something from the 1940s. Modern paper is too crisp, too clean. The coupons wouldn't have looked as good when new, so I didn't even bother trying the aging techniques I'd researched online. Success might come with more experimentation, but for now I can't risk being caught passing forged coupons.

Instead of some hot, delightfully British treat like a Cornish pasty, I pull a boring, cold, 2015-style sandwich from my pocket. Placing it on my lap,

I unfold the waxed paper wrapper. Last night I almost made the mistake of putting the sandwich in a Ziploc bag. Another reminder that keeping everything consistent with the period requires constant vigilance.

I grasp the inch and a half thick sandwich in both hands. Several of my fellow travelers stare at me. What wouldn't they give for the generous slices of premium quality ham, the layer of creamy, sweet butter, and thick slabs of sourdough bread? And I can have as much of it as I want.

Well, it isn't like I'm taking food from their tables. I still feel bad for them, at least a little, especially the small boy sitting opposite me who is staring and licking his lips. But not so guilty that I'm not going to eat it.

I lift the sandwich, but stop before it reaches my mouth. The man who got off with me, the one in the brown overcoat. Didn't I see him on the bus? *Am I being followed?*

I checked the street was empty when I left Miss Rowntree's townhouse. A crew of workmen were removing the rubble of the house across from hers, but I doubt they even noticed me. They were too busy swinging picks, thrusting shovels, and pushing loaded wheelbarrows, all while carrying on a loud but friendly argument with each other — I think over some soccer match. And they were all dressed in working clothes and covered in dust. None of them had on a clean suit and overcoat.

I look around anyway, keeping my head still and moving just my eyes. Mr. Brown Overcoat isn't here. *Nothing but a coincidence.*

I return to my meal. The boy is still staring so I tear a corner off my sandwich and hold it out to him.

He snatches it away and devours it like a hungry animal. His mother scolds him and glares at me, but the smile on his face is worth it.

I smile back then take a greedy bite, one that fills my mouth so full my cheeks puff out, as the woman drags the boy from the room.

— o —

Miss Rowntree purchases a First Class ticket, so I do the same.

It hadn't occurred to me to ride up front on the previous leg, though I can easily afford the few extra shillings it costs, despite missing the chance to make another sale to Riley. Spending money on 'luxuries' might be how she was raised. Not me.

The investment proves worth every penny. The ride from Bletchley to Elverstone is far less crowded than the journey from London, at least in our carriage.

Apart from a few pleasantries passing between us, we travel in silence. Miss Rowntree and I have little in common, and what we do share we can't discuss here where someone might overhear. I use the time instead to go over in my mind what I plan to tell General Rowntree.

Nevertheless, I welcome her presence. It comforts me to have a traveling companion, someone who knows my secret, a co-conspirator, to feel I'm not embarking on this grand, and perhaps dangerous, adventure alone. And every time she looks at me with her sweet, charming smile my heart feels a little lighter.

We arrive at Elverstone Station after 7 pm. She calls the house from one of those classic red telephone booths, or 'phone box' as they call them here.

The summer days are still long, the evening pleasantly warm. While waiting for our ride we sit on a park bench beneath a large, wizened oak tree. Like everything in England, I'm certain the village, and everything in it, including the tree, has a long and interesting story.

"We must discuss your late arrival," Miss Rowntree says before I can ask what she knows of the village history.

I shift in my seat. I doubt majors-general or earls are accustomed to being stood up, and her father is both, so he's probably doubly pissed. Unfortunately, that may undermine his receptiveness to my message.

"How did you explain my tardiness to your father?"

"I informed him you were called away on urgent war business. He understood completely."

"Even though it's not true?"

"That could not be helped. But it must be explained. At least for our own satisfaction and future reference."

She quizzes me on what I did before leaving home, and how it may have differed from my earlier journeys.

I tell her what I can, but I am thoroughly confused. Until I purchased my train ticket and looked at the date stamped on it, I didn't know I'd arrived not a few hours late but four days behind schedule.

She gazes off into the distance, an expression that I now recognize as her performing complex mathematical calculations in her head. I don't know how she does it, working out days and hours and minutes, multiplying and dividing by twenty-four and sixty and adding and subtracting, but her mind and eyes soon return from wherever they went.

She has the answer.

"It appears the ratio changes each time you come back, Professor. On your previous visit it was two to one. Since your most recent return to Princeton it seems time has passed three times as quickly here."

"Does that mean it'll be four times as fast the next time?"

"Not necessarily. There are several mathematical progressions which might fit this pattern. We need more data."

The car arrives while I am still trying to wrap my head around the implications of this unexpected and troubling discovery. If time passes faster every time I come back, will that limit the number of trips I can make?

The vehicle her father sends is a black Rolls Royce saloon. I stand and admire it as it approaches. Struck by its perfect condition, I have to remind myself this is not some lovingly maintained vintage car but a contemporary vehicle, a few years old at most. Though I'm sure it is meticulously cleaned and serviced.

I prepare to climb in, but Miss Rowntree waits for the driver to open the door, so I follow her lead and step back. The hood extends half the vehicle's length — there must be one hell of an engine underneath — meaning the passenger cabin is small for such a large car. But the cramped interior is luxuriously appointed in fine leather and chestnut paneling, all hand-crafted I'm sure, and the ride as smooth as any modern sedan.

After a short but winding trip down several narrow country lanes, the car turns through an impressive stone gateway. The driveway is at least half a mile long. It makes its way in sweeping curves through grounds that remind me of an exclusive country club or high-end golf course. Not surprising, since the landscaping style of these English country estates inspired the design of private and public grounds in many corners of the world, including New York's Central Park.

Could these gardens be the work of the best known proponent of the style called *jardin anglais*, 'Capability' Brown himself? I'll have to check.

At the driveway's end we pull to a stop in front of a stone building far too large to be a house, at least in my world, but not quite imposing enough to call a palace.

Consisting of two tall stories, it is seventy-five yards wide with square towers rising another story at each corner. Tall and narrow rectangular windows fill the facade, each made of many small rectangular panes, giving it a surprisingly light and airy appearance.

In my enthusiasm to see the place, I leap out of the vehicle to find myself standing alone. *Awkward.* I turn to see the driver opening the car door for Miss Rowntree. She climbs out slowly, unfolding herself from the vehicle with all the grace of a ballerina.

A portly man wearing the uniform and insignia of a Major-General in the British Army stands at the main door waiting to greet us. Graying lightly at the temples, Sir Geoffrey Rowntree looks to be in his early fifties.

She rushes forward to kiss her father on the cheek.

"So, my darling," he says while inspecting me, "this is the young man you were so eager for us to meet."

I try not to flinch. The tone of voice and knowing smile lead me to a conclusion I don't like but can't shake off. I fear he misunderstands the reason for our presence. Completely.

"Father, may I introduce Assistant Professor Harrison Seely of Princeton University."

"A pleasure to meet you, Sir Geoffrey," I say as we shake hands. "Or should I say General?" *Or should it be General Sir Geoffrey? Earl, maybe?* "I'm not sure…"

He dismisses my nervous bumbling with a wave of his hand. "The correct form would be Lord Elverstone. But until the war is over my military responsibilities rule all else. So let us settle on General and Professor, if that is acceptable to you."

"Completely."

Her father directs us inside with a wave of his arm.

An older servant—the butler?—leads the way, the driver following behind with my luggage.

"You must forgive me, Professor, but I am taken aback to discover you are an American." He raises an eyebrow in his daughter's direction. "Lady Alicia neglected to share that piece of intelligence."

"It is not relevant, Father."

"I doubt your mother will agree, my dear."

— o —

Though 9 pm is late to dine by English standards, I realize as soon as I enter the dining room that no formality will be spared.

The butler, Mr. Williams, stands waiting to serve. Alongside him is Henderson, the driver. From his change of uniform, he appears to do double duty as a house servant or footman or whatever they call the position.

A massing army of silverware and crystal and an impressive floral centerpiece almost hide the top of the table, filling nearly every square inch of its surface. Each place setting comprises numerous specialized pieces of flatware, enough for five or six courses, and half a dozen glasses of varying shapes and sizes.

For the typical American, even from this era, it would be intimidating. Luckily I learned the basic protocols of formal English dining while a doctoral student at Kings College. I even know how to use a knife and fork English style, the fork remaining in the left hand at all times and held so the tines curve down, the knife always in the right hand.

This British style of eating isn't as practical for moving food from plate to mouth as the American approach—cutting with the knife and fork, dropping the knife and switching the fork to the right hand, and then shoveling the food in—but these people will judge me on something other than the efficiency of my consumption.

If my knowledge of table etiquette is enough to avoid disgracing myself, I cannot say the same of my clothing. Lady Alicia and her parents are 'dressed' for dinner, the General in 'black tie,' what I would call a tux, the women in evening gowns. Even though I anticipated this situation, I can't help being embarrassed by my humble garb.

I considered trying to buy vintage-style formal wear, but decided against it. I understand just enough of the rules of formal dress among the British upper class to know they are riddled with subtle complexities. I would almost certainly miss the mark, a greater indiscretion than wearing my Victory Suit and pretending I did not expect to dine formally tonight.

"The exigencies of war excuse many things," General Rowntree says, accepting my apology with good grace. *My plan worked.*

Despite the positive start, I grow increasingly uncomfortable as the evening progresses. I want to get on with discussing the real topic of my visit, but this isn't the time or place, not with Lady Elver-stone present. Adding to the awkwardness, the secret of my true origins makes it difficult to answer most of the questions Miss Rowntree's parents ask.

Though I say as little as possible, my responses are evasive, bordering on deceptive. I can't even correct their belief that my connection with their daughter is through the field of mathematics, not without raising too many questions, all of them best left until later. I hope they will understand once they know the truth.

Even worse, they show far too much interest in my personal background and family pedigree, reinforcing my fear they have misjudged the purpose of my visit.

Miss Rowntree makes no comment on their mistake though she can't have missed it. Not until dessert is almost finished, when she leans close and whispers, "I am so terribly sorry, but I believe my parents have assumed you are my... beau."

"What took you so long?" I whisper back. "I picked that up when I met your father outside. What on earth did you tell them about our visit? And about me?"

"Only name, rank, and serial number. And that we have a matter of the utmost importance to discuss. I could hardly reveal more over the telephone."

"What are you two whispering about?" Lady Elverstone says with a questioning smile. "Do you perchance have an announcement you wish to share, Alicia dear?"

The anticipation written on the older woman's face suggests she looks favorably on my non-existent relationship with her daughter. I can't imagine why. Miss Rowntree and I are every bit as mismatched as our appearances suggest. My suit is so shabby and ill-fitting people would consider it cheap, even by the loose standards of 2015, while in her elegant satin gown, Miss Rowntree is just about the most fetching creature I've ever laid eyes on. It must be something she owned before the war, because it doesn't fit the current climate of wartime austerity.

Even ignoring the facts not available to her mother, I am an American of moderate means and uncertain origins, while Miss Rowntree is an Englishwoman of noble birth. One of us a history buff, the other a mathematician. We have nothing in common.

But despite our inherent incompatibility, I enjoy her company. Smart, beautiful, sophisticated.

What's not to like? I could easily like her as more than a friend, but such a desirable woman would never be interested in someone like me, even in a less class-ridden world.

My mother raised me to be a 'nice guy,' a label everyone knows is the romantic kiss of death, even more so when combined with my professional interests, which seem dull to most people. Historian is bad enough, but military history is guaranteed to bore most women to tears.

No, I can see Lady Alicia Rowntree with someone far more exciting than me. Someone dashing and debonair, and just dangerous enough to alarm her parents.

From this era, someone like Errol Flynn or Clark Gable. From my own time? No one comes to mind. They don't make sophisticated cads like they used to.

Miss Rowntree places her dessert fork and spoon together in the center of her plate, signaling she is done. Within seconds Henderson whisks her empty dish away.

"Mother, Father," she says, "the hour grows late and we have important matters to discuss."

Her parents, waiting expectantly, both beam back with tight-lipped smiles.

"Official business," Miss Rowntree says, causing her mother's face to fall in disappointment. "Matters relating to the war."

The General's head jerks back in shock, but he regathers himself and says sternly, "Then we best continue in my library."

— o —

The General holds out a box of cigars. I politely refuse. He takes one for himself, snips the end with a silver cutter, and lights it with a matching silver lighter.

My first thought when he doesn't extend the offer to his daughter is to blame the sexist attitudes that no one in this time would even question. But then he produces cognac, which he offers to both of us. Perhaps she just doesn't care for cigars.

To settle my nerves, I prompt the General to pour me a generous portion of the brandy, double the amount Miss Rowntree requests.

Despite my mind telling my fingers to relax, they squeeze the snifter so tight I fear it might break. *Loosen up.* I take a swig. *Wow.* It's smoother than anything I've ever sampled. I hate to think what this stuff costs.

The liquid courage goes to work and I begin. "General, I have to…" As I start to speak the words I've practiced, they seem trite and ridiculous. "General… What I mean… you will find…"

"Father, what Professor Seely is trying — "

I stop her with a raised palm. This is my story to tell. "Thank you, Miss Rowntree, but I've got this."

Ditching my prepared statement, I decide to come straight to the point.

"I was born in 1984. For me the present is 2015." The words spill from my mouth in a breathless torrent. "I have no explanation for the mechanism by which this is possible. Your daughter suggested I share my knowledge of your future in order to help end the war."

He remains seated, his glass frozen in place halfway to his mouth, his eyes fixed on a point across the room, and his expression unchanged.

Did he not hear? He must have. Could I have been any plainer?

He takes a sip of brandy, followed by a long silence, then another sip, and another long silence. "I must say, this attempt at humor is in dreadfully poor taste." He turns to his daughter. "Alicia, how could you allow yourself to be drawn into such a ridiculous charade?"

"It is no charade, Father. I have seen it with my own eyes. The future."

"You have been deceived."

"I have not."

"There is no other explanation, my dear."

"Do you consider me so gullible, Father?"

"You know I do not, but—"

"But nothing, Father. I am certain. But should it prove otherwise, I will do as you and Mother desire—abandon the pursuit of mathematics and devote my every waking moment to securing a suitable husband instead."

"Do you truly mean that, Alicia?"

"I give you my solemn promise, Father, though I do not expect I shall be required to keep it. Allow the Professor to continue, and he will prove the veracity of his claim."

"I doubt that," the General growls. "I will not hold you to your vow, enticing as it is, but I do wish for you to see this man"—he gestures contemptuously in my direction—"for what he is. And so I will give the *Professor* enough rope to hang himself."

"General, I must first correct a misconception," I say, looking away to avoid his frosty stare. "I have allowed you to assume that my connection to your daughter is through a common interest in mathematics. I apologize. My position at Princeton is in the Department of Modern History, my particular field of expertise Britain's military campaigns during this war. I am therefore intimately familiar with events which for you are still the most sensitive of military secrets. For example, I can tell you that Prime Minister Churchill met with President Roosevelt in Washington from May 12 through May 27."

"Hah," he snorts. "You must do far better than that. The visit was hardly secret. The Prime Minister addressed a Joint Session of Congress while in America. Every newspaper reported his presence, ours and yours."

"I doubt *The Times* revealed that during these meetings, codename TRIDENT, Roosevelt and Churchill agreed on a cross-channel invasion to take place in 1944, to be known as OVERLORD. Nor did they report the strong British preference for the main thrust to occur in the Mediterranean, or General Brooke's solemn conviction you should delay the invasion until 1945 or even 1946."

Fear and panic replace the General's attitude of haughty confidence. "Alicia, you must leave this minute," he says. "I will not have you drawn any further into this shadowy business. Say nothing of this to anyone."

She grasps the arms of her chair. "I am a grown woman, Father, responsible for the consequences of my own actions. I will not be dismissed so readily. Please stop trying to protect me."

He starts to object, then demurs, turning back to me instead, an angry fire burning in his eyes as he fixes them on me.

"You have proven nothing, only that you some-how gained access to Top Secret communiques." His mouth moves as he speaks, but in the true spirit of the British stiff upper lip, he maintains a stern and unmoving facade, as if his features are carved from stone. "By revealing this information, you have landed yourself in more than a spot of bother, young man."

"Then let me dig the hole a little deeper." I need to see this through to the end. All I've done so far is expose myself as a potential spy.

"Later this month, beginning August 17, Chur-chill and Roosevelt will meet again in Canada. Quebec City. At that meeting — QUADRANT — the Combined Chiefs of Staff will present detailed plans for the landing on the beaches of Normandy, scheduled for May 1, 1944."

I can see his shock, but I continue. "You must have seen the preliminary plans prepared by Lieutenant-General Morgan." His eyes twitch ever so slightly, confirming my suspicion. "Other topics of discussion will include better coordinating development efforts on the atomic bomb. TUBE ALLOYS you call it on this side of the pond. The Americans refer to it as the MANHATTAN PROJECT."

By now he is ashen-faced. "I do not know what you are playing at or who you work for, but if you think you can trick me into revealing further secrets, you are sadly mistaken."

"I am a loyal American citizen, every bit as committed to Allied victory as you are, General. But you do have a point. These facts could be obtained through espionage. But a spy can't tell you about an operation which hasn't yet taken place. Not the plans, but the outcome."

He scowls but says, "Go on."

"In the early hours of tomorrow morning one hundred seventy-eight B-24 bombers will leave airfields in Libya to attack oil refineries in Romania."

I left home prepared to recite the details of a different operation, one that took place on July 28. I'd be screwed right now if I hadn't packed a detailed chronology of the war. Or if we were meeting a day later. Nothing of significance happened on August 2, 1943, at least nothing with a clear-cut result he would be able to confirm within a day or two.

"One aircraft will be lost during take-off. Another will crash into the sea before reaching the target. One hundred twenty-five will return. You should be able to verify these numbers by noon. The operation is called TIDAL WAVE."

He remains silent as he stands and walks to his desk and picks up the telephone.

"Whitehall 2-5-4-1," he says, followed by a pause. "General Rowntree speaking. Get me Colonel Hanley."

Another pause, longer this time.

"Colonel, I need an urgent report on an American operation. TIDAL WAVE. Specifically, I must know the exact number of aircraft returning to base." Then the muffled sound of a voice on the other end of the phone. "Yes, Elverstone Hall. The minute you have it. Thank you, Hanley, that will be all."

NINE

I wake up to knocking. Not casual knocking, not the gentle kind suggesting you get out of bed, but the aggressive sort demanding compliance. The way my Mom used to pound on my bedroom door on a school day.

I rub my eyes and turn my head sideways to read the watch sitting on the bedside table. 8:30 am. I didn't plan to sleep so late. Yesterday — last night — must have been even more tiring than I thought. Or it's the time travel equivalent of jet-lag. I have no idea what the time is in Princeton, but maybe I'm supposed to still be asleep right now.

Whoever it is knocks again, louder this time, hammering on the door. The next step will be battering it down.

"Just a moment," I shout through the door.

I throw a dressing gown on over my pajamas before opening the door to find Henderson, the driver-footman, standing outside. A young man in battle dress with corporal's stripes on his arm stands at attention to his left, his back to the wall.

"Good morning, Professor," Henderson says,

dipping his head as he speaks. "Lady Elverstone asks if you would care to accompany the family to services…"

Services? Oh, it's Sunday. He means church. "Please give them my apologies. I'm not—"

I almost say 'not religious,' but think the better of it. This is a less open-minded age. "Not Episcopalian. I mean not C of E."

"Very good, Sir. Shall I return with your breakfast?"

"Please."

I visit the bathroom at the end of the hall before my meal arrives.

The house is impressive from the outside, the public areas grand, the works of art hanging on the walls worth God knows how much, and my bedroom finely furnished. But the plumbing is primitive. I skip a bath after I test the hot water and find it to be barely lukewarm, doing my best to clean myself with a damp washcloth instead.

I brought my own toothbrush, toothpaste, and razor, figuring I could keep these modern items hidden in my luggage. But I didn't think to bring toilet tissue. Now I know why the television ads go on and on about softness. There's one modern luxury I'll definitely stop taking for granted. And this rough stuff, barely a step better than newspaper, is what rich people have.

I've freshened up and dressed by the time Henderson reappears. After he sets the breakfast tray on the desk and departs, I turn to the soldier. He hasn't moved an inch since earlier. "Am I a prisoner here?" I ask him.

"No Sir," he barks in reply, still staring straight ahead. "But I do have orders to accompany you should you leave your room." His hand goes to the sidearm on his hip. "And General Rowntree asks you not to leave the grounds of the estate."

In other words I am *a prisoner.*

I push the door closed and turn my attention to the tray resting on the desk.

Lifting the silver dome reveals poached eggs, black pudding, baked beans, fried tomatoes and mushrooms, and toast with marmalade. Accompanied by a pot of tea, of course. The traditional bacon and sausage are missing—*it seems rationing affects even the high and mighty*—but there's still nothing better to start the day than a Full English Breakfast.

I just hope it isn't a condemned man's last meal.

—o—

After breakfast I turn to my chronology of the war, studying it in case the General has more questions.

Around 11 am, Henderson returns.

He stands outside my door holding a neatly folded pile of white fabric in his arms. "Lady Alicia asks if you would care to join her for tennis, Professor." He thrusts the clothing forward. "She suggested you use Lord Jonathan's whites."

I ask him to wait while I change into the borrowed outfit of long pants and a cotton-knit shirt, both of which fit surprisingly well.

The Corporal falls in behind us as Henderson leads me along a meandering path through the house and out across the lawn.

I doubt I'd be able to find my way back to my room alone, but it shouldn't be a problem. If he isn't available, I'm certain my khaki shadow won't let me wander off.

Miss Rowntree is already at the court practicing her serves when we arrive. She's wearing a white, short-sleeved tennis dress that reaches to mid-thigh. Each time she extends her racket above her head, the dress rides up almost to her hip exposing more of her shapely legs. I try not to stare but it becomes a case of looking while trying not to be caught looking.

After serving her last ball she comes to the sideline while Henderson rushes around the court collecting the balls. Did she notice me gawking? A friendly smile suggests otherwise, but if I don't stop blushing…

She looks me up and down, smiling and nodding. "I thought you looked about the same size as Jony. I'm quite chuffed his kit fits you so well."

"The shoes were a little loose, but nothing a second pair of socks couldn't fix."

She picks up a racket and hands it to me. "I hope you will forgive my presumption in assuming you play. I do not know why."

"Well you're in luck. At least a little."

So we do have at least one thing in common. Though I've never had a private court in my back yard. I was good enough as an undergraduate at Stanford to try out for the varsity team though not quite good enough to make it. I still play occasionally. But not for years on grass, and not ever with a wooden racket. They went out in the seventies or eighties I think. Definitely long before I started playing.

"And you?" I add, though I've already seen enough to guess she plays regularly.

"As much as I can, but of late not as much as I would like."

"Then we should get started," I say. "Would you like to serve first, since you're already warmed up?"

"Oh no, that is your prerogative as our guest."

I head to the far end of the court and collect two balls from the bucket Henderson placed there. I put my toe against the baseline ready to serve, but stop.

The Corporal is right behind me. For reasons I cannot fathom he has planted himself no more than three feet away. A racket to the face would teach him it's not a good place to stand, but instead I turn and glare at him, without effect.

"You'll have to move." I point with my racket at the umpire's chair. "How about up there? I promise I won't try to run away."

He looks at me for a moment then wordlessly complies.

With the court now clear, I throw a ball high in the air, swinging the racket forward, but only at three-quarters of my full power.

She returns my insipid serve with a strong forehand drive. *Love-15*.

I gradually increase the strength of my serve, but still lose the first game to love. She plays with grace and style and there's surprising power in her game. Though there's none of the grunting and groaning so common in the modern era, she throws herself around, rarely giving up on a shot.

Meanwhile, I continue to struggle with the feel of the wooden racket with its much smaller sweet spot than the composite ones I'm used to. I'm three games down before I even begin to find any rhythm.

Though I lose the first set 6-4, I rally in the second, once I adjust to the grass surface and the limitations of the racket. At 5-2 in my favor Miss Rowntree approaches the net, summoning me forward to meet her.

"Professor, it appears you are going easy on me," she says disapprovingly.

"Why would I do that?"

There's a pause while she looks at me with an expression that says the answer is obvious. Then with an impatient snort she says, "Because I am a woman."

"I admit I'm not going as hard as I absolutely could." It never occurred to me she'd think I was holding back because she's a girl, but in her world it's the default explanation. "I apologize, but your gender isn't the reason, I promise."

"Then what is?"

"It's no fun if I thrash you. For either of us. I simply enjoy playing. Winning is secondary." That lack of the killer instinct is a major reason I never made it as a serious player.

"Not if I deserve a thrashing," she says. "Adversity is what makes us stronger."

I shrug my shoulders. "If that's what you really want. But they say be careful what you wish for."

I return to the baseline and finish the last and deciding game of the set in a procession of powerful serves, most of them aces.

We head for the row of benches lining one side of the court. It's warm for England, even in summer, and we both glisten with sweat.

"I knew you were better than you pretended," she says. "But I was not quite expecting that."

Moments after we sit down, Henderson magically reappears carrying a pitcher of ice water and two crystal tumblers resting on a silver tray.

"I'm sorry," I say to her as he fills the glasses and presents them to us.

"No apology required." Miss Rowntree sips demurely at her water. "I did ask for it."

Thirstier than I realized, I consume most of my drink in a single gulp. "Yes you did."

I move my eyes in the direction of the servant. I want to speak privately.

"That will be all, Henderson," she says.

"Milady," he says with a slight bow of his head as he withdraws.

"Do you mind if I ask you a question?" I say.

"To the victor the spoils."

"Lady Elverstone's reaction to the idea of us... that we were..."

"Engaged?"

"Your mother didn't really think that, did she?" *Crap. That must have sounded terrible.* "Not that there would be anything wrong with being..."

If Miss Rowntree sees any insult, she chooses to laugh it off. "You were saying? Being...?"

"I was going to say *involved*, which describes something..." What does it mean? "Not necessarily less serious, but less formal, less easily defined."

"Marriage does still exist in the twenty-first century?"

"Of course it does."

She gasps. "You are not..."

"No, I'm still single."

"I have deliberately avoided raising the topic with Mother, but I do believe she assumed the purpose of our visit was for you to request my hand in marriage."

I try not to blush, but my cheeks feel like I've failed. "Sorry to disappoint her. But however wrong her idea, it seemed to please her."

"That surprises you?"

"You bet. I doubt I'm at all the kind of match *the Lord and Lady Elverstone* would want for their daughter."

"I must apologize for my parents. They are concerned I run the risk of permanent spinsterhood by indulging – their word, *indulging* – my passion for mathematics. But I failed to recognize the depth of their anxiety on the matter. It seems they would prefer I marry an American than not marry at all."

She begins to giggle, then collects herself. "Not that there would be anything wrong with that."

"You're not exactly a shriveled old maid." I smile cheekily. "At least not yet."

"At twenty-seven I am in mortal danger of becoming so."

"That's a typical age for a woman to marry in my time." I lower my voice. "Many professional women don't tie the knot until well into their thirties and don't have children until forty or so."

She looks at me with wide eyes.

I return her gaze with a tight expression that says I'm not joking.

"Then," she says, "the future sounds most enlightened."

From the corner of my eye I catch General Rowntree marching across the lawn toward us, his stride determined and purposeful. I draw her attention to his approach and we both stand.

"Corporal Jones, get down from there at once," the General yells at the man still sitting in the umpire's chair. "Prepare my car."

The Corporal jumps from the chair, shouting, "At once, Sir!"

General Rowntree shakes his head as we watch the man rush away. "A good lad, but I wonder where his mind is sometimes."

"That's my fault," I say.

The General waves off my intervention on the soldier's behalf. "I have received the report on TIDAL WAVE, Professor. It is precisely as you predicted. Precisely. In every detail. I cannot believe I am saying this, but the only explanation that comes to mind is you are indeed from the future. I apologize for my skepticism, and for doubting you my darling daughter."

Miss Rowntree accepts her share of the apology by kissing her father on the cheek.

"No offense taken, Sir," I say. "Extraordinary claims require extraordinary proof."

"Extraordinary is certainly the word for it."

"What would you propose to do next, Father?"

"I am entirely convinced. I do not resile from that. Yet I must be certain beyond question and in possession of all the facts before I take this to my superiors. I do not wish to be a doubting Thomas, but is it possible to see this future for myself?"

Miss Rowntree looks to me, asking for guidance. No, she's asking for permission.

I shrug. *It's up to you.*

"It is possible, Father," she says. "The front door of 32 Hartness Street is the… the…"

"Portal," I say, pulling a term from science fiction. "The gateway between here and there, present and future."

"Jolly good. Gather your things. We leave for Kensington within the hour."

TEN

In the General's official car the journey from Elverstone to Kensington takes less than half as long as the outbound trip took me by bus and train. Being so vital to the war effort, petrol — *gasoline* — is rationed, keeping the traffic light.

I ride up front with Corporal Jones. He leaps out and opens the back door as soon as we pull up in Hartness Street. "Should I wait 'ere, Sir?" he asks as the General climbs out.

"Return to the War Office. We may be some time. I shall telephone when ready."

"Yessir!" he says crisply then rushes around to the trunk and retrieves my suitcase.

I thank him as he hands it to me. Nothing online from the period looked in good enough condition to give me confidence it would hold together when used as originally intended. So instead I bought a new handmade leather case, the type with old-fashioned leather straps and buckles to hold it closed. The style is timeless. And expensive. Damn thing cost me five hundred bucks I can't spare right now. I would have been pissed if I forgot it.

The Corporal jumps back in, does a U-turn, and drives away as we make our way up the stairs. I stop at the top for Miss Rowntree to unlock the door, then step forward, grab the brass handle, and wait.

She places one hand on my shoulder, reaching out with her other hand. "Father, we must maintain physical contact as we cross the threshold."

He takes her hand and I take a deep breath. Am I about to be exposed as a fraud?

— o —

A gasp from the General as the door swings open tells me not to worry, even before I see the inside of my own house.

I hang my hat and coat in the entry, inviting my guests to do the same. They leave their hats, but insist on keeping their coats on despite the stifling summer heat. "Come on in," I say, leading the way into the living room.

I expect to need only a few minutes to show the Rowntrees through my home. But every few feet we encounter something requiring explanation. The kitchen alone takes three quarters of an hour, between describing the features of a refrigerator far more sophisticated than anything they have ever seen, demonstrating how a microwave oven works, and then a dishwasher.

Just when I think we're done, Miss Rowntree recognizes the tablet resting on the counter as a larger version of my smartphone. She brings it to her father's attention. First she explains the touch-screen before launching into a discourse on the wonders of Wikipedia and Google. I cut her short for fear we'll be here for days.

An hour and a half after arriving home, I am serving my visitors sodas in my living room. "Have you seen enough to convince you, General?"

"More than enough, thank you."

I detect a slight reservation. "But…"

"A skeptic could say this house is a trick. I should see something more, something outside, to counter such accusations."

"I don't think that's a good idea. Are you familiar with the phrase, to stand out like a sore thumb?"

"My grandfather used a different expression, but the sentiment was the same," he says. "Shows up like a mustard pot in a coal scuttle."

"Compared to you two, a sore thumb and that mustard pot will fit right in."

"In what way, Professor?"

"Let's start there. I am only addressed as Professor in formal settings, or by my students. You and your daughter would normally call me Harrison."

He responds with a derisive snort. "Why don't I go the whole hog and call you Harry?"

"Father, please. The Professor — Harrison — is simply trying to be helpful. When in Rome."

"Yes, right," he says sheepishly. "I do apologize, *Harrison*."

"No problem. But for future reference, only my family call me Harry."

"As is appropriate — "

A stomping foot accompanied by a strident refrain of "Father!" cuts him short.

I am impressed to see a woman from her era stand up to her father so forcefully, especially when he is both a general and a peer of the realm.

"I think I could get away with calling you Mr. Rowntree," I say. "Just. But I can think of no circumstances to explain me addressing your daughter as anything other than Alicia."

"I have no objection," she says. "It is my name."

The General turns his palms up plaintively. "Who am I to argue?"

"Now, to appearances."

I check his outfit. *Where to start?* "I suggest you remove your tie."

"Very well." He carefully unknots the tie, pulls it from his neck, and folds it before placing it in his coat pocket.

"And you'll both have to remove your jackets. And your vest, General."

"People no longer wear coats?" Alicia asks me as she slips hers from her shoulders to reveal a perfectly-tailored but simple white blouse. The small collar, fitted shoulders, and lack of bows or frills are all designed to minimize the use of fabrics so desperately needed for Britain's war effort. Cotton and wool for uniforms. Silk for parachutes.

"They do," I say, "but not in this style, and not in a university town during summer vacation." My explanation meets with vacant looks. "It's complicated. If I asked you to explain the rules for when and where it would be appropriate to wear a morning coat…"

She nods. "I would say, it is complicated."

"And if I persisted?"

"You would force me to explain in long and tedious detail." Her face lights up in recognition. "Ah, I see."

"It may not appear so at first glance, but we still

have rules. Lots of them. They're just not the same rules you're used to."

General Rowntree slips his suit coat from his shoulders. "I will feel somewhat naked, undressed like this in public."

"And the waistcoat too, I'm afraid."

"Incredible." He sighs, then removes it too. "Are we presentable now?"

I inspect them from head to toe. Alicia's dress and short heels are perhaps a little formal, though passable. But her hair screams 1940s. "Alicia…"

"Is there a problem?"

"Women haven't worn their hair like that since my grandmother's generation."

"Is this how you flatter a woman in the twenty-first century, Professor — by comparing her to your grandmother?"

I'm actually a total sucker for female fashions from the forties and fifties. Though far less revealing than much of what women wear now, the clothing was so elegant. And the hairstyles — like hers, rolled up at the back and sides — I can't put my finger on why, but they were so much more feminine.

"I didn't mean it like that," I plead.

The slightest hint of a smile graces her face. She's toying with me.

"Can you… um… loosen it?" I say.

She runs her fingers through her hair, teasing out the rolls.

Oh boy. The looser curls suit her, softening her angular face and allowing her strawberry blond tresses to better reflect the light, so much so her hair almost glows.

I squeeze my face into an expression I hope hides my enthusiasm. "That should work."

Her father's fine woolen pants and long-sleeved cotton shirt are workable too. But the double cuffs with gold links, and his suspenders, don't fit.

"Change of plan. Wait here. Put your coats back on. Without the tie or the vest, General. And no hats."

I go to my bedroom and return a few minutes later wearing chinos, a button-down shirt, and my favorite tweed jacket.

"Add a pipe and you would look every bit the Oxbridge don," Alicia says.

"Is that a good thing, or a bad thing?"

She smiles coyly. "It never bodes ill for a man's appearance to reflect his true nature."

—o—

After I insist on a few more adjustments to their appearance, my visitors are ready for an expedition into 2015. At least they don't look like they belong in a different century.

I'm hoping people will make allowances for their behavior upon hearing the plummy English accents. As long as they don't think they're royals or something and start fawning and asking questions. We need to keep a low profile. A couple of Brits who don't know who Will and Kate are would draw way too much attention.

But will Alicia and the General be ready for what *they* see? How can they be? And there is no way to prepare them. Not completely. I could spend hours or even days telling them about modern society, but it isn't the same as them seeing it with their own eyes.

Hell, what if they make a scene?

"Listen to me carefully," I say. "This is a different world to the one you're used to. I'm not just talking about technology, but more importantly, about social values. Very different. You will see things which shock and amaze and even offend you. Deeply. Are you ready for that?"

Alicia and her father glance at each other before she replies, "How troubling could it be?"

I want to say, 'It'll knock your socks off, sister.' But first, she won't understand what that means, and second, I need a concrete example, something I know will shock them to the core. Make it real.

"How about two men unashamedly kissing each other, on the lips, in public?"

They both sputter in disbelief. The General is dumbstruck but Alicia manages to speak. "Are you saying…"

"Homosexuality is legal and socially accepted. To the point that two men, or two women, can marry each other."

"Outrageous," he thunders.

"Why? No, we'll discuss it later. But that there. You can't do that, express your outrage. Or stare, or make critical comments. At least until we are alone. Unless you can promise me that, we're not going anywhere."

His face softens and he nods. "We have agents behind enemy lines who must pretend to be Nazi sympathizers, though it must turn their stomachs," he says. "If those are my orders, I shall execute them to the best of my ability." He turns to his daughter. "Alicia?"

"If you can manage to face the modern world, Father, I most assuredly can."

"Let's go then." I start toward the back door before I remember I'm not alone and turn back.

"If one of you would do the honors," I say as I approach the front door.

General Rowntree looks confused, and slightly offended that someone he would clearly consider his social inferior expects *him* to open the door.

"If Harrison opens the door," Alicia explains as she pulls it ajar, "it will take us back home to 1943."

My plan is to drive them around, but as we make our way down the steps and along the path toward the street and my car, an ache in my belly demands food. I'm not sure what time it is in England 1943, but it's lunchtime here.

"I suggest we go somewhere to eat," I say as I walk around the car and climb into the driver's seat.

No answer. I turn my head to see them still standing on the sidewalk, like a pair of country bumpkins lost in the big city.

I open the passenger side window and lean across the front seat. "You do know how to open a car door?"

"Of course," they both reply.

"Then get in. And one of you will need to ride up front with me."

Alicia opens the rear door for her father, then slides into the front passenger seat. Sitting upright with her hands clasped together in her lap, she turns and raises her eyebrows at me. *What are you waiting for?* the gesture says.

"Seat belts?"

My statement is met by a blank stare.

Though I'm extra careful to avoid any physical contact, she recoils when I reach across her to grab the belt. I pull it over and click it in, then direct my gaze to the rear-view mirror to check on the General.

Nope, he isn't going to figure it out.

I get out, open the back door, lean in and help him fasten his belt, then return to the driver's seat before slotting my phone into the holder on the dash.

"May we depart now?" Alicia says.

"Yes," I say, sharper than I intend, but this is like traveling with a pair of toddlers. *Be patient.* "Do you remember me explaining the GPS — Global Positioning System?"

"Such a marvel is not easy to forget."

"Would you like to see it in action?"

She claps her hands together like an excited child. "That would be delightful."

"OK Google…"

I wait for the acknowledging ping. "Directions to the Yankee Doodle Tap Room."

— o —

The restaurant — 'gastro pub' as it now markets itself — is located in the Nassau Inn, one of Princeton's oldest buildings, with a history stretching back to the Revolutionary War. That isn't why I take them there. History surrounds them at home; they live with it every day. It was also Grandpa Harry's favorite restaurant. I have good memories of dining with him there when I visited during summer vacations. But that isn't the reason either. I select this place for lunch because of the beer — they have more than two dozen craft ales on tap.

It's a perfect day for sitting in the garden, but everyone else has the same idea, so I ask the hostess for a table inside. Though the room is deserted, I request a booth at the rear for maximum privacy.

Drama unfolds when Alicia and her father examine the menu, vindicating my decision to hide in the back. First, I have to explain that the prices aren't extortionate — the effect of inflation over seventy years is huge — and then walk them through each of the dishes, most of which resemble nothing they are accustomed to eating. Even the sautéed salmon throws them, with its 'saffron couscous' accompaniment. I let the 'GF' annotation pass without comment; I'm not up to explaining the modern fad for self-diagnosed food intolerances.

I pause at the final entree on the lunch menu, a Quinoa Veggie Burger. Is vegetarianism even a thing in their time? Burgers don't take America, or the world, by storm until after the war. And quinoa? I've eaten it before, and I can pronounce it properly. _Keen-wah_. But I can't describe what it is, other than to say it's some sort of grain.

"Order it and see if you like it," I say.

General Rowntree declines my challenge, playing it safe with quiche and salad. To my surprise Alicia insists she wants something exotic. I'm disinclined to believe she is serious, until she settles on the Nassau Wings, undeterred by my warning they come covered in a sticky sauce and are traditionally eaten with the fingers. I order a Reuben sandwich, knowing from long experience it will go well with whatever beer I decide to try.

In the middle of our lunch, a young woman, a

student I'd bet, passes by our table. Her attire isn't out of place in a college town during summer. But flip flops, skimpy shorts, and a flimsy handkerchief of fabric tied behind her neck in a token attempt to cover her ample chest are a bridge too far for Alicia. Her face turns completely red when she catches sight of what to her must be a near-naked woman, though she heeds my earlier warning and says nothing.

Somehow the General misses the show. I think I've dodged a bullet, until he cops an eyeful during the girl's return trip from the restroom. A small kerfuffle ensues — the British term for a fuss seems so apt, given the circumstances — but I kill the drama by reminding him of his promise to hold his tongue and to make an effort to blend in.

The rest of the meal proceeds without incident, and both pronounce themselves satisfied with their selections. I hope it isn't just politeness on their part, but they choose not to order dessert. Since I counsel them against ordering tea, I call for the check.

When the folder returns with the credit card slip for my signature, it is delivered not by our vivacious young waitress but by an older man in his sixties, perhaps even seventy.

I'm relieved at the change in service personnel. I couldn't help cringing at the look of shock on my guests' faces when the waitress introduced herself with a friendly and casual, 'Hi guys, I'm Evelyn.'

But I'm also mildly alarmed. The expression on the man's face, together with his dark suit, says his mission is a serious one.

I'm maxed out again. At least my guests won't understand what's going on, especially if I don't explain it to them.

"Professor Seely," he says, more a statement than a question, "I am William Frawley, the manager."

"Is there a problem?" I fumble for my wallet. "I have another card." At least one of them must have some credit available. I hope.

"No need, Sir. Lunch is on the house." The man reaches into his coat and retrieves an envelope which he passes to me. "Your grandfather asked me to give you this."

I look at the envelope and then at him. "You knew my grandfather?"

"Harry and..." The man glances from me to Alicia and back again, his Adam's apple bobbing up and down. "Harry Seely was a dear friend. You don't remember me. You would have been seventeen or eighteen the last time we met, about to enter your freshman year at Stanford. You remind me more and more of him as you age."

Why does everyone who knew my grandfather say they see a resemblance to him? There is a vague likeness, but it is pure coincidence. Instead of the kindness people intend, it makes me feel like I'm a fraud, an impostor. But I don't correct him. This particular truth is personal, not something I should be obligated to share just to disabuse others of their false assumptions.

"Good to see you, again." I'm embarrassed I didn't remember him. We met dozens of times, but as he said, not in over a decade. "But how did Harry know about" — I make a flat circle with my hand, indicating the three of us at the table — "this?"

"I have asked myself the same question a thousand times," the manager says, "and often doubted he did. But he was so certain, so adamant events would unfold as he predicted, that I never forgot his exact words. 'In the summer of 2015, my grandson will return here,' he said."

Alicia's green eyes widen. "Did he say anything more?"

"I'm sorry." *How rude of me, not introducing them.* "This is my... friend, Miss Alicia Rowntree, and her

father, Sir Geoffrey Rowntree. From England, obviously."

"To answer your question, Miss Rowntree, he
did have something to add."

"Out with it, man," General Rowntree says,
reverting to type.

"He said a beautiful English rose and her distinguished father would accompany Harrison — that
must be you, Miss Rowntree and Sir Geoffrey."

— o —

Alicia makes repeated efforts to engage me during
our trip home from the restaurant, but I refuse to
discuss the mysterious delivery.

My guests put their full 1940s outfits back on as
soon as we enter the house, as if the familiar clothing will protect them from the excesses of the modern world. I remove my coat and turn on the air
conditioner I had installed. July in New Jersey is a
lot tougher than what passes for summer in the Bay
Area.

I make tea then join my guests in the living
room. For several minutes we sit in awkward silence. They both glance at me between sips, waiting
for me to speak.

I put down my empty mug and sigh. I can avoid the issue no longer. "I suppose we should see what's in here," I say as I pick up the envelope. Using my finger I tear it open and empty the contents — a key and a small piece of paper — onto the coffee table.

We all stare at it for a long moment, until I grab the slip covered in Grandpa Harry's handwriting. Though much neater than my scrawl, it has a similar simplicity. The letters, while joined in a cursive script, are square and squat, with none of the loops and curls and other flourishes typical of the style taught when he would have been in school.

I display the key. "It's for a safe deposit box at a local bank."

Alicia asks, "Does the note explain its significance?"

I adjust my glasses before I continue, now reading aloud. "*All my notes are in the deposit box. I hope they help. Don't lose heart. Remember Edison searching for his filament. Every failure tells us what doesn't work and brings us closer to what will. We have only to persevere to conquer* —"

"That phrase sounds familiar," she says. "We have only to persevere to conquer…"

"Prime Minister Churchill," says the General.

"October 1941 at Harrow," I add. I know all Churchill's wartime addresses, many of them word for word. "My grandfather would know I would recognize it."

"Then it must be significant," Alicia says.

"Perhaps. But there's more."

"Do continue."

" — *but beware the Russian.*"

"Do you know to whom he refers?"

"I don't know any Russians. Nobody does, other than diplomats. The Soviet government goes to great lengths to protect its citizens from the corrupting influence of 'capitalist lackeys' like myself."

"It is all rather cryptic," says General Rowntree. "Though this entire time travel business is very irregular."

"Harrison," Alicia says, "you told me your grandfather died in 2004 at the age of ninety-one. Therefore he was born in 1912. On what day?"

The General interjects. "How is that—"

"Father, please. It is entirely relevant, I assure you."

"November 19th," I answer. "How did you remember all that?"

"I have a mind for numbers. A mind which tells

me your grandfather would be thirty years and nine months old in August 1943. And how old are you?"

"I will turn thirty-one in November."

"Also thirty years and nine months old."

"What are you trying to say?"

"You have done this before, Harrison. Not just today. All of it. And I am guessing from your grandfather's note — your note — more than once."

"What do you mean, *my note*?"

"Do you not see the truth of your grandfather's identity?"

I don't know what to say. Or I don't want to say it.

"But how can that be?" the General says.

My face tightens in shock as the answer I already know but refuse to accept breaks through my mental block, hitting me like a speeding train. "Oh my God!"

It takes a conscious effort to push the contents of my stomach back down. "My grandfather is me. My God. He's me. Or I am him?"

"I would surmise he is a previous version of you," Alicia says. "One who returned to 1943 and remained there."

"So I'm destined to do the same?"

"Perhaps we all are, if our foretold presence at today's luncheon is any indication."

It's too much to take in, so I place the piece of paper down on the table, tapping it repeatedly with my finger, as if that will help me understand. No, I understand all right. The problem is acceptance…

ELEVEN

I retrieve the slip of paper from the coffee table in front of me as Harrison sits mumbling to himself. He seems determined to resist the obvious meaning of his grandfather's note.

I bring the document within inches of my face, examining every aspect — the paper, the script, the content. I hope to discover something new, but if a hidden message is present, it does not show itself.

"Alicia," Father says, pointing at the note, "the message continues on the back."

I turn it over.

"What does it say?"

I stare at the document in my hand. My pulse throbs in my temples. I look away, unable to bring myself to utter the words written there. It is as if they are burning my eyes.

Father speaks — his lips are moving — but his words do not register.

He teases the paper from my hand and reads it aloud. "*P.S. The time difference increases each time you pass from the present to the past. Miss Rowntree can explain the ratio. Tell her Licorice says the progression follows the Fibonacci Sequence. And don't try to go past 34. It almost killed me."*

I see in Father's eyes that he understands the momentous implications of Harrison's grandfather using the name *Licorice*. To know that particular term of endearment, and feel free to use it, can only mean one thing: there was, or will be, an intimate connection—

"What is a Fibonacci Sequence?" the Professor asks innocently, ignorant of my distress. "And who is Licorice?"

Father's lips move, beginning to shape an answer, but I stop him with a hand on his arm and an imploring look. A message from the past delivering news of my romantic fate is disturbing enough, but having to explain it to the man to whom I... to a man I barely know, is beyond the pale.

"I regret that this is not my secret to share," Father says.

I examine Harrison with inquisitive eyes. What possible path could bring us together?

Dear God, have I already started down that dangerous route given the familiar ease with which I have addressed him? Thinking of him as Harrison. Admiring his physical appearance, even if I never gave voice to those thoughts. Flirting with him! It must stop this instant. He must remain Professor Seely. No less, no more.

"Alicia, what is it?" the man who will *not* be my betrothed says. "I don't understand. Why are you looking at me like that? What have I done?"

"The Fibonacci Sequence," I say, "is a series where each integer is the sum of the preceding two. It begins with 0, then 1, 1, 2, 3 — "

"Which is what it was this last time," he says. "Three. Then the next number would be five."

"Yes."

"And what about Licorice? I presume he or she is a mathematician. From Harry's note it sounds like someone you know. Perhaps someone you work with? Someone at Cambridge?"

"Fibonacci is simple high school mathematics, though there are many advanced applications. It is also widely found in biological systems."

"So this" — he points towards his front door — "is a natural phenomenon?"

"Perhaps." He deserves an honest answer, a complete answer, not a self-serving partial truth dressed with irrelevant details, but such an answer I cannot give.

"Father, we must leave." My knees wobble as I stand. "Immediately."

He looks at me disapprovingly, but makes no comment on my dissembling. Instead he rises from his chair and presents his forearm, which I take. His gesture is born almost entirely of habit and custom, but I welcome it; at this moment I need something to lean on.

"Before taking our leave," Father says, "we must agree the time and place of our next meeting with Harrison."

Professor Seely leads us towards his front door. "It's too late to go to the bank today, but I can go first thing tomorrow, as soon as they open. Then I'll need time to study my grandfather's papers. He was a meticulous man, known for his attention to detail. His notes will be extensive. But they should explain what's going on."

"Will forty-eight hours suffice?" Father says.

"I'm not sure..." the Professor says. "Probably."

Father turns to me. "How much time would pass in London?"

We have been here 4 ½ hours, so 13 hours and 45 minutes have passed in London. But once we return, time there will accelerate once again, to a factor of five relative to the passage of time here.

5 x 48 hours is ten days. "Early on the 12th of August," I answer.

"That will not work. Our delegation to QUAD-RANT sails for Canada on Thursday. The Professor must brief the Chiefs of Staff beforehand. It is imperative. It may be our only chance to make the Americans see sense."

I wish to depart without a moment's delay, but I have a higher duty than satisfying my own personal desires. The solution comes immediately, the arithmetic simple and undeniable.

"If we return with Harrison immediately *after* retrieving his grandfather's notes," I force myself to say, "we will reach London by Wednesday noon."

— o —

Dinnertime approaches. "Will we dine at the same restaurant again," I ask the Professor, "or at another establishment?"

"This time it must be at my expense," says Father.

"We have no American money," I say.

"Harrison," Father says, "allow me to reimburse you once we return to London. I insist."

"At what rate of exchange, Father?"

"Don't worry about it," the Professor chimes in. "We can eat here. You will be my guests. I owe you

a dinner, General. Although I can't promise anything as fancy."

"But who will cook?" I say.

"That would be me."

His response is unambiguous, but it cannot
mean what it appears to mean. I noticed the absence of domestic staff, though in my mind I explained the lack of a cook by assuming he dines at
his college, as would an unmarried professor at
Cambridge or Oxford.

"Without help?"

"Is that so surprising?"

Yes, it is. In 1943 men do not cook, other than
professional chefs and army cooks. But to say so
would be rude. "How did you learn?"

"My Mom taught me," he says. "She used to say
'Harry, you will want to marry a successful, intelligent woman, so learn to do your fair share of the
housework.' Now, I need to run to the supermarket
first. Is steak with salad and fries OK?"

'Supermarket' is presumably a modern American term for a grocer, but I am less clear what it is
the Professor is offering for dinner. How will he
present the steak? What type of salad? And 'fries'
are a total mystery.

But it would be churlish to quibble. Father and I glance at each other momentarily — he is asking himself the same questions, I have no doubt — before I say, "Excellent."

"You're both welcome to come for the ride."

Father lifts and displays the book he is reading, a history of the war. "I shall remain here, if you have no objection, Professor."

"No problem." The Professor turns to me. "Alicia?"

"Go," Father says, shooing me out with a wave of his hand. "I expect Harrison would appreciate the company."

There is no polite way to refuse. *Thank you for leaving me high and dry, Father.* "Another expedition would be delightful," I say through gritted teeth and a false smile.

— o —

After a tense mile or two in the Professor's car — riding in the front seat still feels less than appropriate — he pulls into an enormous car park. The structure behind it is wide and squat and bereft of any architectural merit, but even before the blackout I had never seen anything so brightly lit.

There must be several hundred motor cars here in such an array of colours and styles and sizes I want to wander between the rows, admiring these unusual machines. But the Professor heads directly for the building, so I follow him.

My spirits lift as we approach the entrance. The perpetual gloom of the blackout has become rather depressing after almost four years of war, especially in winter when I sometimes fear the dark veil will never lift itself from the world. This bright evening I feel lighter. Unburdened.

We enter through glass doors that somehow sense our approach and part automatically! Inside it is brighter still, the interior exploding with a blue-white light so intense my instinct is to turn my eyes away.

We take a few steps forward, enough for me to see what this giant box of a building contains. I stop, rooted to the spot. There are countless rows of shelves extending forty or fifty yards from the front to the back of this emporium, stacked from end to end and eight feet high with food. More food than ever before found in one place I am sure, even before rationing. Mrs. Baker would be in raptures here.

People wander back and forth between the serried metal ranks. Some carry a small black basket, like the one the Professor just retrieved from a stack inside the door. Most push some sort of enormous trolley, freely picking items from the shelves and piling them inside.

My head turns as my eyes follow a woman wheeling a pile of groceries large enough to feed a family for a month.

"What's the matter?" the Professor asks.

I stare at him, open mouthed.

"Of course. Shops in your time aren't self-service."

"And only a fraction this size." This place, in a small university town the equivalent of Oxford or Cambridge, is as large as an entire floor of Harrods or Selfridges.

He leads me up and down the aisles as he selects the ingredients for dinner. I force him to stop in the section labelled CEREAL. In front of me are three varieties of oatmeal, which I determine from the pictures on the boxes to be the American name for porridge: TRADITIONAL, ONE MINUTE, and INSTANT, whatever those labels mean, the latter available in a dozen flavours.

During the next ten minutes I observe the same phenomenon again and again, for all types of products, many of them just as mundane as porridge; a breadth and variety so great it seems almost gratuitous.

What manner of people require twenty-three — I counted them — varieties of milk, including something called 'almond milk.' How does one obtain milk from an almond?

Besides general groceries, the store contains a bakery, a butcher's shop, a chemist, and a greengrocer. I can see why they call it a *'super-*market,' although 'cornucopia' would be a more fitting title.

Another surprise awaits me at the cashier's station. Not the process of paying with a credit card — the Professor explained that at the restaurant earlier today — but rather the 'RFID tags' which allow the register to automatically tally the chosen items without even removing them from the trolley.

I have insufficient physics to even speculate on the essential principles in play. From his muddled attempt to explain, the Professor's ignorance seems equally deep as my own. Though apologetic, he is untroubled by his lack of understanding.

For me, the process is indistinguishable from magic. Perhaps it is a mystery for the Professor as well. But he takes this and so many other wonders for granted. To him they are just a normal part of everyday life, not worthy of a second thought, unless a visitor from the past asks about them.

—o—

Father remains in the living room, his head buried in a book, while I accompany the Professor to his kitchen. I take a seat, perching myself cautiously on a tall stool at what he calls a breakfast bar.

A bottle of red wine appears from somewhere beneath the bench. He pours us each a glass, then realising his presumptuousness, asks if I would like wine.

I answer by reaching for the glass and raising it to the light, examining the colour.

"I apologise in advance," he says as I take a sip, roll the wine around in my mouth, then draw it over my tongue. "It's just something cheap."

Somehow I don't think so. A deep shade of claret, rich and full-bodied, with hints of cherry and black pepper, and a dash of vanilla. A far better vintage than he suggests.

I lift the bottle to inspect the label. Cabernet Sauvignon. From South Australia!

What an alien place this future is. Father's cousin, Reginald Hartley, spent some twenty years in Sydney. I remember his return from what my thirteen-year-old self had imagined to be a great adventure. 'Exiled to the colonies,' he described his experience as instead. 'The frayed edges of civilisation. A cultural desert.' So when do these uncivilised colonials start making wine, and how do they become so accomplished at the vintner's art?

The Professor tackles the cooking with a practised efficiency and a boyish cheerfulness. Sitting in his kitchen, watching him cook, drinking his wine, there is such informality to the scene, such casualness, such familiarity, it ought to make me quite uncomfortable. Instead it is like being wrapped in a blanket, warm and protected. In this moment I have not a care in the world, certain this is the place I am meant to be.

Every few minutes he turns from his work to take another mouthful of wine, smiling at me when he does. I cannot help but respond in kind to his warm countenance.

His performance stirs in me a mixture of fascination and admiration. I have learned some basic domestic skills in my time away from Elverstone, but could not do nearly as well myself. And I cannot imagine any man in 1943 who would be willing or able to cook with such aplomb, even though the process is far less labour intensive than I expect.

Now I begin to see how he can function without any domestic help, between the labour-saving devices in his kitchen and the foods he purchased from the supermarket. 'Semi-prepared,' is the term he uses, as unfamiliar to me as the concept.

My initial expectations of the meal are low. But by the time he finishes cooking I am quietly hopeful. Though the setting is casual — Father makes light of it by describing it as a picnic held indoors — the food the Professor serves exceeds even my growing expectations. The pleasantly surprised expression on Father's face when he takes his first bite indicates he shares my assessment.

After cleaning up — requiring little more than stacking the dinnerware into an aptly named 'dishwasher' — the Professor prepares two beds: his, which he graciously offers to me; and the other, in his guest room, for Father.

"Where will you sleep?" I ask when he finishes explaining the arrangements.

He points to a sofa in the living room.

It looks a poor substitute for a bed. But he seems quite unperturbed by the prospect, and what other option is there? All I can do is express regret at his impending discomfort. Then pleading tiredness, I prepare to retire. Though I truly am weary, I cannot avoid admitting, if only to myself, that I am beating a coward's retreat. But I must. When I am in his company I find it almost impossible to remain aloof.

"Good night, Alicia," Father says. "I shall retire later" — he points to a stack of books on the coffee table in front of him — "when, *if*, I finish these."

"I'll be up for a while too," the Professor says. "I need to dig up just the right documents to prove to the Chiefs of Staff that I'm legitimate."

"Good night to you both," I say before ascending the stairs.

I close the bedroom door behind me then look around. The room is far less dreary than my accommodations in a small village outside Bletchley, and the bed is enormous.

After removing my clothing and hanging it neatly in the wardrobe, I put on a loose-fitting, shapeless garment of the Professor's, what he calls a 't-shirt.' I climb into bed, pull the sheet up, and lie back. *Oh what joy.* The bed is a precise balance of soft yet supportive I did not believe possible. Once again I am struck by the marvellous technology of this era, evident even in simple, everyday things like a mattress. And my unusual nightwear proves as comfortable as the bed.

I ought to sleep soundly. Instead I toss and turn as uninvited visions of a preordained future visit me each time I close my eyes.

Following an unsettled night, I wake soon after sunrise. One dream continues to disturb me, even now when I am no longer asleep.

It is a seductive and enticing dream, a picture of a contented life: a rewarding career in my chosen field; a loving husband who supports my professional ambitions — it must be a dream; and two perfect, adorable children, a boy and a girl, both with my fair complexion and his wild mop of curly chestnut hair...

— o —

I open the front door so the Professor can leave for the bank. He insists on going alone, arguing that our presence will only delay him, a point both Father and I readily concede, though I suspect our motivations differ.

We retire to the living room after the Professor departs. Father pulls his reading glasses from his pocket, slips them on, and picks up another of the tomes from his pile.

I interrupt him as he opens the book. "I am expected back at Bletchley on Thursday, Father. May I trouble you to drop me at Euston Station on your way to the War Office?"

"I would prefer you to remain with us. I anticipate needing your help with Harrison."

He looks down and begins reading. It is a gesture I know well. He considers his statement the last word on the matter.

"I am sure you regard my work as unimportant, Father, but—"

"Nonsense." He looks up, glaring at me over the top of his spectacles. "I know far more than you think about the work at Bletchley. How vital it is. And I have no doubt you make a valuable contribution. But this is far more important. His knowledge is as valuable as ULTRA a hundred times over."

I know Father does not mean to condescend, but I hear it in his voice. I can hardly blame him. My parents understood little enough of my work and studies before the war. The Official Secrets Act prevents me from even attempting to explain my current employment, even to Father. I am surprised he even used the term ULTRA, though I suppose that is preferable to explicitly mentioning what it is — the decrypted German communications we produce.

But to be honest, at least with myself, though my work is important I am just one small cog in the code-breaking machine that is Bletchley Park. Yet I cannot admit to being replaceable, not if I am to avoid being drawn deeper into the orbit of Harrison Seely.

"I do not see why you require my presence, Father."

"Because I do not understand him, my dear. Therefore I cannot fully trust him."

Whatever my personal reservations, the Professor has been honest and forthright. At least following our first meeting. And he provided a reasonable explanation for his initial deceit. Were I to find myself in another time and place, unsure where I was or how I arrived there, I doubt I would be any more forthcoming about my origins until I knew more.

"He has done nothing to earn your distrust," I say.

"I do not mean to suggest he is untrustworthy." The pained look on Father's face says I have misjudged him, unjustly in his view. "He seems a decent chap. For a Yank. Certainly less conceited than the American officers I must work with, always offering advice with such confidence and self-assurance, despite having arrived almost as late to this war as they did to the last one."

"Then I fail to see the problem."

"He is from another world, Alicia. His habits and values, his ideals and motivations, they are as unfathomable to us as those of a Kalahari Bushman."

"I believe you may be overstating the case, Father. But even so, what solution do you imagine I could offer?"

"You seem to have developed a rapport with him. He trusts you. You are, after all, the one who convinced him to share his knowledge, despite his initial reluctance to intercede. Without your assistance I believe I should struggle to manage him."

"I cannot give up —"

"I wish to hear no more of this," Father says, chopping the air with his hand. "I will speak to the man in charge — Commander Travis, is it not? — as soon as we return."

"I will not be bullied."

"In the name of all that is holy, Alicia," he says, raising his voice to me for the first time in many years, "please desist." Seeing me recoil in surprise, he continues in a less strident tone. "I only ask that you do your duty for king and country, as your brother is doing his without complaint, though he risks a great deal more than just a temporary unhappiness. It is not as if I asked you to marry the man."

"But Father, that may be precisely the outcome. You know I have never, ever allowed anyone but Jony to address me as Licorice. How can his grandfather—who is him—know that name? Why does he feel free to use it with such familiarity? Unless, at least in some version of our future, the Professor and I are… are…"

"Are what, my dear?"

"*Involved* is the word he would use," I snarl. "But I want to say *lovers*, just to shock you, Father." Which his tight lips and narrowed eyes tell me I have done, precisely as I intended. "Though you have no right to be shocked when you demand that I expose myself to such dire possibilities."

He does not acknowledge my provocation. Instead he smiles warmly and places his hand on mine. "My darling, you would never surrender your heart lightly. If some version of you grew to care for him, there must be good reason. Trust her judgment—*your* judgment—as I do."

"My head understands, but my heart screams for fear I am destined to marry a man I have known for less than a month. And if the Professor is his own grandfather, what would that make me?"

"I do not… Oh." He nods, acknowledging my point, but all the while chewing his lip as he searches for some riposte. "But nothing compels you to repeat the pattern."

"How can we be sure that is true? But if it is — and I cling to the hope — I am determined to make certain of it."

"And how, my dear, do you propose to do so?"

"It is quite simple, Father. I shall never see him again."

— o —

I hear the front door open, but Professor Seely's sudden appearance in the room still startles me. Then I remember he can pass in *that* direction — from Princeton into his house — without being transported across the Atlantic Ocean and seven decades.

Father and I both stand. The Professor's hands are empty. My heart hammers in my chest. "Did you retrieve the documents?"

He displays a small black object he pulls from his pocket. Three inches square and an eighth of an inch thick, it resembles nothing I recognise.

"That is it?" I say. "What is it?"

"A floppy disk. The documents are stored on it. Electronically."

"All your grandfather's notes are inside that tiny object?" says Father. "How the blazes do you read them?"

"That's the problem. Nobody has used this technology in fifteen or twenty years." The Professor waves the object as he speaks. It appears rigid, despite the name. "I need a specific device to read it, and it will take me two or three days to get one."

For a moment Father looks crestfallen. Then he straightens his back and stiffens his jaw. "We have no choice but to proceed without the notes."

"What would I tell the Chiefs of Staff?" Professor Seely says.

"How the war unfolds. The main strategic errors we should seek to avoid. There seem to be quite a few."

"Can't you tell them that?"

"I have been at this game but a few hours." Father gestures at the books in front of him. "You have spent years studying all this. They must hear from an authority on the subject. Focus on what you would want them to know as they head into QUADRANT."

"I think I can do that," the Professor says.

"Then let us leave at once."

Father and I gather our coats and hats while the Professor retrieves his suitcase and a portfolio.

We approach the front door. Professor Seely steps forward and opens it, stopping at the threshold to reach for my hand.

I recoil. But there is no other way to return to the place and time where I belong. I take Father's hand, then close my eyes and lay my palm in the Professor's, but softly, making as little contact as possible. Thankfully, this will be my final encounter with Professor Harrison Seely, and the most troubling notion that my future is already set.

TWELVE

Alicia and I settle in the drawing room while General Rowntree goes to the telephone in the hall. His first call, summoning his official car, takes barely a minute. The second conversation lasts much longer. Though I can hear only fragments of one side of the exchange, I can guess what whoever is on the other end is saying as the General tries to convince them to schedule an immediate meeting with the Chiefs of Staff Committee.

The housekeeper appears while he is still on the phone. A disapproving glare makes it clear she is disappointed to see me again.

"Lord Elverstone will spend the night here, Mrs. Collins," Alicia says. "And Professor Seely too. Is my brother's room prepared?"

"Yes, Milady. And you?"

"No, I must return to my post."

The housekeeper's expression softens a little on learning that Alicia is safe, at least for now, from my no doubt dishonorable intentions. She picks up my suitcase and trudges upstairs.

I wait for her to be out of earshot. "I don't think she likes me."

"It is nothing personal, Professor," Alicia says. "Mrs. Collins has known me all my life. She is rather protective."

I glance out the window to see the General's Humber pull up right in front. The driver climbs out then stands on the sidewalk, leaning against the car. He lights a cigarette and is soon absorbed in the repetitive process of lifting it to his mouth, taking a puff, lowering it again, and occasionally tapping the ash into the gutter.

A few minutes later General Rowntree returns to the drawing room. "We're in luck, Professor." He looks relieved, but also drained. "The Chiefs of Staff are already meeting on another matter. They will receive us at half past eleven."

I check my watch. "That's only forty-five minutes from now."

"Then we must make haste."

I grab my portfolio from the side table and jump to my feet. "Ready when you are, Sir."

He turns to his daughter. "Alicia, I must apologize, but would you be a dear and find your own way to the train?"

"Of course, Father." She stands, kisses him on

the cheek, then extends her hand to me. "Farewell, Professor," she says as I take the offered hand. "I wish you good luck and good fortune."

— o —

Meeting with Britain's senior military leaders is my dream scenario. But as we ride to the War Office it becomes increasingly real, and my sense of trepidation begins to outweigh my excitement. First, I must get past the understandable skepticism. I'm prepared for that and confident I will. But then there will be the expectation of some earth-shattering revelation. Can I deliver when I'm still not sure what or how much I should tell them?

I distract myself by focusing on the view from the car. Hyde Park passes by on my left then the Royal Albert Hall on the right. London has changed little, at least in appearance, between 1943 and the time, five years ago, when I lived here. Not surprising. In America we love to knock down the old and build anew. It is ingrained in our history and culture. Whereas the English value continuity. Here, it is almost impossible to demolish an old structure, so if there's one thing this city has in abundance, it is buildings steeped in history.

But the reassuring effect of spotting familiar landmarks is no match for the unspoken tension between me and General Rowntree. I try to push it away, but it gnaws at me.

We should clear the air before the meeting. "General…" I wait to be sure I have his attention. "Your daughter's mood when we parted was unusually somber. And her farewell seemed… well, somehow permanent, as if she expected us never to meet again."

He tenses momentarily, but then relaxes back into the seat. "Lady Alicia is under a great deal of pressure," he says in a flat, unemotional tone that betrays a lack of conviction. "The demands of her work, you understand."

"Of course. The work at Blet—"

How much does his driver know? Probably far more than he's supposed to. But discretion on my part would still be advisable.

I lean closer and lower my voice. "The work at that place shortens the war. Some historians argue by as much as two years. In my professional opinion, more like a year, but still."

"I am gratified to hear that. As my daughter will be." He looks away, staring out the window, deep in thoughts of…

I have no way of discerning what. His daughter? The war? Knowing he is about to put his professional reputation on the line?

As we pass Wellington Arch a few minutes later, he turns away from the window, a guilty look on his face. "I owe you an apology, Professor."

"I don't know why, General."

"Lady Alicia's work is demanding, and she does take it quite seriously."

"I'm sure she does. It is important work."

"But not the true source of her troubled mood."

He hesitates. Will he explain? I remain silent in the hope he will.

"It is best you have the truth," he says.

I say nothing, waiting for him to share this truth with me, though his expression says he doesn't want to tell me and I won't want to hear it.

"My daughter does not wish to see you again." He speaks in a rush as if he can't wait to discharge an unpleasant duty. "Not under any circumstances," he adds, slowly and emphatically.

"I knew it!" I say, slapping my knee. "The way she wanted to leave my place in such a hurry, and then the strange way she said goodbye."

We pass Buckingham Palace but I barely look. "I did something to upset her. I don't know what.

But I assure you, I never intended… I tried to explain, standards are different—"

"Professor, if anyone should be offended or shocked it is I. My daughter's generation are far more open in their thinking than are mine. But everything you exposed us to was with the best of intentions, in pursuit of a noble cause. You are guilty of no sin, either of commission or omission."

"Then what is it?"

He looks at me, one eyebrow raised. "What do you know of your paternal grandmother?"

Though the relevance of the question is lost on me, I can see it is important. "Not much," I say. "She died before I was born."

"And her name?"

"Alice. Alice Seely. Obviously. Sorry, but I don't know her maiden name."

He nods, as if my answer is not unexpected. "And her place of birth?"

I still don't see where this is going, not until my answer—"England"—is already leaving my mouth.

It hits me like a brick in the face. I want to yell at Corporal Jones to stop the car and let me out, and then to run away as far and as fast as I can, but I'm too stunned to say anything.

"Yes," he says. "As you can imagine, Lady Alicia also finds the possibility of being both your future wife and your grandmother... shall we say, somewhat unsettling."

Somewhat unsettling? Somewhat unsettling? There's a classic example of British understatement for you. "I can see why."

"I too am experiencing some difficulty," he continues, "adjusting to the knowledge I may be both your future father-in-law, and your great-grandfather. Not because I have identified any shortcoming on your part, you understand."

"If it helps, your daughter is not..."

"What is it, Professor?"

"Alice was not my biological... Long story short, my parents adopted me."

He exhales, long and slow like it will go on forever. "Thank God," he says. "I do not mean that as an insult. But it makes the situation... less disturbing."

"No offense taken." 'Less creepy' is the description I would have used. "But still it's..." Too much to grasp is what it is. I shake my head. "Bloody hell, General."

"Bloody hell indeed, Professor. Bloody hell, indeed."

— o —

We turn into Whitehall. I recognize the Treasury building on our left. I've visited the Cabinet War Rooms buried beneath it, several times. The rooms are furnished exactly as they were during the war. The maps are still there on the walls, filled with pin-holes where Churchill's staff tracked the ebb and flow of the struggle year after year with colored push-pins. They may be doing so as we pass.

Downing Street is a hundred yards further along, also on the left. Is Churchill there, inside Number 10?

Another three hundred yards on we turn right, then left through a tall archway into the central courtyard of a building known in my time as the *Old* War Office. An impressive masonry structure, seven stories tall with a domed tower on each corner, it takes up an entire city block, the footprint a trapezoid rather than a rectangle to use all the available land.

As we leave the car, I push away uncomfortable thoughts about my relationship, or non-relationship, with Alicia Rowntree. There is a different challenge to face right now. It will need all my concentration.

The General and I enter via a grand marble staircase centered in a soaring, sun-drenched atrium. But once inside, the place is a rabbit warren. I read somewhere there are a thousand rooms and two miles of corridors — in an article, I think, about how they're planning to turn the entire building into a luxury hotel seventy plus years from now.

Before long I'm disoriented. But General Rowntree knows where he's going and seems in a hurry to get there. I have to rush to keep up.

Toward the end of a long corridor we stop outside a door. I check my watch: 11:27. I close my eyes and slow my breathing.

At precisely 11:30 am he knocks, then pushes the door open, stopping two paces inside the room. It is a decent sized space, perhaps thirty feet long by twenty feet wide. After the narrow, dark corridors it seems cavernous, helped by a ceiling at least fifteen feet high and an abundance of natural light provided by several tall, narrow windows lining the far wall. On the interior wall, opposite the windows, hangs a portrait of the reigning monarch, King George VI, in uniform.

A dozen people, all officers, all men, sit at a large, solid looking table made of a dark timber matching the wainscoting in the room — oak or mahogany I guess. They are engaged in what appears to be a serious and weighty discussion.

I can easily distinguish the Chiefs of Staff from the other officers by their insignia, while the colors of their uniforms—khaki, sky blue, and white—make it clear which service each man commands. But I need none of that. To me they are familiar figures. I've studied countless photos of each of them.

The commander of the British Army and Chairman of the Chiefs of Staff Committee, General Alan Brooke—later Viscount Alanbrooke—sits at the head of the table. To his left sits Air Chief Marshal Sir Charles Portal, and to his right Admiral Sir Dudley Pound.

Each of these men presents a unique challenge: Brooke for his extreme pessimism on the prospect of a successful invasion of France; Portal for his commitment to the pointless strategy of area bombing; Pound because of his ill health.

Several men also stand against the walls, tensed for the opportunity to render some service or provide some requested piece of information or advice.

The only woman in the room sits two feet behind and a foot to the right of Brooke. Her fingers hover over the keys of one of those machines court reporters use — a steno-*something* — which rests on a three-legged metal stand.

The conversation ends mid-sentence and everyone turns to look at us. At me. A stranger. In civilian dress. An outsider. *Wait 'til I open my mouth and they realize I'm a 'bloody Yank.'*

"Sir Geoffrey," says Brooke. "Please join us." He gives some unspoken signal I miss but the staff understand because they clear the room like a giant vacuum cleaner sucked them out.

The minute-taker alone hesitates. Brooke dismisses her with a quiet, "Thank you, Mrs. Willis." She picks up her machine, folds the stand, and hauls it away.

"Gentlemen," General Rowntree says as he takes the seat to Portal's right. "May I introduce the young man I mentioned to General Brooke. Professor Harrison Seely."

I approach the end of the table clasping my portfolio tightly in my right hand. Less than ten feet away sit some of the most senior commanders of WWII.

I remove my hat and place it on the table. Receiving no invitation to sit, I remain standing. "General. Air Chief Marshal. Admiral," I say, nodding to each of them in turn.

"You claim to be from the future?" says Brooke.

"Yes Sir." Overawed by the occasion, I struggle to get the words out. *You can do this.* I clear my throat. "Seventy-two years from now. The year 2015."

Brooke presses his fingers together into a triangle and taps his forefingers against his lip while he glares at me. "What proof can you offer to support such a fabulous claim?"

I unzip my portfolio and remove a printout. "The Chiefs of Staff Committee, this committee, presents a summary of the war situation to the War Cabinet every week..."

"The Weekly Resume," the head of the Royal Air Force says.

"Yes Sir." I wave the document I'm holding. "This is the issue for the week of 29 July to 5 August." I pause, allowing time for those dates to sink in. "It's from the archives, so I apologize for the poor quality of this copy. But the content is what matters."

Admiral Pound, who looks for all the world like he's asleep, opens his eyes. He stands and goes to the door where he has a brief, inaudible conversation with someone outside before returning to his seat. "The current draft will be here by half past twelve," he reports, "and the final version available at noon tomorrow."

He extends his hand, demanding the document. I pass it to him. "I suggest we keep this under lock and key," he says as he passes it along to Brooke, "until we can compare it to the final version."

"Please do," I say. "In the meantime, may I refer you to paragraph 46…"

I wait while the Chairman of the Chiefs of Staff Committee turns the pages, only continuing when he stops and looks up from the document. "It contains a report on a bombing raid on Romanian oil facilities on August 1st," I say. "I provided General Rowntree with a detailed debrief on this operation—the day before it took place."

The service chiefs all turn to Alicia's father. "Is this true?" Brooke says.

"On my word," he says. "The Professor predicted the *exact* number of American bombers that would return safely, before any left their base."

"Impressive. But let us await definitive confirmation of this young man's prescience before we continue, shall we?"

The other two service chiefs nod in agreement.

Brooke picks up a battered leather briefcase sitting on the floor by his side, rests it on his lap, and slips my facsimile of tomorrow's document into it. "And on that note, gentlemen," he says as he closes and buckles the flap, "shall we adjourn to luncheon?"

— o —

The British officers engage in casual chatter while we wait for lunch to arrive. Though I'm not included, they don't seem to care if I hear their conversation, carrying on as if I'm not even there.

The content and form of the discussion are stiff by the standards I'm used to, but the body language and tone reveal a special closeness between them. *Esprit de corps* it's called, the fellowship of men and women who work together day after day and year after year in pursuit of a common cause for which they are prepared to give their lives.

After a few minutes sitting alone in silence at the other end of the table, I ask to visit the bathroom.

My hosts meet my request with blank stares. *Damn, what's the polite term in 1940s Britain?* I know several modern British slang terms. *Loo* and *lav* are the most acceptable, but I'm certain even those would be inappropriate in this setting. Gaz — Gary, an Aussie colleague and friend at Stanford — called it a *dunny*, but I'm sure that won't work either.

I try *latrine.* Thankfully, that meets with immediate recognition and looks of *why didn't you say so?* The soft chuckles that follow lead me to suspect they knew what I wanted all along and were 'just having a bit of fun with the American.'

Brooke goes to the door and summons a young soldier into the room. "Private Browning will show you the way."

The facilities are only twenty or thirty yards straight down the hall and the Private is armed, so it's obvious he's not accompanying me for my convenience.

It's not pleasant, being the object of such suspicion. But I wouldn't trust me either. Not completely.

I enter the nearest stall and close the door. Since I'm wearing suspenders, I remove my coat and hang it on the back of the door before I drop my pants and lower my naked butt onto the seat to avoid arousing suspicion.

From my inside coat pocket I pull a sheet of paper. With the same care I apply when inspecting aged historical documents, I unfold it silently. It's a letter Grandpa Harry left in the deposit box with the floppy disk. Though I've already read it — while I was still at the bank — I read it again.

I'm still shocked by Harry's message. 'Trying to shorten the war was a terrible mistake,' he says.

He's not telling me it will be more difficult than I imagine, which I half-expected even though I'm already pessimistic on that count, but just plain wrong.

Perhaps it will make sense once I read his notes. For now I'll just have to accept his advice on faith. But it's the next part that worries me most. 'You must put history back the way it was,' Harry's letter says.

OK, but I don't know how history was supposed to unfold, only the way it did in my timeline. Presumably his notes will tell me. But what if there is no way back, no feasible path from my timeline to the one that existed before Harry changed whatever it was he changed? Sometimes you can't put the genie back in the bottle…

—o—

A mess attendant in uniform enters, pushing a cart laden with silver trays resting under domed covers. Stacks of fine monogrammed plates sit on the bottom shelf. It reminds me of room service in an exclusive hotel, at least from what I've seen in the movies.

I expect the food to be equally elaborate, but hiding beneath the elegance is nothing more than sandwiches — granted, they're the dainty little ones with the crusts cut off the way the English like — plus tea and oatmeal 'biscuits.'

While the attendant busies himself tending the needs of Britain's most senior military leaders, I move to serve myself.

He steps between me and the cart. "Pardon me, Sir," he says, "but don't be troubling yourself like that. It's my job to serve you, it is."

He's a lance corporal while I, as a professional, have the status of an officer. An assistant professor isn't anywhere near equivalent to a general, maybe just a captain, or a major, but an officer nevertheless. So his words are polite and deferential. Yet his tone and sour expression leave me feeling like a small boy caught with his hand in the cookie jar.

I step back and wait for him to serve me — after the brass. General Rowntree looks embarrassed for me, and the Chiefs of Staff glare at me disapprovingly. I have overstepped some invisible but sacred boundary, committed some unforgivable *faux pas*.

I can almost hear them thinking something like *uncouth American*. Well, they might think far worse things about me before we're done today.

The conversation while we eat is muted and sparing, and none of it is directed to me. I don't know whether it's snobbishness, scorn, or simply lingering suspicion.

Having learned my lesson, I don't even consider fetching my own tea but wait for it to be poured for me. I even allow the attendant to place the sugar cubes into my cup with delicate silver tongs designed for that purpose and that purpose alone.

Just before 12:30 pm, while I'm still drinking my tea and fighting the desire to dip the hard biscuits into it, a naval captain enters and hands the Admiral a document, which he puts on the table.

"Noses back to the grindstone, chaps," Brooke says as he retrieves my printout from his briefcase and places it next to the first document.

The four officers lean over the table, huddled close. There is a great deal of nodding and pointing as they intermittently turn the pages in parallel, comparing the two reports line by line.

Brooke says something I don't hear and the other three men nod in acknowledgment. As they straighten, there is new respect for me in their eyes.

General Rowntree signals to the server, who clears the remains of lunch away in a flurry and beats a hurried retreat.

This time, as the officers resume their places, I am invited to sit. I take the spot at the opposite end of the table to Brooke. I want to see their faces.

"We have the confirmation we were looking for, Professor," Brooke says. "Whether or not you are from the future, you seem able to predict it with phenomenal accuracy. The benefit to our cause is the same, whatever the explanation."

"I'm glad of that, Sir."

"Perhaps you can begin with the big question."

I stare at him blankly.

"Do we win the bloody war?"

Not as easy a question to answer as he might think. "If you mean will Germany and Japan be defeated, the answer is a resounding *yes*."

"Then I may go to my grave a contented man," says Admiral Pound, "knowing our sacrifices are not in vain."

"Don't be so melodramatic, Dudley." General Brooke sounds surprised by Pound's fatalism. "You've got plenty of life left in you yet, old boy."

It appears the historical record is correct; Britain's war leaders are unaware of Admiral Pound's terminal illness. The Admiral burned most of his papers before he died, so it's not clear from the surviving records if he even knows himself.

Should I tell him? He looks surprisingly well for a man who lost his wife only a month ago and will himself be dead inside two months. But his melancholy statement suggests he at least suspects, and I can't bring myself to tell a man the hour of his death when there's nothing he or I can do to prevent it.

What about Brooke? Or Churchill? Should I tell them?

No. They'll know soon enough with Pound's sudden stroke and resignation next month. Change is going to be hard enough to effect without diverting time and effort into issues which won't alter the broader course of events.

"Professor," says Air Chief Marshal Portal, "your answer seems hedged in qualifications…"

Sweat beads on my forehead. "Your goal is to rid Europe of Nazi tyranny, isn't it?"

"Without doubt. And as you say, Germany will be defeated. I sincerely hope Herr Hitler and his Nazi thugs get what is coming to them. Get it good and hard."

"They do. The Soviets deal with the Nazi leadership in ways civilized men probably can't imagine.

A foretaste of what is to come, because across Europe the Nazi reign of terror will be replaced by a communist dictatorship even more brutal and repressive. Not exactly the victory you seek."

My audience looks mortified, but not surprised. The British ruling classes at this time are far more hostile toward the Soviet Union and Stalin than the British masses, who are highly receptive to socialist ideas, or America's political and military leaders, who are mostly just naive and indifferent.

"How did this happen?" says Brooke.

"The Normandy landings fail. After two days, our forces are driven back into the sea."

"When?"

"May, 1944."

"I told them so!" he shouts, slapping the table. "I told the Americans 1944 is too soon."

"Then how much longer must we wait for V-E Day, Professor?" says Portal.

"September 10, 1945," I say. "V-J Day is a month later."

"Still a better outcome than you have forecast, Brookie," the Admiral says.

General Brooke harrumphs. "How can Germany be brought to her knees so quickly after such a disaster in Normandy?"

"Nukes."

I get no reaction. "Atomic bombs."

The three service chiefs look at me in panicked alarm.

"The Professor is fully aware of TUBE ALLOYS," says General Rowntree. "And of the American project."

The three men relax. "Of course he is," Brooke says. "So how do you explain the subsequent Bolshevik domination of Europe, Professor?"

"After Normandy," I say, "we — Britain and America — refocus our efforts on Italy and an amphibious assault in the south of France. Progress is painfully slow. Once the atom bombs are finally ready, in August 1945, we drop them on Berlin, Munich, Dusseldorf, and Frankfurt, *killing half a million civilians in a single night.*

"The Red Army exploits the sudden collapse of German resistance following our attack by pushing forward to the Rhine. We're far too war-weary to confront them. Despite widespread atrocities committed by Soviet forces, most Germans consider us the greater evil.

"And repeated military failure damages our reputation with the French and Italian populations. After the war, anyone aligned with us — De Gaulle's

Free French forces for example — is so tarnished by association, they can't match the popularity of the local communist parties. Their governments, though elected, soon fall under Moscow's sway. Only Spain and Greece remain free."

My audience sits in silence, shoulders hunched, long faces staring back at me, faces filled with the hopelessness of men buried deep underground and awaiting a slow, unavoidable death.

It is left to General Rowntree to rekindle the discussion. "In light of all that, what advice would you give us, Professor?"

— o —

What advice should I give? I could spend the rest of the day pointing out mistakes, but there's no guarantee they'll listen, or that avoiding them will fundamentally alter the course of the war.

And if I'm not careful, I run the real risk of being dragged into their inter-service rivalries, or inflaming the growing tension between Britain and the United States. It's not a gamble I'm willing to take given the enormous gaps in my knowledge. Changing the course of history is not something you roll the dice on.

When they ask about my hesitation, I tell them about Grandpa Harry — that this has all happened before — and his notes. "To use a military analogy," I say in conclusion, "he warned me the ground ahead is filled with landmines, but I have not yet collected the map showing where they are."

"Unfortunate," says Brooke. "But we do know this much with absolute certainty: OVERLORD *must* be postponed."

"Attempting to sway our American friends is like standing astride the bow of a ship shouting at the storm," Admiral Pound says. "The best you can hope for is a hoarse throat. The worst, to be done in by a dose of pneumonia."

Brooke pulls back his shoulders and puffs out his chest. "We must stick to our guns, Dudley. I have faith that an unwavering conviction," — he presses his forefinger into the table — "grounded in our certain knowledge of the future, will carry the day."

Truly a rousing statement. For a brief moment it seems possible. But reality returns when Pound says, "Brookie, I wish it were so. But in truth, we need a sounder plan than simply giving it the good old schoolboy try."

Brooke sighs. He sinks into his chair as if the

weight of this long-running fight with the American Chiefs of Staff is physically breaking him. "Then what do you suggest?"

"The Professor must accompany us to Canada."

My fingernails dig into the edge of the table. I have a life to get back to. Between travel by sea there and back, the preparatory meetings, and the formal conference itself, they'll be gone nearly a month. I can't be away...

But does anything in Princeton matter compared to this? What could be more important than attending perhaps the most pivotal conference of the war, spending days in the company of Churchill, Roosevelt, the American Chiefs of Staff? What an opportunity!

Brooke shakes his head. "We must keep our powder dry. The picture the Professor paints is incomplete. Once we share this with the Americans, we lose control. They would undoubtedly claim him as their own and do their best to shut us out —"

"I would never let that happen," I say. "I swear."

My interjection is met by skeptical looks. US troops are flooding into Europe and will soon outnumber the British Empire's forces two or three to one. Not to mention the massive imbalance in materiel contributions now that American industry has ramped up to full wartime production. US leaders were willing to defer to British experience in 1942, but they rightly believe America is now the senior partner in the alliance. Their determination to take the lead position is a source of constant tension with the British.

Roosevelt and Marshall would surely regard me, an American citizen, as theirs to do with as they see fit. Would that be such a bad thing? Perhaps not, but at least here in London I have a way home if I choose. If they ship me off to Washington, I'd be at their mercy for as long as they desire.

But I so badly want to go!

"Surely we must inform the Prime Minister," Pound says.

"I would urge great caution, Dudley," Brooke says. "Imagine the wild flights of fancy this stunning new development might launch him on…"

"It is difficult enough keeping Winston focused," Portal adds, "without tempting him with the shiniest of shiny new toys."

I cringe at hearing myself described as a shiny new toy, and the legendary Sir Winston Churchill referred to like he's an unruly toddler. But I get where they're coming from.

Churchill's conduct during the war, though inspirational in public, was often privately erratic, especially as the years wore on and took a physical and mental toll on him, and he chafed at the increasingly unavoidable reality of Britain's fading power. Brooke complained repeatedly in his *War Diaries* of the Prime Minister's love of fanciful, far-fetched ideas, and his romantic obsession with daring side operations which served only to distract from the main battles necessary to defeat Hitler.

"Would it not be wiser to keep mum, as Sir Charles suggests?" Brooke says. "At least until we have a proper understanding?"

"Keeping this from the PM sits poorly with me," Pound says. "Very poorly indeed. But I must concede the point."

"It is for the best, Dudley. Allow us to see what the grandfather's notes have to say. Then we shall revisit the issue—"

A young, fresh-faced army officer is suddenly at the Chairman's side. His aide-de-camp, from the gold braid adorning his uniform. He whispers something in Brooke's ear, then withdraws.

"Unfortunately, gentlemen, we must adjourn." Brooke taps the face of his watch. "Today's Cabinet meeting begins at one."

The Chiefs of Staff stand and gather their papers. I glance at my own timepiece. 12:48. It must be at least a ten minute walk, either to Downing Street or to the Treasury Building beneath which the War Cabinet meets in times of heightened danger.

"If you will excuse us," Brooke says, addressing General Rowntree and myself. "Sir Geoffrey, I leave Professor Seely in your charge."

"I shall take good care."

"Until we return from Canada then." Brooke turns for the door. As the Chiefs rush away I hear him say to his colleagues, "Not a word to Winston about the Professor."

THIRTEEN

I step through the door into my home. There's a strange tingling in my fingers. I open and close my fists a few times. My hands feel normal again.

As I pass through the living room to my bedroom, I glance at the clock hanging on the wall. I've spent several hours in London, but only forty-five minutes have passed here. *Weird.*

I exchange my 1940s outfit for standard summer attire—shorts and a t-shirt—before I head to the kitchen.

Out of pure habit, I open the refrigerator and take a quick stock of the contents. Beer, frozen pizza, a bag of salad leaves, three kinds of cheese. I'm not hungry. I close the refrigerator door and look around the room. What next? I promised General Rowntree I'd return as soon as possible, but the floppy drive I need to access Grandpa Harry's notes won't be here until tomorrow.

I use the back door on my way to and from the mailbox. In my home office, I flick through the handful of mail. Most of the letters I can classify without even opening them. The first is a credit card offer. Just what I need, another credit card. I really should get rid of the ones I already have. They're nothing but trouble. I drop it on the shredding pile.

The next item is a catalog. Into the recycling basket under the desk. Then another credit card offer. **25,000 FREE MILES** it promises on the envelope. Where could airline miles take me that I'd want to go? I've got a door to wartime London. Shred. Followed by coupons for a new pizza joint. It's only a few blocks away. A push-pin secures it to the notice board above my workspace.

I stop and stare at the next item, a windowed envelope bearing the name, logo, and return address of *Streetwise Finance Inc.*

I rip it open and unfold the letter.

Oh crap. **Amount Past Due: $750**. I have ten days to pay or they'll repossess my car.

A quick check of my online banking app confirms my worst fears. There's less than $250 in my checking account.

I've maxed out every credit card, and bills for my new home will soon start rolling in: power, phone, internet, homeowners' insurance, you name it. At least a thousand bucks' worth in the next month. What the hell am I going to do?

— o —

There's a spring in my step as I turn into Alicia's street. Not more than an hour ago I entered *The Hand and Flower* with every pocket of my coat and pants stuffed with razor blades.

True to his word, Riley was easy to find. A quick word to the barmaid and he was at my table before I finished a single beer. I walked out with another £79 in my hand.

When added to the money I still have from my first black market deal, I have more than £200 to invest. I'm hoping it will be enough by 2015 with accumulated interest to cover my expenses until the end of summer. Three thousand should do it.

I pull up when the Rowntree residence comes into view.

Consulting the General means first facing the scorn of the housekeeper again. But I need his help. Or to be precise, the help of a lawyer or stockbroker who can structure an investment in a manner that will allow me — not my descendants, but me — to claim it seventy years from now. In 1943 you can't just find those people in the phone book or online, or walk into their offices unannounced. You need to be known to them or introduced. It's all about trust. Being 'the right sort of chap.' Especially with a request as unusual as mine.

I'm uncertain if the General will be home. But Churchill and the Chiefs of Staff are taking the train to Glasgow this evening, and then sailing for Canada on the *Queen Mary* tomorrow. Tonight, his superiors at the War Office or Number 10 won't delay him. But what if he's dining elsewhere, say at his club? Alicia said he often does. Then I'll come back in the morning. Early, before he heads to work. I'd only need to wait two or three hours at home. Something like that.

At least Alicia has returned to Bletchley Park and won't be here. An encounter within hours of her father telling me she never wants to see me again might enrage her. Her lack of familiarity with the term 'stalking' wouldn't make her any less unhappy about the act itself.

I take a step toward their townhouse. *You don't scare me Mrs. Collins.* If only that were true.

Someone taps my shoulder.

"Professor Seely," he says as I turn to look behind me. "Finally, we meet."

How does he know me? He's not British. Or American. His English is heavily accented. Maybe Eastern European...

Grandpa Harry's warning goes off like an explosion in my brain: *Beware the Russian.*

What do I do?

Bluff. He can't know me. There's no way. Not here. Not now. "I'm sorry. You must have mistaken me for someone else."

"Is no mistake."

"Listen pal, you're way off base. We've never met, I'm sure of it. I've never seen you before in my life."

"Da," he says. "Must apologize for rudeness." He touches the brim of his hat. "Anatoly Gerasimov. First Secretary, Embassy of Soviet Union."

Gerasimov? Can't place the name. But he looks familiar... where have I seen...

Mr. Brown Overcoat!

He has *been following me. Probably the whole time.* That can't be good. How much does he know? Everything?

I sink into my knees, the muscles in my thighs and calves tensing as I prepare to run, but nothing happens. Instead, I'm spinning, then something hard and flat slams into my back with a force that drives the air from my lungs.

"Go home, Professor," he says. His face, now inches from mine, fills my vision. "Stay there."

He's holding me by the lapels of my jacket, pressing me against the brick wall, almost lifting me off the ground. I fight the spasms in my diaphragm, trying desperately to breathe. His voice is icy and his penetrating stare reaches the place inside me where nightmares live. His vice-like grip is the only reason I'm not quivering in fear.

My muscles release. I gasp as air fills my lungs in a rush, the influx of oxygen like a sudden high. Now I can focus on assessing my assailant. Though three or four inches shorter than me, he is heavy set with a barrel chest, broad shoulders, Popeye-thick arms, and the gnarled hands and meandering nose of a bare-knuckle brawler.

I want to fight back, use some of my taekwondo moves. But I doubt this guy fights by the rules. The Soviet Union in the twenty-first century is a terrible place by western standards, dark and oppressive. But far, far better than in the 1940s. The *glasnost* movement of the late 1990s revealed that Russia under Stalin and then Beria was a land filled with horrors beyond anything previously imagined: deliberate famine as a tool of class war; show trials, purges, and mass executions; the gulags; children betraying their parents; men forced to prove their loyalty by shooting their wives. They even nuked their own people to put down a revolt in Siberia in 1953, obliterating the entire city of Novosibirsk.

What must this man have done to survive in such an environment? To thrive even, since he's a diplomat? Unspeakable things. Ruthless and brutal acts.

I might get in one good strike if I'm lucky, but could I kill him? I suspect the answer is 'No,' but my attacker would have no such reservations. Experience would reassure him that he could take a life. This difference would undoubtedly prove my undoing, even if my fighting skills were by some miracle a match for his. My only hope is to talk my way out. "What is this about?"

"Protecting glorious Soviet future."

"What has that got to do with me?"

He slaps me with the back of his hand. Hard. Something in my face — my nose? — cracks. "You think you are only man from future, huh?"

Before I can answer, something, or someone, cannons into him. Suddenly free, I slump against the wall as I try not to collapse into a relieved heap.

He and his new opponent scramble to their feet.

My nose swells faster than an inflating airbag, to double or triple its normal size, or at least it feels that way. A metallic taste fills my mouth. It's like…

the taint of beer drunk from an aluminum can, but different. Don't they say blood tastes of copper? Whatever the flavor, I spit a mouthful of it onto the sidewalk and drag my sleeve across my lips wiping away the rest.

The Russian and the other man square off, fists raised, the second man's back facing me. They circle each other like wild animals, their heads bobbing slowly from side to side as each searches for an opening, a weakness in the other man's defense that can be exploited to deliver a killer blow.

Who is this man who intervened? Where did he come from? A little further… now I can see his —

What the hell?

"Riley!" I shout involuntarily.

Brown Overcoat glances away from his opponent, glaring at me. "Leave and never return, Professor," he says. "For your good health and future of girl. Would be terrible thing if Bletchley bosses learn she is Soviet agent."

He bends in one smooth, graceful movement at odds with his rough appearance, picks up the hat knocked off by Riley's initial blow, and then, like something from a vaudeville act, rolls it up his arm and back onto his head. "This is only warning you will get."

One cautious backward step after another, he moves away. Riley doesn't pursue him, but he holds his fighting stance — soft knees, hard fists, and sharp eyes — until the man disappears around a corner.

My savior relaxes, dropping his fists and straightening his back as he turns to me. "Time to come clean, Mr. Jackson Browne with an 'E.' Or should I say, *Professor*?"

"I have no idea. He just attacked me —"

"Do I look like a garden tool?" Riley barks. "Comrade Gerasimov isn't your average dodgy chancer. And he clearly knows you. The real you. Which is more than I can say."

— o —

I have to get away. My eyes dart about while I keep my head still, assessing my escape route. It's only five yards, maybe six, to the door, though Riley stands between me and freedom. But if I run as fast as I can, take the steps two or three at a time, I might make it. Just wait for the right moment.

Wait... wait... And now!

He grabs my wrist and spins me around, bending my arm behind my back. "Ohhh, no you don't."

"Aargh!" He's twisted my arm so far, my hand reaches the opposite shoulder. The stress on the joint is excruciating. He's about to break or dislocate something. "Please stop!"

He eases the pressure, but only slightly. "Old Riley wants answers, and he wants 'em now."

"All right," I say as I drop to my knees, signaling my unconditional surrender. I doubt I'd do any better in a fight with him than I would have with the Russian, especially starting from this position. Talk about 'out of the frying pan, into the fire.' "Just stop pulling my damn arm."

He releases his torturous grip and signals for me to rise.

I stand and shake the pain from my elbow and shoulder. "I'll tell you everything" — I bend my head toward the door — "but only inside."

He cocks a thumb at the townhouse behind him. "You live 'ere, in this posh place? Yer havin' a lend."

I reach into my pocket and produce the key, then begin up the stairs.

As I lift my foot and place it down two steps up, Riley grabs a handful of my collar. I won't be giving him the slip... leaving me with no choice but to share my secret with him too.

Can I trust him to keep it? Not that it matters. I will never return to 1943 again. I'm done with this. I'll replace the door. Burn the damn thing if necessary.

I unlock the offending structure and swing it open. Riley does a double-take at the mismatch between the interior and the style of the building's exterior.

For a moment I hope he'll rush inside ahead of me for a closer look at this strange phenomenon. I imagine slamming the door shut after him, leaving him stuck... in Princeton.

That's a terrible idea, even if he is dumb enough to fall for it, which he isn't. Still with a firm grip on me, he shoves me through the opening instead.

There's the tingling again.

He pushes the door closed behind him with his foot. "Time ter talk."

Doesn't he feel it, the tingling? Maybe not. "I'll explain everything," I say, "but first I need you to re-open the door."

He squeezes my arm.

"It's easier to show than explain."

He presses harder, his thumb and fingers forcing their way between the layers of muscle. I twist beneath the pain. He eases up, slightly.

"I promise, it'll all make sense soon enough."

Riley glares at me menacingly as he reaches for the door with his free hand and pulls it inward. The outside world—not London but Princeton—comes into view.

He releases me and the door, his right hand flying up to trace a path from his forehead, to his belly, followed by the left side of his chest, and finally the right as he says, "Holy Mary, Mother of God…"

—o—

Riley wants answers but I insist on treating my injury first. He follows me to the kitchen. The ER isn't an option right now, so I fill a Ziploc bag with ice from the dispenser and press it against my nose.

I let out a deep groan of relief as the middle of my face goes numb, easing the throbbing pain.

He chuckles. "A busted nose gives a man's dial some character."

I roll my eyes then launch straight into explaining where and when we are. It takes less than ten minutes to convince him we've traveled to New Jersey and the year 2015. He accepts everything I tell him without question, an interesting reaction given that most of what I've told him to date was untrue. There's none of the disbelief or confusion I expect, just a glint in his eyes as he turns his attention to exploiting the situation to his financial advantage. I should have expected as much from a black marketeer, I suppose.

We start brainstorming and researching money-making schemes. I cooperate on the assumption, or at least the hope, that he'll leave me alone if I give him what he wants. By mid-afternoon he settles on gambling as his preferred path to easy riches. An hour later he has it—printouts of racing results from online newspaper archives—and he's finally ready to leave, my front door open to 1943.

He signals for me to lead. "Let's go, Professor."

I shake my head. "You don't need me anymore."

"I'm not leavin' on me Pat Malone." He waves the stack of paper in his hand. "Not 'til I know fer sure these are good."

"They are, I promise."

He runs his finger down the top sheet on his pile. "I tell yer what. If *Canterbury Lad* gets up in the first at Brighton on Sat'dey, you can leave with me blessing. That's tomorrow by the time we get back to merry old London, right?"

It seems Riley grasps the concept of the differing passage of time. I don't know if his math skills are any better than mine though, so I walk him through the calculation. He doesn't point out any errors in my arithmetic, and I get the same answer he did, so he can't blame me if it's wrong, can he?

"But if annuver horse wins…" — he grimaces, as if it pains him to say what's coming next — "then you and me will be havin' words, Guv, none of 'em friendly."

"He will."

He gently slaps my cheek. "Then there's nuffin' to worry about, China."

"Please, I can't go back," I say. "You heard Gerasimov. He'll destroy her if I do."

"Ah, the girl. Meant to ask you about that. Lady Alicia, innit?"

"Yes."

"And is she?"

"What?"

"A Russian spy."

"Of course not!"

My response is immediate and indignant, but am I really certain?

Before, during, and after the war, Cambridge was a hotbed of communist sympathizers. Often from 'good backgrounds' like Alicia, they were drawn in by the Marxist promise of equality in a better world populated by selfless beings, the much-vaunted but rarely seen 'New Socialist Man.' Many were blind enough to the reality of Stalin's regime to become active Soviet agents. History reveals there were Russian moles in every corner of British intelligence, almost all of them Cambridge men.

"Yer sure?"

It takes a concerted effort to stop myself from shaking at the terrible thought and to convince myself it can't be true.

I stiffen my jaw. "She would never betray her country."

Riley looks at me quizzically. "Who is she to you? I get that it's her door you go in an' out" — he smirks and wiggles his eyebrows suggestively, prompting a desire to punch him in the face, the consequences be damned — "but what skin is it off your nose what 'appens to some toff?"

I'm not sure I can answer his question even if I wanted to, which I don't. My interest in Alicia is not something I want to talk about, especially with him. "Because she's an innocent bystander," I say.

"Nah, there's more to it."

Though he's seen straight through my attempt at a poker-face, I maintain my defiant silence.

"Well, not to worry. Me and me boys will take care of the Russian, then you an' me'll be free to conduct our business unmolested like."

"What do you mean?" I ask as he puts a hand on my back and pushes me through the door. "Take care of him how?"

He raises his right hand, puts his forefinger to his temple, and makes a clicking sound with his tongue. "Problem solved, Professor."

— o —

Canterbury Lad delivers, winning by two lengths, just as the old newspapers said he would. A very happy Riley keeps his promise. We arrived in London on Friday afternoon and I'm back at Hartness Street by early Saturday evening.

Approaching the door, I feel a great sense of relief. It'll soon be over, for good.

As I put one foot forward, stepping across the threshold, the bottom half of my leg goes completely numb, like it's no longer attached to me. My weight collapses onto it and I stumble forward. Gravity pulls me through the doorway and a white veil descends across my vision, like someone threw a sheet over my head.

I stagger across the room, almost falling to my knees, only able to steady myself when I reach the other side and place a palm against the wall. I drop my head, taking deep breaths as I wait for the faintness and blurry vision to pass.

What the hell was that about?

It certainly wasn't because Riley mistreated me. I spent the night in his home lauded like an honored guest, given their eldest son's bed, and plied with some of the best food and finest scotch the black market could provide. He didn't even try to stop me from leaving. He just said, 'As long as the Russian don't know you're 'ere, he's got no reason to cause trouble for yer sweet'art.'

I never imagined a career criminal living a normal family life. His wife must know what he does. Otherwise, where does she tell herself the food comes from? But she and their kids seem to adore him. Her 'lovable rogue,' she called him. I have trouble not thinking of him like that too. He's got charisma, that's for sure. I guess it's an essential personality trait for any successful crime boss. It's not like they can use the law to keep their employees in line.

The disorientation passes after a minute or two. Low blood sugar, perhaps. A glass of OJ should fix that. I straighten my back and look at the clock. I was gone less than two hours. *Hmmm.* Or maybe it's something to do with the time dilation, like an extreme form of jet-lag. But why does it seem to be getting worse?

— o —

I throw back the sheet and roll out of bed. It's pointless trying to sleep when I can't stop thinking about Alicia's safety. Since I have no intention of going back, reason tells me there's no point in being concerned. But my mind keeps wandering toward desperate outcomes.

I have to know.

But where to start? If in doubt, ask the Great Oracle, also known as Google.

I type UK death records.

The first link is to the UK National Archives. I should have thought of that. I've used them extensively in my military history research, mostly online, but during my time in London I often visited the physical archives in Kew. I hadn't really thought of it as a place to find civilian records.

Bingo. I scroll down a page titled: *How to look for records of… Births, deaths, and marriages in England and Wales.* I click on a link to freebmd.org.uk, a site containing all the UK's birth, death, and marriage records. In my current financial situation I especially like 'free' in the name.

I select SEARCH and a new page loads.

I enter the search criteria, choosing the end of 1944 as the latest date to check. If Gerasimov targets Alicia, it's likely to be well before then.

I take a deep breath and press FIND.

Sorry, we found no matches.

Thank God. And no need to apologize.

Next, I check the New Jersey records for Alice Seely's death. I don't remember my paternal grandmother, I was only a baby when she died, but there it is. December 8, 1986, just like it's supposed to be.

What about the Russian? I don't want Gerasimov's corpse laid at my feet, his murder on my conscience, especially when it isn't necessary. I really hope Riley didn't 'take care' of him. I think I talked him out of it last night, but I can't be sure. Riley Cornell is a man who makes his own decisions.

I run the search again, now with the Russian's name and the same time period.

Nothing.

That should be a relief, but there's still a tight pain in my belly. The spelling might be wrong. I try a few variations. Same result. What if Gerasimov was an assumed name, a false identity? Or the Soviets pressured the Brits to cover up his disappearance?

Stop it. There could be a hundred reasons he might have died without there being a record of his death. But you can't prove a negative. I guess I'll never know, not for sure, not without going back. And that isn't happening.

FOURTEEN

Standing outside my parents' house, I reach for the doorbell but pull back at the last second. Mom insisted I keep a key. 'This will always be your home,' she said, 'no matter how old you are.' That was years ago when I first went away to college, but she'll still make a fuss if I don't let myself in.

After I unlock the door, I hesitate again. It suddenly occurs to me that it might lead somewhere else. To some other time and place. Stupid, but who would have thought Grandpa Harry's door would be a passage to wartime London? I'm not entering until I see what's behind it.

With a shove I push the door open. It swings away from me and…

I laugh at my paranoid delusions. Stretching out before me is the familiar entryway of my childhood home.

The house is from the late 1960s, though my parents have only owned it since 1981 when Dad took up his position at Carnegie Mellon. The floor plan and much of the decor are original. Mom likes it that way.

A long, narrow hallway runs down the middle of the house, with rooms off to each side, the opposite of a modern open plan design.

The second door on the left opens into the guest bedroom. There's a double bed in there now and the walls and shelving are free of my posters and trophies and other teenage mementos — only because I packed them away — but Mom still refers to it as 'Harry's room.'

I drop my overnight bag then head to the kitchen, the most likely place to find my parents before dinnertime. They love to cook. "Mom! Dad! I'm home," I call out.

The sound of hurried footsteps is followed by Mom's head poking around the corner. "Harry!" she shouts as she rushes down the hall.

As I suspected, she's wearing an apron. It's covered in a bold, floral pattern. Also predictable. That's her style. She refuses to accept that the 1970s are long over.

Mom throws her arms around my neck, and plants a warm, wet kiss on my cheek before stepping back to look at me. "Oh darling," she coos, "what happened to your nose?"

"It's nothing, Mom." I hate lying to her, but there's no way I can tell her the truth. "Just a stupid fall. I wasn't used to the steps at the front of Grandpa's house."

I follow her to the kitchen. The sweet aroma of whatever Dad is busily stirring on the stove hits me. There are hints of cinnamon and... lemon? Or is it orange zest I can smell?

"Good to see you, buddy." Dad turns his head to look at me, noticing my injury. "What—"

"I've already asked him, Jon, and your son has already avoided giving me a straight answer."

He turns all the way around now. I chuckle at the slogan printed on the front of his T-shirt: 'The Keys to Happiness' above pictures of the computer keys used to type a smiley face.

"I'm OK, Dad. Mom worries too much."

"That's what mothers do." He turns back to the stove. "And fathers."

I perch myself on a stool at the kitchen island. The large granite bench is new. Thankfully, lime green Formica countertops don't last forever. It's a long overdue concession to modernity, if you ask me.

"I like what you've done in here, Mom."

She gives me the sort of disapproving look only a mother can, then pushes a chopping board laden with carrots across the bench and hands me a chef's knife. "Make yourself useful." She leans over the stove inspecting Dad's work. "Why didn't you call?"

"I thought I'd surprise you," I mumble as I grab a carrot and start slicing. I'm too embarrassed to tell them the truth, that I'm here to borrow money. At age 30. I can't decide if it's pathetic or just desperate. Or both.

"Well, it's a lovely surprise," she says, "although we expected a visit sooner. Princeton isn't that far from Pittsburgh, you know."

"Sorry, Mom." I only stopped in for a night on my road trip from Stanford to Princeton, so I promised a longer visit just as soon as I got settled. "I've been busy, with the house and… and everything. You know how it is."

They both stop what they're doing and look at each other, before each pulling up a stool opposite me.

"How is Pop's house?" Dad says.

"Apparently the front stairs are very dangerous," Mom says.

I keep my eyes on the carrots as I answer, "It's fine." *Can't afford to live there, but it's fine.*

There's a hidden agenda here. The tone of Dad's question is anything but casual and my father isn't one for small talk. He's the picture of the shy, retiring, serious computer scientist. Unless he's making dumb math and computer jokes. Then he's the life of the party, or so he thinks.

They're an odd pair, the flower child and the nerd, but they've been happily married thirtysomething years. Their devotion to each other is a cornerstone of my life. It helps ground me. Like gravity.

I imagine it was the same with my grandparents. Dad always says he tries to treat Mom the way Harry treated Alice. Alicia. God, that's Alicia and me he's talking about when he says that.

Mom grabs a dish towel and wipes her hands. "Is there anything you want to share, darling?"

"Like what?"

"Anything unusual?"

"Nope."

"Are you sure?" says Dad.

"I really have no idea what you and Mom are talking about."

Dad stands up abruptly. He points at me and says, "Wait here," before leaving the room.

"What's going on?"

Mom arches an eyebrow. "Are you sure you don't know what this is about, Harry?"

I shrug my shoulders apologetically. "I don't. Honest."

I feel like I'm on trial in one of those totalitarian places like the Soviet Union or India where they don't even bother to inform the accused of the charges. The silence between us is awkward, but I don't dare speak for fear I'll prove myself guilty of whatever it is she thinks I've done.

Dad returns a few minutes later carrying a file box, which he places on the bench in front of him as he sits down. He opens it, fishes around, then pulls out an 8 x 10 photo.

He runs his fingers gently, affectionately over the surface before passing it to me. "Do you know who these people are?"

I stare at a faded black-and-white image of a groom in a morning suit, and on his left a beautiful bride wearing a white satin gown. The day looks gray and dull and cold—England—and their body language says they are waiting impatiently for the photographer to finish so they can go inside. But their faces also say they are deliriously happy.

To the bride's right are an older couple I know, and beside them a youngish man whose identity I can guess. The wedding party are standing in front of a large stone building I also recognize.

The groom is clean shaven and his hair cut very short. Otherwise it's like looking into a mirror. He is even wearing my glasses. I am equally sure the bride is Alicia Rowntree. Her knee-length dress is elegant but simple — no train, a small veil, only modest trimmings of lace — but she is more enchanting than any Disney princess, more beautiful than any supermodel.

Dad stares at me impatiently. "Well?"

"Grandpa Harry, Grandma Alice, and her family," I say, trying not to sound defensive.

"That's not what I'm asking you, Harry. I'm asking if you know who they really are…"

— o —

I slide the old photo across the table and look from Dad to Mom and back again. They know. I can see it in their eyes. But what exactly? How much did Grandpa Harry tell them?

Dad points at the bride in the picture. "You know this woman, Harry. You've met her already." It's a statement, not a question.

I close my eyes, picturing the last time I saw her, only three or four days ago, looking just like she does in the photo. The memory of her is fresh as new snow, the image in my mind sharp, vibrant, and filled with color, so clear I can recall her expression. At the time I thought she was just preoccupied, leaving me blissfully unaware that she was saying goodbye forever. I now realize it was a look of steely determination.

When I open my eyes, my parents are staring at me. "I know that look, Harry," Mom says. "There's something else about her. Spit it out."

There's no point in denying I know her. I'm not that good a liar. And I'd rather admit that than try to put a name to my emotions. I'm too confused to know what I'm feeling at this moment.

"Yes, I've met her. Recently."

Mom gasps. "My God, Jon, it is true, what your father said…"

Dad looks at me longingly as if I hold the key to somehow bringing back his late parents. In a way, I do. I *am* Grandpa Harry. His father. "It was always the only logical explanation," he says, though he shakes his head as he speaks.

"I know Dad's mother as the Lady Alicia Rowntree," I say, "and her parents standing next to her, Dad's grandparents, as the Lord and Lady Elverstone. Actually, I know her father in his military capacity, as Major-General Rowntree."

Dad points at the young man in the photo.

"Her brother, Jonathan," I say. "I haven't met him." *Though I've worn his clothes.* That might sound creepy, so I keep it to myself. "But I did meet his cricket bat."

"You played cricket?"

"No, I was… long story." If only I could go back to that confrontation with Alicia. I'd do things differently. Or more to the point, I wouldn't do them at all. Get the hell out while I still could.

"They're standing in front of Elverstone Hall," I add. "Their family estate. I should say *we're* standing in front of it, because the groom in this photo is me."

My parents are looking at me as if I have two heads. Understandable. How else are you meant to look at someone who is simultaneously your father or father-in-law, and your son?

"We ran a DNA test after Pop told us," Dad says. "Not long before…" His eyes moisten. He tightens his jaw, struggling against his emotions. "Before he passed away."

I place my hand on his arm. "It's OK, Dad."

"Uh, huh." He sucks in his breath. "You and Pop were a match. 'Good enough for a murder conviction,' the technician joked. We always knew in our hearts it was true, but it was such a fantastical story it was easy to tell ourselves it couldn't be."

I pick up the photo and turn it over. There's a date — *24th of November 1944* — written in pencil on the back. I don't recognize the delicate cursive script. Hers?

"A year before this was taken," I say, waving the photo around, "Alicia Rowntree decided she never wanted to see me again. So I don't see how this can be true."

"Pop didn't mention anything about that," Dad says. "But a lot can change in a year. Especially for a time traveler, I imagine."

"It isn't like that."

"Then tell us, what is it like?" says Mom.

"I don't know."

"Please, Harry."

Dad shakes his head. "Leave it, Deb."

"It's OK." I owe my parents some sort of explanation. This must be almost as hard for them as it is for me. "At first I thought it was a wonderful opportunity, to see history unfolding first-hand. You can imagine how excited I was. But I got pulled into something bigger. Alicia insisted I had a moral duty to change the course of events, help win the war, not simply observe — "

"My mother was a woman of strong principles," Dad says. "And very persuasive when she wanted to be."

"She is — was — but I went along with it mostly out of self-interest. Her father, your grandfather, introduced me to the British Chiefs of Staff. Men I've spent years studying. If I'd hung around long enough, I would have met Churchill too. And probably Roosevelt and Eisenhower."

Dad's face lights up like a man suddenly struck by a divine revelation. "I'll be damned. It finally makes sense."

"What does?"

"One day, when I was about seven or eight years old," he says, "Eisenhower came to dinner."

"At the house in Princeton?"

He nods. "It all seemed rather strange at the time. I didn't know who Ike was. Pop told me afterward he was a big general during the war, but I could never figure out the connection since Pop didn't serve in the military. Eisenhower kept apologizing to Pop for not taking his advice. And I remember sitting on Ike's knee."

"Don't be surprised if you wake up tomorrow without that memory, Dad. Grandpa Harry will never meet Eisenhower. I'm not going back again."

"Is that how it works?"

I shrug my shoulders. "All I know about the rules of time travel is what I've seen in the movies, and what do they know? The universe didn't explode every time Grandpa and I were together, so that stuff about not being able to meet yourself is obviously BS. I haven't noticed any changes in the timeline based on what I've done so far. Maybe trying to change the past is a fool's errand. Or maybe I'm just doing what I've already done. Perhaps everything is predetermined."

"Your grandfather didn't think so," Dad says. "He said he would leave you some notes…"

"He did."

Mom looks at me expectantly. "So, what did they say?"

"He wants me to put things back the way they're supposed to be."

"And that is?" says Dad.

"I have no idea." I tell them about the safe deposit box and the still unread floppy disk.

"Shouldn't you at least see what else he said before you make any rash decisions?"

"It wouldn't be rash if I'd had time to think," I snap back. "If I wasn't kept in the dark all this time. Why didn't he just tell me?" I look at them with eyes begging for an explanation. "Why didn't you say something. Anything?"

They respond to my questions with stony-faced silence.

"You lied about your mother's family, Dad."

"That's unfair, Harry," he says. "I didn't know the truth either."

"How could you not know?"

"You think you're the only one Pop kept in the dark? I only met my maternal grandparents twice. Both times here in America. I was young and my curiosity didn't extend past the fact they were the only people I'd ever met who sounded just like my mother. And like you, I never met my Uncle Jony. Mama always spoke so fondly of him, but he never visited. Couldn't travel. Some injury he got during the war was all she told me. And that he had a farm in England to take care of."

I whistle through my teeth. "Some farm. I've seen it. Must be at least ten thousand acres, and the house has like twenty bedrooms. What about the rest of the story?"

Mom glances accusingly at my father. "We wanted to tell you."

"Pop insisted we couldn't," Dad says. "Something about changing as few things as possible. Anything he didn't know at the time he first went back, he said you shouldn't know either. He made us promise to respect a dying man's last wishes. Son, I think you should—"

"Don't tell me what I should and shouldn't do. You're not—"

I grit my teeth, stopping the hurtful words from escaping, the worst thing an adopted child can ever say to his adoptive parents. I've only ever said it once, and I promised myself I'd never say it again.

Tears fill my mother's eyes, a deep hurt my father's. I wave my hands, trying to make my terrible statement go away. "You know I didn't mean it. I'm sorry."

"We're sorry too," Dad says. "But you must—"

"Must what?" As angry at myself as I am at them or Grandpa Harry, I jump to my feet. "I won't be his damn puppet." I storm off, slamming the door to my room behind me, channeling the teenage boy who used to inhabit the space.

—o—

By morning my anger has subsided, replaced by

regret and embarrassment. I apologize to my parents over breakfast for speaking to them so disrespectfully, and they apologize for keeping Harry's secret.

Now we stand in the driveway saying our goodbyes. As I step forward to hug him, Dad signals for me to wait.

He rushes back inside, returning with a manila envelope in his hand. "From Pop," he says as he hands it to me. "He didn't want you to have it until now."

"Figures." *More damn secrets.* I don't understand the reason for all the intrigue, the cryptic notes, the envelopes to be delivered only at specific times and places. All planned out, like some ridiculous fraternity scavenger hunt.

I'm not playing. I throw the envelope on the front passenger seat, unopened, unexamined. I hug my parents and apologize again before climbing into the Subaru.

The five-and-a-half-hour drive home gives me plenty of time to think. Maybe Dad is right. Maybe I am being rash. Except I can't go back. Even if I wanted to. It's too dangerous, for me and for Alicia. But it can't hurt to read Grandpa Harry's notes, can it? Out of professional interest, I really should.

After parking the car, I clear the mailbox, drop my bag in the bedroom and head to the office. There's just one letter—I was only gone a day— a bill for $327, another I can't afford to pay. After the way I behaved, I couldn't ask my parents for money.

I check the due date. Three weeks. I'll think of something before then, before the angry letters start arriving—**BALANCE PAST DUE, PLEASE PAY IMMEDIATELY**—or my power or internet gets cut off. The envelope from Pop might contain money. I could use some luck. He must have known I'd be broke right now.

Damn, I left it in the car. I rush outside and retrieve it. Back in the office, I slice the top open, tipping the contents out onto the desk. There's no cash—did I really expect that?—just a few sheets held together with a paper clip. And three old black and white photos.

The first is a 4 x 6 copy of the one Dad showed me yesterday, the picture of a wedding that will never take place now. The other two, also 4 x 6s, I've not seen before. One is a picture of Grandpa Harry and another man—*I think it's… yes, Eisenhower*—sitting on a chesterfield sofa. My father, seven or eight years old, is perched on Ike's lap, just like Dad said. I go to the living room and hold the photo up in front of the sofa. As I thought, it's the same one that's there now, though the leather has faded and cracked since then.

The men are wearing suits and Dad is in his Sunday best, but there's no stiffness, no formality to the scene. This was a social visit, old friends catching up, although there's a look of regret on both their faces. Did Ike know Grandpa Harry's true story? He must have. Was he someone Harry worked with to change things? What other connection could there be?

I return to the office. The final photo is a studio shot of my grandparents. Alice is sitting, Harry standing behind her, and in front of them stands a boy of four or five. I bring the picture closer. He's younger than in the photo with Eisenhower, but it's the same boy. My father.

What I don't understand is the baby cradled in Alice's arms, wrapped in a blanket, the tiny face barely visible. It could be anybody. Did my father have a sibling who didn't survive? If so, why hasn't he ever mentioned it? Should I call and ask him? Or would he have told me if he wanted me to know? Maybe, maybe not. Anyway, I should wait for the right time and place to raise it.

Next, I grab the documents. On top is another note in Grandpa Harry's handwriting:

Harry boy
Remember the £216 you invested? I spent some along the way, but this should help with the bills.
Grandpa Harry

I flip to the next page.

My brain takes a minute to understand what I'm looking at. I've never seen a stock certificate before. A thousand Apple shares. *Nice*.

The next sheet is also a stock certificate, for the same number of Microsoft shares. Both valuable companies. Even I know that. That would explain why Harry chose them.

But they've only been around since the 1980s. What did he invest in before that? I had no plan for what to buy in 1943, but he must have found something, and I'm glad he did. These should be worth a few thousand dollars, more than enough to get me through the summer, maybe even clear some of my credit card debt.

I wake my computer and open the browser. I've never checked stock prices online before — because

I've never owned stocks — so I type how much is a Microsoft share worth in the search bar.

$42.09 a share. A hell of a lot more than had I expected.

I do the same again for the Apple stock. They're worth even more — a hundred twenty-nine dollars each. The total must be… a lot. A double-click opens the calculator application. Several quick clicks and a startling number stares back at me.

My stake in Apple is worth well over a hundred grand!

I repeat the same steps for the Microsoft stock.

Another fifty Gs.

That cannot be right. Grandpa Harry always seemed comfortably off, but I never thought of him as rich. He lived in the same house for fifty-something years. Drove the same old Buick with a gigantic steering wheel, a bench seat, and whitewall tires for as long as I remember. His idea of a trip was coming to Pittsburgh to visit us. He didn't live the lifestyle of a man with hundreds of thousands of dollars to spare.

Am I sure these documents are what I think they are? I examine them again, reading every line of text carefully, mouthing each word like I'm reading my first picture book. There is no mistake.

Unless the plain meaning of the text is wrong, they are stock certificates. The problem must be my math. I've always sucked at math.

I grab a scrap of paper and a pen from the shelf in front of me. This time I write everything down: the number of shares, the price per unit, the multiplications and additions I need to perform step by step.

Starting with the Apple shares, I enter the numbers into the calculator one slow, deliberate digit at a time, checking the display to be sure I've not mistyped anything before pressing the 'equals' button.

The result is unchanged.

Am I missing something, or did Grandpa Harry really leave me nearly two hundred thousand dollars in shares? It looks that way, the perfect windfall at the perfect time.

But is it too perfect? Are my strings being pulled? Am I dancing again to Harry's tune and not my own? What happens if I don't go back and invest the money? Will these documents dissolve before my eyes, or turn to dust and slip through my fingers, just one more lost opportunity? Or does the fact I'm holding them in my hand mean the past — my future — is already decided?

Not if I have anything to say about it.

—o—

I imagine myself destroying the disk in a dozen different ways. Burning it, chopping it into little pieces, putting it through the shredder, using a strong magnet — if I knew where to get hold of one — to wipe the data forever.

But each time I come up with a new method I waver, thinking about what it contains: alternative histories of the period I study. And perhaps answers to questions I don't even know to ask. Including questions about Harry's life and mine and how we're connected.

No, I'd be opening a can of worms. Do I really want to do anything that might undermine my resolve not to return to 1943?

But actual alternative histories!

After three days, professional and personal curiosity gets the better of me.

Grandpa Harry stored the notes in a basic text file format. Good for ensuring I'd still be able to read them years later, but the single-spaced Courier font and random line breaks make it too hard to read.

It takes a day to import everything into Word, then format and print it. I almost give up again, but

I can't stop once I've got a taste for the content. These notes are to a professional historian what King Tut's tomb was to archeologists — the greatest ever discovery in the field.

The dining room table seats twelve people when extended, the only surface other than the floor large enough to spread the hundreds of pages out.

Alicia's conjecture that I've done this before, more than once, is on the mark. The notes describe six 'cycles.' That's the name one of the Harrys, I don't know which, gave to the process of him returning to the past — six times already — doing what he can to change the course of history, and remaining there until, as an old man, he prepares a younger version of himself to repeat the process in the hope of a better outcome.

When I start reading there is still a lingering doubt in my mind that Grandpa Harry and I are the same person. But the more I read, the more I realize that he thinks the way I do. The options he tried are exactly what I would have done. Even his writing style is clearly my own. It's eerie, like reading something I wrote but can't remember writing.

So yes, I accept that Harry is me. All six of them. And I am him. Them.

First, I read everything from start to finish, in the order he or they created the files. I've reorganized the pages several times since, trying to identify any patterns or themes that would help me understand what it all means. At the moment I have them grouped chronologically, the notes from each Harry mixed together so I can compare what each of them did at any given date.

I can't completely rule out the possibility there were more than six Harrys, but Harry One through Harry Six — the one I knew as Grandpa Harry — wrote everything down, as evidenced by the piles of paper. As I like to do. I already have twenty pages of my own notes. It's hard to imagine there was an earlier Harry who didn't leave any record.

It was exciting at first, reading about their efforts to influence events and seeing the results. Historians love to speculate on the 'what ifs.' Many historians argue that large, impersonal forces — social, economic, technological — determine the broad course of human affairs, that extraordinary individuals only temporarily divert events from an inevitable path.

Others subscribe to the 'Great Man' view of history, believing that events would take a very different path without extraordinary heroes and villains, men, almost always men, like Churchill and Hitler, guiding them in new directions.

Studying these notes only reinforces my pre-existing view that impersonal forces dominate.

As my own experience has already demonstra-ted, none of the Harrys had much trouble convin-cing the wartime authorities that they came from the future. But trying to effect change, even after they accept that astounding fact, has not proved so easy.

Harry One made the mistake of trying to correct the first mistake in the calendar after his arrival — the British plan to capture Rhodes and several neighboring islands off the Turkish coast. He reci-ted chapter and verse the disastrous number of ships sunk and men killed or captured, but the op-eration proceeded anyway. Lives were sacrificed and forces diverted from more important cam-paigns because British military commanders were too exhausted by the constant battles with Chur-chill to deny him this pet adventure.

Harry Three fared no better when trying to con-vince Allied commanders that the strategic bomb-ing campaign was far less effective than they believed. Not in wreaking massive destruction, something it did with frightening efficiency, but in breaking German morale and curtailing the Third Reich's industrial output. He learned how hard it was to overthrow doctrines to which commanders were emotionally wedded and upon which they had built their careers, and for which a massive war machine like the Allied bombing force had been assembled and therefore had to be used.

I stand to stretch my legs, my back, my neck. They're all stiff from sitting so much. Apart from eating, sleeping, and bathing, I've barely left this room in days.

It's amazing how almost everything all six of them tried had the same unfortunate result — reinforcing the Soviet position after the war. Harry Six, my Grandpa Harry, was right. Changing history is fraught with danger. The safest course is to put things back the way they were.

I'm not going back.

But if I did…

Nobody can know how events might have unfolded, *if only*. Except the Harrys know. I know. We've run the experiment several times, each cycle acting as a control group for the other cycles. If I change this, what happens? If I change that? It's the gold standard in the social sciences, almost impossible to achieve.

I'd need to pick my battles, to be far more politically astute than my predecessors. And limit my ambitions, as Harry Six recommends. Don't try to fix everything, just fix one thing right.

The original D-Day, before Harry One, was June 6. A successful landing makes all the difference. With General Rowntree's help, a day or two is surely all I'd need to convince Eisenhower.

But isn't it too risky? Won't the Russian be watching, waiting for my return, ready to make good on his threats?

FIFTEEN

My iPad belts out the distinctive sound of a Skype call.

I'm sitting on the couch, binge-watching a period drama on Netflix. Pure escapism, which is what I need right now. That I shout at the television every few minutes, offended by yet another historical inaccuracy, hasn't stopped me being totally hooked. If you're going to rewrite history, you may as well make it entertaining. Two seasons down, three to go. There's time to finish at least another season today—if I don't get too many interruptions. I ignore the call.

It starts again a minute later. I pause the show then grab the tablet from the side table.

MOM.

What should I tell them about my windfall? Nothing for now. Tell them face to face. I tap the green phone symbol.

"Hello, dear," says the unknown woman who appears on my screen. "It's Mom." She giggles. "Obviously." Her hand reaches for the camera, blocking the view as she adjusts the shot.

"Can you see me?" she says as she sits back.

I could ask her the same thing. My camera is on, but it can't be working or she would see that I'm not her son. "I'm sorry, you must have —"

"Just a minute," she says. "Let me call your father. He's in the garden." She turns away from the camera and shouts, "Geoff, Harry's on Skype!" before turning back to face me. "How is Princeton's newest Assistant Professor?" she says, her voice filled with a mother's pride.

"Ahhh, fine…"

If this is a scam, it's about as believable as those people who call and claim a Windows virus has infected your Mac. Even I'm not clueless enough about computers to fall for that. It's not like complete strangers are going to convince me they're my parents.

I should hang up, but curiosity gets the better of me. Whatever the angle, it must be truly outlandish. I want to see how it plays out, and for the joke to be on the other guy for a change.

"Where are you?" I say.

"At home." She shuffles sideways in her chair. "Don't you recognize the furniture?"

Something moves past the camera in a blur, then a man's face appears beside the woman's.

"Hello, Son," says the man I assume to be 'Geoff.'

I take a deep breath, steeling myself to play it with a straight face. "What time is it there?"

"About 4 pm," he says.

Five hours behind. Which would be where? Alaska? Hawaii, I think. "How's the weather?"

"The weather?" he says with a clear undertone of *why would you ask?* "You know. Same old same old. A perfect 82 degrees every day."

Definitely the Aloha State. "When are you guys coming to visit?"

"Christmas," the woman claiming to be my mother says. "Remember, we discussed it. We'd love to come sooner, but New Jersey's so much further than California."

They've really done their research. I'm playing with fire. "Can I call you back? I'm having trouble with—" I deliberately cut myself off mid-sentence. Then I kill the Skype app so they can't call again.

As scam calls go, this one is extraordinarily unsettling. What the hell is their angle?

The woman looks nothing like my mother. And her generic mid-western sound is nothing like Mom's Boston accent, which is still strong though she's lived in Pittsburgh most of her adult life.

Conversely, the man bears a striking resemblance to my father. They could pass for brothers. He even sounds similar. Not just his accent—New Jersey but educated, like he grew up in Princeton as Dad did—but also the pitch and timbre of his voice.

What if this isn't a scam?

I open the browser and Google 'Geoff Seely Hawaii.'

The first result is a link to a University of Hawaii web page for a professor in their history department. There's a photo. It's definitely him.

His current research focus is outside my area, but still interesting, and his list of publications impressive. I can't deny I'm a little jealous, but I've got time yet to publish more. Probably not on Britain's wartime black market though.

I keep reading.

There's what I'm looking for. The personal bio. Married. Two children. No names given, but the eldest is a son my age.

I read the next line and the words jump from the screen, stabbing me in the chest. To the question, 'Who is your inspiration?' he has answered, 'My father, Professor Harrison Seely, Chair of the History Department at Princeton University for many years.'

— o —

My online accounts — Facebook, email, Skype — are full of friends and contacts I've never met, including Jenny. My sister. We're close, if our daily messaging is any guide. She lives in Philly. Fifty miles away. What if she comes to visit? I've always been an only child, so the idea of a sibling is appealing. And disturbing.

Further Googling turns up a photo of Geoffrey Seely with another unfamiliar relative, his sister, Harriet. My aunt. Their father is definitely Grandpa Harry, but what about their mother? I can't find any mention of Alice Seely. I could call these people, Carol and Geoff, back and —

My God, I've killed my parents!

I didn't really think through the consequences of my choices, or maybe I didn't believe my actions could change the timeline. Obviously they can. They did. But then how can this reality be? If I don't go back, shouldn't Grandpa Harry never exist? Or his son. Either version.

Another search leads me to a document indicating that Alicia Rowntree remained at Bletchley for the duration of the war. So Gerasimov didn't carry out his threat, thank God. But I can't find any

trace of her after 1946. Did some other misfortune
befall her, or did she simply marry and change her
name to that of her husband, some man who was
not Grandpa Harry?

As for me, I should be someone else, shouldn't
I? Or at least have a different name, one given to me
by whatever couple adopted the baby boy that was
me thirty years ago. Yet as far as I can tell I'm still
Harrison Seely, about-to-be Assistant Professor of
Modern History at Princeton University, living in a
house left to me by my namesake.

Does this mean I will go back to repeat the pattern? But then, where's my real father?

Trying to make sense of this bizarre situation is
giving me a headache, and I'm dead tired. It's almost 2 am. I lean back, stretching my arms behind
my head. A slow yawn starts from deep in my
lungs. I should go to bed. I doubt I'll be able to
sleep, but I can't process this right now. It's too con-
fusing. Too overwhelming. Things will be clearer in
the morning…

—o—

By the time I finish breakfast, I've almost convinced
myself that last night was some sort of bad dream.

Or perhaps a mental breakdown. Either that or time travel has messed with my brain. But I have to be sure.

I grab my wallet and keys from the kitchen bench and rush out via the back door to my car.

Four and a half hours later — speeding the entire way — I'm in the street where my parents live, parked in front of the lot where their house should be.

In place of their modest 1960s ranch is a monstrosity of a house, two or three times as big and fifty years newer.

The McMansion stands like a giant, gaudy tombstone to my dead parents.

No, not dead. My mom, Debra Jones, is out there somewhere, presumably married to a man other than my father. Probably a mother to someone other than me — it's my father, Jon, who couldn't have kids.

But even if I find her, she won't know me. She won't… love me. And Dad? He's just gone. Never existed. Not deceased, because you can't be dead if you never lived, but wiped from history.

I can't let that happen. I was never one of those adopted kids who wanted to find his biological parents, or even know who they were. But if there was ever any doubt in my mind about who my 'real' parents are, the events of the past twenty-four hours have erased it completely.

Geoff and Carol seem like good people — Geoff was raised by the same man as my father — but I'll do whatever I must to bring back the mother and father I love. Which leaves me no choice but to return to 1943 and stay there. And marry Alicia Rowntree, no matter how much she protests. Don't ask how I'll swing that, but saving the world would be a good first step to impressing her.

I start the engine, throw the car into gear, and press the accelerator to the floor, determined to make the return trip to Princeton in under four hours...

— o —

It doesn't take long to pack for a one-way trip to 1943. Actually, it's 1944 there by now. There's no point in clinging to the comforts of the twenty-first century. Since I can't carry an inexhaustible supply of toilet paper, I may as well reconcile myself to living 1940s-style sooner rather than later.

The only things I'm taking from this period are my leather suitcase and my glasses. And the photos from Grandpa Harry. I already know how I'm going to use them. He must have put them in the envelope for that specific purpose.

I stop in the entry and look around. It ought to be harder, abandoning my entire life. But I couldn't live with myself if I didn't do everything in my power to bring back Jon and Deb Seely, my true parents, even though I'll never see them again. At least not as their son.

All I can do is leave them a note explaining why I left and saying goodbye, hoping that once I do what I need to do, they'll be here to find it. I place it on the side table, then open the door to wartime London.

It was an uncomfortable experience the last time and I can only expect it to be worse now. Time on the other side will be passing at thirteen times the rate it is here, if I've kept track correctly, at least until I'm there and it resets to the next rate. Twenty-one. *Holy cow.*

My guess is that having one part of your body operating at one speed — blood pumping, nerves twitching — and other parts at a different, much faster pace can't be good for you. I'm hoping that passing through as quickly as possible will minimize the effect.

Time to test my theory.

I take two long steps back then run. Rather than trying to stop on the landing, I dance down the stairs, grinning broadly, so pleased with myself. It worked! There's no faintness, no blurred vision, no collapsing legs, just a little of the tingling in my fingers.

At the bottom of the steps I stop, startled by the sight in front of me. The pile of debris from the damaged house across the street is gone. A dark green tent occupies much of the now vacant site. Two soldiers linger outside, chatting casually between slow, lazy puffs on their cigarettes.

One looks over in my direction. Suddenly he's shouting, "Oy, you there!" and then they're running across the road, coming straight for me.

Primitive instinct — fight or flight — kicks in. I turn to flee back to Princeton, but a third soldier is at the top of the stairs, blocking my path. He must have been standing guard beside the door. *How did I miss him?*

I freeze. The STEN gun he's holding looks more like a caulking gun than a deadly instrument of war, but his stance is unmistakably hostile: feet planted, both hands firmly on the weapon, the first finger of his right hand less than an inch from the trigger.

Now the other two are on me, each grabbing me by an arm.

They haul me across the road to the tent. Once inside, the older of the two men, a sergeant, yells at me to sit.

I don't want to antagonize them, so I do as he says. "Just let General —"

"Button it," he says as he picks up the telephone sitting on a folding table near the back wall.

While he's talking, the other soldier, who can't be more than eighteen or nineteen, goes to the opposite corner and squats in front of a camp stove. I can't quite see what he's doing as he hovers over the cooker, which emits a chuffing sound, but I'd bet any odds he's making tea.

With both their backs to me I could try to run for it. Except the third man will be waiting somewhere outside. He'll most likely shoot me in the back before I make it across the road, up the stairs, and through the door.

The young soldier rises, a tin mug cupped in both hands. Enticing wisps of steam rise from the surface when he blows on it. I stare longingly at his beverage while he sips at it, jealous of the deeply satisfied sound he makes as he sucks in each mouthful.

After a short while he notices me watching him. Given the naked animosity displayed by his comrade, I expect him to yell at me too. Instead he goes back to the stove, pours another cup and brings it to me.

"Thank you," I say as I reach for the offered cup.

Before my fingers can close around the handle, the Sergeant knocks it from my hand. The cup flies at least ten feet, rattling as it rolls along the ground, coming to rest on its side. The tea fans out in a wet, steaming semi-circle, before disappearing into the earth, leaving behind nothing but the empty mug and a damp stain of darkened soil.

"It's just a brew, Sarge," the young man says.

"Nowt for 'im until the General says so," the Sergeant barks. "Now bugger off outside, Billy."

With a hangdog expression the young soldier beats a silent, sullen retreat.

I glare at the Sergeant. Doesn't this stupid Tommy get that I'm here to help? My lips begin to form a protest.

He pokes a finger in my face. "Not a word out of you. Four bleedin' months we've been stuck 'ere in this miserable place waitin' for some Yank. So you can just sit there and belt up, right."

Impatience and boredom explain some of his hostility. But there's more to it. I can understand General Rowntree having men stationed here waiting for my return, but surely he told them I'm a friendly.

Hell. What if the General they're waiting for is someone other than Rowntree?

There's a sinking feeling in my stomach. All in all, there are way too many unanswered questions. And I don't have time to wait for answers. I have to get to Riley before the Russian finds out I'm here.

—o—

I sneak a peek at my watch. Forty-five minutes we've been waiting, the Sergeant sitting across from me the whole time, glaring and growling if I so much as shift in my chair.

He blows another puff of smoke at me. It's not easy to ignore. I protested at first but it only further enraged him. My face burns with anger, at him and at feeling so powerless.

A vehicle stops outside. I hear a car door slam then a shout of "General!" from Billy, the young soldier, followed by "He's inside, Sir."

Footsteps. Mentally I cross my fingers.

I breathe a huge sigh of relief when the tent flap pulls back and a familiar face pokes through.

General Rowntree dismisses my watcher with a tilt of his head and a gruff, "That will be all, Sergeant Barnes."

I wait for my tormentor to leave before rising. "General, what—"

"Sit down," he barks, standing over me with his hands on his hips. "Explain yourself. You promised to return after QUADRANT…"

"I can explain, Sir." But I can't tell him that I only came back now for personal reasons.

I could tell him about Grandpa Harry's notes: how extensive they were, how much extra research I needed to do, and how long it took me to understand and synthesize his experience and the experiences of all the Harrys before him. It's all true, but I'd just be making excuses.

So I'll say something else, not a lie, but something miles from the whole truth. I'll tell him I didn't know what advice to give him and the Chiefs of Staff.

But first I have to make sure Alicia is OK. "General, where is your daughter?"

"I think we have more important—"

"Her life may be in danger. Do you know where she is, that she's safe?"

"Good God, what are you talking about, man?"

I quickly tell him about my encounter with Gerasimov. "I think he's from the future like me. And also trying to change history. Or maybe stop me from changing it. He threatened to kill me, not in so many words but the implication was clear, and to expose Lady Alicia as a Soviet agent. That threat was quite explicit."

"Who would be foolish enough to believe such a ridiculous suggestion?" he says, his bluster unable to hide the color draining from his face.

He goes to the phone in the corner and calls Bletchley Park. After asking for Commander Travis, he spends the next five minutes explaining how a Soviet agent may attempt to discredit his daughter as part of a much larger plot he is not at liberty to discuss.

He hangs up and turns to me with a satisfied smile. "Do not worry, Professor. I have explained the situation to the top man at Bletchley. And you should be perfectly safe with me and my men. We will look into this Russian. If he is attached to the embassy as he claims, he shall be expelled forthwith."

"That's a relief."

"Now, Professor, what advice have you finally brought us?"

I explain the changes needed to the plans for OVERLORD.

He's skeptical at first, but after a few minutes takes a seat. He pulls his chair closer, leaning in. By the time I finish explaining how I came to my conclusion, he is nodding vigorously.

I wait, expecting him to propose some course of action, but he says nothing. "So when do we take it to the Chiefs of Staff?" I say.

He gives a defeated shake of his head. "I do not believe we can. You know as well as I, this is not what Brookie wants to hear. We might still have persuaded him of the merits of this new plan, but you made a bloody fool of me by not returning, Seely. We no longer have any credibility with Field Marshal Brooke. Or the other two members of the committee."

"What are we going to do then?"

He pauses, a resigned expression on his face. It's not the hesitation of a man who doesn't know what to do, but of someone who dislikes the answer. "The only thing we can. Take it directly to the man in charge."

— o —

Soon after my arrival in London I discover that Eisenhower is in Washington, meeting with President Roosevelt and General Marshall. Fortunately, he returns to England two days later. Unfortunately, we spend the next week trying in vain to secure an off-the-record meeting with him, meaning behind the backs of the British Chiefs of Staff.

That is why General Rowntree and I are at Claridge's, where Eisenhower often dines, positioned to intercept him when he answers the inevitable call of nature.

"This is damned undignified, Professor," General Rowntree whispers as we cower in a hidden corner of the hotel's lobby. "It had better work."

The General is running a huge professional risk circumventing the chain of command. While it is a choice he made freely, it took hours of impassioned argument to convince him to approach the Supreme Commander by loitering outside a men's room. Such behavior violates the fundamental rules of decorum the British upper classes hold so dear. Even I feel a little embarrassed. But there is no other way to get a moment alone with our target, away from his protective entourage.

Our quarry approaches the bathroom. "Here he comes," I whisper.

We emerge from our hiding place, the General stepping straight into Eisenhower's path. "Sir, please excuse this intrusion," he says, "but if I may have a moment of your time. It is vital we speak with you."

"Rowntree, isn't it? From Brooke's staff?"

"Yes Sir."

Eisenhower casts a skeptical glance in my direction. "And your civilian friend?"

"Assistant Professor Harrison Seely," I say. "Princeton University."

"Ah, one of ours."

"Yes Sir."

"I suggest you call my secretary for an appointment, General," he says. "I must complete my mission here and return to my dinner companions." He presses forward.

General Rowntree steps back into his path. "Forgive me, Sir, but it is imperative we speak. The success of OVERLORD depends upon it."

Eisenhower's expression turns even more sour at the mention of the cross-channel invasion. "The British view is clear," he says. "As is the American position, which must prevail, no matter how much your superiors dislike it. There is nothing more to say on the matter."

"The Chiefs of Staff are unaware of this conversation, Sir, and would most certainly disapprove. Which is why I have pursued this... unorthodox course of approaching you directly."

"Buttonholing me, you mean."

An American sergeant approaches. "Is everything all right, Sir?"

"Five minutes, Mickey," Eisenhower answers. "Give the Admiral my apologies for the delay."

The sergeant nods. As he turns away, he shoots General Rowntree and me a look that reminds me of a mother bear standing between her cubs and a pack of wolves.

Eisenhower ushers us to a quiet corner in the lobby where we sit.

General Rowntree produces a packet of Lucky Strikes from his pocket — so I'm not the only one with connections — deftly taps the bottom against his hand so a single cigarette protrudes from the top, and extends it in Eisenhower's direction.

The Supreme Commander nods begrudgingly as he slides the cigarette from the pack. With a swift, almost sub-conscious move he places it between his lips, pulls a Zippo from his pocket, and lights it. After several long puffs he says, "What is this about, Rowntree?"

"General, you must delay OVERLORD."

The American commander shuffles forward in the chair, places his hands on the arms, and bends slightly at the waist, ready to spring to his feet. "Sonofabitch. Field Marshal Brooke did put you up to this."

"Absolutely not, Sir. The CIGS doubts the invasion's prospects for success at any time in the foreseeable future. Whereas we are only asking for a month. We know categorically the Normandy landings can and will succeed this year — but in the first week of June, not May."

Eisenhower pushes himself back and slumps into his chair, chewing his lip. He must have expected to hear what he's been hearing from the British all along — delay the invasion until 1945 or '46, or forget about it altogether and attack Germany via Italy and the Balkans instead.

"How could a month make any difference?"

"An invasion in May will be a disaster," I say. "The weather is perfect, the landings flawless, but German units are expecting our boys. Our forces are driven back into the sea within a few days. Whereas in early June a series of storms lash the

Channel, lulling the Nazis into a false sense of security."

"Not much help if we can't get ashore," Eisenhower says. "Or our aircraft can't fly."

"Rommel returns to Germany to visit his family, confident the storm precludes any invasion, while Seventh Army commanders are absent, either on leave or at a military conference in Rennes. The weather clears suddenly on the night of June 5, and our assault the following morning catches the enemy asleep and leaderless."

"You speak of this in the past tense," Eisenhower says. "As if it is a matter of historical fact. Are you claiming to see the future?"

"Not exactly, Sir."

I pause and pull a photograph from my inside coat pocket. "May I show you something that might help you understand?"

Choosing to interpret his grunt as permission to proceed, I pass him the picture.

He barely glances at it, snorting dismissively. But then his eyes dart back, locking onto it like a detective who just discovered the clue that will solve his most difficult case. "What is this?"

"You must recognize yourself in the photograph, General."

"And the man with me?" He looks at the photo then at me with his piercing blue eyes. "He bears a striking resemblance to you."

"My grandfather." I'm not yet ready to explain Grandpa Harry's true identity. Too complicated, and it adds nothing to the believability of my story. "The boy on your knee is my father."

He tears his gaze from the photo. "If this is your father, the photo would need to be from…" He studies my face for a moment. "Forty years ago, at which time I was myself still a boy." He examines the photo again. "If anything, I've aged in this."

"My grandmother" — I glance over at General Rowntree — "shot this sometime in the 1950s." I wanted to say 'will take this' but I don't want to jinx things with Alicia. "I can't predict the future, General. I only know the past. My past. I've come here from your future. Seventy-two years into your future, to be precise."

He glares at General Rowntree, not me. "How can you expect me to believe such a thing?"

"A moment please, Sir," General Rowntree says. He leans close to me. "What other evidence can we present?"

I think for a moment. DC? Three hours each way from Princeton, in good traffic. Too far. But

Manhattan is half that distance. "Sir," I say to Eisenhower, "are you familiar with New York City's major landmarks? The Empire State Building, the Statute of Liberty, Central Park?"

"Of course."

A nod from General Rowntree tells me he sees where I'm going. "Then grant us a few hours of your time," he says to Eisenhower, "and we will prove it to you beyond doubt. If you remain unconvinced following our demonstration, I will pursue the only honorable course and submit my resignation to Field Marshal Brooke with immediate effect."

"I will hold you to it," Eisenhower growls. He turns and looks across the lobby. "MICKEY!" he booms.

The word barely leaves his mouth and the Sergeant is by his side.

"Bring a typist immediately. General Rowntree has an important letter to dictate. Then fetch my car."

SIXTEEN

Being frogmarched from my hut to the main building is humiliating, and more than a little unsettling. My disquiet grows when we stop outside the office of the Deputy Director. Despite the 'Deputy' in his title, Commander Travis is the man in charge at Bletchley Park.

My mind races, searching for dark possibilities, but I have been scrupulous in adhering to every security procedure. There must be a simple explanation, some silly misunderstanding behind this. I will explain, the Commander will gruffly point out some minor transgression on my part to maintain face, and then everything will return to normal.

My escort remains outside when I enter the office. As expected, the Deputy Director is seated behind his large oak desk, but to my surprise 'C' is standing beside him. My confidence in a quick resolution dissolves. The presence of Major-General Menzies, Chief of the Secret Intelligence Service, is extraordinary and suggests a grave matter, not one that will be easily dismissed.

My breathing quickens and my forehead grows

damp. I fight to re-establish a facade of calmness by reminding myself that Menzies, despite his position, is not such an imposing figure.

I recall Father's reaction when informed I was joining the Government Code & Cypher School. "That is part of MI6, is it not, under the command of that buffoon, Stewart Menzies?" he exploded. Then he explained his disdain, recounting an incident during the Great War where Menzies detained an American general for two days because the man's driver spoke with a Greek accent!

Yet I must take great care. Menzies has connections to powerful and influential men through Eton and the Beaufort Hunt, and a close working relationship with Mr. Churchill. It is said he personally briefs the Prime Minister on ULTRA first thing every morning, often while the PM is taking breakfast in bed.

Nevertheless, my innocence must carry the day. I have nothing to hide. With a smile I look Commander Travis in the eye and say, "Good morning, Sir. How may I be of assistance?"

"Please," he says, signalling for me to sit.

I take the only chair available, positioned alone in the middle of the room. I feel like I am in the dock at the Old Bailey, not an incidental effect I am sure.

The sense of being tried for some heinous crime grows as Menzies peppers me with questions.

Determined not to appear defensive since I have no cause for guilt, I answer as honestly and forthrightly as I am able.

The barrage is unrelenting, providing me little time to reflect on the purpose of his inquiries. So it takes longer than it should, at least fifteen minutes and more than twenty questions, to identify the offence of which I stand accused — something so outrageous, I am struck temporarily both deaf and dumb.

"Miss Rowntree!"

I stare at Menzies, or more correctly, at the space he occupies.

"Miss Rowntree," he growls, "you must respond. Are you a Bolshevik sympathiser?"

"Surely you did your homework before dragging me here," I retort. "Or perhaps not. Had you done so, you would know I have never had any connection to communist elements. Now, General, I will answer no more questions unless addressed by my proper title."

"Come now, Lady Alicia," Commander Travis says. "Co-operation is in all our interests."

"Sir, the proposition — that I am a Soviet agent —

is preposterous. Utterly preposterous, I tell you. And quite illogical if you consider the practicalities of the matter. I see such a small part of the whole. Fragments of cyphers, never the clear text. What possible value could I provide the Soviets?"

"Knowledge of an adversary's sources and capabilities is vital in this game," says Menzies. "Were you to inform the Russians which cyphers we can and which we cannot crack—"

"Hundreds of people here could tell them. Assuming the Russians do not already know."

"An allegation such as this cannot be ignored, Miss Rowntree."

I glare at him. "And what evidence do you have, General? None, I will wager."

"The information we received is disturbingly credible in its detail. We have no choice but to investigate. Most vigorously."

"How dare you suggest I would betray my country, based on nothing but unsubstantiated charges. Have you considered the possibility your informant is merely an *agent provocateur* seeking to sow confusion and mistrust?"

"We are considering all possibilities," Commander Travis says. He looks to Menzies who nods in return. It seems to me a prearranged signal.

"Sterling!" Travis shouts at the door. "Nevertheless, we think it best you leave us for now."

My escort opens the door and looks in. "Sir?"

"Corporal, please accompany Lady Alicia to her hut to collect her personal effects. Then to the front gate. She is not to re-enter the grounds."

No, I cannot lose my work. The constant battering of one's head against these infuriating, interminable puzzles wears one down. Until, suddenly, the answer appears, or even just some small crib representing the first step towards a solution. Those moments are rewarding beyond measure. Where else could I, a woman, make such a mark on the world, even if my contribution must remain anonymous?

"Sir, please. I beg you. I am wholly innocent of these charges."

Menzies shrugs. "Someone of your standing, *Lady Alicia*, must see the wisdom in departing without a public fuss."

He is right. I stand and follow the Corporal, an unconscious movement. This predicament descended upon me without warning, events sweeping me along faster than my mind can analyse and comprehend.

Minutes later I am in the hut where I work —

worked — standing before my desk. Corporal Sterling gathers my personal items one by one, carefully examining each object before handing it to me, even going so far as opening my lipstick.

They really are taking this spying business too far. They have no corroboration for the charges against me or I would not be walking free. *But blast it, I said too much.* Any statement, no matter how innocent, can be twisted. They goaded me. Which was their intention. So obvious upon reflection.

I refuse to look at my colleagues as they watch in embarrassed horror. If I meet their eyes I will be compelled to speak, but what would I say? Protesting my innocence would serve no purpose but to dignify this travesty of justice.

Thank the Lord that Dilly Knox is not here. I could not face him, the only one willing to take me seriously. I pray my disgrace does not rebound on him, or the other talented but unappreciated girls he took a chance on, like young Mavis Lever.

Clutching a bag containing my belongings to my chest, I turn away and pass silently out the door, like a thief slipping away into the night. A chill wind whips my skirt against my stockinged legs as I walk slowly along the path leading to the front gate. Tears well in my eyes which I keep to the front, avoiding the gaze of the sentries as I pass through the gate and collect my bicycle from the rack outside.

The ride is as dreary as my digs themselves. The thought of returning to the comforts of Elverstone Hall ought to fill me with enthusiasm, but it means surrendering what little chance I ever possessed of establishing myself as a professional mathematician. Who would have me now, a woman tainted with unresolved charges of espionage and treason?

My future seems as grey as the clouds above. But even the worst storm will eventually clear. Though he is ambivalent about my work here, Father will surely not stand for his daughter being branded a traitor. I raise myself from the saddle, pushing down on the pedals with all my strength, silently cursing the headwind fighting against me. General Menzies is not the only one with the ear of people at the highest levels.

SEVENTEEN

Eisenhower purses his lips when I open the door to General Rowntree's townhouse and show him the inside of my house in Princeton, but he admits nothing.

I quickly explain to him how the door works — the need for physical contact with me, the desirability for speed — then organize the three of us to pass through.

The image of a conga line pops into my mind. I stifle a laugh. "Ready?"

They both nod.

"One, two, three, GO!"

We charge through. Or try to. With two middle-aged men in tow we move at a pace more like a leisurely jog than a sprint. I experience the tingling again in my fingers and my toes. Even in my ears. My head spins.

But the disorientation passes in a few seconds. "Everyone OK?" I say as I close the door behind us.

"Never better," Eisenhower says.

"Perfectly fine," says General Rowntree.

Interesting. They both seemed unaffected by the transition. I don't know why, but perhaps there's some cumulative effect, so it hits me harder.

I ask General Rowntree to open my front door again.

"Voila!" I say, pointing outside. "Princeton, 2015."

Eisenhower raises both eyebrows but still says nothing.

"Really, Sir? You're not convinced?"

"You promised to show me New York City, Professor."

"This way then." I lead them out to the street and my car.

"What type of car is this?" Eisenhower says.

"A Subaru Outback. It's—"

Probably not a good idea to tell him it's Japanese. "Made in Indiana."

I point out the California license plates— I haven't transferred the registration to New Jersey yet—and the steering wheel on the left. "Clearly we're not in England, Sir."

He ignores me and climbs in the back. General Rowntree just shrugs and follows him. *Damn.* I secretly hoped I could convince Eisenhower without the trip to New York.

By the time I slip behind the wheel Eisenhower has lit up. I'm pissed that he didn't even ask permission, but if there's one thing I've learned about the 1940s, it's that nearly everyone smokes, with very few restrictions on when and where. I am so thankful Alicia doesn't partake of this disgusting habit.

Nevertheless, allowing Eisenhower to smoke in my car is a small price to pay to keep him on side, given the stakes. But damn it stinks, especially in a confined space. My left hand drops from the steering wheel, then presses a button in the door.

The sudden lowering of the window startles my passengers, but only momentarily. Eisenhower is soon flicking the ash from his cigarette out the window. By the time we reach New Brunswick, only twenty miles north, he's on his third cancer stick.

My Subaru will smell like an ashtray forever. Though it won't be my problem. Even if I come back, I'm broke. I'd have to sell the car, if the repo man doesn't get it first.

No, it's my parents — Jon and Deb, when I fix things — who'll be left to clean up behind me. I feel bad about that, but it's not like I can call and explain before I go, not now, not in this timeline where they don't exist. But I can leave them a note, once I'm in the past, one they will get before this even happens.

Or did Grandpa Harry already take care of that? Do they already know? What other secrets did the old man swear them to keep?

New Jersey rolls by at a steady 70 mph as we head along the turnpike. Eisenhower fills his lungs and the car with a constant cloud of smoke as he stares out the window, examining the passing landscape. Though he remains silent, his face conveys the sense of wonder anyone would feel seeing the world of 2015 through 1944 eyes.

The traffic is light and the New York City skyline comes into sight an hour and a quarter after leaving Princeton. "Well I'll be damned," Eisenhower says, finally breaking his silence.

I make eye contact with him in the rear view mirror. "General?"

He raises his eyebrows in acknowledgment, but doesn't answer. A few minutes later we approach the entrance to the Lincoln Tunnel.

"There was only one tunnel in my time," he says pointing at the three tunnels in front of us, "though the second is, or should I say was, under construction."

Mission accomplished. The words 'In my time,'

and confusion about whether to use the past or present tense, indicate complete acceptance that this is his future.

Time to head home. "I'll make a quick loop in Manhattan," I say, "and then back through the tunnel to New Jersey."

Eisenhower insists we circle all the way downtown. Now he won't stop talking. He points out every building he recognizes and remarks on every one he doesn't. The detour adds at least forty-five minutes to our journey and then, as soon as we're back on the turnpike, he asks for a bathroom break.

I stop at the first rest area we encounter. As we head inside I fear that two men in perfect WWII generals' uniforms — one British, one American — will attract attention. But nobody gives them a second glance. General Rowntree was never famous and Eisenhower's infamy has long since faded.

I'm in and out in no time so I wait outside.

General Rowntree emerges first. Eisenhower follows a few minutes later shaking water from his hands and scowling. "There is no attendant. And no towels."

I'm about to escort him back inside and show him how to use the electric hand dryer when it occurs to me that every extra minute we spend here is far longer in 1944. Twenty-one times longer, to be precise. Three minutes here is an hour there. An hour and a bit equal to a day.

Jesus.

"I'm sorry, Sir, but we really have to go." I begin rushing toward the car, but then realize I'm alone.

I turn to see the two generals still where I left them, ten or fifteen yards behind. Rowntree says something to Eisenhower, who shrugs his shoulders before they follow in my wake.

"What is it, Professor?" General Rowntree says as I climb in the front and he and Eisenhower in the back.

"It'll be five or six hours elapsed here before we get back to London," I say as I maneuver the car out of the parking area.

"A little longer than we expected, but we should have General Eisenhower back by breakfast, before anyone misses him."

"You've forgotten about the time difference, Sir." Reaching the on-ramp to the turnpike, I flatten the accelerator.

"Dear God," General Rowntree says. "In London that's…"

"Nearly four days."

—o—

We follow the same process returning to London through the door, but one of the men behind me hesitates at the sight of the steps falling away in front of us, slowing our forward momentum at the worst possible time.

The transition hits me harder than a baseball bat to the gut, causing me to collapse like an empty suit. Generals Rowntree and Eisenhower land in a heap on top of me.

By the time I regain my wits, they've climbed off and are helping me to my feet. I brush myself off and look around. A semi-circular wall of GIs surrounds the stairs, a dozen M1 carbines pointing in my direction. Sergeant Barnes brandishes a STEN gun, his eyes burning with a hostility far more intense and personal than the other soldiers show.

A captain holding a pistol steps forward, stopping halfway up the stairs. We tower over him, but he is armed and we're not.

"General Eisenhower, Sir, where have you been?" He waves his pistol at me. "Did this man kidnap you?"

"There was no kidnapping," Eisenhower says.

"Sir, he may be a Ger —"

"What is your name, Captain?"

"Walker, Sir."

"Stand your men down, Captain Walker."

"You too, Sergeant," says General Rowntree.

"But Sir," Walker says, "you've been missing four days. General Marshall is tearing strips off everyone. Even the Brits were worried."

"Captain Walker, that is an order!" Eisenhower growls. He starts down the stairs, pushing past the young officer standing there with a look of frozen indecision on his face. The circumstances are so extraordinary...

But a four-star general gave him a direct order. Walker snaps out of his daze. "Do as the General says," he shouts to his men.

They lower their weapons and clear a path, but I can still feel dozens of hostile eyes on me as we follow Eisenhower across the road to the tent. Before we enter, he speaks privately to the Captain who nods his head so hard I worry it will fall off.

The young officer gathers his men and leads them down the street to several military vehicles parked there. As they load up and drive away, Sergeant Barnes positions himself outside the tent's entrance and we head inside.

Eisenhower pulls a folded sheet of paper from his breast pocket.

"I won't be needing this," he says as he returns the signed letter of resignation to General Rowntree.

"Very good, Sir," General Rowntree says. "And D-Day?"

"Such a decision will be difficult to explain." Eisenhower turns to me. "At least without mentioning you. I have a great deal to consider. Where can I find you, Professor, should we need to speak again?"

I pause — not because I'm going anywhere, but because I can't just invite myself — and glance over at General Rowntree.

He understands what I'm asking. It's the obvious, logical solution. But his daughter won't like it. So there's an understandable moment of hesitation before he says, "The Professor shall be my guest, Sir."

"Good. Best if we keep all this between ourselves for now."

A car squeaks to a stop outside. Seconds later an American sergeant enters the tent, the same one who was so protective of Eisenhower when we collared him over dinner.

"General, you gave us a hell of a scare," he says, sounding like a parent reunited with a child who ran off—frightened, wanting to be angry, but relieved more than anything.

Eisenhower grimaces theatrically, admitting his transgression.

The Sergeant's body language softens and the hint of a smile crosses his face. "Do you remember what my mother told me when I first came to work for you, Sir?"

Eisenhower nods. "Don't come home without the General."

"And she meant it. So please don't go disappearing on me again, Sir, because I dearly want to go home after this is all over."

The Supreme Commander stands and puts an arm around the Sergeant's shoulders, heading toward the door. "Don't we all, Mickey. Don't we all."

—o—

After Eisenhower leaves with his orderly, the General and I move from the tent, where it's cold and damp, to the townhouse.

Sergeant Barnes follows us across the road, his

disposition toward me as sour as ever, and takes up guard duty at the door.

The General calls for his car and we retire to the sitting room to wait. Mrs. Collins brings us tea and delicate cakes, then adds several chunks of coal to the fire.

I don't know whether it's seeing me working so closely with the General, or the fact Alicia is not here, and therefore safe from the attentions of an American, but the housekeeper seems to have warmed to me over the past week. At least she doesn't frown every time she looks at me now.

The glowing heat of the fire gradually drives the chill from our bones while we enjoy our refreshments. Our conversation about Eisenhower, and what we think he will do, is short-lived, dissolving once we both agree there's no way to predict.

I sit in brooding silence, procrastinating about raising the real reason for my return. It's such an awkward thing to ask — not simply to bless his daughter's marriage, but to play matchmaker. But I must say something. If I'm to have any chance with Alicia, I will need the General's help.

I tell him about Jon Seely and his wife Debra, what happened to them in my current timeline, and how I'll do whatever it takes to restore the world in which they are my parents. I close by begging him to help me make my case with Alicia.

"My daughter's modern ideas and your even more modern ways would be well matched, Professor. Though there are many factors to consider, especially for a woman of Lady Alicia's upbringing." He stares at the photo wistfully. "You must think my values antiquated."

"One of the most important lessons any historian can learn is to judge historical figures by the standards of their own times. Your values seem typical for this time."

He chuckles. "Typical? You are such a flatterer, Professor."

"But change is coming after the war. Massive change. Social, economic, political. Isn't it better to embrace it than let it run right over the top of you?"

"I'm afraid I am much too old to change my ways. But that is not the issue. I cannot persuade my daughter to act against her own desires. You have seen how stubborn and headstrong she can be. I give you my word I shall support the match, should you be her choice. Though in that case I doubt you will need it. Once she sets her mind, defying her father is no obstacle."

"Thank you, Sir. You won't regret it. I'll make

her happy. I'm not just saying that. I *know*. It's already happened. Harry and Alice are meant to be."

He shakes his head. "Professor, if you are to have any hope, I counsel you not to follow such a line of — "

We are interrupted by yelling outside. It sounds like Sergeant Barnes.

"Halt!" the same voice shouts even louder now. Definitely the Sergeant. "Halt, or I'll shoot!"

A short burst of semi-automatic gunfire rings out, reverberating in the narrow confines of a street closely packed with brick buildings, followed a moment later by a sharp bang-bang from a different weapon. Then a deadly silence.

— o —

Stunned by the unexpected sounds of violence, we stare wide-eyed at each other before springing to our feet and rushing to the door.

Sergeant Barnes sits on the landing, leaning against the outside wall. His right hand is clamped over his left shoulder, bright red blood seeping between his fingers.

The General turns to Mrs. Collins, now standing in the doorway looking on in shock. "Call an ambulance! And bring something to bandage the Sergeant's wound."

She flinches then rushes back inside.

At the bottom of the stairs, Riley Cornell hovers over a man lying face down in a pool of blood. He removes a pistol from the man's left hand, tucks it in his coat pocket, then steps back and kicks him in the ribs, hard enough for the body to jump.

He looks up at me with a satisfied grin. "Brown bread orright."

While the General tends to Sergeant Barnes, I make my way down the stairs and squat next to the dead man. I can't quite see his face. Carefully avoiding the blood, I roll the corpse over, grunting at the unexpected weight.

It is him. *Gerasimov*.

There's a gunshot wound high in the right shoulder, but the fatal shots were the two in the middle of his back.

I've never seen a dead body before, not in real life. I thought I'd feel something, but I feel nothing except relief. I didn't want it to end like this, but he only gave me two choices — capitulate or meet violence with violence. And the price of surrender was too high. *Live by the sword…*

I stand and lead Riley a few yards along the sidewalk so we can talk privately.

"You shoulda let me take care of 'im earlier, Prof," he says. "Neatly like. It's a right proper mess this way."

"What are you doing here?"

"You've been a goldmine. I dunno how this time travel caper works, but I was worried this bloke would change things. Then those winners you gave me wouldn't be winners anymore, see?"

"You've been watching him?"

"Me boys 'ave. Since you came back. And this place all along. That's how we knew you was 'ere."

"He didn't go anywhere near Bletchley did he?"

"Nope."

"Or contact anyone in British intelligence?"

"Dunno. Spies don't exactly advertise the fact, do they? But he didn't meet with nobody official looking."

Riley's assurance isn't definitive, but I have to hope Gerasimov decided on coercing me directly, with a bullet, rather than through Alicia.

"You're right about things changing," I say. Helping Riley get rich from crooked bets has been weighing on my conscience, but he just saved my life. I owe him, big time. "You have until May to use the information I gave you."

It takes a moment for my warning to register, then his eyes sparkle. "Thanks for the advice, Guv," he says with a broad grin. "I'll make sure I have plenty to retire on by then."

Mrs. Collins returns from inside the house and shoos the General away from Sergeant Barnes, then kneels in front of the wounded man.

"Now, now," she says soothingly, "let's have a look at you."

He groans as she lifts his arm and passes the bandage underneath.

"Don't worry, dear, we'll have you patched up in no time."

The General stands at the top of the stairs and surveys the scene. "What the blazes happened here?" he bellows.

"I'm sorry, Sir," the Sergeant says weakly from behind him. "I warned him. He wouldn't stop." With his uninjured right arm he points at Riley. "We would've been done for if he didn't show up out of the blue…"

Whether it was bad marksmanship, panic, or simply the lack of a killer instinct, Barnes sounds ashamed he didn't take Gerasimov down.

General Rowntree looks Riley up and down, then glares at me. "What is your association with this man, Professor?"

I signal for the General to approach.

When he hesitates I tilt my head and roll my eyes in the direction of the Sergeant and Mrs. Collins. He gets the message — *this is not for their ears* — and moves to join us.

"General Sir Geoffrey Rowntree," I say, "meet Mr. Riley Cornell."

Riley tips his cap. "At your service, Sir Geoffrey. The Prof and me, we're business associates. Of a kind."

The General looks at me with a mix of disappointment and disgust. He's jumped to a conclusion about Riley and me — an accurate one most likely.

"Mr. Cornell offered to take care of Gerasimov for me." I nudge the corpse with my toe. "Which he did."

"This man is the same Russian you mentioned?" the General says. "Our people could find no trace of him."

His expression flips from perplexed to panicked. He turns and races up the stairs past Mrs. Collins and Sergeant Barnes, so suddenly I'm left behind. By the time I realize what he's doing and follow him inside, he's already on the phone. "This is General Rowntree," he says in a deep, authoritative voice. "I must speak with Commander Travis immediately."

— o —

"This must not stand!" the General shouts as he slams down the phone. His face glows, his nostrils flare. For an upper-class Englishman it is an extraordinary outburst.

"What is it, General?" I say. "Is she safe?"

"Lady Alicia is no longer at Bletchley. Commander Travis danced around the issue, but he intimated my daughter was a suspected Soviet agent."

"The Russian must have gotten to him before coming after me."

"I think not. My warning was the catalyst. 'An abundance of caution is warranted,' Travis said."

"That makes no sense. You told him the Russian would make a false accusation."

The General shakes his head in disbelief. "Such cowardly fear of error is no way to win a bloody war."

He picks up the telephone again and calls Elver-stone Hall. Then he calls for his car before turning to me. "Lady Alicia has returned home. We must speak with her."

"Perhaps I should stay here."

"Nonsense."

"She won't want to see me."

"I will deal with my daughter, Professor. There are larger issues at stake. Having given General Eisenhower my word, I am responsible for your safe-keeping."

"But Gerasimov is dead."

"Can we be certain he is working alone? You have an ally here," he says patting his chest. "Does it not stand to reason he would seek local assistance? One of the many NKVD agents operating from the Soviet Embassy for instance."

I hadn't considered that possibility, but it makes sense. "If he has local contacts, Mr. Cornell may have seen him with them."

The General follows me as I head to the front door to ask Riley, but he's gone. Probably slipped away as soon as the General and I went inside.

An ambulance pulls up while we're standing on the landing searching the street for any sign of Riley.

Sergeant Barnes is loaded onto a stretcher. I thank him as he's carried to the vehicle.

"I did it for the General, not you Yank," he says gruffly, though the cheeky twinkle in his eye suggests he too is warming to me. I hope my recent luck in bringing people around extends to Alicia.

—o—

The General and I ride in silence for the first half hour or so, then he turns to me and says, "What the blazes were you thinking, Seely? Keeping company with a ruffian like Cornell. What exactly is the nature of your association?"

"I was selling him stuff. Razor blades and tobacco I brought from the future. It's not stolen, like your typical black market goods."

"That does not change the inherent illegality of the enterprise. The black market. How could you?"

"I did what I had to in order to survive."

"That is no excuse."

"You have to try to understand what it's like, Sir, finding yourself in a foreign land with no money, no place to stay, and no ration book. And that's not even taking into account the added culture shock of being transported seventy years into the past. Remember what Hartley said about the past — "

"Never heard of the man."

"L. P. Hartley? 'The past is a foreign country: they do things differently there.' You don't recognize it? He is English."

He shakes his head.

How can a well-educated Brit not recognize that quote? *Duh.* The Go-Between *wasn't published until the fifties.*

"It's quite a famous line. In my time. But he hasn't written it yet."

"Perhaps my hospitality has been remiss," the General says, "a deficiency I shall remedy immediately. My daughter's sentiments notwithstanding, you are in my charge. Worry no more about lodgings or food. Should you want for anything you must simply ask. And no more shady dealings. Your actions reflect directly on my family, Professor. We have standards to maintain, an example to set."

He pauses and locks eyes. "Do I make myself absolutely clear?"

I feel like a private being dressed down on the parade ground. If a soldier knows what's good for him, there's only one correct answer in that situation. "Yes Sir," I say with all the contrition I can manage. "It won't happen again."

— o —

The staff car crunches to a halt on the gravel driveway in front of Elverstone Hall.

The butler is waiting at the door and rushes out to greet us. "Welcome home, Milord," he says as he helps the General from the vehicle.

"Thank you, Williams. Please ask Lady Alicia to join us in the library."

"Very well, Milord. Shall I have Mrs. Baker bring tea?"

The General glances at his watch and sighs. "The sun is barely over the yardarm. I suppose that will have to suffice."

After the day we've had, I share his wish for something stronger, not to mention a proper meal. But tea is always welcome, and my mouth waters at the sight and smell of the cakes delivered by the aptly named housekeeper-cook.

I manage one delicious bite of a still warm pastry before Alicia charges into the room, throwing herself into the General's arms.

"Oh Father, the most terrible thing has happened," she cries. "I stand accused of working for the Soviets."

"I spoke earlier with Commander Travis. He informed me you were here. We came at once."

"We?" She releases herself from her father's embrace and turns to see me behind her, sitting quietly. "Professor?"

I put down my plate, straighten my clothes as I rise, then run my fingers through my hair, wishing I'd combed it. "Hello again, Miss Rowntree."

"What are you doing here? I thought..."

"The Professor is here as my guest," her father says.

"But why is he *here*, Father? You know my wishes. I do not —"

"Until they bury me beside my parents, I am the lord of this manor, Alicia. I shall entertain as I please. Host whomever I please. The matter is not open for discussion."

"Yes, Father."

"I am sorry to intrude on your privacy, Miss Rowntree," I say, though I'm not sorry at all. I'm so happy to see her again it's difficult maintaining the dour expression the current situation demands. "But I had to return, to complete our mission."

At what point am I going to tell her that completing the mission is merely a means to a personal and selfish end? How can I tell her the truth without further alien-ating her?

"The Professor and I have come from General Eisenhower," her father says. "There's a jolly good chance we've just shortened the war by several months, perhaps as much as a year."

"Wonderful news," she says.

"I'm just sorry that you were collateral dam-age," I say.

She looks at me blankly.

"A modern euphemism… You were caught in the crossfire."

I tell her about Gerasimov and his threats.

"Yet you chose to return. At my expense."

"That wasn't my —" I certainly didn't mean to risk her life, exactly the opposite. But I did secretly hope my efforts would meet with a positive res-ponse. I don't know exactly what. Gratitude. Ad-miration. Something. But if I say any of that I'll piss her off even more.

"To shorten the war, Alicia," says the General. "Risking his own life in the endeavor. The Russian attacked us outside Hartness Street. On our own doorstep, bold as day."

"Oh my. Was anyone hurt?"

"One of my men. Shot in the arm. He will recover."

"And Gerasimov is dead," I add, "so he's no longer a threat."

"We're terribly sorry for landing you in this mess, Alicia," the General says. "I thought by warning Commander Travis I could head off a potentially sticky situation. My intervention seems to have precipitated it instead."

"I was certain they possessed no proof," she says. "Surely you can remedy the situation, Father."

"It will not be easy. Travis seems a decent chap, but I suspect that bloody fool Menzies is involved…"

"He was not only present when they hauled me up, but served as the chief interrogator."

"Then we have our explanation. False accusations are his stock in trade. He sees Bolshevik agents everywhere."

"His paranoia isn't entirely misplaced," I say. "Several Soviet agents are currently active inside British Intelligence."

"Impossible," the General says, his expression despondent despite his protest. "Are you certain?"

He looks at my face. "Of course you are." He pauses, grinding his teeth as he thinks, then his face brightens. "Perhaps we can give Menzies some true communists in exchange for withdrawing these false charges against Lady Alicia. I must have their names."

"Kim Philby, Anthony Blunt, Guy Burgess, John Cairncross, Donald McLean."

"Some of those names ring a bell," Alicia says. "My God, I believe some may be Cambridge men."

"Sorry, they all are. They're known as the Cambridge Five."

"Steady on," the General says. "Did you mention a Donald McLean?"

"I did."

"Son of Sir Donald McLean?"

"I guess so."

"My God. What would motivate a man of his pedigree to turn against his own, to disgrace his family and betray his country?"

"Not to mention tarnishing the good name of my university," says Alicia, her voice dripping with disgust mixed with contempt and disbelief.

"They are true believers," I say. "They share a genuine conviction that communism is the path to a better future."

"The path to a dark future," the General says. "Well, let them hang for their despicable Bolshevik ideals, if they hold them so dear."

"Unfortunately, I have no evidence we can use in 1944," I say. "Even with proof, it won't be that easy. It takes years to remove these men from positions of trust, even after they fall under suspicion, and none are truly held to account. Philby, McLean, and Burgess flee to Moscow evading prosecution, while the authorities allow the other two to resign quietly to avoid a scandal."

"We shall see about that." The General is fuming, his face beet-red, his upper lip and mustache twitching. "The British Empire cannot, will not, tolerate such treachery."

I shrug my shoulders. "All I've got is the historical record."

"But Father, your superiors know about the Professor," says Alicia. "Surely his information must compel them to action."

"After his failure to return last August, the Professor is *persona non grata* with the Chiefs of Staff," her father replies. "And even were they to grant him an audience, they could not act without divulging their source."

"And we promised Eisenhower not to share my story with anyone," I say. "He feels the success of the invasion may depend on keeping this secret."

"I will do what I can behind the scenes to quell their influence," the General says. "But rooting out this ring of spies shall have to wait until we win the war."

Alicia sighs, a sound of a deep resignation, a sign of total surrender. "So the damage is utterly irreparable." There's no anger in her voice, just bitter disappointment.

She stares at the floor as if the pieces of her shattered dreams lie at her feet, mocking her. "After all the sacrifices, my career as a mathematician ends not with a bang but a whimper. Such an ignominious end."

I want to say something to soothe her, but I stay silent. Speaking is only likely to inflame her feelings. And she doesn't give me the chance anyway, fleeing the room in tears before her father or I can say any more.

EIGHTEEN

General Rowntree returns to London and the War Office the same day we arrive at Elverstone Hall.

The following week is one of complete boredom, punctuated only by two visits from Generals Eisenhower and Rowntree seeking more information. In both cases they stay only a few hours.

On the second visit I feel compelled to level with Eisenhower, telling him about the previous Harrys and their myriad failures. Sure, I want to claim success in shortening the war, not only for the lives it will save, but to prove myself to Alicia. But I can't let him make such a momentous decision on my advice without understanding that there are no guarantees about the future. I hope I haven't discouraged him.

The first night I dined with Alicia and her mother, but such was the awkwardness I asked to take my future meals downstairs with the staff.

Lady Elverstone objected, but Alicia supported my request. 'We should not question the ways of our American guest,' she said. 'If such an arrangement will place the Professor at ease…'

I have not seen Alicia since. I don't know how she fills her days, but I spend large chunks of my time in the General's library, reading his extensive collection of classic works. Being surrounded by books nurtures the intellect and the soul, especially important, meaningful books.

But sitting all day is unhealthy, so I punctuate my studies by exploring the grounds of the estate. Now I have the General's trust, I no longer need an armed guard. I wander with no destination or purpose in mind. Alone with my thoughts, I sometimes reflect on what I've read, other times I ponder how to secure the future of these country estates, if possible. But mostly I obsess over the unresolved situation with Alicia.

The first day out I try engaging the estate's farm workers in conversation. Whether they are too busy, or they have as much difficulty understanding my accent as I do parsing theirs, or simply that a farm hand and a history professor have little to discuss, I don't get very far.

After that I satisfy myself with observing the operation of the estate. The work appears even harder than I imagined — farming is far more mechanized in the twenty-first century — and there's a distinct absence of young men to do the heavy lifting, but I find the steady rhythm of farm life relaxing. I especially envy the animals going about their lives without a care in the world.

Each day I walk a little further. Today I avoid the farmers, instead following the path of a small stream running through the estate, the banks thick with rushes teeming with bird life.

Perfect for duck-hunting.

I could return to the house. I'm sure the General owns a shotgun. He probably has an entire armory. But no. Hunting is a ritual here with its proper time and place and form. You don't just grab a gun and start shooting. Anyway, it wouldn't be the same without my father by my side.

I keep walking. After an hour and a half I come to a forest thick with undergrowth. Is this the boundary of the estate? I don't know, but fearing I might become lost in its dark, foreboding interior, I turn around and follow the same path back. Another hour and a half later I ascend a small rise. Elverstone Hall comes into view on the next ridge, framed majestically by the afternoon sun.

How far did I walk in three hours? Ten miles? Fifteen? I have no skill or experience in estimating distances — that's what my phone's GPS is for. Too bad I deliberately left it in 2015.

As I pass the tennis court, I stop and stare at the grand house. Do I really want to go inside? Alicia is in there somewhere. Dare I approach her? Will she hear me out? And what would I say to convince her?

The truth is I don't know the answer to any of these questions. Or if I do, I don't like them. I've had so much time to think, but I still need more. Somehow I must come up with a solution to this seemingly insoluble problem. Failure is not an option.

The benches beside the court are the perfect place for a few minutes of quiet, obsessive contemplation. I sit, lean back and close my eyes, dreaming of the magical moment Alicia and I enjoyed in this very spot. How do I find that engaging young woman who flirted so freely with me then?

— o —

I open my eyes and turn at the sound of footsteps behind me. A man leaning lightly on a walking stick approaches along the path.

I'd pick him anywhere as Alicia's brother, Jonathan, even if I didn't recognize him from my grandparents' wedding photo. My height and weight —

I've been wearing his clothes — he shares his sister's willowy physique. He has her thin neck and long arms and legs, her fair skin and strawberry blond hair, although his bushy mustache is a fiery shade of red.

As he comes closer, I see his right foot dragging slightly. A khaki greatcoat over battle dress and a distinctive maroon beret tell me he's a member of Britain's famous 1st Parachute Brigade. A single gold and red 'crown' on each epaulet marks him as a major. How old is he? Mid-twenties at the most. So much responsibility for someone so young.

"Hello there," he says as he stops in front of me. He points at the empty space on the bench. "Do you mind? Blasted leg is giving me hell."

"Plenty of room." I stand and shake his hand. "You must be Jonathan."

"Major Jonathan Rowntree at your service," he says as we sit. Unable to bend his knee fully, he plops down heavily. "You have me at a disadvantage, Sir."

"Professor Harrison Seely."

He does a double-take. "I wasn't expecting an American invasion, not here. Oh, I won't hold it against you. Are you a guest? You see nobody mentioned you. Or just some rogue who broke in and stole my overcoat? Now that I might hold against you."

"Mr. Williams…" I sputter. "He offered…"

"Well, if Williams approves," he deadpans. Then his face breaks into a broad grin. "You really must call me Jony. Any friend of my sister's is a friend of mine and therefore more than welcome to borrow my coat."

"Harrison." Too formal. He's family. *Great Uncle Jony.* "And you should call me Harry. I'm a guest of your father's. Your sister and I are not…" Not what? Not 'friends'? *Not for want of trying on my part.* "Not that well acquainted."

"Come, come. I've seen that heartbroken expression on many a chap's face. Around here, the cause is invariably my darling sister."

I point at the leg sticking out in front of him. "Bad jump?"

"What makes you say that?"

"It stands to reason." With a nod I indicate his headwear. "You know the Germans call your unit *Die Roten Teufel*. The Red Devils. As a sign of soldierly respect."

"And we wear the title proudly," he says, taking a shallow, seated bow. "But blasted bad luck, I buggered my ruddy knee well and good. It's the home front for yours truly for whatever remains of this war. Brigade Training Officer. He who can, does. He who cannot, teaches." He lifts his stick in the air. "Though it's been four months, I still hope to be free of this wretched thing one day. But I shan't jump again I don't think."

Gazing off into the distance, he adds, "Despite the dodgy knee, I count myself one of the lucky ones."

There's deep pain in his voice. How many men has he lost? Men as young or younger than him. How many letters to bereaved mothers has he written? One would be too many, and I'd bet he's had to send many more than that.

"It must be difficult, losing men under your command, men you're responsible for."

"Responsibility is the nature of leadership, Harry, and loss and sacrifice the nature of war. Which is why armed conflict is not an enterprise to be embarked upon lightly." He takes a deep breath and forces a smile. "To answer your original question, I'm sorry to say it was nothing so heroic. I slipped climbing down the side of a destroyer. Landed like a sack of potatoes in the barge below."

He flexes his right leg, momentarily grimacing in pain, but then chuckles wryly. "It's not right you know. To survive jumps into North Africa and Sicily unscathed, to weather the worst of what Jerry could throw at us in those campaigns, only to be put out of action by the Royal bloody Navy."

"Taranto."

His head jerks back in surprise. "How did you know?"

"I can't think of too many operations where paratroopers landed by ship."

"Yes, well, damn silly business. Much safer jumping out of an aeroplane I say." His brow furrows. "You seem very well informed, old chap. Too clued in to be just another heartbroken suitor to my sister. Perhaps your business truly is with my father. Professor of what? Something quite hush hush. Designing secret weapons or something, I imagine. Well, if you're working to blow Mr. Hitler to kingdom come you have my blessing."

Have his father or sister told him about me, about my secret? They can't have, or he would have known who I was before he sat. My presence here was a surprise to him.

I can't leave him thinking I'm some sort of American Barnes Wallis, inventing wonders like the bouncing bomb. It wouldn't be right. "Nothing so exciting," I say. "Modern History in fact."

He winks at me. "Never fear, your cover story is safe with me."

"I'm afraid you've got it all wrong."

"Perhaps I do have the wrong end of the stick. And perhaps you aren't desperately in love with my sister. But I doubt it."

My face catches fire. I turn away, but not fast enough.

"Aha! Just as I thought. I pity you, old boy. You must be a better man than I, Gunga Din, to even make the attempt."

"I'm surprised to hear you speak about your sister that way."

"Oh I love her dearly, but I doubt Lady Alicia will ever wed. She is more elusive than the Scarlet Pimpernel. Even to her family, Licorice remains an enigma."

My head spins around so fast it almost gives me whiplash. "Your sister is Licorice?"

"Ever since I was two years old and couldn't quite manage to pronounce Alicia," Jony says. "Why do you ask?"

"Just something my gr—" *Whoa. I can't tell him that.* "I heard it somewhere. I knew Licorice was a mathematician, but I didn't realize the reference was to your sister."

Leaning heavily on his stick, he pushes himself to his feet. "Come along."

I stand and follow as he takes a new path, the one around to the left side of the house. I believe it leads to the garage. "Where are we going?"

"Whatever your true purpose here, you look in desperate need of cheering up." He shoots me a wide, mischievous grin. "And I am just the fellow to do it."

— o —

I stand beside the car, an MG, staring at it. It's the sort of old-fashioned machine where you expect the occupants to be wearing goggles and oil-stained overalls. Dark green, with thin, large-diameter spoked wheels at each corner, it is barely the size of a subcompact. The open cockpit sits at the rear behind a long, narrow hood. Making no pretense at being anything but a two-seater, the cabin reminds me of the inside of a bumper car.

Jony is seated behind the wheel, the engine running. "What's the matter, Professor?" he says. "I assure you I can still drive, even with the crippled leg."

I fumble with the door which swings open from

the back, then slip my legs in first before sliding sideways into the seat.

Jony throws the car into gear as soon as I'm in — there's no wait for me to fasten a non-existent seatbelt — and the tiny vehicle leaps from the garage like a racehorse from the starting gate.

We tear along the driveway, the car sticking to the curves like the tires are Velcroed to the asphalt. I've never ridden in a true sports car before, but I can see the appeal of being so connected to the road. Although February isn't the best time for riding in a convertible. Several people have told me they can't remember the weather being so mild this time of year, but it's still as gray and damp as only England can be. I pull Jony's overcoat tighter and higher around my neck to protect my ears from the chill wind.

Out through the front gate, we turn left onto a narrow country lane and he guns the engine.

I tilt my head to the right to see the speedometer. *There's the tachometer. Where's the… That's weird.* They're combined into a single instrument. I study it a minute. *OK, got it.* To read your speed, you have to know which gear you're in…

He pushes the gearstick across and up. Even more impressive than the fluency of his hand movements is the fact the gearbox has no synch-romesh. I've heard about double clutching, but I've never seen it done. He makes it look easy.

The tachometer needle settles back at 40 on the outside ring of the dial, which must indicate 4,000 rpm. According to the inside ring marked **M.P.H. 3rd GEAR**, that's forty-five miles per hour.

The road straightens, and he shifts gears again with two perfectly coordinated pumps of the clutch and downward flicks of his left wrist.

I check the combined instrument again. 4,500 rpm. Sixty-five miles per hour. My teeth clench. It feels like a hundred. My butt can't be more than four inches from the ground, the single-lane road is only ten or twelve feet wide, and the hedgerows perilously close to each side are flashing by in a blur. There's no room for error.

Jony glances over at me. "Relax and enjoy the ride!" he shouts over the throaty whine of the engine.

His wild eyes and crazy grin remind me he's the sort of demented lunatic who likes jumping out of perfectly good airplanes. I want to shout back, *We're about to die*, but what the hell do I have left to lose? Nothing. He's right. Enjoy the ride, for as long as it lasts. "Woohoo, we're flying!" I yell.

He joins in and we're soon whooping and hollering like a pair of over-excited teenagers.

We screech to a halt only a few minutes after leaving Elverstone Hall.

I don't know where we are, but it's not the village of Elverstone. Located at a crossroads, this tiny hamlet consists of no more than seven or eight buildings scattered around the quaint village pub where we are now parked.

The Shearer's Rest looks four or five hundred years old, built in a classic Elizabethan style — sections of whitish daub between an exposed rough timber frame, a steep roof of thatching a foot thick, irregular shaped doors and windows, the latter made from many small, uneven panes, and two chimneys belching smoke, promising relief from the cold.

I climb out and lean on the car. My legs are unsteady, my heart is racing, and my hands are twitchy from the adrenaline pouring through my veins.

He looks at me apologetically.

I rise and straighten my back. "What a blast!" I'm grinning like a kid who just survived the scariest, most thrilling ride in the entire amusement park. "I need a beer or three, to celebrate."

He grins back. "And this is just the place for it." Jony rubs his hands together expectantly. "Come on," he adds as he leads me inside.

— o —

A toasty warmth envelops us as we walk in the door. At 11:15 am on a Tuesday there's only a handful of people in the pub. The interior is dimly lit, the air hazy with smoke from the crackling fires at either end of the room and the cigarettes and pipes most of the occupants are smoking. The ceiling is low enough I keep wanting to duck as I pass under each beam. Every bit as inviting as I hoped.

Everyone, staff and patrons alike, makes a point of greeting Jony as we make our way to a table in the corner, close to a fireplace.

He's clearly a regular here. And well liked. Though they address him as *Milord*, their greetings are warm and friendly. They look at him in his uniform with respect in their eyes, while my civilian attire and long hair elicit wary, disapproving scowls. I suspect I would be unwelcome here if I wasn't in Jony's company.

He signals to the barman and two pints arrive soon after. I bring my glass to my mouth. A pale

ale, malty with just enough hops, it reminds me of *Old Speckled Hen*, a drop I often enjoyed in my past-future days in London.

We pace ourselves, but I'm soon feeling a slight buzz; just enough to take my mind off the impossible situation I'm confronting with Alicia. At the same time, his mood slowly but surely transforms from happy-go-lucky to melancholy. Even the small talk we've been making dries up.

I have to say something. Perhaps I'm overstepping the mark with a guy I've only known for an hour or so, but we are related. And we've just faced the real possibility together of death in a fiery auto crash. "Is the leg getting you down?"

"Not at all." He lifts his glass. "This dulls the pain." He smiles. "I jest. But this will all be over soon enough. Then we shall return to reality. No more jumping from aeroplanes, good leg or bad."

"Do you miss it?"

"The sheer terror of falling from the sky? Not bloody likely. Best to leave the *Boys Own* stuff to the younger lads, I say. But the camaraderie, the special bond with my brothers in arms, I shall miss for the remainder of my days."

I raise my glass. "To brothers in arms."

His glass meets mine. "To brothers in arms."

We both take a generous swig, then in unison, like a choreographed dance, we each wipe the froth from our upper lips with the back of our hands, causing a hearty round of laughter.

"What do you think, Harry? Will we send Mr. Hitler and his Nazi goons packing before the year is out? Wouldn't that be a treat?"

I don't want to say too much, but I don't want him clinging to false hope. "I doubt it." And I don't want to extinguish hope altogether. "But if an invasion takes place this year? Sometime next year, I guess."

"Aren't you a wet blanket."

"Or a realist."

"1944, 1945. Even 1946. That is not the point. Whenever we finally call stumps, have you thought about what comes next?"

I have, but not in the way he means. Do I return to 2015, or do I stay here? There's also the choice of England or America, but that's a trivial detail if Alicia doesn't come around.

"I'm not sure," I say, when what I mean is it depends almost entirely on his sister.

"My parents expected me to read Classics at Oxford, you know."

"You didn't?"

He shakes his head. "I wanted to design aeroplanes, not jump out of them. Aeronautical engineering at Queen Mary University of London, to their enduring horror. They consider engineering 'a trade,' like being a plumber, barely a step above a navvy digging ditches. Nevertheless, I would have stuck it out if not for the war. Enlisted December '39, the day after I finished second year exams."

"Will you go back and finish after the war?"

He shakes his head. "It was a youthful indulgence. Since I was a boy, I knew I was destined to become the 8th Earl of Hamley. But even at twenty I did not truly understand what the title entailed. I thought I could still live my life as I pleased. War forces one to grow up though, rather quickly. I understand my singular burden now."

"And that is?"

"The great estates are dying, Harry. Elverstone is not immune to the forces of change. The place is already running on a shoestring. We have cut the staff to the bone and cannot squeeze the tenants any harder, not if they are to survive. It will fall to me to find the means to preserve the legacy for my heirs, as my ancestors preserved it for me. That will take everything I have. There will be no room to indulge my personal desires."

"It sounds so unfair." In my time living in London as a student I visited many of England's historic estates. Places just like Elverstone Hall. Few remained in private hands. He's in danger of clinging to false hope again. "And hopelessly unrealistic."

"Perhaps it is a fool's errand, Harry. But a man cannot run from his destiny simply because its challenges seem impossible to meet."

— o —

As we approach the car, I step between Jony and the driver-side door. "Are you sure you're OK to drive?" Neither of us is staggering drunk, but he definitely consumed enough to be well over the legal limit in 2015 New Jersey.

He waves away my concern. "I'm perfectly fine, Harry. Perfectly fine."

I matched several of his pints with half pints, so I'm tempted to offer to drive. I've driven on the left before, and I can drive a stick, although I haven't done either in several years.

There's the added complication of the gearstick being on the other side. I close my eyes and visualize shifting gears with my left hand. The real showstopper is the double clutching. We'd be stuck in first gear all the way home. Still, getting in a car with an intoxicated driver…

My lingering unease must show, because he adds, "I'll keep her under forty, how's that?"

I answer by walking around to the passenger side and climbing in. Mildly inebriated and driving slow may well be safer than him going pedal to the metal when stone cold sober.

He keeps his promise, driving back to Elverstone at a comparatively sedate pace. It certainly feels safer than the outbound trip, and we arrive without incident.

As we make our way from the garage into the house, he glances at his watch. "Just enough time for a little something before we dress for dinner." He waves a finger at me. "And none of that nonsense about hiding from my sister downstairs with the staff."

"I have nothing suitable to wear." I can't borrow his tux again, he'll need it, but everyone will understand if I wear my Victory Suit. The truth is I'm searching for excuses.

"We shall find you something that's not too scruffy, old boy. Now, what's your tipple when you're not quaffing ale? Whiskey, brandy, sherry?"

"Whiskey." *If it's anywhere near as good as the cognac…*

But I have something else on my mind, something I must do — speak to Alicia. Jony is right. You can't run away from your fate simply because you feel unequal to its demands. I have to make her listen. "Actually, I think I've had enough for today. Maybe we both have."

For a moment he looks disappointed. Then he smiles and says, "Tea then? For now at least."

Shouldn't I go looking for Alicia? But I have no idea where she is. Perhaps I can grab her right after dinner. "Sure."

"This way." He leads me to the drawing room.

We enter and he rings the bell to call the butler. Mr. Williams arrives so quickly I wonder if he saw us come home and waited somewhere nearby, expecting to be summoned. I'll never get used to that, people hanging on my every need.

The tea ordered, we settle in. When the door opens a few minutes later I look up, anticipation followed immediately by surprise.

Alicia pulls up sharply as she enters. "Oh hello, Jony," she says, while her eyes fix on me in a hostile stare. "Were you expected?"

"Hello, Lic."

He stands and approaches, greeting her with a kiss on the cheek. "My visit is a surprise. I found myself at a loose end for a couple of days. We're about to take a spot of tea. Will you join us?"

Alicia rocks back and forth as she decides whether to come or go. Will the pull of her brother's company outweigh the push of my presence?

Seeing her brother again wins. She moves gracefully across the room, taking a seat opposite him, the one furthest from me. "I see you and Professor Seely are acquainted."

"Harry and I spent a most delightful afternoon getting to know each other at a public house."

She glares at him. "Are you drunk?"

"Not at all."

"And you, Professor Seely?"

"Steady on," Jony says. "Your Professor was the picture of moderation."

"He is Father's guest, not *my Professor*. "

"Harry did mention that, though I don't entirely buy it."

Jony looks at me, then back at his sister, studying our faces, assessing the obvious tension in the room. "I believe you two have unfinished business," he says as he stands, "and I must inform Mother that the prodigal son has returned."

NINETEEN

We sit engulfed in a heavy silence. *What was Jony thinking?* It is almost as if he knows of my unusual connection to the Professor. Did Father say something? Has he seen Jony recently?

When the tea arrives, I dismiss Mrs. Baker, insisting to her surprise that I will serve. Much as I would prefer not to be alone with the Professor, he appears anxious. In such a state, I fear he will say something indiscreet in her presence.

The Professor's eyes follow me as I pour the tea — milk and one sugar cube for each of us — and pass him a cup and saucer.

"You remembered," he says.

"I beg your pardon?"

"How I like my tea. You remembered."

He seems inordinately pleased by the fact. "It was quite easy to recall," I say, "given you take yours as I take mine."

"I suppose."

He looks into his cup as I wait for him to speak.

"I suggest you get on with it, Professor. Say what you feel you must and let us finally dispose of this… Jony said it best. This unfinished business between us."

"What is it you desire, Miss Rowntree?"

"At the risk of seeming indelicate, I believe my Father already relayed my wish to be free of your attentions."

"I meant to say, what is it you desire for yourself? From your life?"

"To be a mathematician."

"Then you're in luck. Do you know what my grandmother did in America?"

I shake my head.

"Alice Seely—she adopted what she thought was a more American name—taught Math at Princeton. I don't know enough about her or the field to tell you how important her research was, but she retired a full Professor. I suspect for a woman to progress so far in that day and age, she must have been pretty damn good."

It does sound impressive, but modesty prevents me saying so.

"Is that not what you aspire to?" he says.

"It is unthinkable now, when my reputation lies in ruins at your hands."

The Professor recoils at my harsh attack. Though uncalled for—he only acted as I insisted he act — offending him serves my goal of driving him away forever. But to my disgust, I am enjoying the pain I inflict; savouring the power I have to wound him distracts me from my despair.

"They have no evidence," he says. "Your rehabilitation is only a matter of time."

"If only I could be so confident. I have no means of proving my innocence."

"Do you not want to be happy?"

"That is an impertinent question, Professor. And ridiculous. Of course I desire happiness. But I believe wholeheartedly that it cannot be gained without control of one's own destiny."

"I know how you feel. I really do."

"How can you?"

"Do you think I don't also feel like a pawn in some cosmic chess game? Looking back, I realize how thoroughly Harry manipulated me. It was my grandfather who encouraged me to study military history. He even paid my tuition at Stanford. He knew I would love it, but more than that, he knew I needed it to complete his plan. But it goes back further than that. Much further. He went with my parents to the orphanage. They picked me of all the children there. I doubt that was a coincidence. So you see, my entire life is his creation."

"Then you should do as I intend. Tread your own path, not one set out by your grandfather."

"I can't," he moans.

"Do you believe your fate is already decided, that your actions are not your own to choose? I cannot, I will not, accept that proposition."

"I really don't know what to believe. My actions, my decisions, they sure as hell feel like free will at the time. And if I can't tell the difference, what does it really matter?"

He removes something from his pocket—a photograph—and passes it to me. "But our actions, whether freely chosen or not, have consequences for which we must accept responsibility."

"What is this?" I say, though I recognize myself and the Professor, both a few years older, and can infer the identity of the boy. The babe in arms is presumably the Professor's uncle or aunt. It is a picture of a smiling, contented family.

"You have made a choice that leads to a different future," he says. "One in which my father— *our son*—ceases to exist. I thought you should see what you are giving up."

"This is an underhand move, Professor."

"All I ask is that you give me a chance. Keep an open mind on the possibility of…" He points at the photograph, still in my hand. "I'm begging you to reconsider, for our son's sake."

I cannot let this continue. If I do, I shall weaken. Who would not, confronted by such a heartrending plea? "Debating metaphysics is all very interesting, Professor, but I have heard nothing to sway my opinion. Now that I have granted you your chance, I would kindly thank you to honour my wishes and take your leave."

— o —

I expect the Professor to argue, to beg, to ignore my plea to go. Instead, he stands without saying a word, though he stares longingly into my eyes.

I turn my face away. "Your photograph," I say, holding it at arm's length.

"You keep it. As a reminder of the consequences." He turns and walks off, an angry, defeated man. I hate to see him so broken, but he will forget me soon enough.

I place the photograph face down on the tea table. Jony pokes his head through the door soon after. I can only assume he was waiting outside for the Professor to leave.

"May I enter?" he says.

"I always welcome your company, silly."

"I only ask because I saw Harry outside, poor blighter. I thought I might be stepping into the lion's den."

"It has been the most trying time, Jony, but I promise not to maul you."

He crosses the room and sits beside me. "Tell me what is troubling you, Lic."

I am at a loss. How could I possibly make him understand? Where would I begin?

"I've seen you break hearts before," he says, "but that poor beggar looked like a widower at his wife's funeral. And I see the same pain etched on your face too. What on earth have you two done to torture each other so?"

"Please, Jony…"

"Is your concern Mother and Father? You know I will support you to the hilt."

"You always do. But that is not the cause of my hesitation. Father has taken the Professor somewhat under his wing. I believe he would approve of such a union. And Mother simply longs to see me married. Any man with a pulse would suffice."

"Then what is the impediment? I've never seen you look at any man the way you look at him, with such admiration. Who the blazes is he, Lic?"

"He is no one. He works with Father. His presence here is not my affair."

Jony takes my hand in his. "I will not rest until you provide a reasonable explanation."

Should I tell him? 'A burden shared is a burden lightened' they say, and who better than my brother to lighten my load? There are two billion or so people in this world, at least in 1943, but none I love or trust more than Jony. Surely Father will understand if I share the Professor's secret with him.

"What do you know of this Professor Harrison Seely?" I say.

"That he's American, obviously, though not condescending towards we English as so many of them are."

"Quite the contrary. He is actually something of an Anglophile."

"Yes, that did catch my attention. An academic, I assume of modest means. Whatever he is doing must be of the utmost importance to demand so much of Father's time. Perceptive and knowledgeable. An all-round fascinating chap."

"Did you find him agreeable?"

"Oh, he's a jolly good sport. Quite unlike the bounders who have come courting you before. Though I spent only a few hours in his company, he put me quite at ease. Made me feel better about my lot than I have in some time. This will sound peculiar, but he almost felt like family."

There is my opening if I mean to speak.

I take a deep breath then exhale sharply. "Not peculiar at all. You see, he is."

Jony looks perplexed.

"Family, that is."

"Perhaps that explains why Father has taken such an interest in him. Descended from some ne'er-do-well relative who emigrated to the New World chasing his fortune, I expect."

"Nothing like that." I gather the photograph from the table and pass it to Jony without looking at it. I cannot bear to do so. "The boy is Harrison's father. His parents—"

"You and Harry!"

His eyes dart from the photo to me and back again, finally coming to rest on me. "Forgive me, Lic, for so rudely interrupting. But they look uncannily like you and—"

"Your initial assessment was entirely accurate. This *is* a photograph of Harrison and me, and our yet-to-be-born children."

His face asks how that is possible.

"Your chum Harry is from the future."

Jony's lips shape an objection.

I hold up a hand. "Before you tell me how ridiculous I sound, let me say it is a future Father and I and General Eisenhower have all seen with our own eyes."

For the next hour I tell my brother everything: about the Professor and his six predecessors; how they travelled between the present and the year 2015; how Harrys One to Six tried to change the course of the war for the better, with mixed results; how this incarnation of Harrison, the seventh, is trying again; what I learned about the future and his modern values, especially his attitudes to women; and finally about the life and profession awaiting me — *Alice Seely* — in America.

"Why would you turn your back on that, Lic?" His expression is even more incredulous than when I showed him the picture, or claimed Professor Seely to be from the future. "It sounds like everything you ever desired."

"Because I cannot countenance the idea that my future is already determined, that others have charted my life's course for me."

He stares back at me.

Oh, what a ridiculous thing to say to Father's heir. "I apologise. That was quite thoughtless."

"No harm done. Being shot at by the Wehrmacht thickens the skin. Anyway, I have reconciled myself to my station. More than reconciled. I stand ready to embrace it."

My tea is tepid by now, but I take another sip while I consider his answer. "But how do you convince yourself to look forward with anticipation to a life of such predictability and limited choices?"

"None of us are truly free." He stands and paces about the room. "Do I really have fewer options than the son of a charwoman born into poverty? Or the daughter of an accountant, destined for a comfortable but humdrum middle class existence?"

Jony spins on his heels, facing me. "We each have our unique burdens and our special blessings, Lic. It is what we make of them that is the measure of our lives."

I hang my head in my hands. "I may have made the most foolish mistake." I look up, imploringly. "Have I made a mistake, Jony?"

He grimaces. "To ask the question, dear sister, is to answer it."

"Oh Lord, it is. I have. A terrible mistake."

"Take heart, Lic," he says. "It isn't too late to reverse course."

TWENTY

The car slows. I lean forward and rap the glass partition with the back of my hand.

Henderson turns his head, glancing over his shoulder. "Professor?"

"Why are we stopping?"

He points to an approaching staff car. "Lord Elverstone, Sir."

The black Rolls Royce and khaki Humber pull up next to each other, facing in opposite directions, blocking the narrow road. Fortunately, there's no other traffic on this country lane, though I suspect any locals who came along would wait patiently for the lord of the manor to move.

The General lowers his window. I slide across the seat and do the same.

"I have come from Norfolk House, Professor. Today General Eisenhower announced that 'due to a shortage of landing craft' the invasion will be delayed until June 5."

"That is good news."

"It is smashing news. Now, where are you off to? We must celebrate."

"The railway station, then Kensington, and then Princeton."

"Nonsense, my boy. I will have none of that. You must return to Elverstone Hall at once. I have something rather special put away for an occasion such as this." He smiles and raises his eyebrows invitingly. "You must try this divine single malt. Seventy-five years old. Perfect with a cigar, though I guarantee you will still enjoy it immensely without."

For a moment I consider sticking around, giving his single malt, and Alicia, another try. But I gave it my best shot with her and failed dismally. And no drink, even if it's better than his amazing cognac, could be worth reprising such a comprehensive rejection.

"I'm sorry, Sir, but my work here is done. I must return home. Where I belong." *Belong? With a family I don't even know? But it's more than I have here.*

"You have abandoned all hope of a rapprochement with Lady Alicia?"

"The situation is beyond hope, General."

"Many said so of Britain in her darkest hour, when the Nazi wave was licking at our shores and seemed set to overwhelm us. Yet here we are on the verge of our long hoped for victory."

"We shall never surrender."

"And we did not. Events vindicated Mr. Churchill's call for fortitude and intransigence," he says. "I hate to see you run up the white flag, Professor. You are welcome to stay as long as you desire... If for no other reason than to see how the remaining days of the war unfold."

"That's a very generous offer, General, but staying here is pointless. The harder I try engaging Lady Alicia, the more I push her away."

He sighs knowingly. "Unfortunately, women are the most challenging of all foes. We will defeat Mr. Hitler with bombs and bullets, but we cannot win the battle of the sexes by force, or even force of will."

"No. Even though I know it's meant to be, I can't make her love me."

"Well, it is a damned shame to see you go. I am at a loss to express the full extent of my gratitude, or England's debt to you. If there is anything I can do before you leave us, anything at all. Anything not involving the affections of my headstrong daughter."

"There is one small favor."

"Anything, my good man."

"It might seem a strange request, but I need the services of a stockbroker…"

He leans forward and speaks to Corporal Jones, who nods then climbs out and opens my door. "Come along," the General says, summoning me into his staff car. "I know just the man. We shall go up to London this very minute."

TWENTY-ONE

I jump to my feet and ring for the butler who appears promptly. "Williams, would you kindly ask Professor Seely to join us? I believe he retired to his quarters."

Mr. Williams' return takes longer than expected, and he is alone. "I am sorry, Milady, but the Professor's room is vacant. I am informed he is no longer in residence. Henderson is driving him to the railway station as we speak."

"Thank you, Williams," I say, dismissing him. I turn to Jony. "What am I to do?"

"Grab your coat, Lic. A heavy one. And a hat and gloves. Meet me out front."

I hesitate, unsure what he is proposing.

"Look lively!"

I leap to my feet and rush to the cloakroom where I gather my warm things. As I wait outside the entrance, I rub my hands together and stomp my feet. The air is not terribly cold for this time of year, but I feel frozen to my core.

The MG screeches to a halt not two feet in front of me. Jony pushes my door open. "Jump in!"

We race along the driveway, a gloved hand resting atop my woollen cap to hold it in place. I usually avoid riding with my brother. He drives much too fast for my comfort. But today I exhort him to go faster still.

In a flash we're at the station. I jump out the moment the car stops and dart up the stairs, across the bridge, and down the steps to the far side where the London-bound trains stop.

I peer up and down the length of the platform, hoping that by some miracle…

The station's only occupant is a thin, stooped man dressed in a baggy, rumpled railway worker's uniform and wielding a broom and dustpan. He does not look up from his sweeping.

I rush over to him. "The London train?" I puff.

The feeble-looking man does not answer, but simply goes on with his task of collecting the rubbish, mostly discarded cigarette butts.

Jony is now at my side. "Has it departed already, man?" he says in his officer's voice, strong and commanding.

The worker looks up, cupping his hand behind his ear. "Eh?"

"Has the London train been through?" Jony says, louder this time.

"The London train?" the man shouts. "Aye, you only just missed it. Never mind, another one will be through in 'alf an hour."

I deflate like a balloon pricked with a pin. Love has slipped through my fingers because I refused to hold it tight when I had the chance.

"Come on, Lic." Jony grabs my hand, pulling me behind him as he runs.

A northbound train thunders by below us as we recross the pedestrian bridge. "Where are we going?" I yell over the din.

"London. We may still reach Hartness Street before Harry — if I drive like the wind!"

— o —

Mrs. Collins must see us arrive because she opens the door before we reach the top of the stairs.

"Milord, Milady, I weren't expecting you today." She looks flustered. While Father comes and goes as he pleases, it is usual for Jonathan or I to give Mrs. Collins some notice. "Are you staying?"

"Has the Professor been here, Mrs. Collins?" I say as we follow her inside. Normally I would say something reassuring, but I am preoccupied with my current mission.

"Professor Seely? No, Milady. I've not seen him since the shooting last week. Ooh, terrible business that."

"Then there's nothing to do but wait," Jony says. "I'm sure he'll be here soon enough. Mrs. Collins, we will take tea in the sitting room."

"Very well, Milord," she says then rushes away.

"Come on." He turns towards the front room. "We'll see him arrive from in here."

By the time we finish our tea, I am growing anxious. "Where is he, Jony? Is it possible he reconsidered and returned to Elverstone Hall?"

"Sounds like wishful thinking, but I'll check." He stands and goes to the telephone, returning a few minutes later.

I look at him expectantly, though his face already tells me the news is not what I hope for. "Is he there?"

"Henderson reports that Harry did not take the train. They encountered Father in his staff car soon after they turned into Fletcher Lane. The Professor returned to London with Father."

"Perhaps they had business at the War Office."

"I checked already," Jony says. "Father left for Norfolk House mid-morning and has not been seen since."

"Perhaps they are with Eisenhower."

"Eisenhower? Supreme Commander of Allied Forces in Europe? Truly?"

"Norfolk House is his HQ."

"What business would they have there?"

"I do not know, but they have met with Eisenhower repeatedly over the past few weeks."

"What are they working on?" He shakes his head. "Never mind. I knew it was something momentous, but Ike? Well, I can't just call and ask, me a lowly Major. Even if they did put me through, when word got back to my CO that I was bothering General Eisenhower…" Jony clicks his tongue and makes a slicing motion with his finger across his throat.

I stand. "Then I will telephone Eisenhower's office myself. Surely they will be sympathetic to a distressed daughter trying to locate her father."

I expect Jony to object, but he does not speak. I turn to find him staring out the window.

"Jony?"

His head whips around. "Lic, they're here."

Peering into the darkness outside, I narrow my eyes. They are there, on the landing. Father and Harrison, shaking hands.

Saying goodbye. *Please, it is not too late…*

I run to the front door and tug it open, so hard it bangs against the stop. "Harrison, I beg your forgiveness, though I do not —"

My legs collapse under me and I slump against Father.

"I am sorry, Alicia," he says as he holds me upright. "Professor Seely is gone."

TWENTY-TWO

BA-BOM. BA-BOM. BA-BOM. My pulse pounds in my temples and my head feels like a giant walnut being squeezed in an enormous nutcracker.

I open my left eye first. Dark wood, almost too close to focus. Then my right eye. My leather suitcase lies on its side. I release the fingers still wrapped around the handle. A foot in front of me is a dark baseboard trimming a pale cream wall. I'm home, in my grandfather's house. My house.

My mouth is dry as chalk and there's something in my mustache and beard. When I wipe my chin with my hand, flecks of dried blood stick to my fingers. I raise my head. A dark magenta pool the size of a quarter lies beneath my face. Grandpa Harry wasn't exaggerating; at 34 to 1 the transition is brutal.

My head is clearer now but my eyes ache, like someone is viciously pressing their thumbs into the sockets. How long have I been lying here? An hour? Two? Longer? The last thing I remember is…

What is the last thing I remember?

Shaking General Rowntree's hand.

I have no memory of stepping through the door. But I must have. I'm here.

With my palms flat against the floor, I push myself up until I'm on hands and knees. I let my head hang between my shoulders and the blood return to my addled brain.

Shakily I climb to my feet. The letter to my parents — Jon and Deb — is still sitting on top of the side table. Where else would it be? I failed. They'll never see it now. I grab the envelope and rip it in half, place the two halves together and tear it in half again. I place the four pieces together again, but the pile is too thick to tear. In frustration and disgust I toss them on the floor.

I open the drawer and retrieve my phone. *5 am Tuesday, July 28*. Two weeks elapsed in London, but just under four hours have passed here since I left with Generals Rowntree and Eisenhower. It gets weirder every time.

On unsteady legs I wobble my way to the bathroom and look in the mirror. Hell, I've seen professional boxers with prettier noses. With the tip of my finger I gingerly touch mine.

"OWW!" *Broken again, damn it.*

Carefully avoiding my nose, I clean the dried blood from my face with a washcloth before

heading to the kitchen to quieten my roiling stomach. No surprise that I'm hungry — it was dinnertime when I left London and it's almost breakfast
here. Either way, time to eat.

I could use a change from tea, so I throw a
capsule in the coffee machine, turn on the air conditioning, then make a peanut butter and jelly sandwich, something you don't get in England and
about all I can manage given the limited contents of
my refrigerator.

While eating my breakfast-dinner, I try to decide what's next. After the ordeal I've been through
I should rest, but I have to keep moving. If I don't,
there's a real danger I'll descend into a dark despair. I'm definitely interested to know how history,
the new history, turned out. But that requires a
clarity of thought I can't muster right now.

Anyway, it can wait. I have a great deal of dil-
igent study ahead if I'm to be ready to teach this
changed history in the fall.

Hell, that's only four weeks from now.

I'll start fresh tomorrow, after I get some sleep.

What about my investment, a Dow Jones-linked
mutual fund? I don't really understand what it is,
I just know what it's called. Mr. Wilkinson, the
General's stockbroker, was reluctant to sell me this

'rather radical product,' concerned about the inferior returns of a passive investment strategy.

Only when the General insisted did the broker acquiesce. Then, demonstrating the discretion British financiers are famous for, he simply explained what my heirs would need to do to cash it in seventy years hence, as if that was a request he dealt with regularly.

He also suggested I track its value in *The Wall Street Journal*, but with a second cup of coffee in hand, I go to my computer and do a Google search instead. It is a simple matter of finding the selling price and multiplying that by the number of units I purchased in 1944.

I can't expect to be as successful as Harry was when he bought IBM stocks and then traded them for Apple and Microsoft shares when the time was right. Unlike his investments, mine had to run on auto-pilot for the past seventy years. But I'm still quietly confident it will be enough.

The unit price doesn't register as I enter it into the calculator. It's just a number. But when I enter the total units and hit the 'equals' button, the answer knocks me for six as the Brits would say. I don't understand how it happened, but my £225 investment is now worth over half a million dollars!

— o —

I wake with a start. Where am I? How did I get here?

I sit up and look around. *I'm on the couch.* But why is it dark? I only planned to close my eyes for a minute. That was the middle of the morning. So I've slept several hours. My body clock must still be keyed to London time.

I'm wide awake now. I may as well get to work. I turn on a lamp and head to the kitchen to put the kettle on, then move to the dining room.

Harry's notes are where I left them, spread across the table, along with a dozen or so reference books.

I find an introductory textbook of twentieth century history and scan the table of contents. It's not the same one I use for teaching freshmen classes — that book, like the timeline it documented, no longer exists — but it's perfect for my current purposes, being organized chronologically, not thematically like more advanced texts.

I flick through the pages until I come to the events of 1944: D-Day landings on June 6; the breakthrough at Falaise in late August; the subsequent rapid Allied advance across France; stalling in the fall; as winter hits, 'The Battle of the Bulge,' a last, desperate German counter-offensive.

I compare them with Harry's notes. The events described in the textbook precisely match the timeline Harry One messed with and that Grandpa Harry wanted me to restore. That I did restore. *Shit*. This new timeline is my responsibility.

I remember the kettle, boil it again, then make tea. Returning to the book, I keep reading into 1945. Germany surrendered in May, the Japanese in August. That's consistent with the pre-Harry One timeline, but Harry didn't tell me about the nukes we dropped on Japan. 200,000 civilian deaths, utterly devastated cities, horribly maimed survivors.

But invading Japan in my timeline cost nearly two million lives, more than half of them Japanese civilians. And no atomic bombs dropped on Germany, saving another million people. Even more could have been saved had Germany and Japan accepted their inevitable defeats sooner, but that is on them.

I jump forward twenty or thirty pages to the 1950s. A war in Korea. Eisenhower elected President! *I'll be damned*. What sort of President was he? That's not relevant right now. There will be plenty of time to explore that and a dozen other interesting questions. Perhaps even write a paper using my inside knowledge.

Back to the book and the 1960s. Another proxy war, this time in Vietnam. None of that happened in my timeline; the Soviet Union was too stretched — controlling continental Europe and trying to foment revolution in the United Kingdom — to confront the US elsewhere. Conversely, the Pakistan-India conflicts in this timeline are mere skirmishes compared to the seven-year-long all-out struggle I'm familiar with, a war that killed tens of millions.

I sit back and take a deep, satisfied breath. Far fewer people have died unnecessary deaths in this timeline than the one I knew. But it isn't just the casualties. The further I read, the closer I move to the present, the more this world seems a better place. Western Europe avoided Soviet domination altogether, and then the Soviet Union collapsed at the end of the 1980s!

I thought I would never live to see that day, but in the end the USSR just folded like a house of cards. Incredible. Twenty-five years ago! Hundreds of millions of people, an entire generation, free from an oppressive totalitarian dictatorship. Even China, while still ruled by the Communist Party, seems to be Marxist in name only.

I may be rushing to judgment. My opinion may change with further study — probably more than once, I am a professional historian after all — but I'd say I've done good. Something to be proud of, even if I can't tell anyone. If only it hadn't come at such a high personal price…

— o —

My phone rings. I glance at the display. 'Mom and Dad' again. I let it go to voicemail. But unless I move house, change jobs, and assume a new identity — in short, live the rest of my life like I'm in witness protection — I'll eventually have to face them. If not them, then my new sister. Jenny could turn up on my doorstep any moment.

I wish they'd stop calling. It's hard to grieve for a Mom who will never know you and a Dad who never existed, especially when a nice, friendly couple who sincerely believe *they* are your parents keep bugging you.

Though perhaps I should embrace my new family. That and my profession are all I have left.

And half a million dollars.

Hell, I ought to be dancing for joy. Money is no longer a problem and I'm already thinking of ways to leverage my unique perspective on the history of wartime Britain to turbocharge my career. But I'd give it all up to see my real parents again.

You can't keep wishing for something you can't have, Harry.

I turn my attention back to the history books. I've completed a quick pass through the new history of the second half of the twentieth century. Now I'm going over it again in more detail, this time considering multiple accounts. Eventually I will compare these secondary sources with the primary documents. Publishing my own findings ought to keep me busy for a few years and hopefully secure me tenure.

Reviewing the campaign to liberate France — from D-Day through August 1944 — takes the entire afternoon. Commentators disagree on the scale of the opportunity lost at Falaise, but I lean toward sympathy for Monty. It's easy to speculate on how he could have acted more aggressively and fully encircled the Germans trapped there. But day-after-victory generals aren't any more heroic than Monday morning quarterbacks.

A war historian must step into the shoes of the commander on the ground, with all the constraints such a position entails: the terrain; the morale of his men; his equipment and supplies; and most of all the lack of knowledge about enemy forces. From the vantage point of the future, the fog of war is often nothing but a light mist. It's easy to forget it can appear an impenetrable cloud at the time. Whatever the plan, the enemy gets a vote too, and it's a secret ballot. You often don't know what he's going to do until he's doing it.

September 1 seems a logical place to take a break, so I stop to hit the gym. After returning home to a shower and a dinner of Thai takeout, I decide to fit in a couple more hours before bed. I'll just cover September 1944.

At midnight I'm still going, wondering how Eisenhower and Montgomery could have blundered so badly.

Despite my contempt for 20-20 hindsight, I have to conclude that MARKET GARDEN was strategically misconceived. Not only did it focus on an irrelevant objective, it was poorly planned and badly executed. Yet even so, with a bit of luck it could have succeeded.

If not for the Panzer units unexpectedly resting and refitting in the area, the men of the British 1st Parachute Brigade might just have pulled it off. Not that it would have mattered. Monty's forces couldn't have exploited a bridgehead without adequate supplies.

The 1ˢᵗ Parachute Brigade! Jonathan Rowntree's unit. How did I miss that? Thank God for his 'dodgy' knee. But how many friends and comrades did he lose? It must have eaten at him, not being there with them.

It takes me less than ten minutes to pull up the Commonwealth War Graves Commission's casualty lists for the action at Arnhem.

There are over six hundred dead, mostly paras, men Jony would have known. His commanders. His subordinates. His friends. I click through to page 33 to find the surnames beginning with 'R' though his name won't... *No! He wasn't supposed to jump again. Why did he jump? He didn't have to.*

I Google his name, looking for some explanation. The first link is to the British Newspaper Archive and an article from *The Warwick and Warwickshire Advertiser* dated September 27, 1944. Makes sense since Elverstone is in Warwickshire.

Thankfully, I'm already subscribed to the site—old newspapers are a historian's best friend. Actually, the cost doesn't matter now. It will take some getting used to being able to spend money freely.

The newspaper print is small and the quality of the scanned image isn't great. It takes me a minute or two to realize it's not an obituary for Jonathan.

Tragedy has struck Lord and Lady Elverstone for the second time this week. After their only son, Lord Jonathan Rowntree, was killed in action in Holland on 20 September, their only daughter, Lady Alicia Rowntree died at 1.12 am yesterday, the result of a direct V1 'doodlebug' strike on Lord Elverstone's London townhouse.

I read it and read it again. The words don't change.

I stand and walk away, returning to the computer to read the article one more time. Then I print it, wandering absently through my house with the article in my hand, glancing periodically at the dark, blotchy letters and shaking my head.

After three or four laps through the dining room, kitchen, and living room I slump into the couch. I screw the paper into a tight ball and hurl it across the room. It bounces off the buffet's glass doors, but I wish it had smashed them into a hundred tiny pieces, shattering the glass the way my heart has been shattered.

— o —

"Sonofabitch," I shout at the gin bottle I'm holding upside-down over a glass. *Empty sonofabitch bottle.* I don't even like gin that much. Still wish it wasn't empty. Like all the other bottles in the sink. I add the gin bottle to the pile. Wish they weren't empty either. Especially the whiskey bottles.

I open the fridge. No beer. The liquor cabinet! Look in the liquor cabinet!

I open the door.

Empty. Empty as the bottles. Emptier. Empty as my soul.

I raise myself on my toes to see all the way in back on the top shelf. Not a drop. I slam the cabinet door shut and lean against the kitchen bench.

I'm not responsible for their deaths. The Germans killed them. Both of them. German murderers. Bastard Germans. How can I be…

Hey, there's a wet patch on the front of my shirt. I pull a handful of the material up to my nose. Whiskey. What a waste. Hope it wasn't the good stuff. It's all good stuff. And I need more…

The liquor store will have plenty of booze. They never run out. That's their job. I pat my pockets. Car keys? Where are they?

The floor moves as I make my way across the kitchen. Earthquake? Or am I drunk? Or is it an earthquake? Only joking. I'm drunk. As a skunk. Ha ha. I'm funny.

Pull yourself together, Harrison. Check the basket where you always leave your keys.

There they are. Wait. That's not my Subaru keyring. This one has a blue and white symbol on the fob. I pick it up.

Try to focus.

BMW. Never heard of that brand. BMW... BMW... I remember now. Motorcycles. The Wehrmacht used BMW motorcycles.

German!

They killed them. The Germans killed them.

"Why the hell would I want a German car?" I mutter to myself. "Who wants a car made by Nazi murderers?"

I swing my arm wildly, tossing the keys. They bounce off the dining room wall and land somewhere under the table. *Stupid.* I get down on hands and knees. Gotta find my keys.

What time is it? I look up at the clock. 6 am. How did it get to be so late? So early. The store won't be open now. Or will it? I don't know the New Jersey liquor laws yet.

It won't. No more alcohol. Good. Nothing but trouble. I should hit the sack. I try to stand, but overbalance and land on my ass. Hard. I laugh maniacally. *Good thing I'm smashed or it woulda hurt...*

I rest my back against the wall, bring my knees to my chest and bury my face in my hands. They're dead. Both of them. Alicia and Jonathan both dead.

I raise my eyes to the ceiling. "IT'S NOT MY FAULT!"

What about your parents? That's your fault.

I roll over onto my side and lie on the floor, tears running sideways down my face, dripping onto the polished wood where they form perfect little circles of brine.

It is my fault. They're dead because of me. All of them...

—o—

My God, something is pressing against my face. Suffocating me!

I recoil, shaking and lifting my head.

It's just a pillow.

I'm spreadeagled face down on top of my bed, fully clothed. My shirt is stuck to my back and my hands and face are greasy with sweat. I had the air conditioning on last night. In the kitchen and dining room. Must not have turned it on in here.

I don't remember going to bed though I do recall being rolling drunk. Or parts of it. None of them pretty. It would have been embarrassing if I wasn't alone.

I take a deep breath. *Ewww*. My clothes reek of sweat and stale booze. And fresh despair. Alicia and Jonathan are gone, and so are my parents.

I grab my phone from the bedside table. 7.13 pm. I sit up, pressing my palm against my forehead. "Ohhhh." My stomach does a somersault.

Note to self: don't ever get that smashed again. Though I'd happily make a drunken fool of myself in public if it would help me forget the image of Alicia's broken body buried beneath a massive mound of rubble. Her unmoving eyes stare at me accusingly, no longer sparkling green but leaden and lifeless, her fair skin even paler with death.

It's not my fault. What can I do about it anyway? It's in the past. Happened already. History.

Emptying my mind of Alicia and Jonathan only leaves a void into which thoughts of my parents rush. *Damn.*

There's no hope for bringing them back — I have to accept that — but there is something I don't get. My actions in the past can change history. I've proved it. And I understand that my failure to win Alicia's heart means Harry and Alice never marry and have a son named Jon, my father. But I had decided not to return to the past even before I visited my parents. So why hadn't the timeline already changed by then? The McMansion should have been there in place of their house the first time I drove to Pittsburgh.

Think, Harrison. What are you missing?

I leap from the bed. Too fast. I spread my feet wide and grasp the footboard, waiting for my head to stop spinning. As soon as I can stand upright without support, I stumble to my office, pick up the remote, then turn the AC on and dial it up to full power.

I stare at my desk for a minute, then rush forward to hunt for the photo. My hands move frantically across the cluttered surface, shuffling the papers. Several documents fall to the floor before I find the picture of Harry and my dad with Eisenhower. I pick it up and examine it, narrowing my eyes as I look closely at the boy, studying every feature of his face.

Shit. I can't be sure that's my father.

What if it's Geoff?

Then that could also be him in the other photo with Harry and Alice. And the baby would be his sister, Harriet. Finally the pictures make sense. At least these small pictures do. The big picture? Not so much.

What did I do between leaving Pittsburgh and receiving the call from Geoff and Carol that could have changed the timeline? Was it deciding not to return? Or was it deciding to go back? Or was it something else entirely, something not even under my control? I don't understand anything about how this works, about the process of cause and effect, if it even makes sense to think of things that way.

I smash my fist into the desk. I have no way to know if there's still a chance to save my parents, and if there is, to determine what I need to do, here or in the past.

It's hopeless, utterly hopeless.

But I do know one thing. I can save Alicia. Well, nothing is guaranteed—she could be run down crossing the road—but saving her from the V1 seems easy enough. Just keep her away from Hartness Street. Away from London altogether would be even better. A few minutes of research confirms the V1s lack the range to reach Elverstone Hall.

Then there's Jonathan. If I do this, I'm going to save him too, though that's a lot tougher. His sense of duty and honor means he'll keep putting himself in harm's way as long as the war continues.

So end the war.

Antwerp is the obvious leverage point, not only to bring the war to a speedy conclusion, but to avoid the specific battle where Jony died. No MARKET GARDEN means no Arnhem, and no senseless slaughter of six hundred paras including Major Jonathan Rowntree.

It would also neutralize the V1 launch sites in Belgium and Holland before the fatal strike on the townhouse takes place.

Wait. What's the date in London now? How long since I came back? Two days, twelve, no fourteen, hours and… roughly twenty minutes. Multiply that by 34.

I grab a pen and paper and start calculating.

Argh! With a frantic left-right motion of the pen I scribble over my flawed arithmetic.

I'm trying to be too precise, working out hours and minutes. All I'm doing is tying myself in knots.

I round it down to an even two days, then redo the calculations. Much simpler. I have an answer in no time. It should be mid or late August there now.

It'll be tight. British forces are due to capture Antwerp on September 4. I can do it. But should I?

The Harrys — all six of them — learned the hard way that unintended consequences can bite you on the ass. Now I've put the timeline back the way it was always meant to be, would I be making the mistake they made?

Like Herodotus, 'the Father of History,' my job is to make inquiries, *historia*, to discover a history that already exists, not to create it. But I'm no longer sure an objective history exists independent of my actions. And if the course of history is what I decide it will be, I refuse to let it crash like a hurtling V1 or a whistling German bullet into the lives of Alicia and Jonathan Rowntree.

— o —

Eisenhower had to know Monty's plan was flawed. Yet he approved it. So I'll need overwhelming evidence to convince him to kill it.

I spend the rest of the evening and all the following day at the University library, conducting

the necessary research, synthesizing the conclus-
ions of multiple historians, and printing over a
thousand pages of source documents.

I've only scratched the surface by the standards
of a professional historian. But compared to most
people I'm now an expert on Allied and German
operations in France, Belgium, and Holland in late
1944. And I definitely know immeasurably more
than the men directing that campaign.

Except you don't know what you don't know.
And that's not my only reservation. The final year
of the war is as important to the post-war balance
of power with the Soviets as it is to the defeat of the
Nazis. Dare I upset that balance? Not at the risk of
improving the Soviet position. But surely a faster
advance on the western front can only weaken the
Communists, preventing more of Europe from falling under their evil spell.

Then there's the fact I'll be stuck in 1944 for sure.
The ratio will be 55 to 1 now. I wouldn't survive the
return journey. Yes, I'd reconciled myself to a one
way trip last time, but I was still clinging to the
belief I could win Alicia's heart. This time I'll be on
my own. But will I be any more alone than I am
here? I doubt it.

I go to the bedroom, pull my vintage disguise

from the closet and quickly dress. Passing through knocked me on my ass the last time. I don't think I can run fast enough to avoid that again if I'm carrying a suitcase, so I grab a small backpack from the hall closet and return to the office. It's not genuine 1940s, but a simple black canvas bag with no logos or designs shouldn't draw attention. I stuff the documents I've prepared inside.

Back to the entry and I open the door to wartime London. It's nighttime here, but the sun is shining outside. For a moment I consider writing another note, but who would I address it to? Jon and Deb? Geoff and Carol? Someone else? I'll take care of that in the past, once I know who my son-father is, if he ever comes to exist.

General Rowntree's staff car stops in front of the townhouse, its silent appearance sudden and unexpected. It's strange that light can pass through the door but not sound. Or smell. I hadn't noticed that until now. Just one more unexplained mystery, but a small one compared to the existence of time travel itself.

The General is smiling as he steps from his vehicle. Why wouldn't he be happy? He knows the war is won, that Germany capitulates in a matter of months. What he doesn't know is that neither of his offspring will live to see that day. I can't let that happen.

My hands tug on the backpack straps, pulling them tight under my arms, then I back up, all the way to the far wall of the entryway. I drop into a sprinter's starting stance—one foot forward, fingers spread on the floor, knees and ankles flexed—and then explode into action, flying through the opening.

I take the stairs in two leaps, landing at the bottom with a thud right in front of the General, startling him. My ankles, knees, and especially my spine absorb the brunt of the sudden, jarring stop, but there's no faintness or tingling or nausea. *Yes!*

"Hello again, Sir," I say as I flex my back and shoulders, working away the pain.

He looks puzzled. "I thought you were gone for good, Professor." His brow furrows. "Is something wrong?"

"Terribly wrong. But I know how to fix it."

TWENTY-THREE

Every time the driver slows the car, General Rowntree orders him to go faster. Under such relentless pressure from his boss he complies, even when there's good reason for caution. Several times I close my eyes, fearing an impending disaster I have no power to avoid.

Once the General realized the stakes, convincing him of my plan took less than half an hour. But contacting Eisenhower at his headquarters in France, and organizing transportation there, took several hours. Between that and me getting the time calculation wrong — it's already September 2 here — we don't have a minute to spare.

Despite our reckless pace, it takes us forty-five minutes to travel to Biggin Hill, an airfield on the southern side of London made famous during the Battle of Britain as a base for the Spitfires and Hurricanes which held the Luftwaffe at bay.

The staff car stops in line with the tip of our aircraft's wing. General Rowntree leaps from the vehicle without waiting for Corporal Jones to open the door.

I follow right behind, determined not to waste a second. It's fifteen yards at most to the plane — very different from the modern airport odyssey of long, painfully slow lines at check-in and security, followed by an endless walk through a crowded, sprawling terminal to the gate.

We rush up the steep, narrow steps, having to duck as we pass through the short hatch. The C-47, the military version of the old DC-3, is smaller inside than I imagined, no wider or taller than one of those regional jets and about half the length. And far more austere. Every surface is cold, hard metal decorated with nothing but khaki paint, the structural ribs and inside of the airplane's aluminum skin fully exposed.

I make my way forward up the sloping floor to take a seat opposite the General on one of the benches running along each side, stowing my backpack underneath. The only padding is a green canvas-covered cushion an inch thick. It seems to do the job — for about a minute. *Damn, I'll be saddle sore by the time we arrive.*

The pilot — or copilot, I'm not sure which — pokes his head out from the cockpit. "We're refueled and ready to go whenever you are, Sir," he says to the General.

"Jolly good, Flight Lieutenant."

"You'll need this, Sir," he says as he hands the General a flying jacket. He then turns and grabs another jacket for me from somewhere inside the cockpit.

General Rowntree dons his protective garment. Military aircraft weren't pressurized or heated before the B-29. We can't fly much above 10,000 feet without oxygen, but I know from hiking in the Sierra Nevadas that it's chilly at that altitude, even in summer. I'll need the sheepskin-lined leather coat soon enough, but here on the ground it's a beautiful late summer day, so I lay it across my lap for now.

One engine sputters to life and then the other. Our plane jerks forward a few feet, then turns almost in place before our taxi begins.

We bounce along, then a hand I can only just see pushes the throttle levers forward and the engines roar like a wild beast unleashed. As we gather speed, the tail lifts until the fuselage is almost level, and then slowly, gracefully we leave the ground behind.

I haven't flown much, and only on commercial jets. Takeoff in this aircraft is a more visceral sensation — somehow more connected to the air — and much noisier.

Five minutes into our flight it gets bumpy as we pass through a layer of low cloud. By the time we level out a few minutes later the sky is clear and the flying smooth. I put on the flying jacket, pulling the woolly collar high around my neck. My toes, fingers, ears, and nose are already tingling from the cold. It will be a long flight.

Still, it could be worse. I imagine Jonathan Rowntree and twenty-five or thirty other men crammed together in this space, dressed in combat gear and loaded down with heavy packs and weapons, waiting to do one of the most dangerous things you can ask a soldier to do.

If the enemy doesn't shoot a paratrooper while he drifts to earth hanging helplessly in the air, or a bad landing doesn't end him, he touches down to find himself in hostile territory, with a good chance he's missed the drop zone. Once on the ground he may be lost and separated from his unit. Without heavy weapons he's certain to be outgunned, and probably outnumbered, by an adversary trying with all his might and ingenuity to kill him. I could never imagine myself being so brave and selfless.

An hour into the flight, somewhere over the English Channel, the sun disappears and we're surrounded by dark, angry clouds. The ride turns rough, far rougher than anything I've ever experienced. I'm discovering the downside of flying low — there's a great deal more weather here than at 35,000 feet.

The aircraft bounces up and down and sways violently from side to side, first one wing dipping and then the other. My knuckles turn white as I grip the bench. I grit my teeth and squeeze my eyes shut, telling myself it will soon pass.

The roller coaster ride continues excruciating minute after excruciating minute, growing more violent if anything. A desperate image forces its way into my mind. It's so vivid it's almost like a private movie, a vision of the plane breaking up, the wingless fuselage plummeting to a fiery end in a bitter sea. *Harrison Seely: Born November 1984; Died September 1944.* What an epitaph.

I force my eyes open and glance across at my fellow passenger. He shut his eyes and dropped his chin to his chest not fifteen minutes after takeoff, and hasn't so much as stirred since.

I lean forward to see into the cockpit. The crew are working to keep the plane straight and level, shoulders tensed and sweat beading on their faces as they manhandle the controls. But there's no sign of panic. They're in the zone, completely focused

on the task, knowing their training and experience
are equal to the challenge.

*There's nothing to worry about. There's nothing to
worry about.*

The positive self-talk has the desired effect, calming me. But soon my stomach has me praying for
a swift and painless end. Despite the cold, my face
is flushed and forehead beaded with sweat, my
breathing shallow and my hands clammy. I'm sure
I look the way I feel — a putrid shade of green.

I fight it as long as I can, trying to bend my stomach to my will, but the acid bile forces its way up
my throat. For the next hour I bury my head in a
brown paper bag, as miserable and sorry for myself
as I've ever been.

— o —

Before the plane comes to a complete stop, I rush to
the back. As soon as the crew have the door open, I
jump out. It's five or six feet to the ground. A hard
landing jars my knees, but I don't care.

A few scrambled steps forward and I sink to my
knees. I've never been so relieved to be reac-
quainted with *terra firma*. I want to kiss the grass
beneath me, but my stomach isn't done yet. It's

empty, so I introduce myself to the French countryside with a dry heave. Twice. No, here it comes again… Three times. My entire torso aches from the convulsions.

I should have stayed in Princeton.

Though the engines have stopped, I can still hear their drone, buzzing like a swarm of bees in my ears. I take a deep breath and climb to my feet. A cool sea breeze soothes my brow, and the sun warms my skin. And I'm standing on a solid, unmoving platform. I might just live.

General Rowntree clamps a hand on my shoulder. "You certainly made a hard slog of it, Professor."

I force a weary smile as he hands me my backpack. "And you must have a bulletproof stomach, Sir."

A jeep pulls up with a tortured squeal of overworked brakes. "Welcome, General Rowntree, Sir," the driver says as he jumps out and salutes. "Sergeant Walsh. I'm to take you to General Eisenhower."

I climb into the rear while General Rowntree takes the front passenger seat. "We must first make a stop at the Officers' Mess, Sergeant," he says. "My colleague needs to freshen up."

"But Sir, the Supreme Commander's orders…"

"I'll be fine," I say.

"Nonsense. I need you at your best. Sergeant, the mess. I'll explain to General Eisenhower."

"Yes Sir," the GI says as he grinds the gearstick into place.

The jeep springs forward like a wild predator starting the chase. I grab the bottom of my seat with an iron grip, afraid I'll bounce right out as he rushes us to our destination, taking every corner at breakneck speed. *Why is everyone trying to kill me in a fiery crash today?*

Twenty minutes later, the vehicle jerks to a halt in front of a white building perhaps two hundred yards long and three stories high. If I guess correctly the meaning of the one French word I think I recognize in the name carved above the entrance — *SCOLAIRE* — this used to be a school.

Inside the sanctuary of the Officers' Club, I splash cold water on my face to brighten my appearance, then drink a quick cup of weak black tea to calm my stomach and rinse the taste of airsickness from my mouth.

Fortunately, Eisenhower's office is in the same building. We still hurry down the long, narrow corridor, conscious we're keeping the man bearing the title SCAEF—the Supreme Commander of Allied Expeditionary Forces—waiting.

—o—

General Eisenhower lowers the phone handset onto its cradle as an aide shows us in. The sign outside said *Le Principal*. The room definitely has that severe, intimidating atmosphere of every principal's office I've ever visited.

I can't help staring at Eisenhower even though I know him. In my time—in the timeline I knew until I helped change it—he was one of history's tragic figures, the man who took the blame for the D-Day debacle before retreating quietly into post-war obscurity.

Dwight Eisenhower is already a hero in this new timeline and, though no one here knows it but me, a future President of the United States. All because he delayed the Normandy landings by a month. Such are the whims of fate.

Eisenhower stubs out his cigarette. He rises from behind his desk and rubs his hands together in anticipation, dispelling my concern our tardiness has offended him. "Professor, I sincerely hoped I would see you again."

"Thank you, Sir," I say as he shakes my hand warmly.

He gestures for us to join him at a small table in the corner of the room. Positioned beneath a large window, the late afternoon sun bathes it in a soft light, the one island of warmth in this uninviting room.

"There were some rough spots early on," he says. "Definitely some moments when I seriously doubted you."

"I suspect June 5 was a very long day, Sir, waiting for the weather to break."

"Our Christian God may be on our side, Professor, but some days I'd swear the weather gods favor the Nazis."

"I'm guessing the storm on June 19 was the low point?"

He shakes his finger at me. "You neglected to warn me."

"I hope you understand why."

"I think so. But losing one of our two Mulberry harbors was still a terrible shock. It was difficult to keep the faith during those weeks when our advance was so laborious. Until Falaise. Since then, progress has exceeded our wildest expectations. You can count me a true believer now. I can only pray that whatever information you came to share today proves as fruitful as your earlier advice. You do have information to share?"

I nod. "I hope it proves useful," I say. "Do you have a current map of the theater of operations?"

Eisenhower retrieves a rolled up map from his desk and spreads it out on the table. About four feet by three feet, the map covers most of the surface. He pulls several clips from his pocket which he deftly attaches to the edges of the table and the map to hold it in place. It is a practiced move. I'm sure he does this frequently, trying to divine the future from maps.

I run my finger across the map, along the line showing the current positions of the Allied vanguard, and the estimated enemy forces opposing them. "Your front is one hundred fifty miles east of where you planned to be at this date."

He nods sagely as he slips another cigarette between his lips and lights it. "We're moving heaven and earth to keep up, but we are fast outrunning our supply lines. All my commanders are screaming for supplies, Monty and Georgie Patton loudest of all."

I place my finger on Antwerp. "British forces will capture the port the day after tomorrow."

I pause for effect. We both know the question he is waiting for me to answer. "*Before* the Germans can sabotage the facilities…"

Eisenhower's face lights up. "You could not possibly bring more welcome tidings." Then his brow furrows and his joyous expression melts away. "But you didn't come here to bring me good news, did you, Professor?"

"No Sir," says General Rowntree. "We came to warn you of a missed opportunity, an impending blunder of enormous proportions and grave consequences."

"A key historian of this period described it this way," I say. *"The fumbled handling of Antwerp was among the principal causes of Allied failure to break into Germany in 1944."*

"So the fight continues into next year," Eisenhower says. "Disappointing, but not surprising."

"Max Harris — the historian in question — is referring specifically to the failure of Allied forces to deal aggressively with German rearguard action in the Scheldt Estuary" — I highlight the narrow forty mile long waterway connecting Antwerp to the sea — "stopping you from opening the port."

I pause and look at Eisenhower. "The first cargo will not cross the docks until November 28."

His mouth drops open in disbelief. "You set me up for a sucker punch there, Professor."

"I'm sorry, Sir, but you won't fix your logistical problems anytime soon."

"Montgomery is convinced a concentrated thrust on our left flank can succeed. He swears he can break through into Germany. But to do so I must give him priority of supply."

"A strategy you will embrace out of sheer desperation," I say. "I'm speaking historically of course."

"No apology necessary, Professor. I have been giving something of this nature serious and increasingly favorable consideration."

"It would be a major strategic mistake, Sir," says General Rowntree. "Even were we to capture a bridgehead, without supply through Antwerp we cannot sustain offensive operations beyond the Rhine. And the greater our success, the more severe the problem grows."

"The point is moot," I say, "because the operation will fail. And on your current course you won't reach Berlin until May."

"That is grim and disappointing news indeed," Eisenhower says. "Though not entirely surprising, at least to me."

He takes several quick puffs on his cigarette, a sure sign of stress. Usually he draws the smoke deep, in long, lazy puffs.

"But I cannot understand how anyone tolerated such a gross failing at Antwerp, me least of all. Everyone in this man's army knows how critical it is to get the port open."

I unzip my backpack and remove the two hundred page document I've prepared for this moment.

I slide it across the table. "You can read the depressing details for yourself. I've included both Allied and German reports."

"The essential problem," General Rowntree says, "is the single-minded and premature focus on driving east into Germany." He illustrates Monty's proposed thrust by moving his hand across the map from left to right. "But sometimes the shortest distance to an objective is not a straight line."

His hand sweeps upward and to the left from Antwerp. "British forces must turn and push northwest instead. And it is imperative they move with the utmost speed and urgency before German forces can regroup and dig in."

"Not only securing the approaches to the port," I say, "but also cutting off any retreat by von

Zangen's Fifteenth Army. They will hound you for months should the British Army allow them to escape."

"Two days is so little time," Eisenhower says. "Our army is like a giant ocean liner, Professor. It takes some time to change direction."

"I'm sorry, Sir," I say. "But I only figured it out yesterday. For me, everything changed after May 1944. The history I knew…" I shake my head. "I've had to relearn it from scratch. I came as soon as I could."

"And what do the previous Harrys say about this new strategy?"

"They don't. The timeline we're in—the one leading to German surrender in May 1945—is where the first Harry started. This isn't a scenario any of them tested."

"Then we're in uncharted waters."

"Ike, you know the Professor is right," General Rowntree says. "His information confirms every concern and misgiving you've felt for the past month."

"Indeed it does."

Eisenhower sits chewing his lip for a few minutes before his face sets in a look of determination. "The risk seems low, the payoff high. Definitely worth the gamble. But Monty will not like it. He is already out of sorts with yesterday's transfer of all ground forces to my direct command. Even his promotion to Field Marshal did not placate him."

I grab the document I gave Eisenhower and flick through it until I find the page I want. "You might want to show him this."

I place it in front of him, my finger resting on the relevant paragraph which reads:

I underestimated the difficulties of opening the approaches to Antwerp ... I reckoned the Canadian Army could do it while *we were going for the Ruhr. I was wrong.*

He scans it and then looks at me.

"Those are Montgomery's words, General. Straight from his memoirs."

"Sir, you know Monty as well as anyone," says General Rowntree. "Those words are as close as he will ever come to admitting error. You must appeal to his concern for his position in history."

"Quite a blunt assessment, Sir Geoffrey."

"But not untrue."

"And quite an ungentlemanly approach you recommend." Eisenhower smiles wryly. "Not something I expect from a British officer and a peer of the realm."

"It is indeed the act of a rotter, Sir. Which demonstrates how utterly convinced I am that we must pursue this course of action. As you pointed out, there is no time to dither, no room for prevarication. MARKET GARDEN — the failed push to the Rhine the Professor mentioned — is merely a more ambitious version of COMET."

"Ah," says Eisenhower, "so it's Monty's brainchild."

"And history regards it as his great folly," I say. "The one really black mark on an otherwise distinguished military career."

"It sounds like a dramatic failure of strategic leadership on my part too," Eisenhower says. "But not if we can help it. We'll leave for Montgomery's HQ first thing in the morning. There isn't a moment to lose."

TWENTY-FOUR

I'm dressed in the field uniform of an American infantry captain. It fits, but I'm uncomfortable in it. I've spent most of my adult life studying military history, but I wear this outfit under false pretenses, never having served, not even ROTC.

I don't know its origins, whether it came from the quartermaster, or if some unlucky officer awoke this morning to find himself short a uniform. All I know is that Sergeant McKeogh appeared at my door at 6 am carrying it. He informed me that his boss was worried the presence of a civilian at Montgomery's tactical headquarters would arouse suspicion and set tongues wagging. Wearing it was an order, not a request.

We were supposed to gather at the airfield by 7 am, but General Rowntree and I are running late. It's my fault; I lost time putting on the unfamiliar clothing, and even more time shaving my face and cutting my hair.

In keeping with this disguise, I've lost the long hair and beard I've had most of my adult life. I feel almost naked, exposed, especially without the beard. At least it's only temporary. I can grow it back after this is all over.

Our driver this morning is not helping our cause. In contrast to yesterday's frustrated racer, this guy drives like he's carrying a precious and fragile cargo or he's at the wheel of a hearse leading a funeral procession. Repeated requests to go faster bring only small and temporary increases in speed.

We make it to the airfield ten minutes late. The plane is waiting. As I climb out of the jeep, I pause to examine our ride, my eyes running from one end to the other. It looks like a B-25. Sort of. The nose is solid metal rather than glass, there are no turrets or guns, and there's a row of square windows in the side of the fuselage. Plus the entire plane is painted a light shade of gray, rather than the olive green or some camouflage pattern I'd expect.

General Rowntree notices me checking out the plane. "Ike had it modified for his personal use."

A little further down the runway are four fighters warming up for departure. They're not the famous P-51 Mustangs but something else with a much stockier fuselage. Thunderbolts? Whatever they are, it looks like they'll be our escort.

"Come along," he says, leading the way to the steep stairs descending from a hatch in the bottom of the fuselage. I guess this is where the bomb bay doors used to be. Behind us the engines fire into life and the propellers start spinning, while ground crew run to their positions ready to remove the wheel chocks.

We haul ourselves up — it's almost like climbing a ladder — and emerge into the space where the payload of bombs would normally go, now converted to carry passengers. There are five seats, nothing like modern airline seats, but rather what I imagine they had in early airliners.

As primitive as they look, I'm not complaining. These seats are several inches wider and at least a foot further apart than typical coach seating. The seat coverings are a blue wool and the interior walls lined with blue and gray plastic. It's an uninspiring color scheme, but one still found on several modern airlines, for reasons I don't understand.

Eisenhower is already aboard. He nods as we enter but continues chatting with his Chief of Staff, Lieutenant-General Walter Bedell Smith, sitting across the aisle from him. General Rowntree takes the seat directly behind them and joins the conversation.

My backpack and a duffel bag containing my civilian clothing go overhead. There's no bin as found on modern passenger planes, just a rack like on a train or a bus.

I take the one free seat, next to McKeogh.

"Welcome aboard, *Captain*," he says with a grin. "General Eisenhower doesn't wait for many people."

I run my hand over my bare chin and then over the fuzz on the top of my head. "Didn't expect this to take so long." I brush the uniform he helped me put on an hour earlier. "Or this. Thanks once again, Mickey."

He glares at me the way a teacher looks at a student who gives an incorrect answer when he should know the right one.

Oops. "Thanks Sergeant," I say, drawing an approving smile.

When the pilots gun the engines I'm thrown back in my seat. We leap into the sky, leveling out at our cruising altitude just a few minutes later. If the C-47 is a bucking bronco, this aircraft is a thoroughbred racer.

Everyone except me stands in one swift movement, as if acting according to a prearranged plan. They move to the front of the compartment, where Sergeant McKeogh folds a table with a map already clipped to it down from the wall. He moves to the small galley at the rear. *Please, let him be brewing coffee.* I let out a satisfied sigh when he pulls a coffee pot from a shelf above.

Eisenhower slips a cigarette between his lips and General Rowntree produces a pipe from one of his pockets. It's not a non-smoking flight.

The three officers crowd around the map. Soon their heads are inches apart as they lean in, engaged in an intense conversation.

I try to listen in, but I can't hear what they're saying. Today's flight is much, much smoother than yesterday's — *my stomach couldn't take that again* — but I swear the B-25 is the noisiest contraption I've ever had the misfortune to ride in. It's like a car with no muffler, but on a grand scale. The two massive engines produce the noise of a thousand screaming devils. If only I had earplugs, though they wouldn't help with the vibrations passing from the seat through my butt and straight up my spine.

Eisenhower notices me sitting by myself. "Please join us, Professor," he shouts over the noise, waving me forward.

I stand and approach the table, but hang back a little, listening in silence. I've done all I can do. This is in their hands now.

The wished-for coffee arrives a few minutes later served in enamel mugs. Eisenhower and Smith begin drinking theirs immediately. The Sergeant must know just how they like their coffee; he would have served them hundreds of cups, but not General Rowntree and me. He offers us condensed milk.

The General declines, but I take the olive green can and pour at least half the contents into my mug until it resembles Vietnamese coffee, thick and creamy and almost sickeningly sweet. Exactly what I need.

The discussion, led by Smith, continues while I'm fixing my beverage. I left them after dinner last night. I was in bed by 9 pm, even with spending an hour making my daily notes, and I still struggled to get up early. Eisenhower's Chief of Staff, a man at least fifteen years older than me, must have spent most of the night working. And probably a dozen other people too. Yet he looks full of energy.

General Smith is presenting a detailed operational plan for a concentrated offensive designed to clear the Scheldt in less than a week. The thoroughness of the research and planning completed in just a few hours is staggering. For every question or objection, Smith has a detailed response which meets with an approving smile or words of praise from Eisenhower and nods of agreement from General Rowntree.

All three officers have studied the documentation I provided. They are across every detail and then some. Especially the primary German sources which provide an unprecedented insight into the disposition of opposing forces, letting them see through the fog of war.

They smile every time they reference the enemy's documents. Even with the benefit of ULTRA, there are still critical gaps in their knowledge which my information helps fill.

An hour or so into the flight, a crew member emerges from beyond the forward bulkhead to inform us we'll be landing within ten minutes.

Eisenhower steps back. "I believe we have a sound plan, gentlemen," he says, bringing the meeting to an end. "For the first time, I genuinely believe we may end this war before Christmas."

We return to our seats while the Sergeant clears away the coffee mugs and stows the table. All three officers are beaming, buoyed by the unprecedented luxury of heading into battle knowing the precise location, strength, and intentions of their adversary. But will it be enough to persuade Monty?

—o—

I don't know exactly where it is we land. When I ask General Smith, he tells me the location is 'need to know' and points out that I have no such need.

I can't and don't argue. It is true, I have no immediate use for the information. But apart from natural curiosity, such knowledge would allow me to cross-reference what I see today with the historical record. So I try to make an informed guess.

We must be somewhere in northeastern France, the theater of operations for Montgomery's Twenty-First Army Group. The runway we're taxiing on is just an improvised grass strip in some French farmer's field. Combat engineers haven't yet laid down those metal grates, which suggests it's new, and therefore close to the front. Given how fast Allied forces have advanced in recent days, we're probably still a hundred or more miles from the fighting. Somewhere around Amiens or Arras, perhaps?

The plane stops. A crew member waits for the engines to shut off then opens the hatch and we climb down. Two Humber staff cars, weather-beaten siblings of General Rowntree's official vehicle, are waiting for us. Eisenhower takes the first one, along with his Chief of Staff and his orderly, while I ride in the other with General Rowntree.

A drive through the French countryside in late summer should be idyllic, but signs of destruction everywhere stop me enjoying the scenery. Damaged buildings and shattered vehicles abandoned by the roadside are disturbing enough, but the sight of dead bodies truly drives home the grisly reality of war.

The bloated remains of young men cut down in their prime and left to lie where they fell, like discarded trash, is an image I will never get out of my mind as long as I live. It matters not whether they are ours or theirs. And the heavy, oppressive, all-present stench of death is an equally confronting assault on my senses. The thick, sweet, sickening aroma fills my lungs and turns my stomach.

Twenty minutes later, the track ascends a slight rise and opens into a grassy clearing about a hundred yards wide, surrounded on three sides by pine forest.

Montgomery's forward HQ consists of tents of various sizes, and trucks that look like different degrees of cross-breeding between gypsy caravans and modern motorhomes, all laid out in a semi-circle skirting the edges of the glade. Add lions and elephants and you'd swear the circus was in town.

As our vehicles pull to a stop, a British officer rushes over to greet us — a Lieutenant-Colonel I see once I leave the car. We gather in a group as he explains that 'the Field Marshal' has gone forward and won't be back for at least an hour.

He leads us to the Visitors' Mess, a large tent hidden beneath camouflage netting, where morning tea awaits. *With real scones!* They're much lighter and fluffier than the crusty cakes we Americans call scones. Actually, the only thing they have in common is the name.

The Brits call this divine combo — tea and scones with clotted cream and chunky strawberry jam — 'cream tea.' So good if you can get the real deal, which means going to England. Specifically the south-west, Devon or Dorset or Cornwall, the true devotees say.

Or a British Army tactical headquarters somewhere in France. It's not what I expected of army food, especially in the field.

I approach the table intending to stuff my face, but as I reach for a scone I find my appetite suddenly lacking. I pour myself a cup of tea instead.

Then we wait. Sitting in a camp chair, I rest my notebook on my knee and jot down everything I've seen today. The others chat or read.

Even when one hour turns into two, Eisenhower seems unperturbed by his subordinate keeping him waiting.

I lean over and mention it quietly to Sergeant McKeogh. He looks up from a letter he's writing to tell me it's not the first time.

Two hours and ten minutes after our arrival, the tent flap lifts. Montgomery enters, silhouetted by the sun behind him.

I've seen a hundred pictures of this man, but never anticipated how small he is in real life. He looks like a boy playing dress-up in his father's clothes, his jacket too broad in the shoulders, and his pants so loose and baggy I'm worried they're about to fall down. His face is fine and narrow, and his hair thinning beneath the black beret of the Royal Tank Regiment that he wears everywhere. He can't be more than 5'5" and 130 lbs. Nevertheless, he has a real presence, like a wiry little terrier filled with energy just waiting to pounce.

Eisenhower does not mention the unseemly wait, but simply greets him with a formal, "Field Marshal Montgomery."

Montgomery seems perplexed by the greeting. "General Eisenhower," he says stiffly in a squeaky voice with a slight lisp.

Eisenhower stares back at him. Just as I think this is going south before we even start, he cracks a smile. "I thought I should address you as Field Marshal at least once, dear Monty."

Montgomery chuckles. "Thank you, Ike," he says. "Now, if everyone has had their fill of tea, shall we move to the command tent?"

$-\circ-$

Montgomery leads us across the clearing to another khaki-colored tent. A large almost square table fills the middle of the space. A long narrow table laden with radio equipment runs along the back wall, and map boards stand along both sides of the room.

Another officer — a British Major-General — is waiting for us there. "I asked Freddie to join us," Montgomery says, referring to his Chief of Staff, Major-General Francis de Guingand.

There are nods of acknowledgment as we take our seats at the table. They all know each other. And I know who they are. But Montgomery and de Guingand don't know me. Are they wondering who the hell I am, or have they assumed I'm just some anonymous flunky? Eisenhower will introduce me when he's ready, I guess.

I remove the plan for MARKET GARDEN from my portfolio and hand it to him.

He in turn presents it to Montgomery. "Read this please, Monty. Then give me your appreciation."

Montgomery's eyes light up as soon as he begins reading. Every few paragraphs he mouths an excited "yes" and nods intently. When he comes to the end he looks up, beaming like he's won the lottery.

"Spot on," he says as he hands the document to de Guingand. "Bold. Daring. Exactly what is needed, I say."

"You should like it," Eisenhower says. "This is the plan you will present to me four days from now."

Montgomery's Chief of Staff thumbs through the document. "It does bear an uncanny resemblance to the plan we are preparing," he says. "Where did this come from?"

Eisenhower signals for me to stand.

As I rise to my feet, I place my hands on the table to stop them shaking, and to steady myself.

Montgomery and de Guingand stare at me like I'm some ghost that materialized out of thin air.

I'm going with anonymous flunky.

"This young man dressed in a captain's uniform," Eisenhower says, "is Professor Harrison Seely of Princeton University."

Montgomery shrugs. "And?"

"And he is from the future. The year 2015."

Amazingly, de Guingand's expression does not change. Montgomery's reaction is more predictable. His beady eyes look like they're about to spring from his head. "You expect me to believe — "

"We do not have time to argue about this, Monty. You will have to rely on my word."

"You are the most trustworthy man I know, Ike, though you must understand how incredible your statement is."

Montgomery's face betrays his dilemma. He sighs deeply, then says, "Nevertheless, I find myself honor bound to accept your claim at face value..."

"Thank you," Eisenhower says. "We have had the benefit of the Professor's counsel for several months now. Every event he predicted has come to pass precisely as he forecast. His latest prediction is that this operation" — he points to the document —

"will fail, with dire consequences for our overall offensive."

We spend the next hour and a half reviewing the history of Montgomery's concentrated thrust to the Rhine. We break for lunch, then they devote two more hours to arguing about the alternative plan developed by Smith and the rest of Eisenhower's staff. I stay silent during this part of the discussion.

Montgomery sits back in his chair, places his hands on his knees and then bends forward until his head is between his knees. I interpret it as a sign he is ready to comply, until he sits upright and launches into a shocking tirade against Eisenhower, who sits silently and takes it.

I'm flabbergasted. I've read about their feisty relationship in the history books. But the behavior they describe—difficult but only flirting with disrespect—is a pale imitation of this outrageous display of gross insubordination.

At the point where Montgomery shows signs of calming down, Eisenhower asks us to leave the two of them alone.

Sergeant McKeogh disappears, presumably to run some errand on behalf of his boss. Always by Eisenhower's side, or somewhere nearby, he seems to have an uncanny ability to anticipate his commander's every need.

The rest of us loiter outside the tent, listening to the battle raging inside. We all look anywhere but at each other, partners in a silent conspiracy to maintain the pretense we aren't eavesdropping.

The fight sounds as fierce and unyielding as anything happening on the front lines. Both Chiefs of Staff frequently shoot each other knowing glances, suggesting they've witnessed such dramatic performances before, and have had to pick up the pieces.

When Montgomery voices a particularly strident criticism of the proposed plan, questioning the parentage of those who prepared it, de Guingand turns to Smith with a deeply apologetic expression on his face.

"It is truly a smashing plan, Beedle," he says. "I'll help smooth things over with Monty, you'll see."

"I have no doubt you will, Freddie. But I wish Ike would punch your boss in the nose when he goes off like this. I'd like to see it just once before this is all over."

General de Guingand rolls his eyes. "I doubt either of them would ever recover from the shock."

Half an hour later the battle ends, or they call a truce at least. Eisenhower emerges looking grim-faced and browbeaten.

My plan to change history has failed. Perhaps I can't save Jonathan, but we can still stop Alicia from returning to London. She's back working at Bletchley — Eisenhower's influence — so it's just a matter of having her stay there...

— o —

General Smith stays behind when we leave. Do he and Eisenhower still hope to change Montgomery's mind? It seems unlikely, but they know him far better than I do.

The other four of us crowd into a single staff car for the ride back to the airfield. About halfway there, out of the silence, Eisenhower says, "Monty came around in the end."

"How did you manage it, Sir?" I say. "It seemed hopeless."

"I told him that for the next ten days he could have all the supplies he needed." He pauses for effect, then chuckles. "And after that, he would receive not a single bullet or gallon of gasoline unless it came through Antwerp."

"He'll see the wisdom of your decision once the strategy proves correct."

"For which he will claim the glory in his own inimitable way." Eisenhower casts me an inscrutable look, a mix of resignation and hard-earned wisdom. "And I will happily allow it should he deliver the swift victory I seek."

I am deeply impressed by Eisenhower's magnanimity. I hope Patton and the other generals react better than Montgomery when told to hold their attacks for a week or two until Antwerp is opened and a strategic advance can be properly supplied. Dealing as effectively as he did with demanding superiors like Roosevelt and Churchill, and hotheaded subordinates like Montgomery and Patton, I can see why history rates Eisenhower's diplomatic skills so highly.

Montgomery offered his C-47 to carry General Rowntree and me across the Channel back to England, a ride I am dreading. It is parked right where the car stops.

The four fighters that will accompany Eisenhower south to Patton's headquarters are lined up in a neat row nearby. But his B-25 is a hundred yards away, parked at an irregular angle to the runway, unlike the tents and the other planes which are all either parallel to each other or standing at neat right angles.

It's hard to identify the precise boundaries of the makeshift runway, but it's clear Eisenhower's personal aircraft has veered off it. The nose rests on the ground and the propellers are bent, not in sharp, harsh angles but into flowing curves like leaves, or the unfurling petals of a giant steel-gray flower. There's a tragic beauty to them.

"FUBAR," the Supreme Commander mutters to himself as he stares morosely at his wrecked plane.

Several men are gathered in the field looking at the wreck, some with hands on hips, others rubbing their chins, some with arms pointing and waving. Eisenhower's pilots, Major Hansen and Captain Underwood, break from the group and rush over as soon as they see us.

"What on earth happened?" he asks them.

Major Hansen steps forward. "I take full responsibility, Sir."

"I didn't ask who was responsible, Larry. I asked what happened."

"Sir. The front wheel dropped into a gopher hole while we were turning her around."

"Then it's the damn gopher who should be held responsible. If you see it, shoot it."

"Gladly, Sir."

"Can't you fix it?" I say to Captain Underwood who stands immediately to my left.

Seconds later, but too late to avoid embarrassment, it occurs to me that this may be the dumbest question I've asked since I was five years old. Even if the plane can be repaired, surely the job would take weeks.

"The drive shafts and cylinder heads were destroyed when the props hit the ground," the copilot says in a matter-of-fact tone. "Both engines and props will need to be replaced."

"It was a stupid question."

"Not at all. You'd be amazed how quickly a dozen nut busters can change those babies out. Even here in the boondocks."

"That doesn't solve our immediate transportation problem," Eisenhower says.

"We can take the C-47, Sir," says Major Hansen. "I've squared it away with the Field Marshal's staff."

"Well, it's only fair. I gave him that airplane." A tight smile on Eisenhower's face provides the only evidence he relishes this small victory over Montgomery. He turns to General Rowntree and me. "Sorry to leave you men stranded."

Major Hansen points to a small, lightly built aircraft parked fifty yards away. "We have an L-5 at our disposal, Sir, and a Brit pilot to fly her. It will be cramped, but it'll get them home."

"Excellent work," Eisenhower says. "Any objections, Sir Geoffrey?"

The high wings and extensive glass surrounding the cockpit suggest this aircraft is designed for observation. If I remember correctly, those types of planes travel super-slow. We'll be crammed into this tiny thing for hours, if it doesn't break into a million pieces in mid-flight. It looks like it's made from balsa wood and tissue paper and powered by a rubber band.

General Rowntree's face betrays the same reservations I have, but he can't contradict Eisenhower, not without something more than unsubstantiated misgivings. "Jolly good, Sir," he replies stoically instead.

TWENTY-FIVE

Eisenhower calls me aside before he departs. He thanks me for everything I've done, tells me I must call him *Ike* from now on, and vows we'll meet again after the war, either in England or back in the States.

I tell him I look forward to it, while wondering if the picture of him visiting with Grandpa Harry was just one of many postwar reunions, or if it will take him a decade to keep his promise.

General Rowntree and I watch the fighters take off, followed a few minutes later by Eisenhower in the C-47. Now it's just us and the L-5.

"My duffel bag," I say, suddenly remembering I left it on the bomber. I don't want to lose my 1940s civilian attire and be stuck wearing this uniform indefinitely.

An airman standing nearby ducks into a tent and emerges holding my luggage before escorting us to our toy plane where our pilot is waiting.

Flight Lieutenant Chalmers introduces himself then opens the door. "Your home for the next two hours, gents."

General Rowntree and I lean in, assessing the space behind the pilot that we must both squeeze into. There's one seat, with about six inches clearance on either side.

"Good God, man," the General says.

"I have an idea." I climb in and stow my backpack behind a small cargo hatch at the back. Then I wedge the duffel bag into the gap beside the seat and sit half on it and half on the seat.

General Rowntree maneuvers himself into the space beside me. "This is going to be cozy," he says.

I push myself as close as I can to the wall, but our hips and shoulders still press tightly together.

"It is fortunate we are on good terms, Captain," he adds with a twinkle in his eye.

Our pilot straps himself into the front seat — I'm already envious of all the room he has — then turns and says, "Ready, Sir?"

"Tally ho, Flight Lieutenant," the General says.

The pilot starts the engine. "Tally ho then!"

We taxi three or four hundred yards before he turns the aircraft around. Our small, high-winged plane uses only a fraction of the runway before it's in the air and we're banking hard to the left.

By the time the wings level out we're heading west into the setting sun. If Montgomery's forward

HQ is where I speculated, the shortest route back to London is due north. But that would take us over territory still occupied by German forces — the Fifteenth Army that Montgomery's forces should neutralize in the next few days. We need to head west first and then make a right turn at some point.

With all the glass I feel like I'm inside a flying greenhouse, not an image that does anything to relieve my anxiety. But flying so low — maybe five hundred feet — I'm drawn into the details of the landscape below. I can make out every house, every vehicle, even the cows and horses in the fields. Large stretches of countryside appear untouched by war, but they're interspersed with random patches of total destruction.

Forty or fifty minutes into the flight and my palms are no longer sweaty, and my heart is beating normally — until I notice we're flying even lower and my pulse quickens.

A man staring at the back end of a horse stops his plowing to gaze up, so close I can see the concerned expression on his face. Is he afraid we will strafe or bomb him? *In this?*

Or is he just surprised at how low we are flying?

Too low. I lean forward and tap the pilot on the shoulder.

"Chalmers"—since our ranks are equivalent, *if mine were real*, I address him as middle and upper class Brits do with their peers, by his surname alone—"I think we're losing altitude."

General Rowntree looks out one side then the other, making his own assessment. "Is there a problem, Flight Lieutenant?" he yells over the noise of the engine and the wind.

"Sir, we're losing oil," Chalmers shouts back. "We must land." He points military style, not with a finger but with the whole hand, to a road at a bearing of two o'clock. "Over there. No need to worry, chaps. Should be quite a smooth landing."

The aircraft banks as our pilot lines it up with the road. The engine throttles back to an idle as we gently descend, almost floating toward our makeshift landing site.

Movement to the left catches my attention. A small, open vehicle is approaching on a road intersecting the one where we are about to land. My pulse races now. They're going to crash into us.

I look again, assessing our relative speeds. *Phew.* I think we'll touch down beyond the intersection.

Now I've stopped thinking of it as a missile aimed at us, I examine the vehicle again, searching for something to indicate who they are and what they're doing. Perhaps it's a blessing. They could give us a ride.

It looks military. The right size to be a jeep. But the color is off. More gray than green. As are the uniforms of the four occupants who sit deeper in it than they would in a jeep. And it has flat, ribbed sides, like it was assembled on the cheap from spare bits of corrugated steel. It kinda reminds me of —

Holy shit! A goddamned kubelwagen!

"GERMANS! PULL UP, PULL UP!"

— o —

The engine surges, the sound of the propeller changing from a deep, throaty hum to a desperate, aggressive whine as we battle for airspeed and altitude.

We climb. I crane my neck, looking past the seat in front of me at the altimeter. One hundred feet. Two hundred. Three hundred.

I'm wedged in so tight my body can't twist, but I swivel my head as far as I can, trying to look down and behind. The kubelwagen is racing along the road after us but we're already half a mile ahead.

I check the instruments again. Five hundred feet and 90 knots. They won't catch us now.

A mile in front the sea comes into view. I hope the pilot has a plan. We can't head out across the Channel with a failing engine. We need dry land, somewhere not under enemy occupation.

As if responding to my unspoken concern, our plane banks gently to the right, initiating a wide sweeping turn. If we can retrace our path, we should reach friendly territory soon enough.

About the time we've turned almost right around, the sinking sun behind us now, a loud clunk comes from the front of the plane and the propeller shudders to a stop.

"Hang on back there," the pilot yells. "Engine's seized. I'll try to put her down on the beach."

The plane banks, first one way then the other, as Chalmers lines it up for an emergency landing. It's eerily quiet, with nothing but the high-pitched noise of the wind rushing over the wings and whistling past the struts and fixed landing gear. It's the sound of the calm before the storm.

Our descent is so gradual it feels like we can glide forever, but we cover no more than a mile before the sand is suddenly rushing up to meet us.

We're moving slowly, maybe forty or fifty miles an hour, when we make contact. There's one small bounce, then we're rolling forward as the tail gear touches down. *Oh my God, oh my God, oh my God.* I see it coming, but there's nothing I can do except brace myself for impact.

The left wing strikes one of those large steel obstacles the Nazis planted all over the beaches of northern France to hinder amphibious landings. It rips off in a melee of splintering wood and tearing fabric. The aircraft twists to the left as the booby-trap seriously impedes its forward progress, then tilts to the right, the tip of the right wing hitting the sand before it jerks upright again.

We hit the ground with a thud as the landing gear collapses. The plane slides across the wet sand on its belly before it comes to a stop, pointing out to sea in shallow water.

There's a moment of incongruous silence before a wave crashes over the nose, smashing the forward windscreen and filling the cabin with water.

I spit out a mouthful of saltiness as I turn to check on General Rowntree. Blood is trickling down the side of his face and his eyes are closed. He doesn't respond when I shake him.

"The General is hurt," I shout. "We have to get him out."

The pilot opens the door and jumps into knee deep water. He grabs the General's feet. I slip my hands under his shoulders and lift, as Chalmers drags and I push him from the wrecked plane.

After I follow them out, we each slip a shoulder under an arm and push our way forward through the water. As we carry him to the beach, we struggle not to be knocked over as more waves roll in, pounding into us from behind.

We lay our unconscious comrade on the dry sand above the high water mark. I kneel and put my ear to his mouth. "He's breathing." *Thank God.*

I drop back onto my rear and close my eyes, hoping I'll wake up any moment from this nightmare. Instead, I hear multiple voices shouting.

"Hände hoch, hände hoch!"

It takes a moment for my mind to register that it's German. I open my eyes. Four soldiers are running across the beach toward us, their weapons drawn and pointed menacingly in our direction.

Chalmers and I look at each other glumly as we raise our hands above our heads.

— o —

Our captors don't respond to English, but hand gestures and pointed MP40 submachine guns convey their orders well enough.

Under their watchful gaze, Chalmers and I carry General Rowntree up the beach and over small dunes to a nearby road where the kubel-wagen is parked. By the time we lay him on the ground his eyes are open, but he's still unresponsive.

One of the Germans drives off, returning soon after followed by a field ambulance and an army truck. Two medics lift the General onto a stretcher and load him into the ambulance which races away. The pilot and I are shoved into the back of the open truck, accompanied by all but one of the remaining soldiers.

A few minutes later we enter a town. It's almost dark now, and the temperature has dropped several degrees. I shiver in my wet uniform. With an act of will I stop it. Then, as soon as I relax, it starts again, my teeth chattering. I wrap my arms around my body.

After two or three miles, we turn into a wide avenue and then grind to a stop in front of a large building. In the failing light I can distinguish only an outline of the structure. Three stories tall and built in the style of so much late nineteenth century French architecture, my guess is it's some type of public facility.

We are hustled inside. In the entrance I see a sign: *Hôtel de Ville, Le Havre*. I mouth "Town Hall?" to the pilot who confirms with a nod.

A port at the mouth of the Seine, Le Havre is one of several pockets of resistance bypassed by the Allied armies as they raced eastward. But not for long. This place is due to be bombed into oblivion a few days from now. If we don't find a way out by then, we're in big trouble…

— o —

I awake to sun in my eyes, streaming in from the only window situated high in the wall above us. I don't know what the original purpose of this room was — storage? — but it makes for an ideal prison cell.

Somewhere in the night, fatigue must have overtaken the discomfort of sleeping on a hard floor in wet clothing. At least they gave us blankets. But I am anything but rested. My uniform is dry, except around the thicker seams, but my skin itches with crusted salt, my throat is parched, and my back and neck feel like a rampaging linebacker tackled me. I don't think the crash did any lasting damage, but some whiplash isn't surprising.

I grab my shoes and put them on. They squelch as I stand and raise both arms above my head. I arch my back, trying to stretch the pain away. It helps a little.

I pace back and forth across the empty room. There must be a way out of this predicament, I just have to figure out where —

"That seems quite pointless," Chalmers says. "And it is rather distracting."

I stop, look at him, then put my back to the wall and slide down it until I'm sitting on the hard, cold floor facing the man propped against the opposite wall.

"Seems like we're in a bit of a fix here, Seely."

"You don't know the half of it," I say. "But please, call me Harrison."

He looks at me as if it's the craziest idea he's heard in a long time.

"Look, I know you Brits don't like any sort of informality. But we're cellmates for who knows how long. You can go back to calling me Seely the minute we're free."

He shrugs. "All right, Yank. David Chalmers."

"All right then, Limey. We have to get out of here. Starting tomorrow night the air force and navy will reduce this town to rubble."

"I won't ask how you know, but I have no doubt it's true. And it's a sure bet the Town Hall is a target. But escape will not be—"

The door opens. Someone slides a metal tray into the room and then closes the door.

Resting on the tray are two bread rolls, two steaming mugs of coffee, and two canteens. I grab a canteen, unlatch the top, and raise it to my lips. Though lukewarm and cloudy, the water is sweet nectar. We've had nothing to eat or drink since our capture last night. I tip my head back and pour the welcome liquid down my throat.

"Steady on there, Harrison. We've no idea how long this has to last."

He has a point. I close the canteen and try the coffee next. I take one mouthful and then spit it out on the floor. *Ugh.* The taste of burned wood lingers on my tongue.

My cellmate lifts the other mug and tastes it. "Chicory," he says with a shrug, then takes another sip. "An acquired taste."

It may be, but I hope I won't be here long enough to acquire it.

We each take a bread roll. I consume mine far too quickly, despite my best efforts to savor every morsel by taking small bites and chewing slowly.

My stomach is nowhere near full. I wish I had filled my belly with those scones yesterday. Well, look on the bright side. There's no need to worry about the impending bombardment. We'll starve to death first.

After our unsatisfying breakfast we share our personal histories. David Chalmers reveals he's from York, an Oxford graduate, and that he had just started working in 'the City' before the war, on something called reinsurance.

The life story I recount is fictional, but based as close as possible on fact. It's easier that way to keep my story straight. I tell him about my parents, a normal, happy childhood in Pittsburgh, and my profession. But I say nothing of my fake military identity, or when the life I described took place.

I would prefer to spend the time making notes, but somewhere along the way I lost my notebook and pencil, as well as my garrison cap. They will be somewhere in the sea with the plane. And my spare clothes.

I hope the Germans will be too busy dodging Allied bombs to search the wreck. The last thing we need is them finding my civilian outfit and my cryptic notes, and deciding I'm a spy…

— o —

The door opens again, but this time a young officer enters. "Gentlemen, Oberleutnant Schier," he says, "but you may address me as Lieutenant. Please, you will come with me."

His English has a clipped, Germanic edge, but is clear and otherwise unaccented. No V sound in place of W, no Z for TH. Together with his pronunciation of Lieutenant as *Lef-tenant*, it suggests he studied in England.

We both stand. "Where is the other officer who was with us?" I say.

"Look here, Oberleutnant," my cellmate adds, "we demand to know what you have done with him."

"Do not worry, gentlemen. Your General is in the infirmary. He is…" There's a pause. "Recovering. I believe this is the correct word, yes?"

"I hope so," I say.

"Do I have your word as officers you will not try to escape, or must I summon guards?"

Chalmers looks at me. I nod. "You have our word," he says.

The Oberleutnant leads us to an imposing room one floor up, probably the mayor's office before the

Nazi occupation, where a German officer sits behind a large, ornately carved desk.

We stand facing him as he sizes us up. I return the favor. I'm not familiar enough with Wehrmacht insignia to pick his exact rank, but his age, fifties, and the fruit on his uniform strongly suggest he's a senior officer — a Colonel or Brigadier is my guess. With narrow, sad eyes and a triangular face, he looks like a man weighed down by a great burden.

He says something in German. Schier translates it as, "Oberst Hermann-Eberhard Wildermuth, commanding officer of the Le Havre garrison, welcomes you."

Some welcome. Does he always feed his guests so poorly?

"Flight Lieutenant Chalmers, Royal Air Force."

Should I reveal my true identity? Under the rules of war a soldier dressed in civilian clothes behind enemy lines can be shot as a spy. Does the same principle apply in reverse? I don't think so.

But I'm still wearing the uniform, so it's best to stick to my cover story. Less complicated. "Captain Seely, United States Army."

The Oberst, equivalent to Colonel, gives his reply, which Schier relays as, "We know an attack is coming—"

"We have no knowledge of those plans," I say, perhaps a little too sharply to be believable. "What we do know is that your defeat is inevitable. You should surrender now."

Schier ignores my interjection, continuing to translate his commander's statement instead. "Herr Wildermuth wishes to communicate an offer —"

"Your surrender?" Chalmers says. "Very well, we accept."

"To evacuate the civilian population." The German Lieutenant points at me. "He has selected you to carry the message, Herr Captain."

— o —

This is it, a chance to escape. I'd be safe. But I can't go. What point is there in saving Alicia if I abandon her father to an uncertain, unpromising fate? She would never forgive me. I would never forgive me.

"Tell the Colonel to send the Flight Lieutenant instead," I say to Schier. "The forces confronting you are British. They are more likely to listen to one of their own."

While the Oberleutnant is busy conveying my message to his commander, David Chalmers leans close and whispers, "I appreciate the gesture, but it isn't necessary."

I shoot him a glance. *I know what I'm doing.*

"He asks why you would be so concerned with the success of this mission," Schier says.

"I don't want to see civilians slaughtered any more than he does."

I wait for him to translate my statement.

The older man looks me right in the eye as he says, "*Nein.*"

I glare back at him. "I *must* stay with General Rowntree. If you send me, I will not deliver your message."

The Flight Lieutenant looks at me questioningly while Schier translates.

"Herr Wildermuth believes you are bluffing. But he is curious about such dedication to your General."

What does he suspect? How to explain? I need something simple, something that might appeal to his humanity, assuming he has any left.

"I am engaged to be married to the General's daughter." The lie rolls off my tongue with surprising ease. "I could never face her again if I left her father behind." At least that last part is true.

The German commander's eyes widen in surprise when Schier delivers my answer. He pauses before responding. When he speaks, one word catches my attention: "*Ja.*"

Does that mean…

"Herr Oberst Wildermuth will grant your request," Schier says.

I look directly at the Colonel as I reply with one of the few German words I know. "*Danke.*"

TWENTY-SIX

The train ride from Bletchley to Elverstone takes no longer than usual, but today it seems excruciatingly slow. Mother refused to tell me anything on the telephone, but it must be something quite terrible for her to insist on my immediate return. *Dear Lord, do not let it be Jony.*

Our motor is waiting for me at the station. Henderson's expression is dark and sombre, and he refuses to meet my eyes as he opens the door. *He knows.* Not officially perhaps, but a servant will have overheard something and word would have spread through the household within minutes. But it is not his place to tell me. The servants and the family must both maintain the pretence that the former remain at all times unaware of the personal trials and tribulations of the latter. I must endure this painful ignorance a few more minutes yet.

In contrast to my rail journey, the drive to Elverstone Hall passes in a blur. We arrive before I even realise we are under way, not one of the many familiar landmarks along the route registering in my mind.

I rush inside to find Mother in the drawing room, sitting by the fire despite the Indian summer England is enjoying.

I sit beside her and take her hands in mine. "Dearest Mother." Her fingers are like icicles, cold and white as the deepest arctic winter, and her eyes and nose red. "Tell me. What has happened?"

She wipes a tear from her eye, and her lips quiver. She does not, cannot, answer.

"Is it Jonathan?" I ask, my heart in my mouth, knowing it is, but hoping beyond hope it is not.

From somewhere behind me a familiar and welcome voice says, "You won't be rid of me so easily, Licorice. I'm like a bad penny."

My head whips around. Standing in the doorway is my darling brother. I jump to my feet and rush to him.

"Oh, Jony," I say as I throw my arms around his neck and bury my face in his shoulder to hide my tears. "I believed you were dead. I did not want to, but I had —"

"Shush. I'm very much alive." He breaks our embrace, holding me by the forearms as he looks me in the eye. "It is Father."

"Father? Where is he? Is he ill?"

"Captured. By the Germans."

"I do not understand." I rub my temples. *How can it be?* "He works at the War Office. In Whitehall."

"They flew to the continent to meet Eisenhower and Montgomery," he says. "Their plane was forced down on the return journey. Over the port of Le Havre, unfortunately still in enemy hands."

Father is a prisoner of war. Meaning he is alive, a condition far, far better than anything I feared for my dearest brother an hour ago.

I resume my seat. I must think this through. "When? How do we know this?"

"The German commander sent the pilot to our lines carrying a proposal to evacuate the civilian population from the city. That was three days ago. Field Marshal Brooke cabled Mother as soon as he was notified. Father was hurt in the crash—"

I gasp in fear and panic, and my breath catches in my throat.

"Not seriously. And the Germans have tended to his injuries."

I exhale deeply, relaxing my body and my mind. "At least he is safe," I say, as much to reassure myself as to comfort Mother or Jony. "The war is almost over. We will see him soon. I just know it."

Jony takes a seat opposite us. "British forces are on the move, liberating Le Havre." His tone is dark. But surely that is positive news? "According to the newspapers, our naval and aerial bombardment has flattened the town."

"Can't we do something to get him out?" I wail. "Do we even know if Father is still alive?"

"There's nothing to be done, Lic. Not until the German garrison surrenders. It is only a matter of time, but for now we must remain strong and steadfast. And pray for them."

"Why do you refer to Father in the plural?"

Mother speaks for the first time. "The pilot said Lord Elverstone was travelling with a young American officer."

She looks at me with eyes filled with a desperate longing for her husband's return. And something else…

What is it? Is it sympathy for me? Pity? But why? "Go on, Mother."

"The pilot referred to the other prisoner as Captain Seely."

I stand and back away, shaking my head. "I admit it is a strange coincidence, but it is not possible, Mother. The Professor returned to Princeton." *And the future.* "There is nothing for him in England.

I made it very clear." *Showing no mercy in dashing his dreams, in breaking his heart.* "Furthermore, he is a civilian." I hear the shrillness in my voice, but continue unchecked. "He has no military —"

Jony kneels before me and grasps me by the shoulders, trying to calm me. "The pilot, a Flight Lieutenant Chalmers, remarked on the fact the American insisted they address each other by their Christian names."

He pauses and looks me in the eyes. "The American introduced himself as Harrison."

Harrison? It must be him. Harrison Seely is not a common name. But no. It cannot be. I simply will not allow it.

"The pilot also reported that the Germans sent him out with the message because Captain Seely insisted," Mother says. "He insisted on staying with... with my Geoffrey."

I twist free of Jony's hold. "Why would he do that?"

Mother has broken down in tears, so Jony answers for her. "He told the German commander he would never be able to face his fiancee again were he to abandon her father."

TWENTY-SEVEN

General Rowntree has recovered from the concussion he sustained in the crash. The Germans moved
us to the basement, along with their command post,
after the first wave of bombing three nights ago.
I don't know if it was concern for our safety, or fear
we'd run off as soon as the walls of our cell came
tumbling down.

We haven't been above ground since, but I can't
imagine there's much of the building left standing.
Just like the history books say, the bombardment is
fierce and relentless. So far we have weathered the
bombing without injury. Our main complaint is
hunger. The Germans feed us nothing but boiled
potatoes and water. We complain, but only in solid-
arity. It's the same inadequate rations they barely
feed themselves.

Hunger and boredom. Interspersed with moments of sheer terror.

Nobody bothers watching us. During our first
night underground we had a brief, whispered discussion about escape, but agreed we wouldn't last
ten minutes in the open, let alone the hour or more

it would take to reach Allied lines. We will hold out here until the battle is over. It's only a matter of time before the British and Canadian forces reach us.

We huddle in an out of the way nook, the floor and walls damp in many places with seeping water, the air musty and filled with the smell of overtaxed latrines. I press my back against the stone wall. It's cold and hard, but I'm glad it's there to hold me up. These quiet hours wondering if we'll die any moment are harder than the minutes we're under attack and I'm certain death is imminent. I've learned that despair is worse than terror.

In contrast, the General appears a man at peace with himself. "How do you do it?" I ask. "How can you remain so serene?"

"Because I have seen far worse and lived to tell the tale. Ypres. The Somme. Now there was a truly nasty business."

"This is nasty enough. Sorry to get you into such a mess."

"Not at all, dear boy. The cause is noble. Worth dying for if need be. No apology is necessary."

He stands and draws himself up. "For years after we leave this terrible place, and I assure you we will, *I shall strip my sleeve and show my scars, and say*

'These wounds I had on Crispin's day.' And gentlemen in England now a-bed, Shall think themselves accurs'd they were not here."

I look up in awe, not at the middle aged man but at the courageous young British officer he must once have been. I almost expect the next words from his mouth to be 'Over the top, chaps!'

"You have spared me the indignity of fighting my entire war from behind a desk, Harrison. I should thank you. Though I would prefer you not share that sentiment with Lady Elverstone."

"Your Mr. Shakespeare understood a soldier's honor," says Lieutenant Schier. He appeared while the General was delivering his call to arms, listening with a smile on his drawn, haggard face. "Herr Wildermuth requires your presence."

I climb to my feet—an act requiring a Herculean effort—and we follow him down a dark tunnel to the enemy's subterranean headquarters.

From behind a folding table covered in scattered maps, the German commander shouts one order after another to his staff. I don't know what he thinks he's doing, but maneuvering his forces is pointless. He's surrounded, outgunned, and outnumbered. And running short on food. As General Rowntree explained to me earlier, fewer hungry mouths to feed is the real reason Wildermuth wants to release the civilians—and also the reason our forces will never agree.

The German defenders are surely low on fuel and ammunition too and the Allies have complete command of sky and sea. It makes no sense continuing the fight. Yet the Colonel leads them onward to an inevitable defeat and avoidable death.

His subordinates seem equally devoted to their hopeless cause, responding to his orders without hesitation or complaint. Perhaps it is a warped sense of the soldier's honor Schier so admired in the Bard's portrait of Henry V and his loyal troops.

"Herr General," the Colonel says, pronouncing 'General' with a hard G.

He continues in German, which Schier translates as, "I wish to send a renewed plea to the British commander to evacuate the civilian population. If you personally deliver this message, perhaps he will reconsider."

"No. *Nein*," General Rowntree says. "The Allied commander will accept no message but your unconditional surrender. And I will certainly carry no other."

Schier translates the answer, then we wait for the response.

"There is no need for further unnecessary deaths," Schier says. "The people of Le Havre are suffering. The French are your allies. Why should you want to let them die?"

General Rowntree takes a step toward the map table and stares directly at the German commander. "Moral responsibility for those deaths lies with you, Colonel. You can end the killing right now if you so choose."

He pauses, allowing Schier to translate, before continuing. "There is nothing noble in sacrificing innocent civilians, or your own men, to a lost cause. Germany is already defeated. National Socialism will soon be but a dark footnote to history. I implore you to forget the past and look to your country's future."

I half expect yelling and screaming once Schier translates the stern and provocative response, but Wildermuth greets the rebuke with a resigned shrug and a sheepish expression. He knows General Rowntree is right. Then his back stiffens, and he dismisses us with a grunt and a wave of his hand.

The German commander is already back to barking orders at his staff before we've even left the room...

— o —

Rumbling that emanates from somewhere deep within the earth literally shakes me from my sleep. I bring my wrist in front of my face. My watch is still working, or at least the second hand is moving. But are the hour and minute it shows correct? There's no real sense of the passage of time when huddled in this burrow where the sun's glow never reaches.

The waves of bombing seem timed to prevent continuous rest. Or any normal human activity. Eating, washing, even visiting the latrine must all be squeezed into the quiet moments of unknown duration between attacks.

If my watch is right, an hour and a half has passed since the previous barrage. Which means I've grabbed perhaps an hour's shuteye since the last round in this fight to the death.

After days of incessant hammering, everyone here is dragged down by an overwhelming fatigue, something I'm sure the Allied commander is counting on to aid his final assault. I'm so tired and weak with hunger that a break of even a few minutes is enough to fall into a deep slumber from which I never want to return. *Let me die in my sleep. I don't care, just let my eyes stay closed.* I can't even sit without nodding off. Except when the bombs are falling. Only the dead can sleep through that nightmare.

Every few seconds there's another thud. The shaking grows more violent as the bombs come closer, a quickening march of death.

I stick my fingers in my ears, longing for some respite from the deafening noise, but like a wildebeest on the Serengeti being chased down by a cheetah, I can't outrun my doom.

General Rowntree and I look at each other as dust rains down on us, knowing speech is pointless, waiting silently for it to be over. Until the next time.

He still seems far more relaxed than is reasonable. Whereas it is only a life-sapping tiredness that stops my body shaking with fear.

As the bombs fall ever closer, the roughly hewn floor beams above our heads bounce up and down, each time jumping a little higher off the stone pillars bearing the weight of the building above.

Is everything going to cave in on top of us?

I look around frantically for an escape though I know there's nowhere to go. My breath catches and my heart races at the thought of being buried alive. I can't think of a worse way to die. Except for drowning. Well, I dodged that fate. I can dodge this one too.

The ground lurches up beneath us. I turn to reach for the foundation wall, for something to steady me, but the wall is coming to me instead.

I launch myself at the General, dragging him forward beyond the path of a crumbling tower of rock and collapsing lumber.

Everything closes in from above, our already tiny world shrinking to nothing. I land face down, my nose pressed against the hard, damp floor.

A high-pitched whistle fills my ears. When I open my eyes the world is tumbling. A wave of nausea washes over me then subsides as the spinning stops. Dust fills the air. I can't see anything. My eyes burn with it, I can feel it in my ears and coating my hair.

Uggh. Pulverized stone and mortar mixes with my saliva, filling my mouth with mud. I spit it out, scraping it from my tongue with my teeth. It's still there. I need water. *Get up!* I have to rinse my mouth. Wash my body. I'm caked in dirt. *Clean. If only I could get clean, wash this terror away...*

I try to lift myself from the ground, like I'm doing a push-up at the gym. My arms don't respond.

I wiggle my fingers. Is anything happening?

There's something pinning me. I'm trapped. I thrash my legs. *Please, get me out!*

Someone places a hand on my back. "Hold steady, old boy."

It's the General speaking, I think, but he sounds so far away, like he's in another room, or underwater. But he was right here, next to me, a minute ago. He wouldn't leave.

"We will get you out." It *is* General Rowntree. "Remain calm," he adds in a voice trembling with barely suppressed panic. "Help us! *Bitte!*"

Other voices now. They shout at each other. Arguing. Why can't I understand them?

A chant of "*Ein, Zwei, Drei*" is followed by a series of guttural groans, then the slow, tortured squeak of wood strained to its limit, pursued by an avalanche of masonry.

The dull pressure on my arms eases, replaced by a searing pain. It begins at my shoulders and shoots like poison arrows down through my biceps to my elbows and my forearms, until my fingers burn with the agony of a thousand needles piercing them. *Make it stop. Make it stop. Please make it stop.*

I turn my head, looking for the source of the pain. Oh God, there's a bone protruding from my left forearm.

I can't breathe. I can't breathe.

Steady. Relax… The pain recedes. Sweet relief.

Everything ebbs, the light dims, sounds fade, life drains away. *So this is how I die…*

TWENTY-EIGHT

Williams enters carrying a silver tray bearing a telegram.

I lay down the article I snipped from the latest edition of *The Times*, a front-page story on the commencement yesterday of the ground assault.

The words in today's reports differ from publication to publication, reflecting the distinctive style of each publisher, but the substance is invariable — two entire divisions, including tanks and artillery, are advancing on the city along a narrow front, their immense firepower concentrated on a few square miles.

Newspaper clippings cover the surface of the secretary desk — everything published in the major dailies about the assault on Le Havre since we received news of Father's captivity. Though I have read every article three or four times, I am reading them again, searching for some important detail I might have missed, some clue to suggest Father and Harrison may still be alive.

So desperate am I for any glimmer of hope, I persist despite the task being both futile and irrational. Whatever facts I glean from the newspaper reports do more to extinguish hope than to nurture it. Today, for example, I read how the embattled population are calling the massive aerial and naval bombing they have endured *La Tempête de Fer et Feu*. The Storm of Iron and Fire. It is a name that conjures an image from Dante's *Inferno*, of Father and Harrison having passed through the Gates of Hell, still to confront untold horrors ahead as they move closer and closer to the centre of pure evil and unending suffering.

Mother lifts the telegram from the tray. "Thank you, Williams," she says, dismissing him.

"Please, Alicia, will you read it?" She holds the telegram out at arm's length, her face turned away, waving it at me. "I cannot bring myself to do so."

She is in a terrible state, continually referring to Father as 'Geoffrey.' Or 'my darling Geoffrey.' Even 'my beloved Geoffrey.' With some effort I can imagine her addressing him by such intimate terms in the privacy of their bedchamber. But my parents, the Lord and Lady Elverstone, are never so familiar with each other in the company of others. Even when alone with Jony and me, they have always been 'Mother' and 'Father,' to us and to each other. Such displays of unchecked emotion are a sign of the depth of her despair, I suppose. Understandable. But it is so out of character it jars me every time I hear it.

I cross the room, taking a seat next to her as I accept the message. "It is from Field Marshal Brooke." My hand shakes as I hold it. "General Crerar believes the German surrender is imminent." I take Mother's hand. "Cousin Alan promises to telephone the moment he has any news of Father."

"Dear Brookie," Mother says.

He is dear indeed. Though only a distant relative, he has gone beyond the call of duty in helping us through this terrible ordeal. At present he is in Canada, attending another conference with the Americans. Not only is he taking time from his demanding schedule to keep us informed of Father's fate, he also arranged with Deputy Director Travis for me to remain here with Mother until Father returns safely to us.

We have settled into a pattern of sleepless nights and listless days spent waiting for some scrap of news. I imagine Mr. Hudson's pigs are eating well, because we only pick at the food we are served. But life in the household goes on around us, following the well-worn paths of tradition and obligation.

Being trapped in the limbo of not knowing is the worst torture imaginable. Not being able to move forward. *Or is it?* Would I rather know for sure they are never to return than hold tight to the hope they will? Perhaps no news truly is good news. Well, it seems we shall know soon enough, whether we like it or not.

I wish Jony were here, for Mother's sake. And mine. He returned to his unit two days ago, something about preparing for an imminent drop. Sometimes I wish his knee had not healed. Is it terrible, to wish one's brother remain a cripple? Of course it is, but this is almost too much to bear. First Father placed himself in the path of death, and then Jony. I could lose every man in the world I care for.

Including Harrison.

I am still reluctant to admit it, even to myself, but the prospect of his death troubles me even more than the thought of losing Father or Jony. For so long I struggled against a future that seemed pre-destined, only realising my mistake when it was too late. Since letting him slip away, I have reconciled myself to another life — unscripted, but undoubtedly less promising. I would give the world to know my destiny lies with him. What a classic fool I am...

— o —

The crunch of tyres upon gravel interrupts my reading. I glance up from a page I must have read a hundred times in the past hour though I cannot recall its content. The book drops onto my lap as my ears prick up in anticipation.

An automobile door thuds shut.

Is it? Could it be? I toss my book on the chair and leap to my feet.

"Alic —" is all I hear from Mother as I dart from the room.

It would never do to be seen running through the house. I move at a pace that complies only with the letter of the rule, not its spirit, but then I cannot hold back. I break into a full-blooded sprint, sliding across the floor as I turn the corner into the entrance hall.

I pull up sharply at the front door. A Humber is idling in the driveway. Khaki paint. It could be any officer's staff car, except I recognise the man standing beside it, even with his back to me. Corporal Jones. Father's driver. He steps back as he swings the door open, providing an unobstructed view of the passenger climbing out.

"Father!" I shout as I rush to him.

"My darling Alicia," he says as I throw my arms around his neck.

"Oh Father, we were so frightened for you." I step back, examining him. He appears unhurt but dog-tired, his face gaunt. Yet there's a spirited fire in his eyes, a *joie de vivre*, missing since this war started. He is undoubtedly as happy to return as we are to receive him.

"I am sorry for the distress I caused," he says, misinterpreting the tears of joy welling in my eyes. "Though it was rather beyond my control."

"You are returned to us safely, Father. That is all that matters."

We begin towards the main entrance where Mother is waiting. She glares at me, an admonishment for my unladylike behaviour, though I suspect she wishes she could throw decorum to the wind too.

Father approaches her, places his hands on the outside of her shoulders, then kisses her lightly on both cheeks before pulling her head to his chest. When he releases his hold, Mother is blushing. This may be his greatest public display of affection in their many years of marriage. But her rosy face also swells with joy.

As my parents link arms and turn to retreat inside, I hear the sound behind me of Father's car driving off.

Where is Harrison? "Father, why…" I gulp, fighting to control the trembling in my voice. "Why is Professor Seely not with you? Is he…" I cannot speak the word. It pains me even to form the thought, yet my mind does so of its own accord.

"He is hospitalised. I'm afraid he was rather severely injured."

Dear Lord, no. Harrison would have happily observed this war from a distance, a safe distance, had I not bullied him into doing otherwise. He should be safe at home in Princeton, not lying broken and alone in some hospital bed.

"Is he…" I cover my mouth with my hand, preventing my despair from escaping. What I want to know, but am afraid and ashamed to ask, is whether he will make a full recovery. What if he lost an arm or a leg, like so many men in this war and the last, or suffered something even worse. Burns. Disfigurement. What if he dies?

"Rest easy, my darling." Father takes my arm, steadying me. "Such anguish is uncalled for. Though his will be a long, slow recovery, the doctors assure me there should be no permanent disability."

I breathe a sigh of relief. But I must see for myself. "Where is he? At which hospital, Father?"

"Coventry. Gulson Road."

I have so much to tell him, so much to say. It cannot wait another moment. I have indulged my obstinate nature far too long. "Henderson," I say, "bring the car." I turn my head. Where is he? "HENDERSON!"

"Calm yourself this instant, Alicia," Mother says. "Remember your station."

"Please," says Father, "visiting hours will be long over by the time you arrive."

"He needs—"

"He needs his rest. There is nothing to be done. Not until tomorrow."

Our driver appears from the direction of the garage, rushing towards us.

Father waves him away. "Come," he says, placing a hand on my elbow, gently guiding me inside. "I have much to tell you both. Including how our daughter's heroic young friend saved my life…"

TWENTY-NINE

The room and its simple furnishings are primitive compared to a modern hospital suite, but without the constant beeping of electronic monitors it is far more peaceful. I am sound asleep until someone enters and I think I hear them mention breakfast.

"Huh?" I say, still dazed.

A waif of a girl wearing a crisp blue and white uniform stands at the foot of my bed holding a tray. "Breakfast time, Captain Seely," she says in a voice as tiny as her physique. She places the tray on the table and wheels it into position over the bed.

I glance out the window. It's barely daylight outside. Why do hospitals do that, wake you up to feed you?

A cast extending to the shoulder immobilizes my right arm, while my left is encased to the middle of my upper arm to stabilize the forearm and elbow. I might be able to hold a spoon, but there is no way I could bring it anywhere near my mouth.

My nurse, a trainee I assume from her tender years, dips a spoon into a bowl of oatmeal then carefully guides it into my mouth. I half expect her to make a sputtering sound and tell me to open wide for the airplane.

Her hands shake and she mumbles something to herself as she refuses to make eye contact. I want to believe she's seventeen or eighteen, but she looks barely fifteen. Despite her youthful lack of confidence I can't fault her attentiveness, or her obvious concern for my well-being. But it still doesn't seem right, being tended to by a kid.

Though the food is satisfying, I signal for her to stop after four or five spoonfuls. "I'm not really hungry."

"Tea?"

"Milk and one sugar, please."

She drops a sugar cube in the cup and adds a splash of milk, gives the concoction a stir, then lifts the cup to my lips and slowly tilts it forward.

I take a cautious sip, trying not to dribble the hot liquid down my chin.

The approaching click-click-click of heels on linoleum draws my eyes toward the door.

The woman who enters is little more than a blurry outline since my glasses are missing. Best guess, they're buried in the rubble of Le Havre's town hall, perhaps to become a source of great confusion for some future archeologist.

Despite the lack of visual clarity, I recognize her immediately, though she is the last person I expect to see. All I can do is stare, not sure what to say.

Alicia Rowntree doesn't avoid my gaze as she approaches, but instead returns it with equal intensity. "Allow me," she says to the nurse as she reaches for the teacup. "You must have other patients to tend."

The girl stares back with frightened eyes. "Sorry, Miss, but visiting hours don't start until 9 am."

"It is all right…" She squints to read the girl's name tag. "Molly, I have special approval from Matron."

"Well, if Matron approves…" She releases the cup and saucer to Alicia's care. "Thank you, Miss." On her way out Molly stops and turns on her heels. "You have to go slow like," she says, miming the gentle tipping of the cup, before scurrying away.

"Hello, Professor," Alicia says in a serious tone. Then a tight-lipped smile spreads slowly across her face. "Or should I address you as *Captain*?"

The tips of my ears ignite, though the experience of the past two weeks makes me far less of a pretender now than when I first donned the uniform. "That was General Eisenhower's idea."

"I would hate to compromise your cover story."

"My war is over," I say. "And it lasted less than a fortnight. Nothing to write home about. *Professor* will do just fine."

With a gesture of the cup she asks if I would like more tea. I answer with a nod. She leans across the bed and raises the cup to my mouth.

I take a self-conscious sip. It was humiliating enough being spoon-fed by a shy teenage girl to whom I am a stranger, but I have so much more at stake in my relationship with this woman. I hate her seeing me so helpless. But I'm a prisoner of circumstances, so I thank her anyway.

Alicia looks at my half-finished meal. "Is this all you have eaten? Do you not like porridge?"

"No, I do. But…"

"You have no appetite?"

I respond with an awkward, restricted shrug of my shoulders.

"Oh, I see. Well, you must resign yourself to being fed, I am afraid."

"It's not that." It is, but I don't want to admit it. "The doctors don't want me overdoing it until my stomach has time to adjust. Though they did say I could have all the liquids I want. Yet strangely, the beer I ordered has not yet arrived."

"Father is under similar orders."

"No beer?"

"You are quite the comedian today, Professor."

"How is your father?"

"In fine fettle. Certainly much better than you." Her expression turns serious, her pale, almost translucent brows meeting in the middle. "Father told me a little of what you and he endured. A plane crash. Capture. Bombed night and day. Starvation. What a ghastly ordeal." She indicates my broken arms. "And then this."

At least I didn't break my nose again. "Tis but a scratch," I say, mimicking the voice of the Black Knight.

I get no response, not that I expected any. But I can't help chuckling at my own humor. She has the joys of *Monty Python and the Holy Grail* ahead of her. And *The Beatles*. And a thousand other wonderful things. *Elvis*. Seeing *Star Wars* for the first time and being blown away.

I joke not out of a misguided belief that I'm particularly funny, but as a poor attempt at outrunning a deep, indescribable sense of unease, a feeling everything could come crashing down again at any minute. I'm not certain what PTSD feels like, but if this is it, I wouldn't wish it on anyone.

Of everything I endured, it was the treatment

received at the hands of the German doctor that haunts me most. He did his best, but with the besieged garrison desperately short of supplies, including medicines, he was forced to set my broken arms with no pain relief, not even a swig of brandy like you see in the old movies. I screamed like a banshee as he pulled and pushed the broken bones back into position, and cried like a baby afterward. Dark, yellowing bruises in the shape of hands stain my chest and legs like unwelcome graffiti, the result of several men holding me down during the procedure.

Many of the German wounded endured far worse. The agonized screams of a man having his leg amputated without anesthesia still trouble my dreams. I didn't understand what he yelled over and over in German, apart from one word: *Mutter*. Mother. No matter how tightly I closed my eyes, I couldn't block out that awful, pathetic sound. Far worse than hearing his pain was the sense his despair was reaching out to touch me, to infect me.

At least I didn't awake in the dark last night drenched in sweat and shaking with fear. I have the morphine to thank for that.

But will the nightmares come rushing back once it stops? God, I hope not. "I'm no hero."

"Father would disagree," she says. "Heroic was precisely the word he used."

"I just did what I had to do in the situation I found myself in. It wasn't something I went looking for. And they don't give out medals for taking friendly fire. Or they shouldn't."

She drops her head, almost like she's praying. "Whatever you wish to call it, we are grateful beyond reckoning for all you did for Father."

I wait for her eyes to meet mine. They glisten with gathering moisture. "It must have been terrible for you too," I say. "The waiting. I can only imagine how worried you were about your father."

"It was harrowing indeed," she says, her chin quivering. She turns away and gently dabs her cheeks with her handkerchief. "But I was equally as anxious for you."

Alicia Rowntree turns back to face me.

I wait. What is it she wants to say?

"I accepted I would never see you again. Then to know you had returned, the thought you would not... that we would not... I do not know how I endured it."

Now it's my turn to look away. I can't let her see the raging storm of emotions lashing my soul — resentment, confusion, desire, anger. I don't want her to realize how her mere presence affects me. "I thought that was what you wanted."

"I thought so too." She chuckles. "As it transpires, I was quite mistaken."

She places a hand on the cast covering my forearm. I only feel the touch indirectly, but it is somehow deeply intimate.

"Harrison, please look at me."

I clench my jaw as I turn to face her. "What do you want from me, Alicia?"

"To allow me to apologize for the way we parted," she says. "My behavior was truly unforgivable. And to know why you are here."

"Where else would I be with two broken arms?"

— o —

Someone enters the room, interrupting us with a throaty "Ahem." White coat. A doctor. He heads straight for the clipboard hanging from the end of my bed. "Good morning, Captain Seely," he says as he flicks through my chart. "Samuel Darlington, Chief of Surgery."

I flap my arms. "I guess I have you to thank for these, doctor?" He bristles, like a cat when you rub its fur from tail to head. *Oh, that's right.* "It's supposed to be *Mr.* Darlington, isn't it?" Surgeons in the UK are prickly about that. Imagine, a Brit who is particular about forms of address.

"Indeed, though you were not to know," he says in a tone far less forgiving than his words. "As for your injuries, the army doctors in France did a competent job, everything considered. Nevertheless, our facilities and personnel are far superior to those of even the best field hospital. I reset your bones, to be quite sure they heal correctly. The compound fractures of the left ulna and radius, here and here" — he taps each side of his forearm in turn — "were of particular concern."

I recall my left forearm, bones poking... My stomach kicks me in the stomach. I swallow hard to force the erupting bile back down. "It's all right now?"

"Not yet, obviously." He pokes and prods my belly.

Stop it! Up here. My arms are the problem. "But will I get back normal use?"

He pulls a small silver flashlight from his breast pocket and shines it in my eyes. "I foresee no serious limitations."

Alicia steps forward into his line of sight. "*Mr.* Darlington, *Lady* Alicia Rowntree."

"Oh, forgive me, My Lady. I didn't notice you there."

"Not at all," she says. "A single-minded focus on the patient seems an admirable quality in a man of medicine."

He responds with an ambiguous "Hmmm," signaling either agreement with Alicia's statement, or a cynical dismissal of the idea. I can't tell which. "General Rowntree's daughter?"

"*Lord Elverstone* is my father," she says with an aristocratic indignation I haven't heard since… since the second time I met her, when she scolded me for calling her 'Ma'am.' But there's a much sharper, less patient tone in her voice this time. Presumably because she understood that I was ignorant of the proper forms, while Mr. Darlington can plead no such defense.

"Then perhaps you could answer a question that is troubling me, My Lady," the surgeon says.

"I shall try."

"Captain Seely belongs in an American military hospital. I am curious as to why your… Lord Elverstone brought him here. It is his pocket that will be the lighter for it, but still, it is quite irregular."

Though it's a good question, it hadn't occurred to me until now. What's the last thing I remember before waking up here? A field hospital. Somewhere in France? That would make sense. Probably close to Le Havre. I close my eyes. Voices hover over me. Not British, but not quite American. 'He's still oot,' one voice said. Canadian.

"Lord Elverstone owes the Captain his life. He wishes in some small way to repay this immeasurable debt." Alicia grasps as much of the fingers of my right hand as protrude from the cast. "And his only daughter wishes to stay close to her fiance during his convalescence."

I try not to jump in shock when I hear myself described as her fiance, an effort greatly assisted by the fact I can barely move.

Why would she say that? Obvious. For the same reason I made a similar claim to the German commander.

"Ah," the surgeon says, as if our fake engagement explains everything.

"When do you think I might get out of here, Mr. Darlington?" I say.

"The cast on your right arm must remain for at least three weeks, the left one for five. During this time you will need a great deal of care. Eating, dressing, bathing, as you have no doubt already learned."

"Five weeks!" I'm so over this place already. "I can't stay here for five weeks."

"Protesting will not change the facts, Captain."

"Is there no other way?" Alicia says. "Could you release the Captain to our care? Elverstone Hall would provide for his every need."

I want to get out of this place, but who would help me dress and bathe? Williams or Henderson? Or worse, the housekeeper-cook, Mrs… What was her name? *Cakes, pastries…* Mrs. Baker.

"That won't be necessary," I say hurriedly.

Perhaps I should return to Princeton and twenty-first century medicine instead. The university provides its employees with excellent insurance — low copays, small deductible — and world class care at its teaching hospital.

But I can't walk into the ER with two broken arms and no explanation for my injuries, or how or where or why I came to be treated with 1940s medical practices.

"I can stay here," I say. "Or, as Mr. Darlington suggests, transfer to a military hospital. They must be used to this sort of injury."

"You will do no such thing," Alicia says.

"Are you certain, My Lady?" the surgeon says. "It would be an enormous undertaking."

"Neither Lord Elverstone nor I would have it any other way. We shall hire a nurse. Several nurses if need be. And anything else the Captain requires for his comfort and recovery."

"Then I see no impediment to releasing Captain Seely to your care in a few days. Assuming all goes well."

"Thank you, *Mr.* Darlington."

"Lady Alicia, Captain Seely," he says before spinning on his heels and hurrying away.

As soon as we're alone I say, "I bet he's not used to being put in his place like that."

Alicia makes a face like she's sucking on a lemon. "What a horrid man."

We both break out in giggles. Laughing in unison I feel so close to her, which only makes me more aware of the distance between us. "Why did you tell him I'm your fiance?"

"Because it cuts short so many questions." She shakes her finger at me. "Anyway, I am reliably informed you instigated the practice."

"You're not upset?"

"When you did so to protect Father? That would be terribly ungrateful of me." She squeezes my fingers before letting them slip from her hand.

"But enough of that. You need your rest. I shall return tomorrow."

Before I can react — not that I know what I want to say — she kisses my forehead and is gone.

— o —

Alicia visits me again the next day, just as she promised. And the next day. And the day after that. Every day for a week, as my discharge is delayed not once, not twice, but three times. Some days she visits me in the morning *and* in the afternoon.

I avoid discussing my French adventure by begging tiredness whenever she raises it. I do the same with anything even touching on our relationship. I'm all around lousy company, yet she sits with me for countless hours without complaint.

Mostly she reads to me. I'm desperate to know if my plan worked, so we start with the newspapers every morning. I learn that Antwerp is open and there's no mention of MARKET GARDEN or any recent V1 attacks, and no reports of her brother's unit going into action.

So if I've succeeded in keeping Alicia and Jony alive, what happens now?

After we check each day's news, she reads from a magnificently bound copy of Shakespeare's complete works. We've completed the comedies. We're now powering through the so-called 'histories' — terrible historiography, but wonderful studies in the use and abuse of political power — though I will have to read them again. Too often my mind wanders under the influence of the morphine, or the soothing sound of Alicia's voice.

Today we're in the middle of *Julius Caesar*. "There is a tide in the affairs of men," she reads.

I recognize the line. Brutus is trying to convince Cassius that they should move against Marcus Antonius now, before he can gather a larger force. Before their tide goes out.

"On such a full sea are we now afloat," she continues. "And we must take the current when it serves, Or lose our ventures."

She stops and closes the book when Mr. Darlington enters. He examines me briefly, then announces without fanfare that he will discharge me today, before leaving without another word.

Alicia's relief is as palpable as mine. I ask if she would fetch a suit of Jonathan's, explaining that the tattered remains of my uniform aren't fit to wear in public. She agrees enthusiastically, though I don't mention that I wouldn't put the military outfit on again even if it were fresh from the tailor. When I said my war was over, I meant it.

— o —

Alicia returns two and a half hours later with the clothing I requested. And with her father. I haven't seen him since Le Havre.

He claps me affectionately on the shoulder, then reaches into his pocket and produces my glasses. "I believe these are yours, Harrison," he says as he delivers them.

I slide them on. "How? Where?"

"The ruins of the *Hôtel de Ville*. Our Canadian liberators were none too pleased when I insisted on returning to search for them. And rather surprised that I found them."

"That wasn't necessary, General, but thank you so much."

I glance at Alicia, seeing her sweet face in focus for the first time since I've been here. I can't help smiling. She smiles back, as pleased for me, I think, as I am for myself.

General Rowntree is smiling too. "Thank you for coming, Sir," I say.

"I apologize for not visiting sooner," he says. "I have had…" His smile dissipates, his hesitation tinged with… embarrassment? Something is wrong, but what?

His face sets and he continues. "I had a great deal of pressing business at the War Office, as you can imagine."

"I understand, Sir," I reply calmly, suppressing my curiosity. "And how is the war going?" I ask casually, though I'm dying to know.

"Splendid, just splendid. At this rate the entire west bank of the Rhine will be ours within a week."

"The V1 launch sites?" The Germans still have the V2 rockets, but I'm not worried about them. They came too late and in numbers too small to be a real threat.

"Captured." He glances at his daughter. "The threat to London is over."

"And Jony? Where is he now?"

"With his regiment. The 1st Parachute Brigade remains on standby."

Not what I hoped for. In the previous timeline — the one I restored like Grandpa Harry asked, before I changed it again — American and British paratroopers undertook one last great airborne operation in March 1945. Like the bomber force, it was a case of commanders feeling compelled to use a weapon because it existed, to justify the resources devoted to building the capability.

Dropped on the far bank of the Rhine to secure a bridgehead for Monty's Twenty-First Army Group, they incurred heavy casualties from German anti-aircraft fire during their descent. Should the Wehrmacht once again make its final stand behind the Rhine, the Allied command will almost certainly resort to a similar strategy. Especially if Field Marshal Montgomery has any influence. He's enamored of airborne operations and the idea of a decisive strike behind enemy lines.

The thought of so many men dying pointless deaths in the final days of the war offends me. Even if Jony survives, and there's no guarantee he will. But I take a deep breath, keeping my concerns to myself. The General would want Jony to do his duty, no matter how dangerous, or how futile.

— o —

Before I can ask the General more about the military plans that may determine his son's fate, Sister Campbell enters. A petite, dark-haired woman in her forties, her appearance fits the image of the stern matron. But not her personality. Not at all. Warm, jovial, and caring, the younger nurses worship her. There's no fear, just respect. I can see why. Though in charge of the entire floor, she hasn't hesitated to get her hands dirty with my care, and I do mean dirty.

She greets Alicia like an old friend, stops and sizes up the General before greeting him warmly too, then asks them to step outside while she helps me dress.

We start with the shirt. She wriggles the sleeves up over my stiff, thick, plaster-covered arms. Next the pants. It's easy enough stepping into them, but I need her help to fasten them. I ought to be over the embarrassment by now — this woman and several others have seen and touched *everything* over the past week — but I still turn my head and look silently away as she fastens the waist and fly.

"You're a bit of a strange egg, Captain," she says as she deftly buttons my shirt, patting my chest affectionately when she's done. "Even for an American. But I shall miss you."

I choke back the beginnings of a tear. "You too, Sister." I won't miss this place once I'm gone — my sentence isn't complete with my arms still out of action, though I am being released on parole — but

I'll always have a soft spot for her and all the women, and girls, who nursed me with such compassion and tenderness.

"You have a long recovery ahead. But you're a very fortunate young man."

"I know. I thought I was a dead man for a while there."

"There is that too." She stretches the suspenders over my arms and drops them onto my shoulders. "But I was referring to you and the Lady Alicia. Have you set a date?"

I owe her the truth, but at this late stage… *Oh what a tangled web we weave.* "Not yet."

"And why not?" She glares at me. *There's the frosty matron.* "I don't have to tell you that life is short, Captain."

"It's complicated, Sister."

I drop back onto the bed. My rump lands with a thud. It is surprisingly hard to lower yourself gently when you can't use your hands. "More complicated than you can imagine."

"You have a beautiful, intelligent, accomplished fiancee, a lady from a fine family, who seems devoted to you."

She kneels to tie my shoes. "And if Lord Elverstone's smile is any proof, he approves, though a person of his station could have any number of reasons to object to this match."

"I did save his life."

She stands and playfully slaps my shoulder, the one not in a cast. "Get away with you." Her smile disappears. "Are you having doubts, Captain?"

I do not respond.

"Do you not truly love her, lad?"

My duplicity and the question's double negative confuse me. If I'd told the truth about the engagement, I wouldn't be in this mess. "No," I say, then quickly correct myself. "Yes." I can't bring myself to answer with a lie. "I mean, I do love her. Of course I do."

More than I realized until now. It isn't about preserving the timeline anymore. That ship has sailed. This time I returned to save Alicia, without any expectation of where that might lead. I no longer believe I can save my parents, even with her help.

"I love her very much."

Matron drapes Jony's coat over my shoulders, the same one I was wearing the day I met him. "Then, my dear Captain, I don't see what's complicated about it at all."

If only she knew the whole story…

— o —

Morphine befogs my mind for days after I return to Elverstone Hall. That's my only excuse for not noticing that General Rowntree hasn't returned to his work at the War Office. Or that I haven't seen him in uniform since he visited me in hospital.

Only one explanation comes to mind, but if I am correct, it is a delicate matter, best approached indirectly. I'll ask him for an update on the war and see how current and complete his intelligence is.

I find him in the library, seated behind his desk. He's alone, for the best if the situation is as I expect. No need to embarrass him in front of anyone else.

I stop at the door. "May I?"

"Of course, dear boy." He stands and waves me in. "So deeply am I in your debt, I would refuse you nothing." He gestures toward the liquor tray on the sideboard.

Tempted as I am, I demur on account of the hour. Breakfast has barely settled. That and the fact that someone would have to hold the glass while I drink. I'm sure as hell not going to ask the General, or even let him offer.

He sits and I maneuver myself awkwardly into the chair across the desk from him, banging my elbow on the arm as I do. Fortunately, the one protected by a cast.

"General, I —"

"I have resigned my commission," he says with a slow, melancholy shake of his head. "You may address me as Lord Elverstone instead. Or better still, Sir Geoffrey."

I'm not happy to have my suspicions confirmed, but not surprised. "Not voluntarily..."

"The Chiefs of Staff were not at all pleased with what they referred to as my 'gross insubordination.' It was either a quiet resignation or the public humiliation of a court-martial. I doubt they would make good on the threat — too many secrets to keep — but they would have been perfectly justified in cashiering me."

I suddenly feel guilty at what I've done, at what he's lost pursuing my schemes, or at least Grandpa Harry's. No, they're mine. I can't wriggle out of it that easily. "You deserve to be feted for all you've done. To go out in a blaze of glory."

"Nonsense. I knew the price to be paid when we approached General Eisenhower directly. To tempt fate once was reckless enough, but twice? Not terribly easy to hide an unauthorized trip to the front lines from one's superiors. Though being wounded and captured did not help that cause, the outcome was inevitable, even had you and I slipped in and out of France as quietly as church mice."

"Do you regret any of it?"

"I regret not a moment of our grand adventure," he says effusively. His face hardens. "I wish only that I could have avoided putting Brookie in such a delicate position."

"He wouldn't intervene on your behalf?"

"I made no such request, nor will I. You and I know in here" — he taps his chest with his fist — "what we did, by God. Winning the war. Saving my son and heir, and my beloved daughter. These are achievements to carry proudly to one's grave. I require no public accolades."

"True enough, Sir. But what now?"

"Devote myself to running the estate with Jonathan. I have neglected it long enough in pursuit of my military career. I must endeavor to put the place on a sound financial footing before I shuffle off this mortal coil. No doubt I will chafe at new ideas, but I can read the writing on the wall. You did warn me change was coming."

He looks at me expectantly. "You could make a contribution too, you know. Helping us prepare for a future you know better than anyone."

I have a sense of being asked to join the family firm. It's an awkward feeling when you aren't part of the family. "I don't know how *this* particular future will unfold."

"Not precisely. But the broad trends, surely they will remain unchanged?"

"Probably. But... well, I don't know if I'll even stay around."

"Ahh. So you have not yet spoken with Lady Alicia?"

"I-I-I can't. What would I say that I haven't already said?"

— o —

I'm in the General's library, holding a book in place on my lap with my right hand, now free of the plaster cast, though my left arm is still encased past the elbow.

Jony rushes in, noticeably excited about something. "Have you heard the news, Harry?"

I shake my head.

He does a little jig. "Hitler is dead!"

"How, when?"

"I'm not sure, but this calls for a celebration." He pours two cognacs and passes me one. I place the book on the side table then receive the glass with my free hand.

"Oh, what a day to be alive!" Jony says.

Sir Geoffrey appears in the doorway. "What a day, indeed."

"Father, there you are. Isn't it wonderful?"

"We will tell your children, my grandchildren, of this day." Sir Geoffrey winks at me. "And even my great-grandchildren."

Jony pours another brandy and hands it to his father. I stand, meeting them in the center of the room, where we form a circle like King Arthur's knights, raise our glasses to meet in the middle, and drink a toast to the most hated dictator's demise. Then one to the King, another to the Empire, and finally to the United States.

"Thank God," Sir Geoffrey says. "Europe's nightmare will soon be over."

"Do you know something more, Father?" Jony says.

"Only that our forces have made multiple crossings of the Rhine to encounter virtually no resistance. It is as if the entire German Army — *poof!* — just dissolved into thin air."

"Withdrawn to the eastern front is more likely," I say.

"What makes you say that?" says Jony.

"Historians in my time speculate endlessly about why the Germans resisted so desperately in the west when they always considered Bolshevism the real enemy of their precious 'Aryan culture.' Perhaps in this timeline they've decided to throw everything into holding the Red Army at bay."

The General casts me a skeptical look. "Eisenhower will accept nothing but unconditional surrender."

"Agreed. I'm certain he will honor the commitment we made to the Russians not to negotiate a separate ceasefire. But if German forces refuse to fight, if they just run away…"

"Then it is simply a question of how fast our tanks can drive," Jony says.

"Exactly."

Today is October 6, 1944. There's been no Yalta Conference yet, not until February. Therefore no discussion with Stalin about the post-war occupation of Germany, and no tacit agreement to let the Soviet Union install friendly regimes in Poland and the rest of eastern Europe.

Who knows how this might turn out if Eisenhower moves decisively. Unfortunately, caution is in his nature and he is determined not to send any more American and British boys home in pine boxes than absolutely necessary. But if nothing else, liberating Holland in the next few weeks will prevent the terrible famine of 1944-45 the Dutch call the *Hongerwinter*.

Yet if the Germans really have decided to throw everything they have at Russia... The Red Army is massive, but it's still fighting in eastern Poland. How different might the post-war world look if Allied forces meet the Red Army at say the Vistula, beyond Warsaw, and not the Elbe?

THIRTY

Mr. Darlington pulls a wheeled stool close to the examination table. The nurse passes him an instrument that looks like pruning shears, but with the blades set at an angle to the handle.

He spreads the handles separating the blades, then slides one blade under the edge of the cast, just above Harrison's left elbow. "Ready, Captain?"

"My military days are over, Mr. Darlington," he says. "It's Professor now. And boy am I ready. This has been the longest five weeks of my life."

"Everything in good time, *Professor*," the surgeon says as he squeezes the handles together and makes the first cut. "Compound fractures are always tricky."

Mr. Darlington removed the cast on this same arm several weeks ago so he could extract the stitches, then applied a new one immediately. A brief taste of freedom snatched away so quickly left Harrison sullen for days. Though his right arm has been free almost a fortnight, there was still much he could not do for himself with only one arm, a situation exacerbated by his left-handedness.

Today, knowing his release will be permanent, his eyes sparkle with anticipation. He's like the Cheshire Cat, all toothy grin, his teeth so white, and so perfect.

I smile back awkwardly, unable to embrace his joy. His happiness should be enough, but for weeks I have dreaded this moment, my stomach churning and heart racing every time I think of it. With this final act of emancipation there will be nothing tying him to Elverstone Hall.

Mr. Darlington moves slowly, deliberately, taking care with each snip not to cut the skin below, while Harrison fidgets impatiently.

Once the surgeon has cut through the full length of the cast, he inserts a device with a wide, flat end into the gap and levers the two sides apart. The plaster separates with a resounding crack.

He peels back the pieces, makes a brief visual inspection, then nods to the nurse as he glides away on his chair.

She douses several cotton balls in alcohol and swabs Harrison's arm. The muscles have withered, the scars are still pronounced, and the skin is a pallid, yellowish shade of grey. But if the experience with his other arm is any guide, it will return to its normal, healthy state within a week or two,

Harrison's dedication to what he calls 'pumping iron' helping the recovery along.

The nurse steps back, her work done, and the surgeon rolls back to the examination table. He grasps Harrison's forearm with his thumb and fingers. "Any pain?" he says as he squeezes and pokes.

"None."

"Jolly good." With one hand on Harrison's elbow and the other on his wrist, he flexes the arm back and forth. "Now?"

"Still no pain."

"Excellent. Everything has healed quite nicely." Mr. Darlington thrusts back his stool and stands. "My nurse will attend to you from here." He peels off his rubber gloves before shaking Harrison's hand. "It has been a pleasure, Professor." He nods to me. "Lady Alicia."

"Thank you, Mr. Darlington," I say.

As the surgeon departs, Harrison and I look at each other with raised eyebrows, our shared distaste for the man having become something of a private joke.

We ride home in silence, Harrison looking pensively out the window, studiously avoiding my gaze. Even Henderson can sense the tension in the confined space of the motor car, periodically glancing at us in the rear vision mirror, his eyes filled with concern. Like all the staff, he has grown fond of the Professor.

I so want to say something, to confess my heartfelt desires, to talk of the future I dream of sharing with this man. But making the first profession of love is not a woman's place. Ironic coming from me when I have so strenuously resisted conventional female roles. But as a modern woman it seems I am a fraud, my views on matters of the heart as traditional as Mother's.

Even were I not such a hypocrite, I would have no claim given my atrocious behaviour, no right to expect more of him. Despite my cruel rejection, he risked his life to save my father. How could I possibly ask him to offer me anything more?

— o —

Craving as much of Harrison's company for as long as I may have it, I invite him to join me for tea when we arrive home.

His acceptance is at once surprising, and pleasing, and unnerving. Will I have the courage to enquire as to his intentions? Should I? I expect the answer to leave me disappointed and heartbroken, but so be it. Only when no glimmer of hope remains can I mourn a true love lost, for I am convinced that is the essence of our connection, at least on my part.

I cannot speak to his feelings with any confidence, but there has been a growing sweetness and deep tenderness in our interactions these past five weeks. I must be deceiving myself, misreading the nurse-patient relationship into which circumstances forced us, but I cannot suppress the desire for his warmth towards me to signify something more profound.

Waiting for our tea in the drawing room, we stare nervously at each other.

Clearly, I must be the one to break this impasse. "What will you do now?" I say, my voice uneven and hesitant.

"Apart from cut up my own food?" he deadpans.

"And dress yourself," I say with an equally affected seriousness.

"There is that."

"And all the other things that must have been so frustrating and embarrassing these past few weeks. Apart from those?"

"I can't go back to 2015." He smiles ruefully.

"I'm convinced that at 55 to 1 the transition would prove fatal."

"So you said."

"You don't agree?"

"If there is any doubt…" I have resigned myself to losing him, but I could not endure the heartbreak of losing him to death's foul grip. "You cannot risk your life again."

"I could return to the States. Eisenhower would help me out."

"Or you could stay here in England. I am certain Father would happily provide the necessary introductions to secure you a suitable position."

"He has already offered. It is tempting. But I'm still undecided."

"I hope… I am confident… I believe I can speak for Father when I say we hope you will remain at Elverstone Hall until you do decide."

"That's kind of you. Of all of you."

"It is the least we can do."

Harrison's expression shifts, from that of a man unsure of himself, to that of someone suddenly decided on a course of action after a long and difficult deliberation. It is a mixture of relief and resolve.

"Do you still have the photo I left with you?" he says.

"It is in my bedchamber." I stand, hoping the relevance of his question will be revealed if I fetch the photograph. "If you will excuse me…"

"Of course."

Upon my return I offer him the picture, but he refuses it. I resume my seat opposite him, placing it face up on the table between us instead.

He clears his throat. "I have to start with an apology."

"No, Harrison. Absolutely not." After his sacrifices for my family he owes me nothing. "It is I who should apologise. You have nothing to —"

"I do. I tried bullying you into marrying me to protect the timeline, to save my parents. It was selfish and insensitive. And not terribly romantic."

"Truly, Harrison, I do understand. Your devotion to family —"

"Was pointless." He leans forward and taps his finger on the boy in the photo. "This isn't my father. It's not Jon Seely."

"Are you certain?" He nods. "Then who is it?"

"Geoffrey. My father in an alternative timeline. Named after your father, I presume."

In a rush he explains his contact with Geoff and Carol Seely, and what he knows of them and his new sister.

He spoke before about his father ceasing to exist, but I understood it to be a possibility, a theoretical outcome. I am stunned to discover that the only family he ever knew was already lost, even then. No wonder his plea was so impassioned, even if completely ham-fisted.

"At least I suspect it's him," he says. "I don't think I'll ever fully understand how this time travel process really works. But it occurs to me that every child is the product of a specific and unique moment of conception. An event that can never be precisely recreated. Of the millions of sperm, what are the chances the same one…" His chin drops to his chest. "So you see, I could never save him, no matter what I did."

I consider the implications. If that is true, it must also have been true for the other Harrys. "Your grandfather…"

"Had to know? I'm sure he did. Logic says he faced exactly the same dilemma. That all six of them did."

"Yet he provided no warning."

Harrison shrugs his shoulders. "I guess he doubted I would knowingly abandon my parents. He was probably right, but I'll never know for sure."

"When did you discover that yours was a lost cause?"

"A day or two after your father and I convinced Eisenhower to delay the invasion. Something about the photos was nagging at me, something that didn't make sense. Until I realised it wasn't Harry and Alice's past they documented…"

"Yet you returned again, knowing you could not preserve your family, even though it was necessarily a one way trip."

"I did."

Bother. His answer provides no insight into his motivation. I must continue to probe. "Do you remember what I asked you that first morning in the hospital?"

He plants his palms on his thighs and straightens his back.

"You asked me why I was there. Not there. Here. In 1944. And like an ass, I fobbed you off with a joke."

"A great deal has passed between us since that day. May I expect a more forthright answer now?"

He pauses, his gaze turning upwards as he considers his words, before he lowers his eyes and locks them to mine. "You have to understand, everyone else I loved was gone."

"I do. I think I do. At least intellectually. I doubt I fully grasp the emotional impact. But your answer, while less jovial, is no more responsive."

Harrison leans forward and takes my hands in his. "I came back to save the only person left that I still care for." He looks at me guiltily. "I gave up the future to save you."

— o —

For Harrison to acknowledge that he still cares for me after the abominable way I treated him — cares enough to abandon forever the wonders of the twenty-first century — is so stunningly unexpected it leaves me unable to form an intelligent response.

"You came back because you care for me?" is all I can manage.

"I came back because I love you, Alicia," he says. "Because I couldn't bear the thought of losing you too, though you were never mine to lose."

He recounts the tragic results of a V1 strike on Hartness Street — my death — and of a military operation called MARKET GARDEN in which Jony would die in action.

Like the history professor he is, Harrison focuses on the facts, his calm, even voice masking his emotions. Only his eyes betray his distress at the thought of our deaths.

I listen in stunned silence, dumbstruck by his direct and unequivocal confession of love, shocked by the brutal reminder of my own mortality, and overwhelmed by the enormity of Harrison's sacrifice on our behalf. Father. Jony. Me. Mother too. Such a loss would have destroyed her. He saved my entire family, but lost his own.

"And Father knew all this?" I say.

"I didn't want you to feel indebted, so I swore him to secrecy." He shakes his head. "Though I have to admit, I never entirely abandoned hope you might..."

"Return your feelings?"

As if it were an unimaginable possibility, he responds with the tiniest and least expectant of crooked smiles.

"Do you know if each of the Harrys married their Alice?" I say.

He nods. "Six Harrys, six Alices."

"Does that not provide a clue as to Harry Seven's fate?"

He grins sheepishly. "I suppose it should have. But with the other changes in the timeline, my parents..."

"Oh, Harrison." I gaze at him longingly. "I see the truth clearly now. Call it fate, call it destiny, call it by whatever label you please. We were always meant to be. Love it seems is far less random than conception. No matter how events moved around them, Harry and Alice were — *are* — the constant thread running through the fabric of time."

"But you made it clear you didn't —"

"My feelings were never in question, my darling. Admiration turned to affection and then to love in such a rush, it terrified me."

"Then why deny it?"

"My courage was wanting. Until Jony's wise counsel forced me to confront my fears."

Now it is his turn to listen in silence while I explain our desperate and unsuccessful dash to London to prevent his departure.

"And what would you have said if you'd caught me?" he says.

It has the sound of a challenge, but a tight smile suggests he is toying with me. I do not respond directly to the taunt; I deserve however much teasing he cares to dish out.

"I would have said I love you too, Harrison. That I love you with all my heart, all my soul, and all my being. Then I would have begged you to stay and told you I was no longer afraid of a preordained future, knowing my future was a life shared with you."

A lump forms in my throat as I wait for his reaction. I try to swallow but it catches. Even breathing requires conscious effort.

He smiles, leans across the table, then cups my face in his hands and kisses me gently on the lips.

A warm flush traverses my spine. I draw back, surprising him. Then I stand, shuffle around the table and sit beside him, close enough that our knees and hips and shoulders touch. Despite the layers of fabric between us, my skin tingles.

His arms encircle me and pull me to him. I lock my lips to his, repaying his kiss with another filled with all the urgency and longing that has built inside me over many months.

When our lips part, too soon, he reaches into his jacket and produces another picture, displaying only the obverse side. "If you've accepted your fate then I hope you won't mind knowing what happens on this day."

Inscribed on the photograph is a date barely more than a month from now. The script is undoubtedly the product of my hand. *Curious. I do not recall writing — Oh, I see. Not yet.*

I raise one eyebrow. "And pray tell, what momentous event occurs on the 24th of November?"

With a dramatically slow twist of his wrist, he turns the photograph over.

Though the people in the scene and the nature of the occasion are instantly recognisable, I take a moment to digest the implications.

Then it hits me all at once. Only five weeks from now Harrison and I will wed.

Wait. My head spins. *Is that what I truly desire?*

I examine the photograph again. The bride's face is awash with joy. A beaming smile, eyes glittering with happiness, glowing skin. The woman in the picture has no reservations about her chosen future.

Harrison said these images did not record his grandfather's past. They are a record of our future, his and mine. The joyful bride is therefore not simply a version of me, another Alicia Rowntree from another timeline, but the Alicia Rowntree who exists in this timeline. She is me and I am her, or I will be this bride very soon.

What woman would ignore such incontrovertible evidence of her future happiness? I certainly will not, though I need no such reassurance. My heart tells me all I need to know. No longer can I imagine any other path for my life than marrying this man. My heart aches, I love him so deeply and want him so desperately.

Only five weeks. Thirty-three days until I am completely his, and he mine. If only it were one day. No, an hour. Even a minute is almost too long to wait.

My lips begin to form the shape of a word—

He stops me with a raised finger and a shake of his head. A gentle nudge with his elbow signals for me to rise.

As I stand, he drops to one knee and takes my hand. "I don't have a ring, and I should speak to your father first... I'm sure I'm doing this all wrong..."

"None of that matters, Harrison."

"Are you sure?"

"Yes," I say, impatient for the *Yes* I truly long to utter.

"Ma'am," he says with a mischievous grin.

I try meeting his gesture with a scowl, but giggle nervously instead.

My laughter is infectious, or perhaps he shares my nerves. I hope not. By now he must know my answer to the question I expect and hope so desperately he will ask.

He takes a moment to compose himself before continuing. "Lady Alicia Rowntree…"

"Yes…"

"Alice…"

With as much sternness as I can muster — granted it is not a great deal — I say, "I believe Alice Seven would be the correct form of address."

"Alice Seven," he says, "would you do me the honour of being my wife?"

"Yes!" I say again. "Yes, Harry Seven, Yes. Yes, for the seventh time. Even for the hundredth time the answer would remain unchanged. *Eternally Yes*."

I pull him to his feet, wrap my arms around his neck, and smother his face in kisses, punctuating each kiss with another '*Yes*,' not stopping until we are both laughing and crying with total abandon.

EPILOGUE

1954

Saturday, May 15
Princeton, New Jersey

Geoffrey turns from the living room window. His face lights up in innocent wonder and anticipation as only a child's can. "He's here! He's here!" he shouts as he rushes into the entryway.

"Calm down," I call to my son, though Alice and I leap to our feet and follow. Placing my arm around his shoulders, I hug him to me so he doesn't bolt outside.

I open the front door, an ordinary oak door that perfectly matches the style of the house. Secret Service agents loiter on the front lawn and in the street, looking far more relaxed than they probably are.

A massive black Lincoln convertible with huge whitewall tires is parked in front, sandwiched between two equally black but much smaller Chevy sedans. The plexiglass roof on the President's vehicle is only a few weeks old, but his car is already widely known as 'The Bubble Top.'

President Eisenhower looks up as he approaches along our front path and bounds energetically up the stairs. His forced smile confirms my worst fears. This is far more than a social visit.

"Professor Seely!" he says, clamping his left hand on my shoulder as he shakes my right. "Wonderful to see you again, Harry."

"And you too, Mr. President," I say, less than convincingly. Though I'm pleased to see him again after all these years, and honored by his visit, I can't help wondering what crisis caused him to take time from his demanding schedule to come to Princeton.

"Lady Alicia," he says, extending a hand to my wife.

She shakes his hand with the same delicate refinement I still recall so fondly from the very first time she held mine. "It is just plain Alice Seely now, Mr. President."

"There's nothing plain about being an Assistant Professor, Ma'am," he says. He turns to me. "Is there, Harry?"

The signs are subtle — addressed as *Ma'am* several times a day, Alice is practiced at disguising her annoyance — but my wife still chafes at this title.

"Please, do come in," Alice says, summoning the President inside.

He follows us to the living room. "And who is this handsome young man?" he says, patting Geoffrey on the head.

My son throws back his shoulders and looks up at the President towering over him. "My name is Geoffrey Seely, Sir," he says in his best grown-up voice. "I am eight years old, Mrs. Carlton is my third grade teacher, and I am very pleased to meet you."

"I am very pleased to meet you too, Geoffrey Seely." He sits and lifts our son onto his knee. I take a seat next to them. "Do you know who I am, Geoffrey?"

"Yes. The President of the United States. Papa said the President is a VIP. That means a Very Important Person."

Eisenhower chuckles. "And did your father tell you he is a very dear friend of mine?"

"No Sir."

"Well he is."

"Smile," Alice says.

I look up, barely catching sight of the camera before I'm blinded by a flash.

So this is the photo with Eisenhower.

"Come along, Geoffrey." She glances over her shoulder at us as she ushers our son into the kitchen. "I'm sure your father and the President have important matters to discuss."

Eisenhower pulls a packet of cigarettes from his jacket. "Do you mind?"

In this time cigarette smoke is ever-present. I only notice when I come home to air free of the stench. I want to accommodate him, but this house is my only real sanctuary. I can't hide my reluctance.

Eisenhower returns the offending item to his pocket. "You're right, Harry. Disgusting habit. I really should give it away."

"Thank you, Mr. President."

"A man's home is his castle," he says.

"Mine isn't as impressive as your current castle," I say. "I would have come to the White House had you asked. But you know that. So there's a reason you came here instead."

"I could say nostalgia," Eisenhower says as he glances around at my home.

"But I wouldn't believe you."

"Neither would I. You know I was horrified when you told me of the other timelines in which we used atomic bombs on Germany and Japan. I have devoted my presidency, almost every waking moment of the past six years, to preventing the world — this world at least — from ever knowing the horror of nuclear war."

"It is a proud legacy, Sir," I say, "even if the world doesn't know the bullet it's dodged."

"Not much of a legacy," he says glumly.

I look at him questioningly.

"Despite our best efforts, the Soviets have developed an advanced nuclear program right under our noses."

Oh shit.

"How advanced?"

"They could have as many as a hundred operational warheads. And it's only a matter of time before they use them to break the stalemate with Germany."

I hide my face in my hands. With the worst of the Nazis purged, Germany is a military state run by the OKW, the German High Command. Though not officially an ally, we support them as the main bulwark against Soviet communism. The United States won't stand by and let the Russians turn the place into a glowing post-nuclear wasteland. The apocalypse could be upon us. Hundreds of millions dead.

I look up, my eyes pleading with him not to ask of me what I expect him to ask, what he has to ask.

And what I have to accept. This is my fault. The price of saving Alice and Jony.

"You've already given so much, I hate to put you in this position, Harry. But I need you to retrieve that blue door from your father-in-law's townhome in London. If worldwide nuclear war is unavoidable in this timeline, Harry Eight may be our only hope..."

AFTERWORD

The genesis of this story was reading about a decision taken in January 1944 by the newly appointed Supreme Commander Allied Expeditionary Forces in Europe, General Dwight D. Eisenhower, to delay the Normandy landings from May to June of that year. The reason given was the availability of additional landing craft a month later.

I couldn't help asking myself two questions: first, what would have happened had the landings occurred as originally scheduled in May; and second, how many extra landing craft could the Allies have secured in a month, and did it really make a difference? Or was there more to the decision than meets the eye? The influence of a time traveler perhaps?

On a more serious note, research is an important part of writing any story with a historical setting, even one based on alternative history. I have listed at the end of the book a number of sources I found particularly helpful in understanding WWII during the period in 1943-44 when Allied leaders were making critical decisions about the final defeat of

Germany. The task of the historical writer is made much easier now by the availability of extensive on-line archives and other records. Anywhere in this story that Harrison Seely uses these resources to find information, I have done the same.

I am indebted to several friends for help with this story, but three in particular.

The first is Peter Rixon, one of the first friends I made at military college, way back when we were both seventeen years old. Peter has an extensive knowledge of military history. He assures me I haven't postulated anything too ridiculous, but of course any errors are mine.

The second is my neighbor Bob Subr, who is old enough to have served at the tail end of WWII but still going strong. A retired military aviator, Bob logged many hours in both the C-47 and the B-25 before becoming a fighter pilot. And yes, his B-25 also had an unlucky encounter with a gopher hole.

The third is Tom Kelly, a retired bond trader who advised me on long-term investment strategies for the time traveler.

Thank you to my sister-in-law, Melina, for proofreading, and finally, as always, thanks to my darling wife, Marie, for her editorial services and everything else she does for me.

SOURCES

Armageddon: The Battle for Germany 1944-45.
Max Hastings.

Crusade in Europe. Dwight D. Eisenhower.

Eisenhower: Soldier and President.
Stephen E. Ambrose.

If Chaos Reigns: The Near Disaster and Ultimate Triumph of the Allied Airborne Forces on D-Day, June 6, 1944. Flint Whitlock.

The Lost World of Bletchley Park. Sinclair McKay.

My Silent War: The Autobiography of a Spy.
Kim Philby.

The Secret Life of Sir Stewart Menzies, Spymaster to Winston Churchill. Anthony Cave Brown.

The Secret War: Spies, Ciphers, and Guerrillas, 1939-45. Max Hastings.

War Diaries: 1939-1945. Field Marshal Lord Alanbrooke.

Winston's War: Churchill 1940-1945. Max Hastings.

Also by D.A.Hill

The Emulation Trilogy
Newton's Ark
Fuller's Mine
Book 3 - coming in 2018

Cerelia's Choice
(an award winning space romance)

If you enjoyed this story, please let other readers
know by leaving a review on Amazon.com.

Made in the USA
Columbia, SC
02 September 2020

18480837R00267